# Kartoffel Noggin

**Other Books in the Prairie Preacher Series:**

*Prairie Preacher*
*Victoria's Nest*
*Rainbows and Rattlesnakes*
*Z*
*Coot and the Gophers.*


*Check out www.PJHoge.com*

# Kartoffel Noggin

## Fifth in the Prairie Preacher Series

P. J. HOGE

iUniverse, Inc.
Bloomington

**Kartoffel Noggin**
**Fifth in the Prairie Preacher Series**

*iUniverse books may be ordered through booksellers or by contacting:*

*iUniverse*
*1663 Liberty Drive*
*Bloomington, IN 47403*
*www.iuniverse.com*
*1-800-Authors (1-800-288-4677)*

*ISBN: 978-1-4620-5506-7 (sc)*
*ISBN: 978-1-4620-5508-1 (hc)*
*ISBN: 978-1-4620-5507-4 (ebk)*

*Library of Congress Control Number: 2011916851*

*Printed in the United States of America*

*iUniverse rev. date: 10/04/2011*

# Contents

*This book is dedicated to all the men who fought in the Vietnam War on behalf of our country. There is of course, no way to truly thank those who put their own lives on hold. Some sacrificed their futures, their health and their lives. They were honorable men who deserve our respect.*

*I would also like to thank many friends for their input and sharing their personal stories: Ken, Tom, Wayne, Darrell, Mike, CJ, John, Jim, Chris, Danny, Don and Al.*

*I also would like to thank my dear friend Tho Trinh Huy for the cover photos.*

*I would like to offer a special thanks K. Kincaid for his diligent and thoughtful input of the book.*

# 365 days left

Andy Schroeder leaned back on the webbed seats of the C130. Comfortable was not the word that came to mind, but it wasn't too bad. It was cold in the plane. He wondered how cold it was back home. He was from central North Dakota and it was very cold when he left the end of February.

He closed his eyes. Andy wondered how his little friend, Ginger Ellison was doing. Still in the hospital when he left, she was six and got the crazy idea to get rid of her freckles with a mixture of spot remover and Hilex bleach. It almost killed her and left her with severe burns on her face, damaged her eyes and both hands. She was doing better, but still faced a long recovery.

He and Darrell, Ginger's uncle and Andy's best friend, sat with Ginger at the hospital most nights after the accident. Andy loved that little kid. He reached in his pocket and retrieved a little braid of her hair. Ginger said that he could look at it whenever he wished she was there. Well, he didn't wish she was with him, but he sure wished he was with her.

He put the braid back and felt the laminated card that his pastor, Ginger's dad, had given him the night he left. He didn't read it then, because he was having a hard enough time saying goodbye. He took it out and read it. It was Ecclesiastes 3. He took off his helmet and ran his hand through the brown stubble left by his buzz cut. He put the card inside his helmet and put it back on his head.

His Dad and his brothers had all pretty much said the same thing about being in the war. 'Do what you have to do and get back home. Don't drive yourself crazy thinking about it all; just do it and be done with it.' Sounded so easy, but none of them said it would be.

They had all served in the military and now it was his turn. He wanted to prove to his family that he too could take on adult responsibilities. He had always been 'little Andy' or the little brother. He always felt like a little boy, even though they never said that. Although the whole reason he was there would refute how responsible he was. He graduated from junior college with a good grade point average. He had decided to study law and filled out his application to the University of North Dakota in Grand Forks. He threw the envelope in his pickup, but didn't have any postage. He kept forgetting it and when he finally got it mailed in, it was too late. The Selective Service smacked their lips and wasted no time to invite him to join the ranks of the Army.

Andy was upset, but figured he deserved it. What a stupid, dumb thing to do! He decided to be a grown up about it; even though he hated every minute of it. There was no way he wanted his big brothers to think he was a wimp.

He had attended more than a couple funerals of friends, relatives and classmates killed in this mess. He had one friend who took off to Canada to avoid the draft. Andy could see no good end to it and wondered of the virtue of the whole thing, but like his Dad said, "Doesn't really matter how you feel about it. Your job is to do it. The leaders of all sides send ordinary folks to do the dirty work. Most of the ordinary folks just want to be home."

Andy had to admit that was true. 'Too bad the politicians couldn't just duke it out and leave the rest of us out of it.'

He decided he would go and do the best that he could. He would serve his country, come home and go to law school. Maybe then, everyone would realize that he had grown up.

He looked at the picture of his dear Annie and shook his head. If he had his way, he would be married to her and living in the little old rural town on the northern prairies. It was important to him that she think he was a real man. Annie was a widow and her first husband died in Vietnam. While Andy didn't want to repeat history, he certainly didn't want her to think that he was a coward. He put it back in his helmet and then tried to fall asleep.

"Hey Spud," the guy sitting a few men away from him said, "You sleeping?"

"How could I sleep with your yelling around here?" Andy grumped, "What do you want now?"

"A smoke," Jackson Fielding answered. Jackson and Andy had become friends during basic training in Ft. Leonard Wood. Jackson was from a small town in South Dakota and so they had a lot in common.

"Thanks Spud. I owe you one." Jackson took the cigarette.

"For the record," Andy grinned, "You owe me a carton."

"Yah, Yah, don't get yourself all French fried, Spud."

Thanks to his little sister, Andy was called Spud by Jackson and most of the men in his squad. During basic, Pepper always put Kartoffel Noggin on his letters and one of them saw it. Then he had to explain that Kartoffel was potato in German. She was calling him a Potato Head. She thought it was funny. Apparently, so did the guys.

They started calling him Potato Head and by the time basic was over, it had been shortened to Spud. Andy was glad of that. Potato Head sounded like something to call a little kid. At least Spud sounded a little more grownup.

Everyone called Jackson 'Crazy Horse' or just Horse. He was a Lakota Sioux from the Pine Ridge Reservation in South Dakota. It seemed that everyone had a nickname. Those that didn't usually were not of a humor to have one anyway.

Horse was a good-looking guy a taller than Andy with a lean but good build. They could talk for hours about the prairies, farming and mechanics. Andy enjoyed his wacky sense of humor and his good spirit. He was one of those guys that always could find something good or funny in any situation. There were times when that was a valuable asset.

Everyone was nervous but no one was really talking about it. It wouldn't do any good anyway. Andy knew they were all worried what hazards the future would bring. They had heard the stories of horror that the war had produced. They had seen the photos and film clips of the wounded and the fighting. It was not going to be a picnic, for certain. Finally, Andy fell back to sleep listening to the drone of the aircraft and the quiet talk of his platoon.

The plane landed and they all stood up. It took a few minutes to get the numbness out of their legs and gather their equilibrium. Andy thought he would be eager to get off the huge cargo plane, but he wasn't certain of it either. The first thing that hit Andy when they opened the door was the deafening sound.

Da Nang was a major airbase in Vietnam for the US Military in 1970. It was a busy place with tremendous activity. Sorties were taking off and landing, helicopters moving back and forth and the idling of aircraft engines and trucks. In the distance was the sound of explosions. Andy was

3

surprised they could hear it so well. It was almost too loud to be on the tarmac with all the air traffic.

When he descended the plane, he looked around. The sky was gray and overcast. To the west, some tall green distant mountains were draped in low cloud cover and blanketed with smoke from the carpet-bombing and explosions. The air was thick, still and sultry. Before they got to the ground, their clothes were clinging to them from the humidity.

The smell was unforgettable. His nostrils nearly burned with the smell of JP-4, the mixture of kerosene and gasoline that fueled the jets. It stunk of kerosene. The asphalt was hot and the air smelled of tar, diesel and sulfur. It was so overpowering that it caught in his throat.

Army trucks pulled up and Andy's platoon boarded the back of the vehicles. As he was climbing in, there was some artillery fire on the west side of the two thousand acre base. Andy looked at Horse.

Horse shook his head, "What the hell did we get ourselves into, Spud?"

The Army trucks laden with green uniformed troops traveled in convoy south from Da Nang and followed the coastline for some way. Being from a landlocked state, the Pacific Ocean fascinated Andy. He was amazed that the same body of water that lapped these shores, washed on the beaches in South America, California, Hawaii, and Japan. He could hardly fathom anything that huge.

Most of the way to Nha Trang, the coastline had narrow beaches of sand and palm trees. South of there, most of it was hills covered in vines and grasses that curved down the hills into the ocean. When the convoy passed by Cam Ranh Bay, the overcast hazy gray sky blended into the outline of the distant seaside peninsula that created the bay. The mountaintops were nothing more than a faded shadow in the gray haze. The ocean was also a blue gray, deeming the horizon indistinguishable.

Cam Ranh Bay was one of the best deep-water ports in the world. It was a valued port of the United States Navy and one of the main distribution points for supplies for the military in country. Traffic in and out of the Bay was tremendous.

The entire trip, awed by the amount of air traffic, Andy was amazed at the smoke in the air. He could not decide if it was the low hanging clouds, air traffic or explosions. Even though he knew intellectually there would be a lot of people and hardware over there, to see it was overwhelming. He was struck by the thought there were one heck of a pile of people fighting over this piece of geography.

The air was so humid it was almost tangible and Andy could feel every thing on him becoming wet and clammy. Missouri had been humid by North Dakota standards, but this was ten times worse. Andy scratched his chest where his tee shirt was sticking to his body.

Horse looked at him and groaned, "A guy could damned near wear this air!"

Chicago, one of their buddies in the platoon, chuckled, "This is like a hot summer day in Chicago. You flat land farmers are wimps."

Chicago's real name was Leon Washington. He was even shorter than Andy, but very muscular and black as the ace of spades. He always had the devil sparkling from his eyes and dimples that looked like a smile even when he was mad. No matter what happened, his smile was there. He was a prankster and loved a good joke. He came from a large inner city family and most of his brothers were in the Army.

"You just don't know what good air is all about," Horse retorted. "See, it's supposed to be dry. You're supposed to drink water and breathe air! You need to some good Dakota air."

Andy started to laugh, "That is if you can catch it as is blows by at thirty miles an hour!"

"Don't forget, I'm from Chicago. The Windy City," Chicago boasted.

"It's probably called that," Swede pointed out to his bragging friend, "Because the citizens are all filled with hot air!"

Swede was a tall, lanky kid from northern Minnesota. Andy wasn't certain what his real first name was, but knew that his last name was Swenson. He was a calm, very quiet guy from a small Minnesotan town on the shores of the Lake of the Woods. Half of the Lake of the Woods was in Canada. Swede often told them that it was so tempting. Just paddle a little ways and no worries about the draft, but he didn't. His family had a strong sense of duty and so he did what was expected. He never denied that he thought about it every day when he was home. Just get in his canoe and paddle, just a short ways.

There was actually very little conversation on the truck. Andy was taking in all the new sensations. His mind tried to get a grasp what was ahead and just how miserable this was going to be. Filled with anticipation and trepidation, Andy decided it was easier to not think about home or anything like that. He didn't want to think about any of it.

Some distance past Cam Ranh Bay, the trucks turned toward the western mountains. Only a few miles from the coast, the heavy, oppressive mist had turned to rain. Within a few miles, it turned into a heavy, non-relenting downpour.

Inland from the coastline, there were many rice paddies and the land was rather flat. The neatly tilled squares of land fascinated Andy. Some people were working in them, seemingly oblivious to the rain. They stood in their fields bent over from the waist, planting what looked like small sprigs of plants in water that was ankle deep. It must have been back breaking work. The women had bags on their back that held the seedlings and other bags that held their small children.

He shook his head and couldn't imagine what it would be like to have to go plant a crop in the middle of a war zone. Then he thought of his Aunt Gilda. She would. She'd say "It ain't going to grow by itself! If you want to eat, you'd better get your butt out there and plant it!"

Yah, he was sure she would. He guessed eating is a strong incentive for all sorts of things.

The land changed as they traveled further inland and the elevation increased. The rugged terrain was thick with trees and vines. There were areas with livestock, mostly goats. He thought of his best friend back home. Darrell milked goats and sold it to a cheese factory.

To say that Darrell was a best friend wouldn't be totally fair. Darrell was more like a brother, or a twin. They were the same age and had spent most of their childhood together. Their families were each other's families. They knew each other so well that one only had to think and the other could answer.

Darrell had some very bad heart problems when he was only eighteen and nearly died. After some surgeries and a lot of medical care and prayer, he was okay; but he could never go to the service. Darrell felt like he was a shirker. Andy assured him that he was doing his fair share for his country. Taking care of the home front was important, too. Andy could count on him to keep an eye on his Annie while he was gone and his Mom and Dad. Darrell had given him is word. If Darrell gave his word, you could count on it. There is no one in the world that he could trust more.

About an hour later, Horse yelled, "Hey Spud, got a smoke that isn't soaked?"

"Yah, I do. Why do you ask?" Andy taunted.

"Just give me one, you idiot."

Andy handed him the pack and then Swede said, "As long as you are passing them out."

"Me, too," Chicago said as he took one from the pack before handing it back to Andy.

"Damn. You guys!" Andy grumped as he looked into his nearly empty pack. "You all owe me one."

"Yah, Yah, Yah." No one seemed too worried about it.

Andy wasn't certain how far they had gone before it was pitch dark and still raining. Then they pulled into the base camp in the Cu Chi region, which was west and north of Saigon. It was east of the neighboring country of Cambodia.

The wet and tired troops finally found their way to their barracks. There were wooden floored buildings built about three feet off the ground, in case of the monsoon flooding. From what Andy had already seen, he was certain that it could definitely flood with the way the water was draining from the sky.

The soil smelled different there than at home; maybe because back home, it was frozen most of the year. Here, one could almost hear vegetation grow. He wondered if he would get used to this place in this year.

The walls were made of screen and tarp, while the roof was corrugated metal. The drenching rain rattled the metal. The tarp was heavy with rain and stuck to the screen. It was nearly as damp inside as out.

In their barracks or hooch, they were assigned their beds. Andy was glad that he had the bunk next to Horse. After putting their things away and drying off, the troops collapsed into their racks.

Andy closed his eyes and tried to forget where he was. He was really tired. He had slept sitting up in the plane or truck for the last forty-eight hours and it felt good to be horizontal. It wasn't nearly as comfortable as his room back home.

He wondered what kind of a mattress he had there. He decided the Army should invest in a pile of them. In his mind, he could the smell the kitchen of the farmhouse; his Grandma Katherine baking bread and meat roasting on the stove.

"Hey, Horse," Andy asked quietly, "Does this count as our first day here or is tomorrow the first one?"

"Dunno, Spud. Does it make a difference?" his tired friend asked.

"Well, yah. I'd get home a day earlier if today was the first day. You know?"

"You idiot! How can you worry your brain about that now? Count it part way, then you will be mostly right and only a little wrong," Horse said half-asleep.

Andy picked up a pair of folded socks and lobbed them at his friend, "You are worthless, you crazy Indian."

"Maybe so, Paleface," Horse threw the socks back, "But I'm going to sleep. So, tomorrow, I'll be less worthless than you."

"Yah, I guess."

Chicago groaned, "Will you two shut up!"

# 364 days left

Andy woke up exhausted. The weather hadn't changed one bit and everything felt damp. He felt like he had soaked in a swamp overnight.

"What's wrong with you today?" Horse grinned, "Not enough sleep? That's what you get for yakking all night."

"Yah, yah." Andy agreed, yawning, "I think I have jet lag."

Horse cracked up, "It looks to me like everything else is lagging, too!"

Andy punched his friend in the arm. "You know, there are days when I don't even like you."

Horse chuckled, "Ah, just give me a smoke."

Standing in line to get their food, the young men looked around the mess hall, which was an amazing building. Built from packing materials and scrounged supplies, the roof leaked like a sieve and there were buckets in various places collecting the drips.

Swede made the observation, "This building looks like it has been used for target practice."

"You must be a newbie," another soldier answered. "This mess hall has been burned down twice and destroyed by mortar fire once. It is under fire as much as we are! Hell, the enemy probably found out what they're serving here!"

The MP behind the serving line gave him a filthy look and the soldier quickly added ingratiatingly, "And they're jealous that we're being fed so well."

The MP nodded, but didn't smile. It was obvious that he had no sense of humor that morning with the rain leaking into everything.

Andy was excited at mail call, naively hoping he would get some mail. He was disappointed because nothing had wormed its way through the system. However, no one else in his squad got anything either.

He mostly wanted to hear how Ginger was doing. He and Horse talked about his little friend who was in the hospital and he had shown him her

9

picture. Horse thought it was especially neat that she loved Indians and horses so much.

"Spud, I'll get Mom to send her a medicine bag. Okay? Tell your Mom so she knows what it is when it comes in the mail." Horse said thoughtfully, "Would that be okay?"

"Man, that would be great! She'd be so excited!" Andy agreed. The two soldiers worked out the details.

Of course, he was disappointed that he didn't hear from Annie. His sweetheart, Annie Grover had been married before a few years back. Within a couple months, her husband was killed. Annie was terrified that history would repeat itself; even though she wasn't a superstitious person. It was one thing for him to be nervous about being in this mess, but Andy hated that she would to be, too.

His sweetheart worked as a paramedic at the Bismarck Fire Hall and stayed at the station four days a week. The rest of the time, she stayed at the farm with his family. Her family was spread all over. Her Mom had passed away and her father lived near Dickinson. One of her two brothers was in North Dakota and worked as an addiction counselor in the northeastern part of the state. The other brother was in the Marines and stationed in Vietnam too, which added to her unease.

Then they got the word. They were going on their first mission, expecting to be gone four days. Their platoon would be inserted into an area near the Michelin Rubber Plantation and then move west. It was mostly recon but also S & C, (search and clear). There had been a lot more Viet Cong activity in the area and it was vital to disrupt the movement of enemy supplies into the south. That had been an expensive lesson learned during the Tet offensive in 1968.

The North Vietnamese had an underground tunnel system throughout the country, but it was extensive in the Cu Chi area. Munitions, supplies and manpower were transferred from North Vietnam on the Ho Chi Minh trail, down through Laos and Cambodia into South Vietnam by the North Vietnamese Army. The Viet Cong, which was the guerilla army of the National Front of the Liberation of South Vietnam, moved sometimes above ground, but it also moved readily through the underground tunnel systems. The NLF or Viet Cong were devoted Communist citizens who wanted South Vietnam to join with the North under Communist rule.

It was relatively quiet as the newbies were packing their gear for the mission. Everyone was mostly lost in his own thoughts. Andy packed extra socks, another pair of trousers, a couple changes of underwear and shirts. In his helmet was toilet paper, bug spray, matches and cigarettes along with the oil required for his grenade launcher. The rest of his gear was all specified; ammo pouch, machete, knife, grenades, shovel tool, rucksack that included a shelter half, first aid kit, canteen and mess kit, extra shells for the M-60, about 100 rounds, and extra grenades. By the time a troop got all the gear on, it was anywhere from fifty to seventy pounds of extra weight!

The troops began to consider the value of even their flak jackets (fragmentation vests). Every little ounce became something to debate. After carting it around for a couple days, its value was as dependent as much on the weight and the ease to carry as anything else. What was necessary was necessary; however the heavier it was, the less necessary it seemed to become.

So this was it. The moment that they had all trained for, been told about and dreaded. Andy had most of his breakfast lurking in the back of his throat. He had tried to avoid it, but finally, he looked at Horse.

Horse nodded back at him, "Just think, Spud. Tomorrow, this day will be history! We'll never have to do the first time again!"

Chicago shook his head, "It's sad, but you almost make sense! Tomorrow!"

"Yah," Swede agreed, "Tomorrow."

Andy repeated, "Tomorrow."

By mid-afternoon, the platoon of forty men was dropped at their insertion point. It was an area of trees and short grasses, but not dense vegetation. It had stopped raining and almost instantly became muggy and too warm. The mosquitoes swarmed the troops as they moved into the dense vegetation.

The men had moved about seven klicks (kilometers) before the vegetation became thicker, which also meant more mosquitoes. The trees were larger and thicker. It was difficult to see anything more than a few feet ahead.

The gear was heavy, but walking through the dense vegetation made it even more difficult. Andy crawled over roots and vines, brushing the low hanging branches from his face. He had to be careful that his equipment didn't catch in the vegetation.

Andy was the grenadier, the man who carried the grenade launcher. He had a M203 which was a combination weapon. It combined the M16 with the N79 Grenade Launcher, so he had to only carry one weapon instead of two. The M16 was built with the tri-prong near the end of it. It could catch on foliage while the troops were walking through dense areas. The M16A1 had a birdcage flash suppressor and was easier to move with. However, since Andy's weapon was the M203 which combined the older M16 with the grenade launcher, his weapon had the tri-prong. It caught on every vine it was near.

It was a toss-up which was of more value. To only have to carry one thing that caught on vegetation, or two things that didn't. He finally decided he was happy with what he had. At least, he might as well be; there was little he could do about it now anyway.

Andy carried his Thumper, the grenade launcher and more grenades than the other guys because he was the grenadier. He could have carried a sidearm, but preferred the M-203. A handgun would be just another thing to carry.

He also carried smoke grenades, used to allow helicopter pilots to gauge wind direction and friendly positions. He carried flares also, to lighten a dark area and signal. When he was all ready, his load was well over 70 pounds.

Swede was the RTO, or radio operator. All RTO's were enemy targets of choice. The antenna made them easily identifiable. If the soldiers lost their radio contact, they were in big trouble. Swede carried his radio as concealed as he possible and usually bent his antenna to make it less visible. He carried flares, maps and as many batteries for the radio as he could.

Chicago was the M60 gunner and Horse was his assistant gunner. Chicago carried the 'Pig', the M60, and as much ammo as he could. Horse carried a spare barrel to use when the first was overheated, asbestos mitts and cleaning supplies for the Pig. He also carried as much ammo as he could. Chicago and Horse worked together like they had one mind and could anticipate each other's every move.

The platoon had two medics. Andy only knew one personally. He was from Boston and always teased about his accent. His last name was Bertrande, which soon became Bandaid. Andy never knew his first name. He was a pleasant fellow and they seemed to get along pretty well.

A medic was also a favorite enemy target and, as such, had long since quit wearing the red cross on their helmets. The M-5 medic bag was the most identifiable thing about them and the medics tried to conceal it as much as possible. They also were allowed to carry a handgun, but many carried a M16 instead.

Every soldier carried some of the ammunition for the M-60 and extra grenades for the grenade launcher. The men assigned to carry that equipment had their hands full with the weight of it all. The radiomen and medics were also weighted down even more than the usual gear with batteries and medical supplies, so others tried to help out. Every man carried as much as he possibly could.

The platoon leader was 2$^{nd}$ Lt. Hamilton and his PSG (assistant) was a Staff Sergeant Bolenksy from Michigan. Most guys called him Bole and he seemed like a nice enough person. Swede knew Hamilton and Bole better than the other guys because he worked more closely with them as he was the RTO. The RTO had to stay within arms length of the Platoon Leader and PSG as much as possible and be at their disposal at all times while on patrol.

While Andy was trudging along in line with the others, he thought about his brothers. Keith has served on the ground in Vietnam while Kevin was in the Navy and off the coast. Keith had always been a hero to the rest of the kids. He was the oldest and most sensible. No one ever considered him irresponsible. Andy didn't care if he was a hero, but he really wanted Keith to respect him. He hoped Keith was proud that his baby brother was a grenadier, but he had never said so. He sure didn't want to embarrass him.

And started wondering what he was facing, when an old Bible verse popped in his head. That verse Pastor Byron had given him from Ecclesiastes 3 came to him:

> *"¹To every thing there is a season, and a time to every purpose under the heaven:*
> *²A time to be born, and a time to die; a time to plant, and a time to pluck up that which is planted;*
> *³A time to kill, and a time to heal; a time to break down, and a time to build up;*

> <sup>4</sup>*A time to weep, and a time to laugh; a time to mourn, and a time to dance;*
> <sup>5</sup>*A time to cast away stones, and a time to gather stones together; a time to embrace, and a time to refrain from embracing;*
> <sup>6</sup>*A time to get, and a time to lose; a time to keep, and a time to cast away;*
> <sup>7</sup>*A time to rend, and a time to sew; a time to keep silence, and a time to speak;*
> <sup>8</sup>*A time to love, and a time to hate; a time of war, and a time of peace."*

'Well,' he thought to himself, 'I guess I have done most of it already, there are just a few things I still have to get out of the way. I would much prefer this to be the time to embrace.'

# *363 days left*

Andy smelled the chocolate chip cookies baking in the oven and his mouth was watering. He was all set for them when he woke up out of what passed for sleep. He was in the boonies and C rations were not exactly chocolate chip cookies. He thought a minute about being cranky about it but gave up. He looked around the group. 'Hell, if I had fresh cookies, I' have to share with this crowd. I wouldn't get any anyway!'

Horse sat next to him, "Well, we made it through day one without anything."

"I thought it was day two," Andy frowned.

"Man, you get wound up about the darnedest things! Got a smoke?"

"I'm beginning to understand why the Indians sent so many smoke signals! I know for sure, they weren't burning their own!"

"Some of us are kind of crabby this morning, aren't we? Chicago taunted.

"I hate it when people talk that way. There's no we to it! This humidity is a bitch," Andy grumped.

"Oh heaven forbid," Horse said, "Now Chicago will tell us about how humid it is in Chicago."

Chicago looked up from his eating and nodded, "Well, it is so humid-,"

"Put a sock in it, Washington," Spud retorted, "I'm not in the mood."

"You're testy this morning," Chicago winked at Horse. "Hmm, Spud doesn't like his accommodations."

Before too long they were back beating the bush, traveling through even denser jungle. It was becoming nerve racking. Andy had the feeling they were being watched but could not see anyone. It was very quiet, quite warm and clammy. The only sound was the incessant buzzing of those damned mosquitoes. Bug spray quickly became was everyone's favorite cologne.

Sweat began pouring off the soldiers and soon Andy had his neckerchief tied around his forehead to keep the sweat out of his eyes. His shirt and pants were soaked through with sweat. His neck was chafing from the weight of his load and he folded his towel into a pad under the straps. That was more comfortable.

The walk seemed endless, through trees and then clearings. The clearings were usually the sharp-leaved elephant grass, the first pioneer of the jungle trying to retake previous tilled lands. There was some sign of the Viet Cong. A few trails but nothing major.

That was okay with Andy. He was wondering if it was possible to make it through the year without seeing any enemy soldiers. He doubted it.

He couldn't shake the feeling of being watched and watched the tree line like a hawk.

They were moving across the middle of a large clearing of three-foot high elephant grass. The point man was moving ahead cautiously. Every so often, he would squat down and wait, then give a thumb's up signal for the platoon leader to move ahead again. Then he suddenly squatted out of sight. Almost instantly, he moved back to the platoon leader as fast as he could. That was unusual. From Andy's position, he could see the fear on the man's face. Andy immediately thought of Viet Cong.

The point man was talking rapidly to the platoon leader and the medic moved up quickly. The word spread rapidly what had happened. When the point man had squatted down, he accidentally stepped on a very irritable small Krait, which had reciprocated by biting him. The krait was a poisonous snake, often given the dubious honor of being called the Three-Step.

Vietnam was home to a goodly share of them, in fact all kinds of snakes. In training, troops were told there were about 140 snakes indigenous to Vietnam and only 30 were poisonous. For Andy, that would be thirty too many.

The men weren't taught to differentiate which was poisonous and which wasn't. They were taught to treat them all as if they were and then not worry about making a mistake. In training, they were told that 'most of the snakes in Vietnam are poisonous; the rest will crush you to death.' It wasn't true, but it gave everyone a good basis to work from and developed a healthy respect for the creatures.

That wasn't hard for Andy. He had what some people called an unreasonable fear of snakes. In his mind however, there was no fear too unreasonable when it came to snakes. He had heard the stories of the Vietnamese Three Step Snake. Legend was if it bit you, you would die before you could take three steps. They were assured that in reality, no snakebite could kill you that fast. Andy knew that was a lie. He knew he personally could die of a massive heart attack instantly if one was even too close to him, let alone if its big fangs sunk into his hide.

At any rate, this was not the news Andy needed to hear that morning. Horse knew of his fear, figured he would be freaking. He moved up beside him, "Spud, at least it's not a cobra."

Andy frowned at him, "Shit Man, I was having enough trouble thinking of the Krait, now you reminded me of the cobra! I think I'll go home now and leave this business to you guys. Okay?"

Horse snickered quietly, "Good idea. I'll be right behind you." Then he moved back to his position. Andy really appreciated Horse thinking about him, though.

Someone asked how the point man was, but no one seemed to know. There was a new man taking that position. They began moving forward again.

Now Andy had more to think about. Snakes, mosquitoes and Viet Cong! That should keep his little mind occupied so he didn't think about his lack of chocolate chip cookies.

He was trying to decide what to look for. Should he watch for the enemy at a distance or in the grass or where he put his feet because of snakes? He moved on with the platoon. A few men were dispatched to the rear with the injured point man. Andy figured he would be brought to a LZ (landing zone) and then evacuated.

There was a sound ahead and Andy listened carefully as they all crouched down in the thick jungle area mixed with scrub trees. They stayed there for a time and nothing else happened. Then they were given the signal to move on.

By late afternoon, the platoon encountered more trails and more signs of activity. It was hotter than Hades and most of the men had stripped any clothing they didn't deem necessary to be wearing, usually wedging it under gear to prevent chafing.

2<sup>nd</sup> Lt. Hamilton told the men to camp for the night because the next day would be 'more productive'. He wanted them well rested; which brought a smile to most of their faces. Rest and patrol were not words used together with any degree of sincerity. Other than guard duty, they did try to get cleaned up and sleep.

Andy didn't dream about cookies, instead he dreamt of snakes and muzzles of rifles pointing at him through trees. It wasn't restful, but it was sleep.

# 362 days left

It was still dark when they woke up. Andy had to admit that he did get a lot of rest and was grateful that he felt so much better. So were Horse and Chicago.

"I wonder if your girl knows what a grump you are when you're tired?" Chicago asked.

"She likes it," Andy grinned. "What about your woman? Oh, that's right. You don't have one!"

"I do to! Chicago answered. "I don't want her to pine away for me."

Horse just about cracked up, "Pine away for you? Where did you get that word? Boy, are you dreaming!"

"You got a woman waiting for you, Horse?" Chicago asked.

Horse grinned, "A policeman with a warrant is about all that is waiting for me! Nah, I had a girl. That went to hell about a year ago. Anyway, we need to get our butts in gear."

Andy actually felt good. He was rested, the weather was cooler and his strength was back. Today his mind was clear and alert. That gave him his confidence back. He was anxious, but not scared. Even the thought of a cobra didn't bother him quite that much this morning. Well it did, but today he felt he could run fast enough to make it almost to Hawaii before his body sunk to the bottom of the ocean!

The platoon divided up into four squads of ten, each coming from a different direction to converge on the same area. First Squad was in the lead, with Second Squad on the left, Third Squad on the right and Fourth Squad in the middle rear. They were all about 20 yards from each other in a rough diamond shape. In the dense jungle, it was amazing that even though he knew his comrades were there within a few feet, Andy couldn't see them. Then why did he feel his every move was being watched?

The air was still and the fog was like soup. It was cooler and almost eerily quiet. Too quiet. Andy's team, Third Squad, moved about 15 yards to the most northern position and then it turned to the west. They would be the right flank on the north. They encountered a lot more trails which all disappeared into nothingness. How could a well-worn trail just disappear?

They moved along for about forty-five minutes. The sun was just beginning to dimly light the eastern sky and gave everything the appearance of a black and white cinema. In the jungle, it was still dark. In the clearings, it was a little lighter. Nothing had any color, except shades of gray and vague hints of green. The fog permeated almost everything.

Andy began to sweat, not from the heat, but from anxiousness. The foreboding feeling of doom made it difficult to breathe. He almost wanted something to happen to take his mind off the dread. Everything was too quiet, too calm. The fear was palpable. Andy looked to Horse, who was rather fearless, and saw that he was serious and tense.

They crossed an area of tall grass. It had once been a rice paddy now being overtaken by jungle growth. There was a semi-circular growth of dense trees to the west and maybe 35 feet to the north. That is when Andy heard a sound.

There was a long, slow thhhhupppppddd. A single motion from their team leader and they all hit the ground and covered their heads before a grenade went off not ten feet to the north of them. A barrage of artillery fire followed quickly from the west and north.

Adrenaline set in immediately and the newbies all reverted to their training. Without a word, everyone knew what to do and how to do it. There was no thought. Thank God for their repetitious training. Their actions were nearly automatic.

Andy moved into position and lobbed off the first grenade toward the north. Then he moved the barrel forward on the Thumper to reload. They were taking a lot of fire, mostly from the west.

Andy could see that Chicago's Pig was firing into the western trees. Horse was beside Chicago feeding rounds of shells into the ravenous gun. When the barrel would get too hot, he was ready to change it.

Andy kept busy firing back and forth between the M16, which was now on 'rock and roll,' full automatic fire and the grenade launcher. He could see only shaded outlines in the trees ahead as the blasts flashed sporadically. He returned the fire in that direction. The only things visible were muzzle blasts, tracers, small explosions and bright flashes. The people were simply transient shadows. It seemed as though the underbrush had become alive, popping off without any order.

It was difficult to determine how many men were in the trees, but it didn't take a rocket scientist to figure out the platoon was vastly outnumbered. Andy was shooting into the dark more than aiming at anything. He aimed where the most fire was coming from, which seemed to be from the west. Then it would lull and the north would take up the slack.

The yelling and screaming with lots of profanity, was mostly drowned out by the firing of the weapons and the sound of explosions. Within minutes, First Squad overlapped them, moving swiftly to build up their defenses.

Andy continued with his shelling and kept as low as possible in the weeds. At one point, machine gun fire hit the soil so close to his right arm that he watched the shells land not a foot from him. He was almost shocked to realize that he, little Andy, was really in a battle. "Holy Shit! They're getting downright serious about this." Andy mumbled to himself.

Time was in a warp. It seemed like it had been an eternity, but the firefight continued for another ten minutes after First Squad moved in, maybe twenty minutes total. Now, it was daylight. As quickly as it started, the firing stopped. Dead silence.

That was almost more frightening than the steady fire. Everyone knew the enemy troops weren't all dead or gone. The firing had stopped suddenly and completely. No, they had chosen not to shoot anymore. Why?

The squad moved on toward the west to an area that afforded more cover. After a few minutes, the medics tended the wounded. Thankfully, no one was killed and only two men had wounds bad enough to warrant being taken back to the LZ. That of course, meant that four men would have to go with them. Since they had started their patrol, six men were gone from the firefight and three with the snakebite. Their platoon had shrunk by a fourth. Worse, the location of the two squads was well known to the enemy, who had gone down in the secret tunnels to rest, reload and regroup. Andy just knew they were having a cup of coffee. The bastards.

Now joined by the First Squad, the Third Squad, Andy's squad, moved out again. They were concerned when they moved past the grove of trees where the firing had come. There was not a soul around. Ominously curious.

As he walked along, Andy wondered if he had actually injured or killed anyone. One thing he was certain of, they wanted to injure or kill him. The rounds in the soil a foot from his arm had convinced him of that!

His first firefight was interesting as he thought about it. It was frightening to be sure, but not as much as he had worried. That must be the work of the adrenalin, but also the fact that he was too busy to think much while it was going on. He was really getting into this not-thinking mode.

The squad moved on for another hour before they took a break in an area that afforded better protection. No one talked, but everyone assessed his ammo and supplies. While they were doing this, Sgt. Bole showed up and checked with the men. He assured the newbies they had handled themselves well. That made them feel better but there wasn't a man among them that wouldn't have rather gone back to base camp then and there.

After half an hour of down time, they were back on their feet again. They were still heading toward the west. The going was slow and the vegetation was becoming very cumbersome. About half an hour into some not so dense trees, the squad leader summoned one of the smaller men named Franklin. The point man had discovered an opening to an underground tunnel. The opening was very small, barely two foot square if that. It was covered with vegetation and when closed was totally unnoticeable. The point man had simply noticed this one by accident.

The platoon leader ordered a gas injected into the tunnel to kill anything that was down there. They replaced the cover and left for a few minutes. After judging the gas had done its deed and dissipated so it was no longer a threat, someone would be sent down the tunnel to check it out. The task of the tunnel rat was to retrieve any papers or necessary information.

The tunnel rat was usually a smaller man, someone who was about the size of the Vietnamese. Many of the Americans were too large and couldn't get around in the tunnels. The assignment fell to Franklin. He took off all his equipment and then tied a rope around his waist.

He took his flashlight and a handgun. Since the tunnels were tight, there was little point to take more. A person could no more than slither through many of them and could only reach what he had in his hands. Franklin went down the hole with his comrades holding on to the rope. There was no light and little air in tunnels. Many times, they were booby trapped by the entrances, sometimes with poisonous snakes or insects.

Once down the hole, it was usually up to the tunnel rat which way he wanted to go.

Franklin was gone about twenty minutes before he came back up. He came out another opening not two feet from where a soldier was standing. Needless to say, that soldier almost had a heart attack. He had been standing right next to the mouth of a tunnel and had no idea. It threw the fear of God into all of the newbies. The feeling that there was no 'safe place' took hold of the squad and made a huge indelible impression.

Franklin had found little; some spent ammo and not much else. It was clear that everything else had been removed. When he emerged, Franklin reported that there were several branches of the tunnel and several layers. He had only checked out two. He reluctantly asked if he needed to go back down.

"No," said the Squad Leader, "We know this place is crawling with the tunnels. I don't want you coming up in the middle of something nasty. This is a pretty active area."

Franklin was visibly relieved. Even though it had not been his first trip down a tunnel, he didn't relish having to go back down again. The squad moved on.

The fog had rolled in again and looked like it would be a repeat of the night before. Andy curled up trying to write to Annie. He couldn't think of a thing to say. His Dad had told him about when he was in WWI freezing in some Russian snow bank and his brother Keith had told him about how he had spent many nights in the Vietnamese jungle. Andy didn't know which would be worse. Before he went to sleep, he decided that neither amounted to a damn.

# 361 days left

Sometime during the night, the soldiers returned from taking the wounded to the LZ. Everyone was encouraged to see them back and know that their numbers had increased again by seven. The men reported the wounded were evacuated without any further problems although one of them was in very bad shape. Now Andy's squad was only down by two and First Squad was only down by one man. Things reverted to normal.

Andy slept about as well as one could under the circumstances. Between nerves and the damned mosquitoes, he was worn out when he took his stint at guard duty. However when he went on guard duty, so did the mosquitoes. Whose big idea was it to create those stupid things anyway? Their only purpose on this earth, Andy decided, was to make his life totally miserable and they excelled at it.

That morning, everyone's nerves were on edge until the fog lifted. The fog wasn't as thick as the day before and the temperature was enough warmer so it cleared off much faster. The platoon continued on its mission heading west. There were myriads of trails, more than the day before and a few more tunnels were found.

Second Squad encountered some fire in a very dense forested area about three o'clock, but it was brief and no one was injured. It was another case of starting abruptly and then quitting just as abruptly. It was very unnerving. It was just enough to remind everyone that the enemy knew exactly where they were and probably how many of them there were.

This had become their reality.

About five, the platoon converged on an area that had obviously been a VC command of some sort. There were numerous tunnels and trails, and even a shredded hammock still swinging between two trees not too far from the entrance of a tunnel. Apparently, they had felt confident there for some time.

Inspections of the tunnel complex below them revealed no papers or documentation. However, there were the remains of a 'factory' that fashioned land mines from scavenged materials and another that had been making sandals from ruined rubber tires. There were several larger rooms below ground, which led them to believe that it had been an area of some importance. Of course, there was nothing remaining that would confirm this. It had been cleared of anything of value to the VC, North Vietnamese Army or the US.

Without confirmation, Andy knew their every move was being monitored and that the VC could return whenever they wished from below ground. It was not a comforting thought. It meant that they had been allowed to find what they had found and to do what they had done so far. It was a deadly mind game.

It reminded Andy of a mouse being tormented by a cat. The mouse had to know that he was totally at the mercy of the cat for his survival and that the cat was also fully aware of it. It was not pleasant.

The men received orders to secure another area where there was a clearing. Andy had developed an extreme dislike for clearings. However, he wasn't all that happy with wooded areas either. But from this cleared area once it was secure, they would be distracted by helicopter. That was truly an incentive. The men completed the work in a short time and there was no sign of VC anywhere. It was unusually quiet.

Maybe he was crazy, but it reminded Andy of how the weather felt minutes before a tornado. The bile was resting right below his tonsils and he had a real sick feeling.

Before dusk, four Chinooks came toward the clearing. Andy could remember no time in his life when he was as glad to see some sort of transport. They began loading while keeping vigilant the area was secure. Things were going well while the first fifteen men loaded. Andy was still on the ground as part of the 'fire team' which would be among the last to board because they afforded protection for the others.

The area was surrounded by trees about fifty meters away. Two sides were dense jungle forest, but one side was a much thinner forest with some open areas. The area had been cleared and had been secure as it could be, but that wasn't all that comforting, considering the odds could change whenever the VC decided to return by way of the tunnels. No tunneled area was ever considered actually cleared or secure.

When the first Chinook was ready to lift off, all hell broke loose in short order. They were suddenly surrounded by heavy fire and some large artillery. The ground around them churned into craters and flying mud. The sky also filled quickly with the Huey gunships that had escorted the Chinooks. They were able to keep the VC occupied and hunkered down while the rest of the troops loaded into the Chinooks. It was a very fierce firefight.

Finally, they were lifting off amid fire. Before they were out of sight, the fixed wing aircraft, gunships came in and obliterated the area. Most likely, the VC had allowed the platoon deep into their area to draw in the US helicopters so they could disable them. They had likely hoped the airplanes would not follow.

It was a given that the air fire could not destroy the tunnels, especially the multilayered complexes. However, it would take time for the VC to reinforce them and that was an advantage the US wanted.

Once they felt more secure in the bird, Horse looked at Andy. "I always knew you were a religious guy, but I didn't know how much."

"What do you mean?" Andy questioned his friend with a frown.

"Man, every step you took, you said Jesus, Jesus, Jesus!"

Chicago laughed, "I heard a few 'Oh Jesus' in there, too. You praying or swearing?"

Andy punched Horse, "You dumb ass. The 'Oh Jesus' were prayers, I don't know, I suppose the rest were swearing. Hell, I've no idea what I was saying."

Chicago grinned, "Well I was saying Holy Mother of God and I'm not Catholic!"

Horse cracked up, "Is that what they call a battlefield conversion?"

"What were you saying, Horse?" Andy asked.

"I didn't say anything. I was just thinking that if we Indians had spent more time with shovels than on horseback, things might have worked out better for us!"

"You're such a jackass!"

When they finally got back to their barracks and had time to really look things over, they realized that most of the last grunts to load had cuts or bits of shrapnel. Nothing serious, but it was enough to tear some of their clothing. They cleaned their weapons and got everything in order.

The M-16 were advertised not to requiring cleaning. However, that was very wrong. The first ones were sent over didn't even have cleaning kits with them. After a few dirty guns blowing up in soldier's faces, the Army changed things. A comic book featuring a sexy lady giving instructions on cleaning the weapon was dispatched. Although met with very derisive comments from the troops, but it did work. They all started cleaning their M-16's regularly and there was a lot less jamming. There were enough other things to kill a soldier over there that it wasn't necessary to have his own gun blow up in his face.

For Andy's part, he was just glad to be on his way back in camp. He was even thinking that leaky old mess hall looked like a fine dining experience. And coffee. Oh my God, he could have a cup of good coffee!

The men enjoyed their meal at the mess. It might not have been so great and no one could remember what it was except, damned good. Andy got his coffee. He held his cup in both hands and just absorbed the smell for a while. Finally, Horse couldn't stand it anymore.

"Are you going to drink it or take a steam bath in it? Good grief, just chug it."

"What does it matter to you?" Andy squinted at him. "This isn't a cold beer."

"Speaking of which," Chicago said, "I be thinking I want one after dinner. What about you?"

Both men agreed, and Horse said, "A few of the guys decided to drink their supper."

"I'd just get sick. Time I spend puking, is time I'm not sleeping," Chicago pointed out.

"You're so right. Eat, then drink," Andy laughed, "And then sleep. Oh, sleeping. I almost forgot about that. How does that work again? I mean the real kind where you don't wake up thinking someone might put a bullet in your ass."

# *360 days left*

Although it was not as comfortable as his bed back on the farm, his rack was a big step up from curling up in some mosquito-infested hole in the boonies. Andy decided he could learn to like his rack a lot.

The so-called shower that morning was not exactly what Andy anticipated. It was a cold-water, canvas-sided rig, but it did get the muck off. Sometimes the soldiers from the camp would billet into an area that provided good hot showers, but they did not have any at the camp. Swede learned that there had been one, but it was destroyed during the mortar attack that burned the mess hall to the ground. Andy didn't like the idea of not having a hot bath, but consoled himself with the idea that maybe this would allow him to build up multiple layers of bug spray that those damned mosquitoes wouldn't be able to penetrate.

Andy was really bummed when mail call came and went, and none of the guys in his platoon had received any mail. He was dying to hear how Ginger was doing and he really wanted to hear from Annie. He wondered how the big shots could organize a war, if they couldn't even get a letter to him. He knew the mail would catch up with him eventually, but he wasn't in the mood to wait. Since he didn't have any letters to read, he wrote a few and got them off in the mail.

Andy, Horse and Chicago took their clothes to a laundry pick up run by a Vietnamese family. There were no laundry facilities available at their camp. A young man from the family would come by the base every morning and pick up the clothing. He would return with the clean clothes, either that night or the next morning. The family did a good job and even repaired the little cuts and tears on any material.

These nationals were 'approved' through the Army command, although no one ever knew for certain what criteria was considered for approval. Some bases had many problems with VC infiltrating in construction crews and such, but some did not. It might have been just the luck of the draw.

At any rate, this young man seemed very pleasant and careful to take care of the soldier's clothing. He gave them tags to identify their things and left. After he left, Horse commented, "I wouldn't want his job. Can you imagine what would happen to him if the VC found him with a bag of grunts clothing? His life wouldn't be worth a damn."

"Did the Indians do that?" Chicago asked.

"Do what, you moron? Laundry?" Horse shook his head in amazement.

"No, long ago did some Indians work with the American soldiers?" Chicago asked seriously.

"Well, of course," Horse grinned, "Otherwise the Palefaces would still be lost!"

Even Andy had to laugh. Chicago gave them a dirty look, "You know what I mean."

"In our area," Horse answered seriously, "It was mostly the Crow who worked with the soldiers. They had signed a peace treaty before my people did."

"Oh. Never heard of the Crow," Chicago answered.

"There were a lot of them. Regardless, I still wouldn't want his job," Horse replied and the others agreed.

It was in the morning, when Andy saw the first one. He had already heard about them, but had to admit that seeing one did make an impression. The jungles are good places for rats. The weather, except the monsoon season, is compatible for them and there is a lot of food available. The rats were probably the most grateful of all creatures for the war! (Although Andy thought the mosquitoes were right up there on that list!) The soldiers on both sides brought food into areas of wilderness. That was easy pickings for the rodents. They grew to enormous size with the change in their environment. The humans even dug holes and stored food in them! For a rat, it was almost like Santa Claus delivering the packages to his door! What more could he ask for? Sure, there were some drawbacks, like bombs and so on, but for the most part, the war was a blessing. The rat population not only proliferated, but they also grew huge. Some weighed about five pounds. They took over at night and had the run of the place.

Andy was not afraid of rodents, although he had heard that they might decide to chew on your extremities while you slept. That did not intrigue him but he had given so much blood to the damned mosquitoes that he didn't think that could be one whole hell of a lot worse. At least, a rat bite would wake you up and the rat would only get one crack at you. Those damned mosquitoes worked in league with each other. While you were swatting one, fifty others were swarming in for the kill from another side. He really hated them. Besides, it wasn't likely that a person could inhale a rat.

The men were in line for the mess hall when an exceptionally large rat came running out from a pile of boxes near the entrance. One grunt laughed, "He must have read the menu!"

Andy was surprised how large it was. The rats back home were miniature compared to this thing. Horse looked at it and grinned, "Shit man, if you skinned that sucker you could make a whole coat!"

Chicago laughed, "Back in Chicago, rats are so big—!"

Andy punched him and he glared back at him, "Damn Spud. You'll never be learning anything about Chicago if you don't let me talk."

"I could tell you about the Boston rats!" Bandaid offered as he joined the guys, "You interested, Chicago?"

"Okay!" he grumped. "But you will never learn anything."

"Hey," Horse asked, "Did you hear how the guy with that snake bite did?"

"I never heard. I think I would've heard if he died, so apparently he is okay," Bandaid shrugged. "Did you guys get any mail?"

"No," Andy answered, "Did you?"

"No There was little mail for the whole camp today. Must have been a disruption somewhere. I know that would be hard to believe!" Bandaid said sarcastically.

"You waiting for something special?" Horse asked. "You sound like it."

"My dad was going to send me his good luck charm that he had in WWII. I just hope it didn't get lost somewhere along the way," Bandaid explained.

"That wouldn't be very good luck," Swede responded, "Spud is waiting to here how his little friend is doing. She was burned before he left."

"House fire?" Bandaid asked.

"No, chemicals," Andy answered, "Ginger has mahogany red hair and freckles. Pretty kid, but some jackass told her that freckled-faced redheads were worthless. Then he said he had to shoot his horse because it was sort of red and freckled. He said it was so horrible he had to put it out of its misery. It scared the hell out of the poor little kid. She took some spot remover, mixed it with bleach and smeared it all over her face. She almost killed herself. She burned her face and her hands that she applied the solution with. The acid ate all the muscle and stuff off some of her right hand and she had to have her little finger amputated. Her eyes were really messed up."

"Wow! That's really bullshit!" Bandaid answered. "Did you beat the hell out of the guy that said that? I would have."

"Nah, we were too worried about Ginger." Andy reached in his pocket to show the guys the braid that Ginger had given him. He panicked when he couldn't find it. "Oh shit!"

"What's wrong?" Horse asked.

"Dammit to hell, I think I left her braid in my other pants that I sent to be washed. Well, I will never see that again! Crap! I promised her that I'd keep it," Andy felt all the blood leave his body and he could have cried.

Horse knew that he was really bent out of shape, but no one said any more about it. Andy was just sick. He paid no attention to dinner or to most of his afternoon.

He hated this damned place. Everything was a pain in the ass and there was no way to make it better. He had been irresponsible and let Ginger down. He would never amount to anything. He couldn't gain the respect of an adult, until he acted like one. It was obvious that he didn't. He was getting a real pity party going for himself when Horse pulled him aside.

"Get your shit together, Paleface! It is only a piece of hair. She'll send you another one, got it? You have more important things to worry about. You just write home and ask them to send you another one. I don't want to see you dragging around here acting like a baby!" As soon as he said it, he was afraid he had said too much.

Andy looked at his friend and then started to nod. "Thanks, man. I needed that. One thing that Ginger really hates is what she calls blubber babies!"

Horse punched his friend, "You'd better thank God she didn't see you a few minutes ago then! Let's go see what we can find to do. I almost hate having so little to do."

"You won't feel that way for long. I'm pretty sure they are plotting something while we wait!"

It was about five when the laundry man returned. The men went over to get their things. but were not certain that it would be back so soon. They were relieved that it was and Chicago was delighted that they had carefully repaired a tear on his sleeve. They moved a few feet from the line of soldiers gathering their laundry and admired the work done on Chicago's sleeve. Andy felt a touch on his elbow.

He turned to see the young Vietnamese, "Hello. You soldier for these clothes?"

Andy nodded yes and the man continued, "We find thing might be for you. Maybe throw out, I think you want."

The fellow reached in his pocket and pulled out Ginger's braid. Andy looked at the braid in the man's hand and jumped for joy. He put his arms around the shocked man and spun him around. "Thank you so much! God bless you! You have no idea how much this means to me."

The shocked guy was glad to be released and gave Andy a funny look as he stepped back from him, "I think so."

Andy looked at the braid carefully, beaming all the while, "Thank you so much. This is a gift from my favorite little girl."

"You have daughter?"

"No, my friend's daughter," Andy smiled. "This is a braid of her hair. She has red hair."

"Very nice. I happy I find."

"How much can I pay you for this? What can I give you?" Andy asked.

The Vietnamese man looked at him with a great smile and said, "Nothing. You happy. That good. No money."

"Thank you so much," Andy said. "I really appreciate it."

"Must go take care of things," the young man turned back to his work.

"Have a great evening."

The guy looked back with a surprised smile, "You too, soldier."

Andy grinned, "You can call me Spud."

The Vietnamese started to laugh, "That is my name."

"Your name is Spud?" Swede asked.

"Oh, no. I think you say Suds. That is what soldiers call me. You know—washing clothes. Suds."

"Oh. No, I am Spud, another name for potato," Andy grinned. "Have a good evening, Suds."

The guy smiled back, "You too, Spud."

# 359 days left

The next morning on work detail, Andy saw Suds loading the sacks of laundry. Andy waved at him and Suds returned his wave with a huge smile. "Hello, Mr. Spud."

Chicago heard this exchange and corrected Suds, "He is just Spud, not Mr. Spud. Mr. would mean that he's important."

"You make joke to Suds, right?" the young man asked.

"Yes. But really, call him Spud. I am Chicago," the soldier grinned.

"And do not call him Mr. Chicago!" Horse answered, "He will get a big head."

"Big head?" Suds asked.

"That just means that he'll think that he's important," Andy explained.

"You make many jokes, you grunts."

"Yah, we're kind of crazy," Andy explained. "Now this guy is Horse."

"Horse?" Suds shook the Indian's hand. "Suds not real name. Is Horse real name?"

"No, and neither is Chicago. That is just the city that he comes from."

"I hear about Chicago. It is big city," the Vietnamese said.

"Yes," Chicago agreed. "These two guys are from the Dakotas prairies."

Suds smiled, "I hear of prairies. You see tornadoes?"

"Yes, we do get tornadoes there. How did you know that?" Andy asked.

"I read in book. I never see tornado. You see?"

Horse and Spud both said they had and assured Suds that he really didn't want to see one.

"I have take care my things," Suds smiled. "Must go now."

"Thank you for stopping to say hello to us." Andy clapped his back, "You have a great day."

Suds looked at him in surprise, "You too, Spud."

That afternoon, there was some mail. Andy was so relieved. He got three letters from his Annie and one from Grandma Katherine, Mom, Pepper and Darrell. He read Darrell's letter first and was able to find out that Ginger was improving, but the news on her health was still very old. She was still in hospital and the doctors were debating if she would require more surgery. He wished he had a more current update.

Grandma told him about how his Dad's broken hand was healing and his efforts to take the cast off every time someone wasn't watching him. She also said Grandpa Lloyd was failing more with his Alzheimer's. He was still wandering around at nights and getting into all sorts of predicaments. He managed dismantle Dad's radio and mix up the ingredients in Mom's pantry. Dad put in an alarm, nicknamed the Pa Bell, so he couldn't wander off at night into the frigid nights without his shoes on.

Pepper's letter of course, had Kartoffel Noggin written all over the back of it. It afforded his little sister a great deal of glee to do that to him. He knew too well that complaining would only encourage her. She told about her trials with trying to get Dad to keep cast on, his brother Kevin who was running the gas station and shop while Dad was healing from his broken hand and then all about what she and Annie had been up to. Then there was an entire two pages about Pepper's boyfriend, Chris.

Then he read Annie's letters. He missed her so much. He could read between the lines she was having a difficult time. She was worried sick about her brother, Travis, in Vietnam and him. She told all about her work, but there was an emptiness that she couldn't cover up.

He wanted her so much. Damn. If he had just sent in his papers to UND a little sooner, he wouldn't be over here! They could be together. Why had he been such an idiot? She was worried, his Mom was worried, his family was dealing with a lot of work because he wasn't there. It was all his fault, and they were all bearing the brunt. He hated that. He started to get bummed. He had to fight back the tears he had earned with his stupidity.

Then he read part of a letter where Annie told about how Ginger was trying to be a brave soldier like her Andy. The little girl was determined she wasn't going to be blubber baby. Andy thought about it. That small child had put up with more than he had and wasn't being a blubber baby. Okay. He wouldn't be either. He just hoped he could be as brave as she was being. He hoped he had it in him.

About then, they received their orders that they would be moving out on a patrol the next morning at 4:00. They got their dinner at the mess and went to bed early. There was little conversation that night. Everyone wanted to get as much sleep as they could before they headed back out to the boonies. Andy answered the letters with short notes and wrote to Ginger. Then he hit the rack.

He dreamt about the farm and his family. He thought about Annie. Too much, in fact, way too much! He wanted to be with her more than anything. He was almost as terrified of her finding someone else or realizing he was irresponsible, as he was of getting killed over there. In fact, that would be preferable. Oh, what a hell of a thing to even think about. Dear God! Why hadn't he sent those stupid papers in a week earlier? He should've just went to town and bought more postage. What a stupid reason to end up drafted! He could have done it and avoided this whole thing.

Then it came to him. There must have been a reason. He didn't know what it was yet, but his Dad and Uncle Byron would say that God doesn't make mistakes. He tried to convince himself, but not very successfully. Maybe He did make a mistake this time. Or maybe it wasn't God's mistake, but his. After all, he did have free will. Nothing stopped him from getting more postage.

'Just keep your cool, Andy. It will be okay,' he thought to himself. That is so damned easy to say and so much harder to believe. 'Don't be a blubber baby.'

# 358 days left

They loaded into the trucks and rode to the helicopter pad. They filled the birds and headed out some god-forsaken hunk of jungle in the middle of nowhere. They always had one order. 'Kill more of them than they kill of us.' They all knew their mission would not bring peace to the world or make a pile of difference to anyone in a day or two. It was fruitless, but seemed to be the par for the course.

Everyone was rather quiet. Andy wished he had some good coffee. That would have changed his spirits. He watched the dark trees pass by below the aircraft and wondered what it would be like to have his home blown up. He couldn't imagine how Suds must feel. Of course, he really knew nothing about him. It was definitely a beautiful country, if you are into vegetation and green. Andy almost missed the white of the frozen tundra he called home.

"Whatcha thinking, Spud?" the fair skinned, blue-eyed Swede asked. "You look like it must be something profound, for sure."

Andy grinned, "I was thinking how much I missed snow!"

"Yea gads, that isn't profound. That's more like pathetic!" Swede retorted. Then he looked out of the helicopter, after a minute he said quietly, "You know what? So do I."

"Oh shut up, you boneheads," Horse grumped. "You shouldn't get any mail, any of you! It makes you all sappy."

Andy punched him, but then said, "Yah, you might be right, huh?"

"Better shape up, because I can't be babysitting for all of you. What with keeping an eye on Chicago! He's all bent that he didn't hear from his woman! Half the time, I feel like Ann Landers!" Horse grumbled.

For that comment, he received punches from almost everyone within reach. Andy just cracked up in laughter. "You are completely insane, you crazy Redskin."

"Paleface!" Horse listened to the helicopter's engine, "Me think big bird land."

He was right and soon they were trudging off into the boonies again. Andy was delighted to know that his own flock of mosquitoes had found their way to him. He would have felt lost without them. He hated them so much, it was almost comforting to have them around.

It was unusually warm and sticky that morning. The ground was soft, but not quite muddy. Tall grasses and trees in the distance filled in the rough terrain. The soft ground made the walking extremely heavy and difficult. It was more tiring than usual.

They moved along until about noon when it became unbearably warm and humid. Before too long, it was pouring rain. They took out their ponchos to protect themselves from the deluge. Within a few minutes, the ponchos soaked up the water and weighed a ton. Andy took his off, as did several of the other soldiers. If you were going to be wet anyway, you might as well be wet and light as wet and heavy.

At least, it was too rainy for the mosquitoes. Andy wondered where they all went when it rained. Probably down the tunnels with the VC. That made him smile. He was wondering if the tunnels leaked with this downpour, when the squad leader gave a signal to drop and freeze.

After a couple minutes, they moved forward, but within another minute, they were down again. There was definitely something causing concern up front. They didn't have to wait long.

The woods directly in front of them erupted into a chaos of flashes, explosions and yelling. Andy got his grenade launcher into position in the mud. The ground was soggy and spongy. There was little one could do to secure anything in the soup.

They were definitely in the enemy's kill zone. There was little they could do but to inflict as much damage as possible, before they were overrun.

As happened so often, the fight raged for some horrific minutes of incapacitating terror and then quit, just as it began. Instantly. Out of nowhere and with no warning.

The squad rapidly moved for better cover and checked their situation. One man had been injured in the leg, but Bandaid thought he could continue.

It made Andy sweat just thinking of how many enemy were watching them every minute. To not be annihilated but still know, beyond any doubt, that you were at the mercy of their very whim was immensely disconcerting. Hamilton had told them the enemy liked to do that to keep them on edge. Andy had to acknowledge they were damned good at it. It made him doubt the US slogan; we own the day but Charlie owns the night. Andy wondered how much they really owned the day, or if the enemy just let them think so to entice them into another trap. It almost made his head spin to think of it.

When Andy caught himself thinking that, he gave himself hell. 'You are doing exactly what you have been warned repeatedly not to do! Don't fall into it. Quit thinking! Just do what needs to be done now. Don't dwell on it. Just remind yourself, there is a cup of coffee waiting for you at the end of this patrol. Hot, steamy coffee. Don't think about anything else. Just your orders, your training and your coffee.'

Andy shifted the load in his hands to reach into this pocket. He retrieved Ginger's little braid. He looked at it and made a promise. 'No more blubber baby.'

Then he put it back in his pocket and thought about his coffee. He was debating whether he should have it black or with cream, when the squad leader had them in the mud again.

They waited for quite a while, but nothing happened. Andy decided he wanted cream. The first cup, he'd have with sugar, two teaspoons full. After that, just cream.

By that evening, Spud was dug in and trying to sleep while waiting his turn on guard duty. The mosquitoes were buzzing to their little hearts delight and Andy felt totally immersed in bug repellant, not that it worked. Andy figured the money the military spent on camouflage was wasted. The VC only had to sniff the wind and they could place an Army squad a mile away.

He did sleep a little before guard duty. Then he took his post and watched the black trees nested in the copious vegetation from the ground midway up the trees. He watched for any unusual movement, a metallic reflection or mostly, the deafening quiet that comes upon the jungle creatures when humans are sneaking around.

It was tense and frustrating. Everything made noise, or made quiet. Everything moved and seldom at random, but random wasn't good either. After all, if random was planned; was it random? There were reflections. Dew on a leaf reflecting in the moonlight looked amazingly like a rifle barrel. Andy decided to go back to thinking about his coffee before he lost his mind. How many days did he have left?

He was glad to be relieved from guard duty and go to rest again. He knew he wasn't doing a good job. He wouldn't want to be counting on him. He would have trusted either of his brothers, but not him.

Then he looked at the grunt who took his place, Andy realized he was in no better condition. No worse, but no better. "Shit, we're doomed," he mumbled as he went back to his spot to try to get more sleep.

The sleep seemed to help and Andy actually woke up feeling fairly good and in a much better mood. The day was almost a repeat of the day before, with only a brief contact with the enemy. No one was hurt and the soldier who had been wounded the day before was doing much better. He was trudging along with the rest of them.

That night was not so quiet. It wasn't while Andy was on watch, but while he was sleeping that he heard the order. Immediately, they were taking fire from three directions. There was a bedlam of profanity, noise and confusion.

Andy found an especially lucrative place to lob the grenades, and Chicago gave the VC a 'mad minute' of artillery fire. Whatever they hit, there was a massive explosion. After the pandemonium, there was the sound of frantic shouting and then it was quiet.

They did not move out, but held their position. The time seemed endless until it was breaking daylight. Men were sent to search the area from which they had taken fire. It was all quiet.

The men that moved to check out the right flank saw some action and lit up an area. They called in the Zippo (flame thrower) and after a few chilling screams and some M-16 rounds; it became extremely quiet. Andy tried not to think of what had happened, even though he knew.

After full daylight, the many tunnels were inspected in the area. Of course, there was no one in them or anything of value. By late afternoon, they blew the tunnels and went to the LZ. The birds came in and lifted them out. Before long, they were back in their trucks and headed back to their own little corner of paradise. The ramshackle mess hall looked like the Coffee Palace to Andy.

That night, Andy was just about asleep, when Horse poked him. The lean fellow was down on the floor next to his rack whispering to him.

"What?" Andy whispered back.

"Spud, do you think this is what it will be for a year? Just go out, get shot at and come home. Over and over?"

"Looks like it."

"I don't know if I can take it. I would feel better if we were burning a fort or something. This seems futile."

"Maybe we are just practicing so we can take the fort next time," Andy tried to encourage his friend. "Just don't think about it. You can't crap out on me."

"You either and don't speak with forked tongue!"

"I won't. No forked tongue! Get to sleep before we get in trouble."

# 355 days left

The morning in the barracks erupted early when one of the grunts woke everyone yelling at the top of his lungs. "Son of a Bitch! The bastards! They're everywhere! Kill them! Kill every last one of them. We can't even see all the bastards!"

Everyone sprung out of bed in various stages of consciousness—some nearly comatose and some combat ready, having grabbed their rifles. Chaos reigned for the couple seconds it took to figure out what Bradley was having a fit about.

He had stepped out of bed to go to the head and almost tripped over a rat. Then he put his other foot down on the tail of another rat. He went ballistic. He grabbed the piece of wood about the size of a baseball bat, which he had squirreled under his rack for just this purpose, and began beating the floor trying to kill them! Swinging frantically, he broke anything in his way. He missed one of the soldier's heads by only an inch or two. The frenzied, irrational man pulverized his piece of wood. Splinters flew all over. Everything around him was knocked over and smashed. A couple other guys tried to calm him down and take the remaining bits of crushed wood from his hands that were now slivered and bleeding, but he was still swinging wildly.

Some of the other guys were yelling at him to shut up. While most of the men in the room felt the same way that Bradley did about the rats; no one appreciated being awakened that way. One of the soldiers finally put his fist in Bradley's face. That settled him down.

The men put the place back in order enough so they could go back to sleep. Andy just shook his head and crawled back in his rack. He pulled the blanket over his shoulder and mumbled. "Stupid ass place!"

Over breakfast, Swede brought up what Bradley had done. "He is a hell of mess. He has been here almost four months and I think he is cracking."

Chicago nodded, "I'm glad he was after the rats and not me. He is one mean ass. I don't want to get on his bad side, no way."

"Was he always hot-headed?" Andy asked.

Horse shrugged, "Don't know. I hope he can keep it together when we need him."

"What are they going to do with him?" Swede asked naively.

Horse looked at him in disbelief, "You idiot, they're going to give him a loaded gun and send him back out with us! What the hell do you think they are going to do? This isn't a nursery school."

They all nodded and ate in silence.

That evening on their way back from the mess hall, the men noticed Suds. Andy went over to say hi to him. Suds looked at him with a grin. "Suds not see, think grunts to boonies."

"No, we done a work detail today," Chicago answered. "How's the laundry business?"

"Much work. Much dirt!" Suds grinned, pleased with himself that he made a joke.

Andy laughed, "I have a whole bag to bring in the morning. I was wondering how much extra would it cost to get you to make them smell nice?"

Suds looked at him seriously for a minute, and then got a devilish gleam in his eye, "Big joke, right? No way nice smell! Suds cannot do!"

Andy cracked up, "That's what I was afraid of. Hey, I have to know, do you guys drink coffee or tea?"

"Yes. And beer," Suds smiled. "What Spud drink?"

"All of that," Chicago answered, "But Andy he be loving his coffee! He thinks about it all the time!"

"Like girlfriend?" Suds' eyes twinkled. "He like coffee like girl? You have wife, Spud?"

"I have a girlfriend. How about you, Suds?" Andy asked.

"No more wife. She die. Suds very sad, but have to do washing you know."

"I'm so sorry, man," Andy put his hand on his shoulder. "I can't imagine your loss. I hope things get better."

Suds looked at Andy, "You nice friend for Suds."

"You are a nice friend for Spud, too."

At dinner, Chicago said, "I wonder how old Suds is. I can't no way figure out how old these people be. They all look like fifteen. I thought he was a kid."

"No," Swede answered, "I think he is almost thirty."

"Who the hell you talking about?" Bradley interrupted their conversation as he belligerently pushed his way to sit down on the other side of Swede. "That monkey bastard you were talking to!"

Horse saw the look in Andy's eye and gave him a look to keep quiet.

Swede replied, "Suds, the laundry guy."

"Yah, that bastard," Bradley expounded, "He should be put in a cage with the rest of them. Can't trust a single one of them. He would slit your throat if he had half a chance."

One of Bradley's friends piped up, "I don't know, Bradley! He has been coming here since before we got here and I never heard a bad thing about him."

"Sneaky sons of bitches," Bradley wouldn't back down, "He is just waiting for the right time. I better not catch you talking to him again. I saw Spud talking to him like a long lost friend."

Andy glared across the table, but Horse kicked his foot. Everyone looked at each other, but decided to change the subject. Andy and his friends finished eating in silence and then headed back to the barracks.

"I couldn't take being around that Bradley much. I had a bad feeling about him when I first saw him, and it hasn't changed yet," Andy stated.

"I'm warning you," Horse stopped walking and looked straight at Andy. "Don't antagonize him."

"My sentiments exactly," Swede agreed. "Hey, want to play cards?"

The next morning, on the way back from the mess hall, the men brought their laundry to Suds. He took their bags and then smiled, "You get coffee now, Spud?"

"Yup, on my way to the mess hall. Did you have your coffee?"

"Suds have Cohn coffee. Grunts say weasel poop coffee."

"What is weasel poop coffee?" Andy asked.

Suds started to answer, but the men behind in line were getting impatient. Andy grinned, "Talk later. Have a nice day."

"You too, Spud."

At the mess, Bandaid sat with the guys. They talked about Bradley. Bandaid just shook his head. "He was nuts when he got here. Granted, time hasn't worn well on him, but he isn't hooked together right in the first place. I mean, when he loses his temper, he loses all sense of reason. He has a real rotten streak. Just flat out cruel."

Then Chicago told him about what he said about Suds. Bandaid nodded, "I know. I have heard him go off on him. He hates him, but then he hates all Vietnamese. It is not uncommon, you know. Course, you get a few of your buddies killed, you develop a different outlook on things. Some folks forget to differentiate. The Vietnamese do the same. Some hate us just because. I'd hate to think that they thought we were all like Bradley! There are good people of all kinds, and bad people of all kinds. You know?"

Chicago smiled, "Hey man, I am black. I know."

"Ah shit," Andy said, "If you want to look for something to hate someone about, you can find it. I am more interested in this weasel poop coffee."

Horse laughed, "You would be."

Bandaid smiled, "Well, I can help you with that. Seems that there are these weasel-like things, civet cats which eat the coffee bean berries off the tree. The civet cat is related to the mongoose. In Thailand the coffee is called Kopi Luwak after the palm civet, but here in Vietnam it is called caphe cut chon which means fox dung coffee. Guess the Vietnamese think the civet looks like a fox, or something. Anyway, the beans pass through this weasel in a short time and come out partially digested. Then the beans are harvested. The coffee is excellent. It is very rich almost syrupy and tastes like it has chocolate in it. It is not bitter at all. I love it."

Swede was spellbound, holding his fork in his hand without moving. "My god, you drank that? What the hell were you thinking?"

Andy burst out laughing, "This from a guy that eats lutefisk! Codfish soaked in lye! Man, if you can eat that you are more of a man than I am! I can't take the smell of the stuff and it looks like slime!"

"And you guys give Indians a bad time about puppy stew?" Horse shook his head. "I don't know about the rest of you, but I'm done eating for a while."

# 354 days left

Andy got a couple more letters from Annie and one from his mom. His brother Keith wrote from Wisconsin. Keith was encouraging and told Andy to not let the job get him down. He told him that he knew he had what it took to handle things. Andy only wished he was a certain of that as Keith sounded. Most likely, he was just trying to encourage his little brother.

Uncle Byron wrote and enclosed a letter dictated from Ginger. She wanted to tell Andy she was being as good and as brave as she could be but was getting tired of it. She didn't think a person should have to behave for a long time. It was too hard. Andy was in total agreement with that.

Annie sent a couple pictures. One of her and Marty, Andy's cousin, who was her partner in their paramedic uniforms standing by their new ambulance. Then another was her and his Grandpas, Bert and Lloyd. Those old guys always thought that Annie was their girl and were very possessive about her.

Horse, Chicago and Swede looked at the pictures and they all agreed that Annie was a beautiful girl. Chicago didn't think that she was a beautiful as his Sonny. He was happy because he had finally received a letter from her. He had received a picture which they all admired before he put up on the shelf by his rack.

"Thank God this mail call was better," Horse observed. "Another one like the other day, I'd have put a halt to you guys ever getting mail."

"What did you get today?" Swede asked as he offered them some of his mom's cookies.

"Letter from my Mom. Good news," Horse teased. "She'll be off parole soon, and Dad is drying out in rehab. My sister finally figured out who the father of her kid is and they are thinking my brother's sentence will be reduced."

Swede punched him, "You dumb shit! Are you ever serious?"

Horse chuckled to himself, "Nah, Everybody is fine. Still colder than a well digger's ass and more snow forecast. Almost makes a person glad he is here."

Then he looked at the damp tent and sighed. "Or not. Just think, it has rained this much and it isn't even the monsoon season yet! Wonder what that will be like?"

That evening before going to eat, they went to pick up their laundry. Suds was extremely quiet. He smiled at Andy, but didn't say anything.

Andy looked at his friend and asked, "Is everything okay, Suds?"

Suds just nodded and then hurriedly gave him his change. Andy could tell he was nervous. When Andy took his clothing, he caught his glance briefly, "You need something? Something I can do?"

Suds answered quickly, "Talk later."

Andy nodded and moved on. As he and Horse walked away, they heard some men yelling. One of them was giving Suds hell over some shirt and chewing Suds out mercilessly. Andy turned immediately and was going to go back, but Horse grabbed his arm. "Calm down. The MP's are coming over. They'll handle it."

Andy watched while the MP's came and stood near the laundry guy. The four soldiers settled down. As Andy turned back, he noticed that from a distance, Bradley had been eyeing him like a hawk. Andy just gave him a dirty look and headed off with Horse.

"You'd better watch it," Horse pointed out. "You are getting on Bradley's bad side."

"What the hell did I do? I've never said more than hi to the psycho," Andy got mad. "He can keep out of my business."

"Look, Spud," Horse got serious. "I know you. I can't keep an eye on you all the time. You're letting him know how to get to you and he'll use it."

"I've never done a thing to him!" Andy defended himself.

"I know that, but it doesn't matter to him. He needs to have someone to harass and if he knows how to get to you, he'll do it. Mark my words. Steer him a wide berth. We'll both be happier."

"I'll think about it," Andy grumped.

"I have to meet your sister. What is her name, Pepper?"

"Why?" Andy was surprised at the abrupt subject change.

"You always say she is a hot-head. Man, if she is a hotter head than you, she must be a real spit fire!"

Andy shook his head, and then they decided to find someone to challenge to a game of cards.

When the friends came back from the mess, Chicago went to his bunk to look at his picture of Sonny. He couldn't find it. He looked all over and started to panic. Swede, Horse and Spud were all helping him. They knew where it was when they left. They thought it might have fallen behind the cot. As they were moving it, Andy happened to notice Bradley. He was watching them with an arrogant smirk. Andy knew right away what had happened.

He stepped toward Bradley and yelled, "Hand it over, Bradley. Give Chicago the photo back. Now."

The entire barracks froze. Everyone stared in shock. Not a man even breathed. It wasn't until then that Andy realized that he was half the size of Bradley and not a tenth as strong. But he was furious.

Bradley snarled at Andy. That made Andy even angrier. "Hand it over," Andy continued.

"What makes you think I would want his picture?" Bradley gloated while crossing his arms.

Andy moved toward him, "Dammit, hand it over!"

Bradley laughed, "Watcha gonna do about it, monkey lover?"

Then one of Bradley's friends grabbed the small framed photo and threw it back to Chicago's bed. "Here take the damned thing. It isn't worth wiping up blood over."

Chicago grabbed the photo and wiped it off. Andy sat back down on his rack. He hoped no one knew how his legs felt like rubber. Horse just stood there thinking.

After lights out, Horse moved over by Andy's rack and sat on the floor. "Spud? You awake?"

Andy whispered back, "Yah. You don't need to say anything. I know already."

"I'm afraid there could be big trouble over this. Watch your back, Man."

"Thanks."

"Ah, Spud?"

"Yah."

"Do you have any idea how small you are? I mean, did you even think about that?"

Andy grinned, "Not until I had my big mouth going."

Horse nodded, "I figured. Looks like Tonto will have his work cut out. Even though it was a dumb thing to do, I was proud you did it. Just don't do it again."

"I'll try not to."

"Not encouraging. You better watch you back."

Bradley was on guard duty that night. As was the case with him, when he came back, he managed to wake up everyone in the whole hooch. He kept saying 'Excuse me', in a loud whisper, but everyone knew he did it on purpose. No one said anything because it wasn't worth it. Andy started to open his mouth and Horse gave him a dirty look. Andy turned over and put his pillow over his head.

Thunder woke them and it was pouring rain when they got up. They had orders again that they would be leaving in a few hours for patrol. After breakfast, Andy wrote some letters home and organized to leave. Andy and Horse were both relieved to learn that Bradley was not on this mission.

Bradley and some guys were raising hell about the rats again in their corner and Andy tried to ignore them. They were blustering about all the things they were going to do to the rodents, ranging from poison, being set on fire or disembowelment. It was getting more torturous with every new idea. The laughter had taken a turn from merriment to evil glee.

It was killing Andy. His father would have had his hide pinned to the back wall, if he had ever carried on like that. He didn't like rats either. However, there was no reason for how they were acting.

Horse stopped what he was doing and his look penetrated Andy, "Listen here, Schroeder. You keep out of it. If you get your ass whipped over a rat; so help me, I will let you bleed!"

"But-,"

"Dammit. I mean it," Horse glared.

Andy stopped and thought. Horse wasn't messing around, besides Andy knew he was right. He knew that he and Bradley were on a collision course and he needed to back off. That was totally against his nature, but it was stupid to get into a confrontation with a jackass like Bradley, and over a rat, no less.

"You're right," Andy conceded. "You know, I'm almost anxious to get out in the boonies! How bad is that?"

"I'd say there is no hope for you," Horse raised his eyebrows.

Before long, they loaded into the back of an Army truck heading off toward the rain-drenched jungle. An hour or so later, they were inserted into the forest. The terrain that they were humping through was very dense and seemed almost devoid of clearings. This time, they had received explicit warning to keep alert for booby traps. Many had been reported in that area.

As they traveled along, they saw a few. Treacherous things. A few Pungy pits were found that had been covered with the vegetation to be disguised perfectly. Inside the narrow five to six foot deep Pungy pits were deep enough to allow for the necessary impact and the penetrating sharp bamboo spikes were long enough to impale a human being. Horrible things. Some of the spikes were smeared with poisons or feces to cause infections if the victim managed to survive the fall onto them. It made Andy cringe to look at them. He was rather certain one wouldn't necessarily die immediately if you fell on it, unless you were lucky and a spike hit an artery. Anyone would play hell trying to retrieve a person impaled in such a manner. It was too deep and if the body was stuck on—.

'Knock it off,' Andy reprimanded himself. 'With any luck, I'll hit a land mine instead. I know I haven't talked to You in a while, God; and I should have, but please promise me that if I land in one of those damned things that I puncture something vital and go quick. Please God.'

Andy almost felt reassured that he and God had an agreement about that, so he was able to put it out of his mind. Well, pretty much.

The good thing, it was raining hard enough, so the mosquitoes were not out. Andy grumped to himself. "They are probably in shelter somewhere partying and breeding!"

That night when he settled into his mud pie for some sleep, he actually manage to put Bradley out of his mind. He thought about Ginger. 'You are right, little girl. A guy shouldn't have to behave for too long.'

# *351 days left*

Right after daybreak, the men were on their feet again. They moved out of the wooded area and began climbing. The going was difficult because of the dense vegetation, but by ten or so, it was easier because the landscape was previously sprayed with defoliant. The early fog had lifted and the sun was bright. It was starting to get warm.

They came out of the woods and on to a dirt road. They followed the road a couple of klicks and Andy could see a small mountain village ahead of them. There were about twelve or fifteen twig-thatched huts, mostly wooden buildings. Goats and chickens grazed leisurely around the buildings.

There were several people in the village. Some men were repairing the roof. A pregnant woman was giving a small child a bath on a porch in front of one of the hooches. An older woman was cooking something on a short burner while she squatted next to it. Little children stopped their play and peeked around corners or doorways to watch the soldiers go by.

Lt. Hamilton talked with an older man of the village, while the soldiers kept a keen watch. There had been VC through the day before and had caused the damage on the roof of the building they were repairing.

Andy felt everyone watching them from under their coulee hats. Expressionless, no one made eye contact. The villagers didn't look afraid but everyone was; the soldiers and the civilians. The children were mostly curious and a few whispered to each other. Andy thought of Ginger and her little brother Charlie.

He wondered how those kids would react. At their home, Ginger and Charlie would run out and talk to anyone who came into their yard. They would find out their names and how many kids the strangers had in a matter of minutes. Charlie would probably take their hand and walk them back to the house so his Mom could give them coffee. But they had never had soldiers with guns come in their yard, men who destroyed buildings and killed people. It would only take one go-round of that and they would no longer be welcoming either.

Andy watched as a dog ran out from one of the huts and a little boy grabbed at it, trying to get it to come back by him. Andy could tell the child was worried the dog would get into trouble. The kid panicked and Andy was relieved when the dog returned to stand by his master. The little boy reached down and petted his dogs head. Andy smiled. The little boy shyly smiled back and then went back to his vacant expression.

A few more men from the village were now talking to Hamilton and his translator. Then they all moved toward one hooch on the edge of the village. First Squad leader directed his men inside to search. Everyone else stood at the edge of the village in a protective stance while they did it. Apparently, they found nothing. Within minutes, the soldiers all moved on.

It wasn't until they were down the road about fifteen minutes when Andy realized that his heart had been in his throat the whole time. 'Man,' he thought to himself, 'We were right smack in the middle of forty people with no cover. That can't be good. Any trouble at all and we been dead for sure.'

He glanced over toward Horse who returned his look. Andy knew he felt the same way, without having to say a word. This was some scary shit. Andy decided that he liked the jungle better. Then he thought about it, maybe not. Hmm. Now he didn't like clearings, jungles or villages. Yah, things were definitely narrowing down.

They walked along another half an hour and then entered into lightly wooded area where they stopped. While they were eating their C Rations, which the guys always joked were older than they were (since it was rumored they were made for the Korean War). Horse sat next to Andy.

"Spud, I was freaking out in that village. What about you?"

"Yup, if someone hiccoughed, I'd have opened fire."

They began moving along again. Within a short distance, they came into another village, not unlike the one they had passed through. However, this village was empty. There was no one around, not a human or a dog. There were some chickens and a couple goats, but all other living things were gone. The platoon inspected the situation and on passed through. It was eerily quiet.

As they came into the next clearing, they saw the smoldering remains of what had been another smaller village. The smell met them before they actually saw anything. There must have been eight buildings still in piles of smoldering ash. There was one dead man lying in the village center. He had been shot execution style. Not ten feet away lay a woman and a toddler; both shot dead.

It was so quiet that other than the trudge of soldiers' boots, the only sound was the buzz of mosquitoes and the flies that were dining on the dead. Between the repugnant odor, the humid heat and the dead, Andy started to feel light-headed and nausea was emerging.

Then there was a sound. It sounded like a twig cracking and adrenaline immediately took hold. They all listened for another sound. Nothing for a minute and then there was another set of sounds. There was no question now, but that there was something just out of view in the wooded area to the right.

The pucker factor of the situation must have been a plus one hundred. Andy could not remember ever having been so terrified in his life. Why had they been ordered to march smack into the middle of a burnt village with no cover? Was this a trap? Were they surrounded? Would they end up like the village, totally decimated? How long had they been followed? How many tunnels were under the very ground they were standing on? Andy started to panic.

Then for reasons unknown, his mind clicked off. Everything went into slow motion, as if his brain was giving him more time to think. He was more alert than he had ever been in his life. His senses were all at full capacity. It almost felt good. He watched the tree line and listened for the sound.

He didn't look at his friends, or think about home, God or any of the things one hears about. He just watched the trees, ready to react. Granted he was frightened, but it would be futile to worry at that point. He would just react the best he knew how and right now, he felt confident that he could. It was a weird feeling.

The men all stood for what seemed to be a decade when they heard the sound again. The underbrush beneath the trees rustled and Andy heard the men move their guns to react.

Out from the brush came two goats, totally oblivious to the situation and the near heart attacks they had caused. There was a feeling of relief and a few chuckles, but everyone was still tense.

The men checked the remnants of the village and found a couple tunnel entrances. Franklin was sent down one and another smaller man was sent down another. There was nothing of any value in them, but Franklin reported that one of the tunnels headed back in the direction of the village they had just passed through.

"Ah hell," Hamilton grumbled, "They are all bloody connected. These people have more roads underground than New York has above ground! Let's move out of Indian County before we get our asses scalped."

A few men laughed, but everyone agreed with his sentiment. They left the decimation that was once someone's home and moved on.

It became very hot and the soldiers were beginning to strip off anything they could to keep cooler. They came to a dirt road with clearings on either side. It became obvious that the intent was to go right down that road. Andy thought it was ludicrous. They would be in clear sight, lined up like so many slowly moving targets, waiting to be picked off. He thought it was nuts but then what he hell did he know. Lt Hamilton looked none too happy about it, so Andy figured it had been a direct order.

Maybe the mucky-mucks knew it was secure. After all, they had the comic books (military maps) and the Intel. Of course, that could all change in a flash. Everyone knew that no area was secure if there were tunnels and this place was crawling with them!

Damn, why hadn't he just got those damned papers mailed off to the University of North Dakota in time? What an idiot. Ah hell, there was no point in thinking about that now! His Dad said, 'just do what you gotta do; do the best you can and don't think about it.' He wondered what his Dad would say about this. Then he grinned, 'Nothing good, I'm damned sure of that.'

He envisioned his Dad standing in the barn with a cup of steaming coffee in his hand. His Dad loved his coffee, too. He wondered if he had thought about coffee while he stationed in Northern Russia at the end of WWI. He'd told him how miserable cold it was. He was sure that Dad would've needed his coffee to keep warm.

He looked at the tree line and wondered if those coffee eating weasel things lived in these trees. Maybe they were chewing on some beans while he was walking by. Maybe those villagers made their living gathering up those partially digested beans.

As they were almost out of the cleared area, but still on the dirt road, they got the signal and all hit the dirt. There was instant terror as there was a cacophony of incoming mortars. Bole signaled for them to get up and move as fast as they could off the road.

Some men were incapacitated with fear. Paralyzed, they were unable to move. Bole and the squad leaders started yelling, "Move, you stupid sons of bitches. Get your sorry asses off this road. Keep moving! Move! Move!"

It seemed like an eternity, but actually it was within seconds, the men that were moving were pulling at the others and they were all off to the edge of the trees. Andy had slipped back into this mode. The mode of slow motion, reacting and not thinking that afforded him to think clearly and sharply as it took over his mind. He could make split second decisions, but actually felt that he had the time to think about them. It must have been his training or the fact that when it comes down to it, survival is dominant and extremely powerful. Survival is a primal motivation.

This fight did not end in a few minutes like the previous ones. There were many wounded and the fight was furious. Enemy fire was coming from every direction. It was erratic and devastating.

Heavily engaged, all the men worked to keep the munitions coming and giving first aid to the wounded. Andy saw Swede talking frantically on radio. There was no doubt about it; they were pinned down. They would not be able to get out of this one unless the enemy decided to let them go. It didn't seem they were of a mind to do that.

One of the grunts handed Spud some of the extra grenades he carried. Andy nodded thanks. The soldier was moving back, no more than seconds later, when he was hit in the chest and abdomen with a grenade. Andy watched as the man was blown apart directly next to him and felt he concussion of the explosion. Bits of the man's body landed not two feet from where he was laying. Andy's eyes opened wide and he immediately returned fire in the direction he the deathly grenade had come from. He slipped back into his mode.

What seemed like a century later, the Puffs (gun ships) arrived and opened fire on the area around the men. The odds changed dramatically and almost instantaneously. The enemy fire stopped within a minute or two, but the Puffs continued to shell the area. The sound was deafening. Then two Slicks (medivac helicopters) came in and moved the wounded out. The dustoff was completed and graves registration had taken the three dead away.

Andy looked at the spot where the soldier had died beside him. "Holy Jesus!" Andy muttered. Whitmore seemed like a decent fellow, but Andy didn't know him very well. Now he was thankful that he didn't. He shook his head. He never wanted to see something like that again.

Then he remembered that Pastor Byron said the reason that he became a minister was because his best friend was killed by a grenade a short ways away from him while he was in Korea. A chaplain had helped Byron deal with it. Afterwards, he felt called to help others.

Andy looked at the bloody dirt and the bits of human flesh beside him. He didn't make him feel anything. That was horrible. He didn't feel sad or mad, though certainly not happy. All he felt was sick and repulsed.

# 350 days left

That night curled up in this little hole, Andy thought about the day. Three men killed and seven were seriously injured. The war was over for the dead but for the injured, who knew what battles they still had to fight?

He thought about Whitmore. He had died fast. There was no doubt about that. It was quick. He literally never knew what hit him. Andy figured he would prefer to go that way himself. He thought he should feel worse about Whitmore. Shouldn't he have cried or something? He knew there was no helping him. There was nothing he could have done. However, he should have felt worse. Andy thought about it, he didn't have time to cry.

Then he thought, in that Bible verse that kept going through his head—that one from Ecclesiastes.

> *¹To every thing there is a season, and a time to every purpose under the heaven:*
> *²A time to be born, and a time to die; a time to plant, and a time to pluck up that which is planted;*
> *³A time to kill, and a time to heal; a time to break down, and a time to build up;*
> *⁴A time to weep, and a time to laugh; a time to mourn, and a time to dance;*
> *⁵A time to cast away stones, and a time to gather stones together; a time to embrace, and a time to refrain from embracing;*
> *⁶A time to get, and a time to lose; a time to keep, and a time to cast away;*
> *⁷A time to rend, and a time to sew; a time to keep silence, and a time to speak;*
> *⁸A time to love, and a time to hate; a time of war, and a time of peace."*

In that verse, mourning and weeping were not on the same line as a time to kill. On that line, was a time to break down! Andy thought to himself, 'figures!'

Swede reported that Lt. Hamilton had not been at all happy with the orders about that road and had tried to explain to the brass that moving across that open road was suicidal. They said there was a reason, but it made no sense to him. He had told Bole that he wished the jackasses with the big ideas were actually out there. He didn't think that they would have trotted down the middle of the road if they had been.

After they were hit so hard, as soon as he could, Hamilton wasted no time in telling them what he thought of their stupid ass plan. Not that it did one iota of good for the three dead men and the injured. At any rate, Hamilton didn't seem any more pleased with the rest of the mission that was before them. They would receive some reinforcements however because their numbers had been effectively gutted.

Horse sat next to Spud for a time without talking. Then his friend asked, "You okay, Man?"

"Yah, you?"

"Okay. Now I know how Custer and his boys must have felt. You know, if I had been one of Custer's men, I'd have shot him myself."

Andy looked at him and dropped his head, "I always wondered if he didn't die by 'friendly fire."

"You mean fragging, don't you?" Horse replied. "When an officer gets nailed by his own men. Yah, I bet he was. He was a stupid, arrogant bastard."

"Yah. That he was," Spud agreed.

The young soldier leaned back in the hole. "I figured this was it today. My last stand for damned sure. I knew it once we got on that stupid road. I just knew it," he spoke quietly. "Did you hear about that Fredericks guy? The one with the Southern accent?"

"He was wounded today, right?"

"Yah. Blew off one of his legs and his family jewels," Horse reported. "Even if he lives, he will never have kids. I think I'd rather be dead."

Andy glared at him, "No, you wouldn't. Don't crap out on me. I don't even want to hear that."

Both young men sat quietly for a few minutes, then Horse spoke with great gravity, "Andy, will you promise me something?"

"What is it Jackson?"

"If that happens to me, or if I get killed, will you name one of your kids after me?" His eyes penetrated the importance of his request to his friend. "Then at least someone would know I had been here on this earth."

"Of course, I would be proud to name a child of mine after you." Andy said quietly. After a minute, he put his hand on his shoulder, and then broke into a grin, "I always wanted a little girl named Horse anyway!"

Horse punched him, "You sorry ass, I wouldn't want any of your kids named after me! So forget it!"

Andy got serious, "I give you my word, but I have a better idea. You just get out of this mess in one piece. Horse, would you ever name a kid after me?"

"Yah, but his name would have to be Jackass!" Horse cracked up at his joke.

The guys laughed and never mentioned it again, but both knew they had made a solemn promise. Horse moved over to his hole and both men tried to get some shuteye before guard duty.

While Andy was on guard duty, a bird brought in more troops, supplies and some mail. When he was relieved, he went back to his hole and opened his two letters. One was from his brother, Kevin. Kevin was seven years older than Andy and the family cut up. When Andy was home on leave, he was groomsman in his wedding this February. He was working with their Dad at the family gas station and repair shop in Merton. Not only was he doing most of the work, since Dad had broken his hand; but he was also helping with the chores on the home place. Andy would have turned in his flak jacket and rifle for a milk stool in a heartbeat. Poor Kevin. He was actually taking the brunt for Andy not mailing his paperwork into the University of North Dakota on time.

The other letter was from his Annie. She seemed in a much better mood than she had in the previous letter. She was excited about their new ambulance at the Fire Hall and about Ginger's progress. Seemed the little girl was doing well and the skin grafts were finally healing. The doctors thought she wouldn't require any more surgery. Her eyesight, which they had first thought would be okay, was in jeopardy, however. They were now worried that she would ever be able to see very well.

The whole family had become quite close to Ginger's doctor, Zach Jeffries. Andy and Darrell had met him while sitting up at the hospital with Ginger and they had started to hang out together. Darrell had given him the nickname Smitty, which only Andy, Ginger and Darrell ever called him. Zach had come out to his going-away party and stayed overnight at the farm. From what Annie said, it sounded like he was rapidly becoming a family fixture.

Andy's family tended to do that. If they liked someone, they soon became part of the family. Now Zach was spending most of his spare time at the farm. He was helping his Dad and little Charlie build a model helicopter. They had started it before Andy had to leave. He would have loved to work on it himself, but knew he didn't have time.

He folded the letter and put it in his pocket. He envied Zach. He wished he was helping with the helicopter, milking and talking politics with the Grandpas. But he did like Zach and he was a good guy. He was glad that he was there. Andy just wished he was there, too. They were taught all their lives, that there is always room and time to include someone else. He did believe that. He was just jealous that he wasn't there himself.

He remembered how Zach used to bitch about the hospital coffee. Actually, they all did. It was some real rotgut. He wondered if he had ever tasted this weasel poop coffee. Zach was raised down South and had told them once that he had tried that chicory coffee and hated it. He thought it was bitter. When Andy got back to Ft. Leonard Wood, he had made it a point to taste it. He was in total agreement.

Finally, he fell asleep. He felt like he did when he had slept by Ginger's bed at the hospital. He woke at every sound and never really slept hard. However, the little real sleep he got was helpful.

Before dawn, a barrage of gunfire awakened the troops and the trees lit up like a Fourth of July celebration gone awry. It only lasted a short time and no one was injured, but it had its desired effect. The men all knew that the enemy was still there and the enemy knew exactly where and how many of them there were. Now they had a good idea how many reinforcements were brought in. Andy almost wished the VC would just blow them all to kingdom done and be done with it.

The entire next day was just like the day before, minus the fierce firefight. There were a few short mad minutes, just to let everyone know they were still in a damned war. In case, anyone could forget. They moved through more trees, clearings and the terrain was just like before. It had become tedious, tiring and boring. Andy had never been aware before that terror could become boring. Besides that, his feet hurt, he was tired and he still didn't have a good cup of coffee. And those damned mosquitoes!

He saw a couple snakes, which perked him up. Someone told him they weren't poisonous, but he really didn't care. They only found two of those booby-trapped Pungy pits, but no one could guess how many they had passed just missing by inches. One tunnel entrance was located and one of the replacements went down into it. Of, course nothing was found, except more tunnels. Since there was no way one could follow all of them, Andy wondered about the virtue of going into them. For the most part, he was just glad that no one had noticed he was about the same size as Franklin.

His mosquito friends were back in full force accompanied by their new generation. Andy wondered why they still bothered him. Certainly, he couldn't have any blood left. He felt like Pig Pen in the Charlie Brown comic strips, accept that instead of being in a whirlwind of dirt, he had his own little cloud of swarming mosquitoes.

He wondered if anyone appreciated just how much he really hated them. Yah, they probably did. He certainly bitched about it enough. Chicago wasn't very sympathetic pointing out that when he was nearby, the mosquitoes stayed off him. Andy grumped that if he was a mosquito, he would prefer his smell to Chicago's, too. Horse had to break up the argument. "You guys are worse than a bunch of two-year olds!"

"How old are you, Horse?" Andy asked.

"Older than you. How old are you Spud?"

"About twenty."

Chicago had a fit, "How can you be about anything? You either are or you aren't. Are you twenty or not?"

"Okay, I'm twenty. How old are you?'

"Nineteen. See, that's how you should answer. So, what are you?"

"You guys don't want to know. You'll just get mad," Horse answered.

"Why would we get mad?" Chicago demanded. "I guess you are thirty!"

"Thirty? Hell, I'm eighteen!"

Chicago went into a total tailspin! "Here I thought you were older and wiser. Shit, you ain't nothing but younger and dumber than me."

Horse grinned, "I may be younger, but there is no way I'm dumber."

Then it was up to Andy to break them up.

# 349 days left

The next six days continued on the same pattern. There were a few mad minutes but nothing of any significance. They had gone around a couple clearings, instead of crossing on a road. At first, the men all thought it was a brilliant plan. However, there were so many of those impaling Pungy pits, other assorted booby traps, tunnels and land mines, that it took an eon to get around any clearing. It probably wasn't a heck of a lot safer. One of the men pointed out, "At least on the road, it would be quicker."

At one point, about halfway around the clearing to get back to the road in the jungle, they were deluged by enemy fire. One grunt threw himself on the ground and landed a little over half way onto one of those Pungy pits, or tiger pit. In his adrenaline-induced slow motion, Andy watched as he rolled into the pit. There was not a damned thing anyone could do for him.

After the short firefight, Bandaid went over to the pit. The soldier was dead. One of the spikes had penetrated an artery in his leg and another stripped an artery in his upper chest. Without being asked, Bandaid answered the question that all had in their mind when he said, "He went real fast."

Everyone nodded and then had to work like hell to get his body out of the pit.

The mission became monotonous and miserable. They could point to nothing to make them feel they had accomplished something. They all knew they hadn't. That is, except for Andy. He knew he had personally given blood transfusions to at least three million of those flying syringes. He was convinced that he even had a mosquito bite inside his mouth! Horse told him he was nuts, but after all, it was his mouth. He should certainly know if he got bit there!

Even his eyelids were swollen with mosquito bites. There was one evening, when he actually lay in his hole hoping for enemy fire. He would

63

stand up with a neon target on his chest, just to get away from those damned mosquitoes. He was going to write to Smitty and ask him if he had ever heard of anyone dying from insect repellant poisoning. He knew the repellant didn't keep bugs away and it surely made them breed. Just how much of that mosquito venom could a human body take? Maybe it didn't cause physical disease, but he knew it definitely caused madness. He didn't need medical advice on that.

He decided that he wouldn't study law when he got back to the world. Now he reconsidered and decided to become a chemist. Yah, that would be good. He would develop something that would keep those relentless antagonists from ever flying again. Good grief, they almost drove him mad. Only the heavy rain kept them away.

The rain gear, ponchos, became extremely heavy when wet, so most men just forgot about wearing them and walked in the downpour. Andy didn't enjoy slopping through the mud, but rain was so much nicer than those damned mosquitoes, he was glad that the monsoon was not that far away. With any luck at all, it would start early this year.

When they were plucked out of the boondocks six days later and the army trucks rolled up, the men had all they could do to keep from kissing their drivers! It had been long enough. There was not one of them who was not glad that little adventure was over. Even though the talk was filled with testosterone bravado, everyone knew the other guys were just as glad as they were heading back to camp. Maybe that is why they didn't say it. What was the need?

They returned to camp about time to hit the cold water showers and then mess hall. When Andy smelled the coffee, he almost ran the last few feet. He was convinced their mess crew contained the best cooks in the entire world. Their food was hot, they had real coffee and there was a table to sit at. It was like a dining room in Heaven and he didn't have to share it with a single mosquito. No matter that none of the guys were certain of what they were eating; it was real food. Real hot food.

After the shower and dinner, they had a couple beers and then went back to their beds. As Andy crawled into his rack, he decided that life was good and he was glad he had not jumped up with a target on his chest. Even Bradley didn't bother him too much. Bradley had not been on their mission, so they had some time apart. He felt he might even be able to handle being around him.

He reread his favorite letter from Annie and looked at her picture. Then he stretched all the way out in his bed. It was dry, not rain soaked or covered in mud. He had a pillow. It was like paradise. He even liked the sound of the other men snoring. Things were wonderful.

Sometime during the night, Andy had a very erotic dream about Annie. He could feel her close to him and curling her legs around his. She was slowly moving her leg up his thigh. He became quite passionate and it almost felt real. It was wonderful.

He was almost awake, but not quite. Suddenly, she was tightening around his foot so much that it hurt. He wondered to himself why she was choking his foot. How could she be doing that? She was still moving slowly closer to his privates which were now at full alert.

His foot was starting to hurt a lot. He wished that she would stop doing that. It was beginning to ruin what was a fantastic erotic experience. Then it got too painful and he couldn't stand it anymore. He told her no. She didn't quit. Why wouldn't she stop?

Then it got even worse. Surely his beloved Annie wouldn't want to hurt him like this. Finally, there was nothing erotic about it anymore, it was just plain excruciating pain. He woke up, let out a painful yell and threw the blanket back on his cot.

There was a nine foot boa constrictor wrapped around his leg. It was a good thing that Andy had yelled before he saw the snake because he was speechless after he did! He was terrified. It was the biggest, ugliest thing he had ever seen. Its head was about three inches from his privates but if he had had a gun in his hand, he would have shot it regardless.

Nearly catatonic, he was fighting to keep breathing. Horse and a couple other guys had awakened when he yelled. Thank God. They worked mightily to pull the damned snake off Andy without causing any more damage. Andy, for his part, between fear and mortification, was unable to say a word. In fact, he wasn't even thinking anything other than that he just wanted to die. Then and there.

Once the men got the snake off him and threw it out of the tent, one of the other grunts shot the damned thing. Then Bradley, who had been laughing like a hyena at the whole situation, became livid and belligerent.

"Why did you kill it? You stupid bastard. I purposely brought him in to keep the rats down!" Bradley yelled at the soldier.

The MP's arrived after hearing the ruckus in time to hear Bradley admit he had brought the snake in, so they heard him for themselves. If they had not heard it, there was not a man in the tent that would have had the courage to tell them Bradley had brought it in intentionally.

"You purposely brought a large boa constrictor into the barracks?" one MP shouted, "You stupid bastard. That is about the dumbest thing I have ever heard. It could have killed somebody."

By the time the lights were back out, Bradley had new sleeping accommodations courtesy of the MP's, and would have to face the consequences for his actions in the morning. He knew what he had done was against the rules but he felt no remorse, except that the snake was dead. He would get another one. He knew he would be in trouble, but not that much. The Army needed him more than he needed them, so he figured he was in a no lose situation. "If I end up in a brig, so? They can get come other jackass to do their fighting."

As for Andy, he had almost literally been scared to death! He was not only embarrassed, terrified and madder than hell at Bradley, he really had no desire to crawl back in his rack even though he wanted to sleep.

He tried to act like it was okay and that he wasn't dying, but he was. He couldn't look at Horse because he knew that Horse would know. Hell, Horse probably knew right away. He guessed he didn't care if Horse knew he had thought it was Annie; but he hoped no one else did.

He lay there trying to think of something that would make him feel better. He started to think of Annie, but after that experience, he couldn't do that. Then he tried to think of Ginger and Charlie digging holes all over, but that only reminded him of the Viet Cong tunnels. He thought about his sister, Pepper. If she had been there and saw what Bradley did, she would have been all over him like a cold sweat.

Then he thought of his Mom. He hated to even think it himself, but he really just wanted to cry into her arms like a little baby and have her tell him it would be okay. Yah, he would really have the respect of his brothers! Who the hell was he kidding? He decided he was going crazy. Finally sometime before time to get up, he fell asleep.

# 342 days left

Incoming mortars interrupted the early morning peace. The whole camp was under attack. It lasted only a matter of minutes, but in the aftermath the devastation took hours to calculate. Seventeen dead and about thirty to forty seriously injured, there were many minor injuries they didn't even count them. Three of their makeshift buildings were totally destroyed and everything was damaged in one way or another. There were a few small fires and one rather large one in the mess tent. The men each took that as a personal affront. It only took them a short time to put the fire out, but what was left was dismal to say the least.

Andy only received a cut on the leg, Horse a couple cuts on the arm and Swede took a piece of shrapnel in his shoulder, but once it was removed he required only a bandage. Hit by a falling rafter, Chicago sustained an injury to his head. It required stitches, but he was on the mend.

It was about eleven that morning when Andy received word that Bradley had been killed in the mortar attack. Andy stopped what he was doing and didn't move while absorbing the information. He never answered Swede when he told him but stood in stone silence for a minute and then went back to work. Swede finally turned and walked away.

Andy's head was spinning. He couldn't say he was sad about it because that would be a flat out lie. He couldn't help but feel if someone had to die, it might as well have been him. He wasn't happy about it either.

He had to admit to himself that he was glad for the attack in a perverted way. Everyone but him seemed to forget about the night before. He had been terrified about the guff the men would have given him that morning about the snake. He knew it and they knew it. Bradley was the ringleader of a bunch that were not much of an improvement over him. Any one of them would give him grief about being aroused by a snake at the drop of a hat, and think it was hysterical. Now, all their attention was on the attack.

He was glad for Bradley, too. He could go home a hero, instead of an embarrassment to his family. Andy wondered what his family would think of him. "Not much," he mumbled to himself. The only honest thing Andy could give him was to hope that he died quickly.

Andy sat by Horse during lunch but only mumbled mundane sentences. Andy knew that Horse was very aware that he was about two inches from going over the edge. As they went back to their work detail, Horse clapped him on the shoulder, "We need to talk. Just you and me. Okay?"

Andy looked away, "Not necessary."

Horse tightened his grip, "Damn right it is. Don't give me any grief. You can't crap out on me. I won't have it."

Andy stopped walking, "Really, I'm fine."

"You're a lying sack of shit. We'll talk. Hear?"

"Yah. I hear."

All afternoon, Andy tried to work out things out on his own. He just couldn't do it. He had nowhere to start. He always thought he was a normally sympathetic, God-fearing person. He knew he didn't like to see suffering. Yet he had watched Whitmore get blown to bits and never even reacted. He watched the guy fall into the impaling pit and didn't react. Some of the men threw up, or cried. Not him. He did nothing. He heard that Bradley was killed and only thought it was probably for the best. What the hell was wrong with him? What kind of a unfeeling monster had he become?

How could a person mistake a snake for their lover? It was bad enough to be so scared he could hardly breathe. He never had known fear like that before in his entire life. He wasn't adult, or brave. He was still that little brother.

How could he be so mortified the other guys knew what he had been thinking last night that he thought an enemy attack was a good thing!

All he had to do was think of it, and his face would turn red from embarrassment. Thank God, no one noticed because he was moving debris in the heat, but he knew. He was dying of embarrassment and humiliation.

He was certain that neither of his brothers or his dad would think he was acting like a responsible adult. He was acting like a spoiled teenager.

He hated himself. Andy thought to himself, "Bradley still came out on top. He is at least dead, but I'm left to face it."

After last night, he wondered if he could ever feel the same about Annie. Would he always think of that snake? How could you think of Charlie and Ginger and not immediately associate them with Viet Cong tunnels? He was definitely losing his sanity. No doubt about it.

It didn't seem to Andy that the Army was sending anyone who was crazy home, or else they all would have been gone. Everyone was some form of insane over there. Maybe he had lost his ability to feel emotions? Maybe he never really did and just pretended that he had because everyone else did?

He had gone to church his whole life, believed and prayed regularly. Since he had been here, he prayed twice—both times asking for a promise to die quickly. Last night, he didn't even think to pray. He didn't even think about God, Jesus or any of it. He was certain God was embarrassed at his behavior Himself. None of it was very Christian.

That seemed like a joke. Christian? Andy felt like religion was something for another time. Faith really had no connection with this life. This was survival. Faith was something that Ozzie and Harriet people had. The meek inheriting the earth seemed a far cry from grenades and mortars! Turning the other cheek did not appear in the Army's SOP. When you were told to kill, you did. No questions asked. And yet, the country thought it was noble. Andy shook his head. 'I guess it isn't if you kill, it is who you take the orders from. And then you go nuts like Bradley, everyone is glad you are dead!'

Hell, nothing out here made sense. Soldiers carrying big guns marched into decimated villages, tramped unwavering by a dead family and were afraid of goats in bushes! He knew he hadn't encountered a lot of the stuff that he had heard about from the other soldiers who had been their longer. Some of that was horrific. At first, Andy had wondered how these grunts could talk about stuff, or even make sick jokes about it. He had been so self-righteous. Now he was doing it himself.

The only pure emotion he had felt was that of wanting to cry like a baby last night. God, what he'd have given to be able to do that. He couldn't let even Horse know that. That would be the end of him. He knew that he was not even close to being that responsible, respected adult.

He hated this whole damned thing but now didn't even know if he could go home and still feel good about himself. How could he want to be home when he knew people like Bandaid, Bole, Chicago, Swede and Horse were over here? Who did he think he was that his sorry ass should be saved while these guys were here? They were more together than he was. At least they had some semblance of sanity.

He hated everything. Every single damned thing. There seemed no point to anything and he still had so long before he went home that it seemed closer to forever. He couldn't even count that far.

Then a tiny mosquito bit him on the back of the hand. Andy stared at the miniscule insect and then slapped it. "Determined little bastards," Andy grunted, "I will give them that."

If only he could do that. Could he be as determined and single minded as a mosquito. They had very little going for them. They had no armor, nothing that would kill anything, but they certainly would make their presence known. They flew into every little crevice, knowing their targets were ready to retaliate with the audacity to make quite a noise doing it! They didn't sneak around! Hell no! They went bzzzzz, bzzzzz, like a tormentor taunting his prey, building dread in his victim before injecting the needle!

"Quit sluffing, Schroeder," one of the guys next to him yelled, "You have been standing there for five minutes!"

Andy looked at the man and apologized. "Sorry, I guess I was lost in thought."

"What were you thinking about that got you that far away?"

"You won't believe it, but mosquitoes."

"Knowing you, I can." The man went back to digging away debris.

After mess that night, Andy and Horse went for a walk around the camp. Chicago had hit the rack early because he was still nursing a horrible headache. The men walked to the far end of the camp and then sat down for a cigarette on some junk piled up there.

Horse was quiet for a bit, waiting for Andy to say something, but he didn't. Finally, he said, "Look Spud, I know last night was a bitch. I think you should talk about it."

"Don't want to."

"I already figured that. I could hear you talking to yourself before you yelled. I think I know that you thought it was Annie but no one else could hear you. You are the last one on the end and then it's me. No one else heard it. Chicago didn't hear because he snores so loud, he couldn't hear a C130 land. Okay? So don't let that bother you. Got it?"

"I feel like such an ass. How could I make a mistake like that?"

"Easy. Why do you feel like you're an ass? You are a human being! You weren't the guy who brought a boa constrictor into the tent. That thing was big enough to kill someone! Bradley was always two logs short of a cord. Hell, when I heard he died, I thought to myself, 'Probably the best for him. At least his family will never have to know what an idiot he was.' That wasn't very nice of me, but man, he almost killed that guy from Alabama whipping that piece of wood around after that rat the other night. He was dangerous."

"You thought that too? I thought I was the only one who felt that way. I was giving myself hell for not feeling bad he was killed and I didn't even care."

"Why would you? Good grief, man. You didn't hurt him and you didn't make it happen. So don't go around trying to find a reason to feel guilty about it. Hear me?"

"Yah man, you are worse than my Dad."

"I thought you really thought a lot of your Dad," Horse furrowed his brow.

"I do."

"Thanks, then," the Indian grinned.

"Don't get a big head over it, Tonto," Andy answered, and then became quiet, "Jackson, can I ask you something? Do you believe in God?"

"Yup. You white guys might not think so, but I think my God the same God as yours. We call him Wakan Tonka. Why?"

"I thought you did. How does believing in God work with being here?"

"Spud, this is all His world, The whole damned joint. He made it all, even your mosquitoes. And he made people, all of them, the good, the bad and the deranged. I thought you knew that."

"I do," Andy shrugged, "But I don't get this killing some of them and then defending others that are even worse."

"I thought you were the one that always says we shouldn't judge each other. We are not killing anyone because we personally think they should be killed. We are doing it because we got to. This is our job now. We can't stop and mourn over every fallen soldier or we would be dead ourselves. Sure, I felt horrible for that family in the village but I couldn't help them and they wouldn't have wanted me to bury them anyway. That is for their family to do. We felt bad and we didn't like it. That's all we could do."

"Doesn't seem like much."

"No. It doesn't but that's it, just the same. We accept that Wakan Tonka is all things mysterious and impossible to understand. We don't pretend to, and it is a lot easier if you accept that. We can't understand everything. I don't think that you can understand everything about your God either. If He wanted you to figure it out, He would let you. Apparently He doesn't think you would get it yet."

Andy watched his friend, "That's for damn sure."

Horse frowned, "Don't you think that the VC sometimes feel a little sick when they look over our dead? Don't you realize that some of them don't want to kill us? They have their sadistic Bradleys and their jackasses, just like we do. But they don't have a corner on the market. Hell, you white men always think that your motives and feelings are so superior to the Asians, the savage Indians or anyone else, for that matter. I'm here to tell you, people are pretty much just people. My great granddaddy was the biggest sentimental slob you ever could meet. He fought in wars. He didn't like it and he used to tell my uncle about how sometimes he cried. Sort of messes up the picture of a brave Indian chief, huh? You know, Spud, dead people are not fun to be around. I think it's a biology thing. It makes you sad, but sometimes we just can't be bawling about it. That won't make them well again. We gotta keep going, so there aren't more dead people."

Andy looked at him, "I can't believe all that is swirling around in your head! I don't know what I would do without you!"

"Probably end up as crazy as loon. Now when we get back, will you write a long letter to your Preacher friend? You don't even have to mail it, but write it. You can burn it when you are done."

Andy was puzzled, "Why do it then?"

"To get all this crap out of your system. You might want to send it, but just don't keep it bottled up. You were always weird and I kind of like you that way. Sullen doesn't look good on you," Horse said seriously.

"Okay." The two men started to head back to their hooch. "Jackson, thanks."

"No problem."

# 341 days left

Andy felt a lot better. Maybe it had worked writing that four paged letter to Pastor Byron or maybe it was the fact that he had a long talk with God last night. Or it could be just because he finally got some rest. He had slept like a log.

On the way to the remains of the mess tent, the guys noticed that Suds was not in his usual spot. Andy was concerned that something had happened to him because of the mortar fire. At breakfast, they overheard some other grunts grumping because he hadn't brought back their laundry yesterday.

Even though he was worried, a tune kept going through his head but he couldn't remember the words. He knew he was very familiar with it. If he could just get the words maybe it would quit bugging him.

On their way back from breakfast, Andy noticed that Suds had arrived. He was so relieved to see that he was okay. He ran on ahead to get his dirty laundry and talk to him.

He stood in line and when it was his turn, Suds looked at him and gave him a big smile. "Suds very happy to see Spud okay. It bad yesterday. I worry."

"Well, I worried about you too. Are you okay? Is your family okay?"

"Yes, we okay. Trouble in village. Suds not come here and many explosions. I happy you okay. Spud, try not to lose your spirit like many grunts. That would be no good. Suds like your happy spirit."

Andy was taken back, "Thanks. I'll try not to. How do you keep your happy spirit, Suds?"

"I burn paper to chase bad spirits away."

"How does that work?" Andy was taken by surprise.

"Okay," Suds nodded.

"No," Andy grinned, "I mean how do you do that?"

"Roll up some paper and set it on fire. Shake where the bad spirits are and they go away. They don't like smoke."

"I might try that. You said it works for you?"

73

"You have to look too. Many things to be happy about. Spud needs to look. They are sometimes, too close to see." The man held his hand up at the end of his nose and smiled.

"Good point. You know one thing. I am happy I have you for a friend, Suds."

"Thank you. I like Spud for friend too."

As Andy walked away, he thought about what Suds had said. He said he liked his spirit. Just like that, it came to him the tune that was going through his head. He had sung it in church almost every Sunday as part of the liturgy. He thought it was from Psalms:

*"Create in me a clean heart, O God, and renew a right spirit within me.*

*Cast me not away from your presence and take not the Holy Spirit from me.*

*Restore unto me the joy of your salvation and uphold me with thy free spirit."*

He felt like a huge weight had been lifted off his shoulders. He looked up and smiled. It really was a nice day. He had a lot to be grateful for, things weren't that bad and Ginger was getting better. He had made it this far. He even had good coffee this morning. He smiled to himself. Things could be a heck of a lot worse.

Cleaning the camp and repairing the wreckage from the mortars took up most of the day. He enjoyed that kind of work. It reminded him of home. Fixing and repairing. Something that you could look to at day's end and feel good about.

The mail came that afternoon and Andy was delighted to receive letters. Of course, Annie and Mom had written, but there were other letters too. There was one from Darrell, Zach, Pepper, Kevin and a little package from Ginger.

He could hardly stand it but made himself wait until after dinner. Then he went back to his bunk and started to read. First, he read the letter from his brother Kevin.

Kevin and Carrie had written to tell him he was going to be an uncle. He was very happy for them. Now he would be uncle twice. Keith his oldest brother was expecting around Halloween and now Kevin about Christmas!

Darrell wrote to say that he was keeping Annie as busy as he could and that she and Jeannie were getting to be good friends. That was a relief to both guys because they were so close they wanted their wives to be friends too.

Then he read the one from Zach. Zach told about all his adventures at the farm, his dating Andy's cousin Suzy and how much good Andy's parents had done for him. It made Andy feel good. He knew that his Dad and Mom were special people.

Then he read Pepper's letter. His dear goofy sister, Pepper, of course had to plaster Kartoffel Noggin all over the envelope! She thought it was so funny. She even drew a potato with feet and eyes. He hated to tell her but it looked more like Mr. Peanut.

She told him about Keith moving home in June and Dad buying the gas station in Bismarck. She explained the whole business end of it all, since she was the business manager under Dad for the family business. She reported every detail, more than Andy ever needed or wanted to know, but at least no one could say she was holding anything back.

She reported that Zach had thought the family should build Mom and Dad a new dining room and that she had used his vote and voted for the idea. He nodded while he read the letter. That would be a good idea. They really needed to quit carrying those chairs and tables up and down those basement steps every weekend.

Then Pepper told him about Chris, her boyfriend. She went on and on, and Andy could just imagine seeing her say the words. She thought Chris was the best thing since canned dog food. Then she told how she and Annie were sharing an apartment in town, since both of them were at the farm so much it was silly for them to each pay rent on a place they hardly used. He liked that idea.

Next, he opened the letter from his Mom. Grandma had written a nice note and told about the Grandpas. His Mom had promised to send cookies the next day, but when Andy checked the dates, he realized he had received them a week before. They were already gobbled up. His Mom told him all the neighborhood news and then there was a surprise.

Dad had written to him too. Dad wasn't much of a writer, but took the time to write just the same. He told him to keep his faith. "You only need a little tiny bit, you know Andy. An iota will be enough, if you let it. Remember Andy: We don't always know where God is heading when He takes the reigns, but He is getting us somewhere. Don't get off the wagon until the ride is over because you might miss the point of the trip. I know it is a bitch, but I also know you can do it. I am so proud you are my son."

Andy didn't even realize that he had tears rolling down his cheeks until they hit the paper. Then his Dad went on to tell about how he almost sawed his cast off. He would have too, but Zach caught him with the Dremel saw. Andy could just envision the whole scene. He burst out laughing. He would have given anything to see that! If anyone would be ornery enough to saw off the cast on their broken hand, it was his Dad.

Then he opened the package from Ginger. It contained a little note and a small tape player, batteries and a couple tapes. He was so excited he could hardly put the batteries in it. He finally got it put together and put in the tape was marked one. It was from Ginger. As soon as he heard her tiny little voice, the tears started to flow down his cheeks. He poked Horse and told him to listen. Soon Chicago, Swede and Horse were gathered around as well as a few other guys, to listen to the tape. They made so much ruckus getting settled, they asked Andy to start it over again.

"Hello Andy. This is Ginger. Smitty is helping me make this tape because I still can't use my hands so pretty good. I really wrecked them up. Smitty had to take off my little finger, but Uncle Eddie says that is okay because I have spares. Do you think so? Mommy said she'll sew my gloves shut on that hand so my finger won't flop. Isn't that good? I was pretty mad about it, but Daddy says I can't say bad words. So Uncle Eddie is saying them for me. I know he really is because Smitty said that when he told him that he had to take off that finger, Eddie said bad words right away. I sure hope that doesn't mess up my digging.

"And you know what else? That graffing stuff when they move your skin to a new place, well, they wanted to use foot skin on my hand! Can you imagine? It would be so stupid because my hand would smell like dirty feet! I cried and your Daddy talked to Smitty so they took skin that didn't stink. I was really lucky your Daddy told them about that, huh?

"I'm still in the hospital but Smitty says I'll get to go home before very long. I told him it is not nice to keep saying that, because it's been a too long already. He told me to be a brave soldier. Do you get tired of it? I sure do. I want to bite somebody. I suppose Mommy would get pretty mad about that!

"Oh guess what we missed? Charlie asked Smitty to sit by him in church and Charlie got Smitty into trouble. Charlie took the button off his shirt and put it in Smitty's hand. Then Smitty laughed. Mommy gave them both the look. You know the red fire one when she is at her wit's end! Now Smitty and Charlie aren't allowed to sit together any more. I bet that was funny, huh?

"Guess what? Everybody is working on my present for when I get home from the hospital. It's a surprise and no matter which way I try, I can't get Smitty to spill the beans. He gave me some clues, but they don't make sense. I asked Darrell, but he won't tell me. I tried to get it out of Katie, because she's a blabbermouth, but she was even more mixed up than me.

"So I have a good idea. I talked to Dr. Lassiter and he is going to find out for me. It is a secret and Smitty doesn't know it. Promise you won't tell him. Smitty and Uncle Elton think they are so smart.

"But you know the bad news? Smitty said all this stuff about how I can't dig this summer because of my hands, but then he said I still have to go to school! Can you believe that? I said I was too sick, but he said that Jeannie would help me and come to my house with her books. I would ask Uncle Eddie to say bad words about that, but I don't think he'll do it. Darrell won't do it because he likes Jeannie, but maybe you can do it for me? Nobody would even hear it over here, so you won't get into trouble. Can you help me be mad about having to go to school?"

"Well the light thing is blinking so I had better be done talking. I miss you. I hope you still have my braid with you. I have a little dream catcher over my—."

Then the tape went dead. All the guys looked at each other. Some were giggling, some were emotional; but they all agreed she was quite the kid. One of the men volunteered to cuss for her if she wanted. Then another said he would too. Pretty soon, she had about fifteen men who were dedicating all their bad words to help her out because she was sick and still had to go to school.

Andy laughed. "I will write and tell her. She'll really like that. Thanks."

It was late, so he hit the rack. Andy put his letters from Annie in order. This mail was such a mess. Some came right away and some took forever. It was impossible to figure out if what was going on, but he loved every one of them. He read his last letter from Annie and then went to bed. He lay there and said a prayer of thanks, the first one in a long time. It felt good.

# 340 days left

Late in the morning, there was a memorial ceremony for those killed in the mortar attack. Andy dreaded going to it, but of course, everyone would attend. It was simple but very moving. The roll was called and when the fallen soldier's names were called off and there was, of course, no answer. The name was called three times, and there was no answer. That especially got to Andy. He was finally able to feel the grief that had evaded him. By the time the Taps played at the end of the ceremony, he was beginning to realize that he hadn't lost his ability to care.

It was weird, but he actually was very glad he felt that bad. Maybe he had never lost it or maybe he got it back, but he did feel that he had human emotions again. At least, he didn't feel dead inside.

He decided that maybe this not feeling thing was a gift from God meant to help him get through all that he had to face. Maybe he needed to not think and feel about everything, at least for a bit. Sometimes it wasn't an appropriate time to grieve.

Rebuilding and repairing the camp and getting things back to normal occupied the next ten days. No one was sent out on patrols for a week, so there was a bit of peace that went with that. By the end of the time however, they were all getting anxious to be doing something again.

Andy had spent most of his spare time answering letters and making Ginger a tape. Several of his buddies said hello to her on the tape and assuring her the bad words were being taken care of and they were helping her be mad. Andy knew she would be pleased.

Andy asked Horse and Chicago to be sure to say hi to little Charlie too, since Andy knew that he'd be bent out of shape if no one said hi to him.

When he mentioned it, Chicago immediately decided that he would send him a tape of his very own. Chicago loved to sing, much more than most folks loved hearing him. He thought it would be great idea to send a musical tape to Charlie. He sang some popular songs of the day and did a fantastic, in his mind, rendition of *Little Green Apples*.

Andy just hoped that Charlie would contain himself enough to not hurt Chicago's feelings and tell him how it really sounded. After all, it was from the heart. Then Chicago asked him to sing him a song back and send it to him. Andy didn't know about that either. Those two could do a wonderful duet! Maybe they were both so bad, it wouldn't matter.

The other tape that Ginger had sent in the package was from the whole clan. Everyone said a couple words and it made him homesick but it was neat to hear them. They had made it at a Sunday dinner and there was all the usual commotion around. When Grandpa Lloyd got his turn, he told him to hurry home. "I need you to help me fix my Ford. Elton really messed it up. You can help me when you get home. I know you are in Iwo Jima taking care of things. Get it done and come home."

Andy almost cried and Horse asked him what that was about. Andy explained that his grandfather had Alzheimer's and he was pretty mixed up most of the time. But he and Bert, another grandfather, would sit and argue about politics and wars all day, every day.

"Do you have any of your grandparents, Horse?" Andy asked.

"Only my grandfather. The rest have all passed on. You know, us Indians don't often make old bones," Horse said quietly. "You are lucky you have both of your grandfathers."

Andy grinned, "Oh, I am not related to either one of them. Bert is really Ginger and Charlie's grandfather. Lloyd has always been like a father to my stepfather, but we aren't related."

"I didn't know your Dad was not your real Dad."

"My real father died before I was four. Mom married Elton when I was five. He's been a good dad."

"I never thought that he was only your stepdad. I thought your family was perfect," Horse commented.

Andy grinned, "It is just about! Dad isn't *only* a stepdad. He is the best guy anyone could ever get for a father."

"Sounds like it."

"What about your Dad? You never mention him," Andy asked.

"My father died of alcoholism when I was just a kid. I have been lucky though. I have some real good uncles. One of Mom's brothers is the one that slaps me up when need it. Dad has a brother that is a good guy too.

He has tried to keep all his nephews and nieces in line. There is a bunch of us. It's good that I have my uncles."

Andy looked at him, "Both my brothers are my uncles."

"Huh? Good grief, how did that happen?"

"Keith and Kevin are Mom's youngest brothers. When their folks died, Mom raised them. After Elton and Mom got married, he adopted the all four of us kids. We don't even try to keep it straight anymore," Andy chuckled.

"Confusing as hell, I'd think," Horse laughed.

"What about your family?"

"Well, the White Feathers are a rather big bunch. I suppose when we all get together there are about forty of us," Horse calculated.

"I thought your last name was Fielding."

"It is. Some white man sneaked into the teepee. Most of Mom's family are White Feathers," Horse looked a bit wistful. "You know, I miss the crazy bunch. We're nothing to brag about, but it's my family. They're why I joined the Army."

"How so?"

"Unemployment is ridiculous on the reservation and I couldn't find a job. Mom needs help with the little kids. This way, I have money to send home."

"How many brothers and sisters do you have?"

"Steps. They are my stepdad's kids. There are five of them."

"Wow. What does your stepdad do?"

"Drink, mostly. He works as a laborer from time to time, but not much. Anyway, they can use the money."

"It's good of you to do that. Family is important. I wonder what Suds' life is like?" Andy asked, "I can't imagine what a mess that must be. Half his country wants one thing, the other wants the total opposite, all these other countries are fighting over it and he is just trying to keep his happy spirit. I don't know how he can do it," Andy said thoughtfully. "But he seems to be a pretty decent guy, don't you think?"

"Yup. I agree. I wouldn't want to walk in his moccasins. Who could you trust? Must be hell," Horse shuffled the cards. "I do think he's a decent guy though. Hey, wanna get beat at cards? Maybe we can draft Swede or Chicago."

At the end of the ten days, new men had replaced those that were lost. It was a constant turn around. Even though he hadn't been there more than two months, Andy could already see the signs of a newbie. He recognized how green they all must have been when they got there. He felt for these new guys, but realized that the only preparation for their new life was to live it. No one can explain it to you in advance.

The orders came for his platoon to go out on patrol. They would be gone about a week. The men were actually excited to leave the next morning. This was truly a crazy place. One was either bored to death or scared to death.

# 328 days left

That morning in the mess hall, one of the guys was telling about the tank battle in Ben Het, in the remote area of north central Vietnam in 1969. It was situated not far from the Ho Chi Minh trail, which was just over the border in Laos and Cambodia. It was a main supply route for the Viet Cong. One of the main branches of the trail passed not too far from Ben Het. The Special Forces, ARVN and members of the 69th US Armored division held Ben Het.

The men of the Armored division lived in their tanks for their almost two-year stint they were in Vietnam. The thought of living in a tank made all the grunts feel their accommodations were almost palatial.

The assignment was to protect Ben Het at all costs. If it fell, it would give the North Vietnamese Army and the Viet Cong a clear road into north central Vietnam. Tanks were seldom used in Vietnam and until then, there hadn't been a tank battle during the war. Granted, tanks were used effectively, but mostly for guarding bases, covering transport areas and making clearings for roads.

The American troops at Ben Het reported up the chain of command that they heard enemy tanks moving in the surrounding valley. Intelligence assured them there were none there. They must have heard bulldozers.

When the men at Ben Het could see the tanks less than 1000 meters from the base, they told the intelligence people they were the damnedest looking bulldozers the 69th had ever seen!

The Spooky's (aircraft) had just left the area and were called back. They needed them because they were surrounded and taking a lot of fire from those 'bulldozers'. It took some convincing, because everyone had been told intelligence had not reported any tanks! Finally, however, the Spookys did come back. The battle was very costly, in life and treasure. In the end, the base was held.

It only reinforced that the North Vietnamese Army was made up of imaginative and willing, tenacious fighters that should not be underestimated. To many American troops, it also underlined that the US intelligence they received was subject to change and interpretation. It was to be considered, but could not be relied on. Conditions changed faster than things were reported.

The breakfast conversation was a little depressing. It was not enough to think about mosquitoes, snakes, tunnels and Pungy pits; now they could consider the possibility of enemy tanks. Andy thought about it and decided it would just put his brain in overload. He felt good that morning and had no intention of getting all bent out of shape again.

They loaded into their trucks and went to where they boarded the birds. The LZ was out in the jungle and before long; it was as if they had never left—trudging along, swatting mosquitoes and wondering what was beyond the next clearing.

The first couple of days were almost boring. Aside for sore feet and muscle aches, there was little excitement. Their mission was to enter villages and remove any munitions they found. It could be quite a challenge, but this time was not. Then it started to rain in earnest. The monsoons were beginning.

At first, Andy was delighted and envisioned millions of mosquitoes begging for miniscule life jackets in some swollen stream. However when the rain stopped for a moment, the newest swarm of his flying nemeses descended on him. Then he realized the little devils loved it. That put him in a very foul mood.

The water and mud became a way of life. Everything was wet and muddy. Walking was horrible because the grunt's boots sucked into the soft mud. Every step was ten times more difficult. Andy's calves ached but he figured he was building some huge muscles.

On the fifth day, they had a few mad minutes with the enemy, but other than that it was extremely quiet as far as the Viet Cong was concerned. Most of the grunts figured they were probably trying to keep from drowning too.

The soldiers all had their weekly pills to ward off malaria, and most took them religiously. It wasn't uncommon, however, for some men to become so discouraged they would quit taking their pills hoping they could get malaria and be sent home. Andy didn't think that would be a wise idea.

Before landing in country, they were warned about the fungal infections. During the rainy season, many did not wear underwear because of the chafing around the waist band soon led to infections. The feet, however, were another problem.

Jungle rot was considered a foot disease, but it occurred anywhere a scratch or cut that became infected, which occurred frequently on their feet but elsewhere too. The men got it in their armpits and behind their knees. The wet and humidity extrapolated the disease. One fact was that where ever you got it, it wasn't fun.

Ringworm was common. It was not the kind that most soldiers were familiar with in the States, or world as the grunts called it. It was a penicillin resistant variety and displayed oozing lesions. There were antibiotics such as erythromycin that helped. Many men became so infected they had to be hospitalized.

Bandaid told the guys that about seventy percent of the sick calls were due to skin infections and lesions. Dry socks, boots and sleeping conditions were the best prevention and that was nearly impossible.

However all that considered, Andy still preferred the rain. What he didn't like was the flooding. Everything flooded and the soldiers spent a lot of their time wading waist deep in muddy, dirty water. The leeches loved to see them show up. They would cling onto the soldier's bodies and suck their blood. They were all over and everyone had their experiences with them.

They were just about Andy's undoing. He finally found something he hated worse than snakes and mosquitoes. That was leeches. This damned war was determined to drain his blood, one way or the other. He missed the snow covered winters of the northern prairies. He vowed never to complain again about thirty below. Ever.

When he told Horse of his new creed, Horse rolled in laughter. "You'll be whining like a jackass the minute the temperature drops below freezing!"

There were a few firefights and several caches of munitions found in civilian villages. For the most part, the patrol was quiet. When they returned to base camp, they all dried their feet and crawled into their dry racks. They enjoyed being dry.

Andy was also delighted that he was now only two weeks from being one-third the way through his tour. He read his favorite letter from Annie, said his prayers and went to sleep in his dry bed covered with his dry blanket with his head on his dry pillow. Wow!

# 314 days left

It rained every day, all day for the whole time they were back in camp. The mess hall leaked even more than before but it was still better than eating outside.

Suds visits dropped to once a day because it took much longer for the laundry to get dry. He always greeted Spud and Horse with a big smile but was a lot quieter. Obviously, something was bothering him, but they found that it was almost impossible to talk to him. On the third day, they were walking by when he was gathering his things to leave. There was no one else around.

Spud went over to him, "Hello, Suds. How have you been? We've been worried about you? Is there something wrong?"

Suds looked at him in surprise, "Hello. You get clothes?"

"Yah, we got all them. We were just wondering if everything is okay with you."

Suds looked back to the bag he was packing with dirty laundry. "Is okay. Grandmother has sickness, maybe die soon. Suds say thank Horse and Spud ask."

Horse put his arm on his shoulder, "I'm so sorry, Man. Is there anything that can be done for her?"

"Suds think no. She see doctor. He say she old and body no good long time. Suds know, but sad."

"I'm so sorry," Andy nodded with compassion. "I'll keep her in my prayers."

Suds smiled, "Suds thank good friends."

Horse reached in his pocket, "Here. Give this to her. It's a medicine bag that my tribe believes will help bring good spirits to the person who has it. It is a small one, my mother made for me to carry over here."

"Horse need," Suds said as he held the small beaded leather pouch in his hand. "Thank you, you keep."

Horse smiled at him, "No. If she is passing over, she needs it now. I can get another one from my Mom. I insist."

"Very kind. I give her," Suds said, quite moved. "With bag and Andy prayer, she have good luck for journey. You good friends for Suds grandmother."

"You take care of her and yourself, Suds," Andy said.

"Bye, Suds need to go now."

"Good bye, Suds."

On their way back to their barracks, Andy said to Horse, "That was very kind of you."

Horse laughed, "You aren't the only one that can be nice, Paleface."

"I know," Andy said thoughtfully, "Believe me, I know."

"Well, there's work to do, so we had better get to it."

The next day, the men had to have their gamma globulin shots. They had to take them every three months and most men hated them. They would rather have been in firefight because at least there was an opportunity to fight back. Not only did this require an injection, it also left you with a welt on your rear the size of a golf ball that lasted a week. None of them had hepatitis but they all wondered what the hell kind of disease it must be if the prevention was so awful.

Horse and Spud saw Suds and he waved at them from across the yard. They made a detour and walked to where he was.

"Suds grandmother smile when get gift and tell her you pray. She very happy. She sleep good at night. Not so much pain like before. Suds know it from you. Thank you."

"Thank you, I'm sure God is watching over her," Andy agreed.

"Suds and Horse, I bring you gift from family. Weasel poop coffee." He shyly handed him a small packet of coffee grounds.

Andy was delighted as he took the package. "I've been wanting to try it."

"Suds hope you like. Must do work now."

Andy said anxiously turning the packet in his hands. "We'll try it tonight."

Horse grinned, "I'll probably only get to smell it because Spud will drink it, but thanks."

The men talked to Bandaid who offered to bring his coffee press over to their hooch and make it for them that evening. "He must really like you guys. That stuff isn't cheap even with their prices."

"He is a good person, that Suds," Andy declared. "I really like him."

That night the men enjoyed their Cohn coffee. Andy couldn't wait for his father to taste it. It was the best coffee he had ever tasted in his life and he didn't care what had digested it beforehand! Andy was convinced he was going to take some home to his family.

Andy packed his gear for the next patrol and wrote a few letters. In the wee hours, the platoon was dropped into a hot area. They knew this would not be a lazy experience like the last patrol.

Andy tried not to worry because it changed nothing and put him in a funk. He didn't need that. He had learned enough about himself to realize that did no good.

The rain continued. The water levels rose all over and there was a great deal of flooding. It was going to be a muddy mess, again. They all knew it, but they were resigned to it.

Andy envisioned the leeches tying their bibs around their necks, just waiting for his sweet blood. By God, he should charge them. It seemed to him that everything in this beautiful country either bit, sucked or stung.

The helicopter approached the LZ in the rain-drenched moonlight. It was a small grassy clearing in the middle of the jungle. When their boots hit the ground, they sunk in to their mid-calves. Pulling their legs out of the slop was a real effort.

Andy looked around. All they would need was incoming fire and they would be dead, still standing where they landed. They could hardly move. If he picked a country to have a war in, it would not be Vietnam, or Northern Russia where his father had fought. Oh hell, there was probably not a good place to fight a war.

# 308 days left

Between the rain and soil that was a close cousin to quicksand, Andy knew this would be a crummy trip. There had been a lot of enemy activity in the area and it seemed to be increasing. They were to join up with another platoon that had been inserted into the area a few days before.

It took them a full half an hour to move out of the grassy clearing and be able to stand on some solid dirt. By then they were already soaked through and caked in mud. It was a real challenge keeping their weapons in firing condition. The word was the M16 was good unless it got wet! No one mentioned how that goal was to be obtained.

They moved out through the jungle and toward the west. By noon, they were worn out but had seen nothing except vegetation and a pretty parrot. The platoon sat down, ate their rain soaked rations and then got back on their feet.

It was beginning to get warm. Warm and wet. Andy could feel his feet squishing in his shoes and his skin rubbing raw under his arms. Before long, the skin behind his knees was chafed. He had put his towel around his neck to protect his neck from the abrasiveness of his gear but it became soaked developing an abrasiveness of its own.

However, he was in a good mood. He and Horse had joked around over rations with Swede and Chicago. They were all four in a goofy mood. Even Swede, who was usually the quietest of the group, was on a roll. They laughed until some of the other men looked at them like they had lost their minds. No group of people could have ever had more fun trying to light rain-soaked cigarettes than they did that noon.

About two hours later, they entered a small village and as was their usual pattern, checked the hooches for caches of munitions, signs of tunnels or VC. Then they moved on. They only thing they had found there was a feeling of foreboding. There was nothing to put their finger on, but things were ominous.

Another hour out of the village, they were given the signal to hit the dirt. Within seconds, the platoon was taking heavy fire from three directions. They were definitely in the kill zone.

Andy's mind slipped into its adrenaline-induced slow motion. He did notice that the position that Bole, Swede and Hamilton held was taking a lot of fire. He lobbed a few from his Thumper in the direction the fire was coming from before he realized that it was coming from everywhere.

He knew that they were taking casualties. He could hear the yelling, cursing pleading and moaning in between the explosions. He wondered if he would ever enjoy another Fourth of July fireworks. What a stupid thing to think, since he was two inches from the Pearly Gates!

He saw Chicago and Horse feeding the Pig. The barrel was so hot; they were changing the barrel as fast as they could. They knew they were bringing smoke to the enemy, but they also knew they were in deep trouble. The mad minute lasted about fourteen minutes; and then as was the usual, it stopped as abruptly as it began.

The men began to look around. The ground was churned up like summer fallow, mud flung all over, pieces of flesh and grunts were lying chilly or motionless. This was definitely by their calculation as Numba Ten (with Numba One being the best on a scale of one to ten).

The platoon called for a dust off and the medics did the best they could. However, two men were dead and four were seriously injured. One was Swede. Swede Swenson's left arm was blown off. One of the men who put him in a litter found his part of his arm and placed it beside him before the helicopter lifted off.

Andy was beside him when they lifted him onto the helicopter. Swede, who was in shock, looked at his detached arm, shook his head and said, "Hell of a deal."

Andy said, "God bless you, Man. You go home now. We'll meet up again when this mess is over."

Swede mumbled, "Tomorrow."

Andy watched as the dustoff was completed and then he broke down in tears. He shook his head and cried, "He should've just paddled off to Canada, you know. That's what he should've done. This damned war is just a bunch of shit."

Horse was in no better shape and this time, Chicago that pulled them back together. "Dammit, shape up! He might be better off. He gets to go home. I have to sit here and listen to you two! Come on! There's a war to fight!"

Andy had little time to dwell on anything, as they were back on the move again. In a little over an hour, the signal was again given to hit the dirt. This firefight was shorter and no casualties were taken.

In the minds of the platoon, they had inflicted heavy damage on the enemy because they were so angry. However, there was little actual sign of it. It served mainly to take the platoon's mind off their fallen comrades.

The night was a battle of nerves. Guard duty was hell and everyone thought everything was something. They were eager to meet up with the other platoon in the morning.

Morning light was difficult to distinguish. The rain was torrential with no let up. Apparently, their formidable enemy was not enjoying the weather any more than they were. There was no sign of them.

Mid-morning, they met up with the other platoon. As they came up to them, Horse's glance caught Andy's. It was obvious these poor bastards had seen hell up close and were worse for the wear.

The men all rested a bit while the platoon leaders talked their situation over. The plan to stay in place and fortify where they were rather than be caught out in the open. The men didn't like the sounds of that but spent the afternoon securing their encampment. The squad leaders wanted their men in the best condition possible for the next day. That pronouncement was met with sardonic laughter from the men.

They took their turns at sleeping, eating, re-enforcing and standing guard duty. When Horse and Andy had a chance to visit, they worried about their friend. Swede was always rather quiet, a kind person with not a mean bone in his body. Their hope was that he was on some hospital ship with some good-looking nurse.

"Do you think they can sew his arm back on?" Horse asked.

"Doubt it. Hell, even if it isn't dead, there's so much of it missing it would be six inches shorter than the other," Andy shook his head. "You should've seen the look on his face when he looked at his own arm. I'll never forget that expression as long as I live. God, I sure hope he makes it."

"Come on Spud, what is it that Suds always says about keeping your happy spirit?" Horse asked, and then was overcome with discouragement. "Sounds kind of dumb now, doesn't it?"

Andy shrugged, "Sure does. Ah, hell, Horse, one thing about it we can count on. If we die here, no matter where we go—we know we'll be in a better place!"

"You jackass!" Horse thumped him.

After mulling it all over, Andy said, "I guess it's better what happened to him, than if he landed in one of those damned Pungy pits. They make my bones quiver."

"I doubt Swede thinks he won a prize," Horse pointed out.

"I didn't mean it that away, Horse." Andy apologized. "I only meant . . ."

"I know. Ah hell, let's not waste our sleeping time. I wish just once they would point to a fort and say—you guys take it. Just once. This cat and mouse is driving me crazy."

"You told me that you'd keep it together!" Spud retorted.

"No, I said I would try."

# 305 days left

Activity filled their morning. The platoons were digging in more than they had ever done before on a patrol. Without being told, everyone was aware that something was coming and that it wouldn't be fun.

They had built up barricades of sandbags and dirt within a perimeter of landmines and trip wires. Another squad of men was inserted with them with more supplies. Horse confided to Spud that maybe Command had decided to let him build a fort instead of take one.

The morale was very low. Before noon, their encampment was nicknamed the Alamo by the men. They all wondered why they had not heard a bit of scuttle about what was going on and that only added to the trepidation. That night, two more squads were dropped in and a lot of armaments and supplies. Whatever was going on, the feeling was they were in it for the long haul. A platoon of ARVN joined them and the camp was further expanded and fortified.

The second day, they were relieved when they learned from Bandaid that Swede was doing okay. His arm couldn't be saved but he was doing well otherwise. His Army stint was over and he would be heading home as soon as he could make the trip. They were all relieved and happy for him, but they missed him.

There had been zilch in the way of enemy movement or activity since the day Swede was shot. Nothing. That was very odd. Everyone knew they were in the middle of enemy territory and there should have been something. Instead, they continued to fortify.

The morning of the third day, their mission was revealed at a formation. This was indeed in the midst of enemy area. They had uncovered one of the larger command areas for the NVA in this region and in fact, were now encamped almost on top of it.

The enemy had withdrawn to the east for the time being. They were assembling and preparing to take it back. They were determined to take it back.

The assignment was to thwart those attempts. Under no circumstances was the enemy to regain control of the area.

They would be joined by another platoon of men later that afternoon and then they were to wait it out. Their job was to not be uprooted. Andy and Horse looked at each other. Chicago looked at other two and shrugged. He said quietly, "Sure hope they have a back up plan."

It began on the fourth night. It started with just one small report of movement on the north. Nothing followed for about an hour. Then there was a short firefight on the west side of the encampment. It lasted only a minute or two and then stopped. Everyone was now on alert.

The fighting started in earnest about an hour later. It was not a firefight. It was a major attack. The enemy was well-enforced, heavily armed and ready for a long fight. It continued incessantly into the next day.

The NVA was minutes from penetrating the west area when the gun ships came in. These were the US Goonie birds, gunships, also known as Puff the Magic Dragon, because of all the devastation the huge airplanes were capable of inflicting.

When the fighting ceased and the dust off completed, the actual number of casualties was high. The Army had lost about seventeen men and the ARVN about ten. The morning of the sixth day, there was short memorial service for those who had died in the battle and then everyone went to work. Their area was expanded. Some of the surrounding areas were drenched in defoliant. There were many tunnels to be searched and destroyed.

This time Andy was not so fortunate. It was noticed that he was the same size as Franklin. He was among seven men were designated as tunnel rats that day.

When they called him to come forward, he almost passed out. He dared not look anyone in the eye so they could see the fear. It didn't make him feel any better to know that the enemy was gone. He knew the tunnels were often rigged with the booby traps, poisonous snakes, scorpions and spiders. He was truly, sincerely was scared to death.

His palms sweating, he numbly took off his gear and kept looking at the tunnel lid that had been pumped full of gas to kill any poor soul that still was down there. They had all heard of stories when the tunnel rat was sent down too soon before the gas had dissipated and succumbed to the gas. There was nothing about this that Andy even vaguely liked.

Franklin came up to Andy and said quietly, "Look. It isn't so bad. When you are going down, make sure that they keep the rope on you."

"Why?" Andy could barely speak. "To retrieve my body?"

"Yah, but also you might want to have them pull you back if you encounter something poisonous or get hurt," Franklin said, matter-of-factly. "When you get in there, try to keep breathing as normally as possible. Don't hyperventilate."

He gave him a short briefing on how things usually worked out and tried to encourage him. Then he said, "Give any of your important stuff to a buddy 'til you get back up. Just in case. You'll do fine. If I can do it, you sure can. You are a good man, Schroeder."

Andy only wished he had the confidence that Franklin had. Then he looked at the man. Andy shook his head and thought, 'Who the hell am I to think this guy has to do the dirty work. It's about time I earned my salt.'

Horse looked at him when he took Andy's stuff. "Tomorrow, this will be past history."

Chicago agreed, "Tomorrow."

Andy nodded, "Tomorrow."

After the platoon sergeant figured the gas had safely dissipated; they opened the lid and Andy went down into the two foot square hole, head first. He had no more than put his head in hole when he was engulfed by the gas fumes. He would have backed out except that he was upside down. Once he adjusted to the gas smell, he gathered his wits and got his bearings. The tightness of the tunnel was oppressive and the pungent smell of the damp earth nearly overcame him. It was stifling warm down there and a few feet down, became very tight. He had all he could do to wiggle down the hole. The only light was the beam from his flashlight, but all he could see was blackness.

Then he thought, "This has to be the tunnel of death." He stopped himself with instant pep talk. Franklin had done this numerous times and he was okay. Other guys did it. They were okay. He would be too. Hell, these Vietnamese flew up and down these tunnels all the time, and they were okay. He would be fine. His arguments didn't convince him, but he just wanted to get it over with.

He slithered along a shaft that angled downward about ten feet, with his arms outstretched in front of him. In one hand he held a flashlight and in the other, a handgun. The tunnel was so tight, he would not have been able to put his arms by his side. His body was covered in perspiration and now dirt.

At the bottom, he looked it all over as carefully as he could with his flashlight for booby traps. Some dirt fell from the top of the tunnel down the back of his neck.

Andy quit breathing. He couldn't reach it, so he lay still until he was certain that it wasn't moving like a snake or spider. After a few minutes, he felt nothing and decided to think it was just dirt. Hell, if it was an insect, there was absolutely nothing he could do about it anyway.

When he got to the bottom, he found himself on the floor of a small room. It was about five feet tall, so he could get himself upright, even though he couldn't stand up straight. There he saw some empty containers and a pile of ammunition boxes that were empty. He looked to the other side of the room and there was a dead man. He had been wounded but was now dead. Andy wondered if it was the gas that had killed him.

He moved into the next tunnel only stooping over and he didn't have to crawl. When he got into that room, there was another dead man and a dead woman. The man had a packet around his neck and Andy checked. There were some papers in it, so Andy put if over his shoulder.

He entered the next tunnel and crawled along until it branched. Now he had a dilemma. Since the bag he was carrying made it more difficult to move to the left, he turned right. He entered the pitch-black room and decided it had been a map room of sorts. He rolled up the maps and put them inside his shirt. He looked around the place with his flashlight.

He noticed nothing else and crept back into the tunnel. This time he passed the way he had come and checked out the other direction. The tunnel opened into a room about six by six. In the room were four badly wounded soldiers, now all dead. They looked so young. When he turned to look around the room, he saw a dead woman bent over face down like she was kneeling in prayer. He went over to her and moved her back. She had been covering a small baby, dead in her arms. Andy threw up, then and there. He had no problem crying this time. It just made him sick.

Finally, he pulled himself together and continued his search. He found nothing else and there were no other tunnels, so he went back to where he had entered. Before he started to crawl back out the hole, he looked around one last time. He wiped his face and then said, "May God bless your souls."

Then he went up the tunnel and pulled himself out onto the ground. He turned the maps and pouch over to Sgt. Bole and reported the number of dead. Bole said "Good work, Schroeder."

Andy went to Horse and put his gear back on. He never said a word. He never wanted to do that again as long as he lived. Ever. Andy never said anything else about it until later that night. He was in his hole, when Franklin came and sat down by him.

"How did it go?"

Andy nodded, "Okay."

Franklin looked at him with disbelief, "No, really."

"I wasn't expecting dead people. Will they come back to get them for burial?"

"We blew the tunnel about a half an hour ago. No one will find them," Franklin said quietly. "These were individual tunnels, the big, connected ones, the NVR usually move their fallen out as fast as they can, like we do. You have to remember, it is war. Not everyone is found and given a decent burial, no matter what the big shots try to say."

Andy stared ahead and then said quietly, "One was a baby. The mother had tried to cover it with her body."

"Schroeder," Franklin took his shoulder, "Listen. That might be and it rips you up, but that mother would have thrown a grenade or shot us with an AK-47 in a heartbeat. That is the way of it. Try not to forget that."

"Do you see a lot of stuff down the tunnels?" Andy's eyes searched his face.

"Sometimes, lots; sometimes, nothing. Just depends. You'll never get used to it. Every time you go down one; it is different. Some of them are so connected it's like a cobweb and some have just one entrance. Some you can stand up in and some you have to be a damned earthworm to move around. Sometimes there is a lot of stuff, but mostly there is not. It is crapshoot. They are all darker than dark.

"I don't like it when there are dead people, but I sure don't like it if they are alive. That only happened once. The guy was wounded and he died in front of me. If he'd been in better condition, he'd have killed me.

He was trying to when he died, but didn't have the strength to hold his pistol." Franklin shook his head, "It's those damned snakes I hate. You get to the entrance to a room and they'll have one tied there. Usually the gas will get them, if they gas the tunnel first. They aren't all gassed, you know. Once I came out into a room and damned near fell into a Pungy pit. The only thing that saved me was that a lid from a case of some sort had fallen on it and stopped my fall. I tell you, I almost filled my drawers. After that, I always take a second to flash the light down on the spot I would land before I come out of one of those tunnels."

"Good thing to remember. I hope I never have to do it again," Andy said, almost as a plea.

"Sorry, kid. You will. Now they know you fit. Sure makes you wish you ate more when you were a kid, huh?" Franklin chuckled. "You'll be fine. Ever want to talk, look me up. I know you got what it takes. Okay?"

"Thanks Franklin," Andy was truly grateful. "I really appreciate that."

Franklin went off into the darkness and Andy sat thinking about the day. He had always thought Franklin was a nice enough guy, but such a nervous, jumpy wreck. Everyone used to joke about how if a spoon dropped, Franklin would spring twenty feet into the air. Now, Andy understood. He couldn't imagine why the guy hadn't lost his mind a hundred times by now. He was one hell of a guy.

# 300 days left

The next few days, Andy went in and out of more tunnels than he cared to count. They retrieved some information, although nothing that important. One of the other guys found another blind tunnel that contained a few more wounded dead. There were no booby traps. It was apparent that they had left in a hurry.

After each tunnel was thoroughly investigated, they were blown. Andy thought it would have been decent of them to pull out the dead before they blew them, but he never opened his mouth about it. He doubted that his input would have been appreciated.

He couldn't shake the vision of that dead little baby in his mother's lap. It penetrated his sleep. Poor little kid never had a chance. However, he knew that Franklin was right. The only point of them being there at all was to kill the soldiers. Wars were like that. After all, that is why he was there, too. None of them were sent there to open a lemonade stand.

Going down into the tunnels made the war more personal for Andy. He could see that people had been there. In one room, there was a cup of unfinished coffee. His wondered if it was weasel poop coffee. In another room, a pair of sandals and a dirty shirt that someone had spilled on. Things like that made him realize that the enemy was not a shadow with a gun, but a real human being. Andy had to admit though, that when they were on the other side of a weapon; they still wanted to kill him. Of course, they could honestly say the same about him.

Horse noticed that Andy was quieter than usual. One night, he had a talk with him. "Are you crapping out on me again?"

Andy shook his head, "No. I'm not. I just hate this. I know, so does everyone else. I'm really not feeling sorry for myself. It just makes me sick that we spend so much time and energy trying to kill each other. Just think what we could do if we spent half of it trying to be good to each other."

Horse nodded, "True. But that is not the way of things. I know you mentioned about that mom and her baby. Andy, you have to realize, those people were not Suds or his family. Hell, they might not have even been Vietnamese. Don't get all distorted in your thinking. It is why they call it war. It is not nice."

Andy stared at his friend and thought. "You're right, I know. I just liked it better when they were shadows without a face."

"Don't we all," Horse nodded, "Anyway, you told me once that your Aunt Gilder or something like that . . . ."

"Gilda."

"Gilda, yah. That's right. The one that says that you should enjoy the good as much as you can because that's what makes the bad bearable. I've thought of that many times since you told me. I think you should remember it too."

"Yah. You're right. Dad says I should just do the best job we can here and get back home."

"Amen," Horse grinned, "Now, I know what would cheer you up. You could let me beat you in rummy."

Andy frowned, "How would that cheer me up?"

"You could tell yourself that you let me win because you were trying to be good to me."

"You have no idea how much I hate you!" Andy groaned as he punched his friend. "Let's find Chicago. We can gang up on him."

One of the platoons was lifted out by the Slicks, so the rest of the men had high hopes of getting the same helicopter service. However, that was not to be. The ARVN and one of the squads were assigned to stay at the encampment for some time. Andy's platoon was to move out on foot to the north.

The first day of trudging along in the rain was rather boring and there was no sign of anyone. The second day, the telltale signs of NVA activity became more apparent. The night of the second day, there were a few brief firefights. Nothing major, but it was just enough to make everyone nervous.

The third afternoon they arrived at the pickup zone. The birds landed and the men made it out of the boonies. Everyone was relieved and delighted. It was the longest they had been gone and the nastiest time Andy had spent in country. The thought of getting back to his rack brought him pure joy.

When they arrived back at camp, they noticed that things had started to change. As part of the plan of Vietnamization of the war, many bases were being turned over to the ARVN, the South Vietnamese Army. Andy's camp was one that was to be turned over within a few months.

The new system of individualization of the troops meant that troops weren't necessarily transferred en mass as units. One man might be assigned in the north and another to the south, as needed. It was a disruptive and unsettling feeling.

Andy, Horse and Chicago had all arrived the same day and we all due for R&R about the same time. They knew that wouldn't happen. Some of the men already knew that they would not come back from R&R to Cu Chi but be sent to another place. The camaraderie prevalent in most wars was certainly threatened by this. For the time being, there was no change. The three guys were still together and there were no definite plans for anyone to get R&R or transferred. They put it out of their minds.

They missed Swede and were delighted when they got a letter from him. They were all glad to hear that he was going home within a month. He told them he was looking forward to getting out in his canoe and paddling on Lake of the Woods. "I am going to paddle up to Canada. Just because." They all knew what he meant.

The time at camp was good because it would be nice to let their feet dry out. Andy's feet really took a beating this last go round. He developed sores on them, especially his right foot. They oozed and even bled. No matter what he did, they just didn't get any better. Finally, he went to sick call. The medics gave him some medicine for it and told him to keep them clean and dry. He nodded, and thought to himself. 'Okay then. Just don't send me out on patrol.'

The next morning, they got their orders. They were leaving on a patrol that afternoon. Andy looked at his socks when he packed his stuff and thought sarcastically, 'Hmm. That lasted a long time.'

They were inserted into an area to the west and south of their camp. There was a lot of jungle, rain, streams and villages. Andy was sure there would be tunnels. Everything from the wild kingdom that he loved was there; mosquitoes, leeches and tunnels. He was pretty sure he could drum up a snake or two if he really looked.

There was more activity in some of the villages that had previously been quiet and non-aggressive toward the Americans and the ARVN. Things were changing. They were to do search and clear, trying to locate pockets of resistance and signs of tunnel activity.

They moved in and around the villages while the inhabitants watched them suspiciously from under their coulee hats. The atmosphere had never been friendly, but it was much less so now. The distrust was palpable on both sides. The soldiers found caches of armaments and tunnels that ran on endlessly. No one in the villages ever knew anything. The citizens were afraid to speak and wouldn't say anything, for any variety of reasons.

On the fifth day in the morning, they had passed through a small village of only a few hooches. The tense atmosphere could be cut with a knife. The hair on the back of the soldier's neck stood straight up. Nothing was found, not even a tunnel opening, but there was definitely something going on. As they left the village, the soldiers were all nervous.

They entered another village down the road just a few miles from the first, later that day. There were only a few people there; a very pregnant woman, an old couple and another woman with some small children. The little kids, of course, peeked around corners and gave nervous little smiles to the soldiers.

The pregnant woman began to hold her belly and grimace in pain. Before long, it was apparent that she was in labor. The other woman took her to one of the hooches and the four young children went along. The old lady motioned for a soldier, as if asking for help from their medic.

The Sergeant hesitated, conferred with the translator and then gave the order for Bandaid and a couple other men to go in to help with the delivery. It seemed the decent and proper thing to do. Still prepared for anything, the soldiers felt good to do something good. It seemed downright noble.

The men assembled in the hooch with the lady in the full throes of delivery. The men put down their weapons to help. The woman in labor and the other woman, with the children gathered around, both pulled the pins on their grenades and destroyed them all.

Shock was the first thing that struck the soldiers outside. Bole was not five feet from the hooch door when the grenades went off. He was injured, but not severely. Nearly everyone inside the hooch died. One soldier and one child were still alive, although the child was in terrible condition.

Immediately, the trees to the north exploded into artillery fire. It only lasted a short while, but it was very devastating. Out of Andy's platoon, two were killed besides the four in the hooch. Their friend, Bandaid was among the dead. Besides Sgt. Bole, there were four others injured. All the villagers with the exception of a couple children were dead. The old man had been killed by the fire from the trees. It was hideous.

The dust off was completed and graves registration did their work. Andy helped load Bandaid's remains with tears in his eyes. He hated this damned war.

The soldiers moved on toward the west. Before sunset, they had moved across a stream that had risen with the monsoonal rains. It was at least four feet deep. The water was soaked into Andy's boots and his right foot burned with pain. He had a difficulty walking on it.

That night, he checked it. It was oozing blood and infection. It was swollen and bluish red up past his ankle. He dried it off as best he could and put the salve on it. The medic gave him some pills and told him to keep it dry. Andy nodded.

The infection seemed better in the morning and he was able to hump along with the rest of the guys. He missed Bandaid. He missed Swede. Hell, he even missed Bradley. It was easier not to think these days because there was little good to think about. It had become a matter of keeping going just to keep going. It was two days later when they finally were picked up out of the jungle to go to camp.

When he got back to camp, he was on sick call. His right foot was bad enough to require care. He was put in bed and his foot was dried and medicated. Horse and Chicago gave him grief about being a slacker but they knew it was not a joke. The jungle rains did horrendous things to feet. He would be laid up for the next couple days. During this time, he only got up once and that was to go to the memorial service they held for the soldiers who had died in the village. He didn't want to miss the memorial for Bandaid.

# 291 days left

"Whatcha thinking, Spud?" Horse asked as he shoved his cigarette pack toward his friend as they headed out on patrol again. "How's your foot doing?"

"Actually, pretty good," Andy grinned. "Either that or I have gotten used to it feeling funny. At least I can still feel it, huh? I was thinking about Bandaid. I miss him. He was a good guy. I don't think that he knew what hit him, do you?"

"No," Horse agreed.

"At least he died doing something good for someone," Andy nodded, "I guess that's a lucky break. I'll probably croak being a real ass. Then I'll have lots of explaining to do!"

"Yah, you can about count on that. Hey? Have you noticed how quiet Chicago has been?" Horse asked as the bird they were in carried them back into the boonies. "He has been awful quiet lately. I worry about that. It's not good."

"I noticed he was like that since I was on sick call. I thought you knew about it. Think it was Bandaid's death? They were pretty tight."

"Don't know. I know he got a letter from home. I thought it was from Sonny. He is so stuck on her. I sure hope that he didn't get dumped. Man, last mail call was a bad one. Two guys got Dear Johns."

"Someone said it is usually around the fourth month. That guy said the last place he was, they called mail call the Dear John Roundup. Surely Chicago would have mentioned it, wouldn't he have?" Andy asked hopefully.

"Who knows? People are funny about that kind of stuff. Anyway, if you get a chance, see if you can find out what's eating him. I will too. Either that or we are going to have to corner him and beat it out of him."

Before long, they were back in the jungle. It seemed to them that they were wandering aimlessly, but they knew there was a bigger picture. At least, they clung to that hope. One of the men insisted that they should be told everything and some of the other guys said they didn't want to know any of it. As far as Andy was concerned, he truly doubted it would make any difference to him one way or the other.

It wasn't raining for a change, but it was hotter than usual and very muggy. It took no time at all before his clothes were sticking to him. Two of the guys passed out from the heat, which was unusual. After the second man passed out, the Sergeant had them hole up for a while. Whatever the temperature was, it was too hot to be skipping around in this jungle and he didn't relish having all his men lying in a heap.

While they were stretched out in the shade, the three men had a chance to talk. Horse was a blunt guy. He didn't spend a lot of time with gently giving someone an opening to voluntarily say something.

He handed Chicago a cigarette and asked, "What's eating your ass?"

Chicago looked at him with surprise and said, "What?"

"You've been so quiet lately. Something's wrong. Sonny dump you or something?" Horse put it out there as plainly as possible.

"Why you are always so sure that Sonny would dump me? You always think that. Not even close," Chicago retorted, "I resent you thinking that."

"Sorry. Didn't mean to get your dander up, but you know one of the guys in the barracks next to us shot himself when he got a dear john letter from his girl. I don't want you doing that on us!" Horse tried to explain. "If that's not it, what is it?"

"I'll not be shooting myself, although I might consider shooting you," Chicago frowned, "But yah. Something is wrong. My little brother's fifteen and the doctors think he might have muscular dystrophy. It makes me sick."

"Man, that is horrible," Spud said. "Why didn't you tell us? You should have."

"You'll do what about it?" Chicago asked. "Got a magic cure?"

"No, we don't, but it isn't right to try to carry this alone. We are tight. If you have trouble, we have trouble. We're friends." Horse pointed out, "Does he have a good doctor?"

"Sonny and Mom are taking him to the Mayo Clinic. Our doctor wasn't sure. He mostly just scared the hell out of them," Chicago related. "This way, they'll know."

"We'll pray about it and listen, if you need to talk, grab one of us. This place's shitty enough, we don't need to carry anything extra we don't need," Spud patted his friends shoulder. "You're one of the Musketeers, man."

"That is right," Horse laughed, "In fact, I think we'd make a fine television series! I can see it all now. The little white guy, the burly black guy and the strikingly handsome Indian hero."

They both whopped him. Chicago laughed, "It would be more like the Three Stooges."

"Nah, with these hair cuts, who would be Curly?" Horse asked.

"I'm going to talk to people I don't even know. I'd be happier," Chicago groaned. "I came over here so I could make enough money to move my family out of the city. They need to be in a safer place. I was hoping to move them soon. Now this."

"Look you need any help," Horse slapped his friend on the shoulder. "I can chip in."

"Me too," Andy offered.

"My brothers are helping. We think we can get them a house in Wisconsin. I want my Mama to have a garden, you know."

"Look, anything we can do to help, just say the word," Andy repeated.

Horse smiled, "I'm real sorry about your brother. Let's keep our fingers crossed that it all works out okay. And Chicago, thanks for telling us."

Chicago nodded. "Yah, we're tight, bro."

It was the usual search and clear patrol. They found a few hot areas and caches of ammo. For the most part, it was what they had gone through a thousand times. There seemed to be more activity than there had been, but that was also becoming routine.

After the seventh day, the platoon walked past a tiny village of about six houses. As usual, the little kids peeked curiously at the soldiers and gave little smiles. As Andy went by a hooch, he noticed a little boy with his mangy dog. Andy noticed him because the boy was holding him with a short rope around his neck to keep him from running after them. The boy smiled at Andy and he smiled back. He figured he must be about the age of Charlie, Ginger's brother.

As Spud passed and was about twenty feet ahead of the kid, the boy let the dog go or it may have broken lose on its own. The dog ran right for the soldiers and the hand grenade attached around its neck went off. It killed two soldiers and very badly wounded one other. The soldier behind them shot the boy dead within seconds.

The moments immediately following the encounter were ones of mass confusion and a devastating but short firefight. It was over in minutes. The village was in ruins and only two buildings were still standing. All the residents were dead including three children and the two soldiers.

When the Slicks arrived to evacuate the dead and wounded, there was another shorter firefight with shadowy characters in the trees. Later, when they were moving again, they found the entrance to three more tunnels. Franklin, Andy and another guy were chosen to go down.

One of the tunnels was a factory for landmines. The North Vietnamese Army often used unexploded ordinates and fashioned some lethal weapons from them. The tunnel that Franklin went into contained a reloading equipment and rounds of ammo that they had recycled.

The tunnels were not gassed. As Andy entered the tunnel he was assigned, it went straight down and then moved horizontally about ten feet. He was about to step into the room, when for some reason, a voice reminded him to check out for a Pungy pit like Franklin had said. As he moved the flashlight downward, he saw it. There was a huge cobra, tied to the entrance of the room. He backed away as fast as he could.

Andy watched it for a second. The creature didn't seem to be moving, but it didn't look dead either. However, considering how he felt about snakes, he couldn't trust his judgment. Even though he knew that shooting in a tunnel usually rendered you deaf for a while, he did it anyway. Better deaf than dead.

This room had been used for a melting down metals. How anyone could stand the heat in there amazed Andy! This enemy was very ingenious and tenacious, even though Andy didn't think much of some of their tactics.

He couldn't come to grips with people who would loosen the pin on a grenade so that a little kid would be able to pull the pin. They had to be started by the adult. The adults knew the results. And that pregnant lady! He couldn't get over that. It was awful to think of what war could get people to do. Why would they do that? At what point could he be coerced to do those things? He just didn't know. He had already done a lot more things than he ever thought he'd do. And at the time, it made sense and he didn't even question it! How much further would he go?

107

Then he thought of his sister. If North Dakota was invaded, Pepper would be digging tunnels, throwing grenades and right along with the men. He knew her that well. He decided that war just does that to people, but he still hated it.

He had just smiled at that little boy and the little boy smiled back. He couldn't believe that the kid knew that he was about to become a killer. Or could he? Hell, anymore he didn't know who or what you could trust. Then he looked at the dead snake while he shook his buzzing ear drums. He looked around and said aloud, "Nobody."

When they got back to camp, he was told that his Mom had called the Red Cross that morning. His Grandpa Bert had died the night before. Andy was stunned, although not really surprised. He had really hoped to get to see him again, but he also knew it might not be likely, because his health had been poor for years.

Grandpa Bert had been every bit like a real grandfather since he was five years old. He and Grandpa Lloyd had babysat for the kids, took them fishing, given them hell and played with them. He would always remember the men sitting on the stool whittling away arguing about politics.

Andy worried about Grandpa Lloyd. Who was he going to talk to now? He was getting so mixed up with his Alzheimer's and that seemed to be the only joy of his life anymore was arguing with Bert. Those old guys had argued every political decision and war at least three times in more detail than any historian. They never agreed, even if they did and it was never resolved. It had kept them occupied for a long time.

After dinner, he wrote a couple long letters home and then fell asleep with tears in his eyes. He couldn't believe how much he hated this place. He didn't know what God thought He was teaching him, but at this point, he didn't give a damn. He just wanted to go home and be with his family.

He wondered who would be the pallbearers and who would dig Grandpa's grave. He was in basic training when Grandma Ida died and now he was Cu Chi when Grandpa Bert died. He really hated it.

# 280 days left

## 29 days 'til leave

The following day, Andy got some good news. His R&R was set up. He had hoped for Hawaii and he got it. He would leave Cu Chi on the 23rd of July to arrive in Hawaii on the 26th. Then he would have seven full days of leave. He would have to check in on August 2nd. He was so excited he could hardly stand it. He immediately wrote a letter to Annie and his parents. They had promised they would come over to see him, if he got Hawaii.

According to the rules, Command sent the soldier out on leave. The soldier had a choice of where they wanted to go, if there was room there. They were not always able to comply; but in this case, they were. If someone refused their assigned leave (to get a chance to go to a different place), he would lose his place and have to go back to the end of the line and start over. Andy was very grateful that he got Hawaii.

If there was ever a letter than he wanted to travel fast; it was the one he wrote to his family and Annie that day. He asked Annie to marry him while they were there. He was certain and she had said that she was certain that they would spend the rest of their lives together. At this point, he didn't care if it was going to be a long life or a short one, but he knew he did not want to leave this planet without having been her husband. He hoped that she agreed and was willing to take the chance.

A unit was not able to deny a soldier's leave set by the command. Even if the soldier was in the field in a battle, when it was time, he was taken out and sent back to his base to drop off his things.

Andy would go to Cam Ranh Bay and be there about a day to get things organized. He would exchange his money for US dollars instead of the MPC's. They weren't allowed to wear military clothes on R&R, they would change their clothes in Cam Ranh Bay. In Hawaii, they could wear some military clothing, but definitely not encouraged to do so. From Cam Ranh Bay, he got on the 'freedom bird' and flew to the R&R center.

These freedom birds were like regular commercial airplane with a stewardess and everything! There they had to endure a two-hour lecture about what they could or could not do on leave and then were released. They could rent civilian clothes there at the R&R center. In Hawaii, unlike other destinations, they could rent or drive a car. He knew his Dad would rent a car, but he sure wanted to be able to drive it at least once while he was there.

Now he kept another countdown. He was also counting down the time until he would see his Annie again. It was a much shorter countdown, 30 days, and seemed a lot more real than the 279 days until he could rotate out of Vietnam.

Chicago got a letter from his Mom and didn't open it for a whole day. Finally, Horse had to get rough with him. "Will you open it, Chicago! You are walking around thinking the worst and you don't even know what it says. It you don't open it, I will!"

"You're being a little pushy there!" Chicago snapped back.

Andy looked at his friend, "You know whether or not you read it, the news won't change. You might as well know what's going on."

"What if it's bad news?" Chicago's face fell.

"Then you will know it. Come on, you're always willing to face stuff. Just get it over with. Remember, tomorrow you'll already know." Horse reminded him.

Spud poked his arm, "Yah tomorrow."

Chicago shook his head, "Okay. Tomorrow."

Chicago looked at the letter and started to open it. Then he handed it to Andy. "Here Spud. You read it and let me know. I can't do it."

Andy took the letter and opened it. He read it and then smiled. "It is kind of good news, Chicago. Mayo says that he has a weird spinal infection and it is mimicking some of the symptoms of MD. However, it is not muscular dystrophy. He is in the hospital there and is on these strong antibiotics. They seem to be working. He'll have to be there at least a week."

Chicago put his head down and cried. "What a relief. I was being so damned scared, bro. I was dying."

"That's okay," Horse rubbed his back, "We all have things that get to us. That's when you need someone to lean on. See, he'll be okay after he gets this treatment. So, now you can go back to being your obnoxious self. We kind of like that guy."

"I need to get tight with some decent folks. You guys are the weirdest people in Vietnam!" Chicago retorted. "Anyway, I'll be buying you supper at the mess."

"Real big of you, there, Chicago," Spud laughed. "Don't be putting yourself out any. Hey, when do you get your R&R?"

"Oh no!" Horse groaned, "Now we get to hear all about Spud's big leave again. I feel like I've lived through it twice already! You think Annie will want to get married? I mean, if it is a Justice of the Peace thing; that wouldn't be a big wedding or anything. I can't see your family going for that."

"Don't care," Andy grinned, "Mom and Dad got married while Mom was in the hospital. They had a big ceremony later. We can do the same thing if they want a big whop-dee-do. But if Annie says yes, I want to get married."

"Spoiled white boys!" Chicago chuckled.

"I suppose if you had your way, you wouldn't marry Sonny first chance you had!" Andy pointed out.

"Of course, I said you be a spoiled brat, I ain't like that I ain't one, too! That's exactly what Sonny and I plan," Chicago nodded. "And then Horse won't be giving me no guff about her dumping me. Right?"

Horse smirked at him, "It happens all the time, my friend. I seriously doubt that would slow me down one bit."

"I don't know why I hang with you," Chicago grumped.

"As I always say, who have you got waiting for you, Crazy Horse?" Spud raised his eyebrows and asked again.

"I will tell you all about it sometime. Until then, you two just enjoy with your womenfolk," Horse grinned.

"Really, Horse," Andy said, "You have never said much except that you broke up about a year ago. What happened?"

"It was over a year ago." Horse repeated. "That sums it up."

"How long did you go together?" Chicago asked.

"A long time," Horse's tone became serious. "And you aren't getting any more out of me, so don't put yourselves through the turmoil of trying. Got it?"

Andy and Chicago looked at each other, "Got it."

That night as Andy lay in his rack, he wondered what happened with Horse. He never said any more about the breakup with this mystery girl. He never even made a vague reference to it. It was curious, because he was rather open about everything else.

When Andy thought about being in Hawaii, he mostly just thought about seeing his Annie and his parents. He wanted his feet to heal up by then, but there wasn't any more he could do than what he was already doing about that. They were okay, if it didn't rain. Which was like saying, you will be okay if you don't breathe.

A few days later, they were out on another patrol. This was a recon of the area just north of where they had encountered the boy and his dog. When they encountered some villagers and there was a little boy with them, the kid smiled. Not a single soldier smiled back and more than one cocked his weapon. No wonder things got so hateful.

They came upon several more tunnels and of course, Andy got to do his favorite task. This time, the tunnels were empty, but that he only knew after he had crawled into them and felt the fear and anticipation of disaster that always accompanied him when he started down in those dark places.

They had no contact with the enemy and it was all-in-all a boring patrol. Nice and boring. They all were glad. When they got back, Horse and Chicago received their orders for R&R. They would be leaving at the same time two weeks after Andy. Chicago got Hawaii which he wanted.

Horse got Sydney, Australia. He was excited about that since he had no one to meet and wanted to be someplace 'western'. Australia had always intrigued him. He decided his character in his fantasy television series would be cool as an American Indian hero with an Aussy accent!

Chicago received another letter from his Mom saying that his brother would be released from the hospital in a few days and heading home. He was worlds better and they were so thankful. Chicago looked forward to seeing his Sonny just as much as Andy was his Annie, and they were planning to get married on Oahu.

Horse had heard from Swede who had arrived back in Minnesota. He was in Minneapolis yet at the hospital, but would be able to go home in a couple weeks. He asked Horse to give Spud and Chicago his home address. The three fellows were actually happy for the first time in a long while.

# 270 days left

## 18 'til leave

One of the other units went out on patrol and had met some serious resistance. There was a memorial that morning for the two fallen soldiers. It seemed as though there was no end to the number of these damned things they had to attend. Most of the GI's believed that things were worse now than they had been just six months before. The animosity of the villagers was much more evident than when Andy had first arrived. No one knew for certain the reasons, but it was the way it was.

The newbies brought news that confirmed by what some family members had written, of the political unrest back in the world. Seems everything was upside down. Men were still being drafted and sent over to the war, but fewer wanted to be there. The country was torn apart about it. As for the soldiers, everything was exploding around them. Some had gone home to be treated like lepers after having been drafted. And others were treated horribly for evading the draft. It was a no win situation.

The civil rights movement and the accompanying violence disturbed many of the men and caused some of them to wonder why they were fighting and what they would go home to when their tours were over. It was very disconcerting for everyone.

Had it not been for their personal good news of late, the trio of friends might have been more discouraged. As it was, their personal near futures looked good and they were able to smile and mean it.

They were all taken by surprise the next morning, when they learned that one of the more quiet, responsible MP's had taken his own life overnight. At first, they all speculated that he had received a Dear John letter or that had somehow learned that his wife was unfaithful. However, it turned out not to be the case. He had been on leave two months before and had only four months left before he could go home. However, some of the guys he was tight with reported that he had to use his machine gun on a young Vietnamese girl about eight, right after he got back from leave. He never really got over it. No matter that she indeed fired a loaded weapon in his direction, he couldn't get past it. Some folks were just not able to handle the hatefulness and insanity of it all. Bad, ugly business.

The next day, they went on a two-day patrol. It was routine until the last afternoon. They were forging a swollen stream in the pelting rain, when the came under heavy fire. It lasted only a few minutes, but when it was over, one man was killed and two were seriously wounded. For them, the war was over.

Andy couldn't get over how routine it had all become. He agreed with Horse. He wanted to take the fort! Hell, he would have been happy if they could just keep the same trail clear for more than a week. It seemed to him, this whole thing was like trying to control the ocean tides with a teaspoon. Sure, you could cheer every so often when the tide went out to sea, but wait a few minutes. It would be back again. It was depressing as hell. When they got back to camp, it was a relief to stand down for a while and let their feet dry out. Knowing full well, they would be back out in the boonies, chasing the elusive enemy all over again in a few days.

Suds had been very quiet the last few weeks. After his Grandmother died, he had been down for a while but seemed to bounce back. About the time that Swede was injured, he became more withdrawn. The guys were in their own funk, so no one seemed to talk about it. He was still friendly, but they talked little about more than business.

A couple days after the last patrol, the trio was on their way to breakfast when they saw Suds packing laundry into the bags. He was alone so they went over to talk to him.

"How have you been?" Andy asked. "We haven't had a chance to talk for some time."

"Suds know grunts in boonies many times," the young Vietnamese nodded. "Friends okay?"

"We be going on leave soon! Cool, huh?" Chicago smiled. "Guess what? Spud and I be getting married."

Suds grinned devilishly, "Suds think Army not like you to marry Spud!"

Horse just cracked up, "Ha! He got you there, Chicago!"

"Funny guy," Spud laughed. "No, I am going to marry my Annie and Chicago is going to marry Sonny."

"Who is Horse going to marry?" Suds asked the Indian soldier.

"Horse is not going to get married," Horse smiled. "Horse has no girlfriend."

"Like Suds. No wife. No girlfriend. No fun for Horse and Suds."

"Amen Brother," Horse laughed, "But we have no one to tell us what to do all the time, either."

Suds smiled and nodded emphatically, "Yes. Suds think good. No boss."

"How are things going for you these days?" Andy asked.

"No good. Much trouble in village. No trust for anyone. Very sad."

"I can about imagine. I'm very sorry for that," Andy put his hand on Suds shoulder and he flinched.

Andy jumped and asked, "Did I hurt you? I'm so sorry."

Suds became very nervous, "Suds have to hurry with dirty clothes. Must go now."

Andy grabbed his hand, "What's going on Suds?"

Suds looked down and pulled back his shirt over his shoulder. There was a large bandage. "Suds have accident. Better now. No worry for Spud. Suds okay."

Horse blurted out, "Liar."

Suds looked at him in shock and then said very quietly, "Suds have trouble. Please, no talk anymore. Friends no talk, no worry. Suds must go now."

"What the hell?" Andy asked. "Is it trouble from a GI?"

"No. Suds must go. Suds happy friends get married. Must go."

With that, the young man nearly ran off. The three guys stood there in wonder. Then Chicago said, "Think we should be reporting to any one? And who?"

Horse thought and then said, "Hell, we don't have any idea what we'd even say. I think it's more to it than an accident, but we have to trust his judgment. He said to keep quiet and I think we should honor that."

The other two thought a minute and then Chicago said, "Yah, you're right. I hope that he's not in trouble in his village because of his job with us."

"With all the unrest lately, I wouldn't be surprised. I hope he's going to be okay," Andy said.

The next day, Suds did not come to the camp at all and the three friends were very worried. They wondered if he was ill or if there was trouble for him. He said a mouthful when he pointed out there was little trust left. The soldiers knew it from their perspective and could easily imagine the villagers felt the same way.

They had passed through villages with one or two dead. They were messages to one alliance from a faction on the other side. There was no question about that and recognized by all.

Suds going back and forth daily once or twice to a US camp put him in the position of distrust by everyone. Some folks thought he was a turncoat, working for the enemy; some thought he was a spy for either side; but even the villagers who took no side, did not relish the fact that someone as controversial as he, lived amongst them.

While the guys didn't know how old he was, they had all wondered why he wasn't in the military. Was he a spy? Was he covert? Was he somehow privileged to stay out of the war while others had to go? None of the questions or the answers made him any easier to be seen with as a friend. He wasn't trusted by his neighbors or the soldiers. It must have been a miserable existence.

The following morning again, there was no Suds. That morning at breakfast mess, they heard some of the other soldiers talking about him. They had clothing they were waiting to be returned and inquired when he was expected back. After asking around, the trio found a MP who was vague, but told them who to ask.

The man who handled civilian employees told them that Suds was injured in an incident in his village and became quite ill. He was expected back when he recuperated in a couple days.

Horse asked the other soldiers, "Does anyone know why he isn't in the military?"

"Nguyen Van Tri, or Suds as you grunts call him, gets seizures caused by an injury he got while in the ARVN. That was a few years back. So, he took care of his mother, grandmother and his wife. She was killed by the VC a year or so ago. His grandmother died recently. Poor devil has had a bad time of things. Seems like a nice guy."

"How old is he, do you think?" Horse asked.

"He is in his mid-thirties. Anyway, he is supposed to be back in a few days. I have to get back to work. Talk to you later."

After he left, the three guys sat quietly until Chicago said, "Hmm. Mid-thirties, huh? I would have thought he was just a kid."

"I know. I think they are all really young or very old," Andy said. "I feel bad for Suds. I bet he could tell us a lot if we had the time and the place to talk."

"Yah," Horse agreed. "I bet he could. I hope he's okay. I get nervous about this 'trouble in the village' he mentions. It makes me very nervous."

"It's a mystery," Chicago nodded. "Like another mystery I want to understand."

"What's that?" Horse asked.

"What happened with your girl? You're always making us talk to you, but you never tell us about your girl. We would no way make fun of it, you know. We're tight and share everything. I think you should tell us."

"Ah, it is just the usual," Horse tried to change the subject.

"I don't believe that for an instant," Spud retorted. "We know better than that."

"Well, you aren't going to find out. So, save yourself the trouble of trying. Please, leave it alone."

# *261 days left*

## *9 days 'til leave*

Andy's feet were getting worse again because of the incessant rain. He was disappointed that they had another recon patrol. It was hot, rainy and miserable. They saw little activity with the exception of overly active leeches and mosquitoes.

As luck would have it, the Sergeant came upon some tunnel entrances about sixty feet apart. Andy and Franklin got the privilege of each getting their own tunnel to investigate. They stripped to their waists and headed to the tunnels which had not been gassed.

Inside the tunnel, it was tight, pitch dark, damp and very warm. Andy had to crawl on his belly, wiggling himself through. He came to a small room and it was empty with the exception of a little debris. He entered another tunnel at the other end of the room and was crawling, forcing himself into the tight passage. He held his flashlight in one outstretched hand in front of him and his pistol in the other. It was miserable.

He thought he heard something but inside the tunnels, movement were easily heard from the ground above also. He was sweating and having a difficult time pulling himself along. Then he saw a flicker of a light ahead of him.

He switched his light off, quit breathing and he froze in place. He wondered if he should back up. The tunnel had a turn to the right and the light came from around the turn. His mind, that he usually counted on to slow down and think, went numb. He just lay there trying to figure out what to do. His entire body was drenched in sweat of fear.

Apparently, the enemy had seen his light too. There was no sound or movement from that direction either. The air was dank and there was no longer a glimmer of any light. The sound of his own breathing resonated in his ears. It seemed like an eternity. Finally, his brain started to work again.

'Okay. Whoever it is, already knows I'm here and knows I know that he's there,' Andy tried to reason. 'I really didn't want to buy it a week before leave! Damn it all!'

Then he heard the other person cock his pistol. 'Shit! That's exactly what's going to happen, too. Sure as hell. I couldn't back out fast enough to save my ass. I guess this is it. Son of a bitch.'

He cocked his pistol. 'How long can we lay here? One of us is either going to have to back up or we're going to have to shoot each other. Or stay here until we die of old age.'

A few more minutes drug by while his mind was swirling with visions of his squad deciding it would be too difficult to retrieve him and blowing up the tunnel with him in it, like those other folks. That would really make his Mom upset about not getting him back.

Then he got mad, for no specific reason. How could this happen when he was so close to getting leave? What a dirty rotten trick! So close to marrying his Annie! Dammit. It wasn't fair and it wasn't right! If he was going to die, he'd rather hurry up and do it. And by God, when he met his Maker, he was going to make Him explain why He didn't let him get to be married to Annie for just one week! Good grief, was that be too much to ask!

Andy decided to get it over with and find out what he was dealing with. Then he remembered the code. His mouth was so parched he could hardly say it. The response was something that even Vietnamese who knew English had a difficult time pronouncing. Andy said, "Sixteenth President."

"Abraham Lincoln!" Franklin burst out laughing. "I've never been so glad to hear anyone's voice in my life! I thought I was dead, Man. Damn, we almost blew each other away!"

Now both GI's were laughing and thanking God that they not only weren't confronting an enemy, but that they had not panicked and killed each other. After the relief, they both decided to back out of their end of the tunnel and go up the holes they came down.

When they emerged from their holes a good sixty feet apart, they were both shaking but almost giddy. "What happened down there? You two are both acting crazy," Sgt. Bolinsky asked.

119

"We damned near killed each other," Franklin chortled. "That would have really pissed me off!"

"We were each coming in the other end of the same tube. Those folks really need to put lighting in those things," Andy added in fits of hysterics!

"Or at least, passing lanes," Franklin guffawed.

Bole just shook his head. "Be better if they quit building them altogether."

Andy and Franklin looked at each other and grinned. Today, they didn't care. They were both glad they were alive and that they hadn't killed each other. Sometimes, it takes very little to make a person think he had a good day.

That night, Bolinsky stopped by where Andy was sleeping. "Schroeder, I just wanted to tell you that you handled yourself very responsibly today. A lot of guys would have freaked and started blasting away. That would have been a disaster. but you kept your head. I am proud of you."

Then Bolinksy shook his hand, handed him something and moved off. Andy was stunned and sat there for a full minute without moving while trying to absorb what he said. After he pulled himself back together, he looked at the card Bole had handed him. It was a hard paper card about the size of a playing card. Andy read it with his flashlight.

## If
### Rudyard Kipling

If you can keep your head when all about you
Are losing theirs and blaming it on you;
If you can trust yourself when all men doubt you,
But make allowance for their doubting too;
If you can wait and not be tired by waiting,
Or, being lied about, don't deal in lies,
Or, being hated, don't give way to hating,
And yet don't look too good, nor talk too wise;
If you can dream—and not make dreams your master;
If you can think—and not make thoughts your aim;
If you can meet with triumph and disaster
And treat those two imposters just the same;

If you can bear to hear the truth you've spoken
Twisted by knaves to make a trap for fools,
Or watch the things you gave your life to broken,
And stoop and build 'em up with wornout tools;
If you can make one heap of all your winnings
And risk it on one turn of pitch-and-toss,
And lose, and start again at your beginnings
And never breath a word about your loss;
If you can force your heart and nerve and sinew
To serve your turn long after they are gone,
And so hold on when there is nothing in you
Except the Will which says to them: "Hold on";
If you can talk with crowds and keep your virtue,
Or walk with kings—nor lose the common touch;
If neither foes nor loving friends can hurt you;
If all men count with you, but none too much;
If you can fill the unforgiving minute
With sixty seconds' worth of distance run—
Yours is the Earth and everything that's in it,
And—which is more—you'll be a Man my son!

Andy was dumbfounded. He couldn't remember anything that ever meant so much to him. He wiped the tears away from his eyes and reread it. Then he carefully placed the card behind the card of Pastor Byron. He never told a soul about it. He fell asleep one very grateful man.

They got back to camp on the fifth day. Andy's feet were raw again and he saw the medic. He gave him some more of the ointment and some antibiotics. "You need to stay off your feet for a day or so."

"I am going on leave in three days," Andy pointed out. "I want to be well."

"I hope you can be, but don't count on it. If you take it easy for the next day or so, we should have you in good enough shape to go back on patrol. If you are well enough for that, you are well enough for R&R."

Andy frowned, "Sounds like convoluted logic to me, but whatever."

The medic nodded, "It is whatever. If it gets worse, come right back to see me. You are pretty close to being in the hospital."

"Not necessary," Andy was definite, "It was worse the last time and I didn't have to go to the hospital. I'll be fine."

The medic looked directly in his eyes. "If you want to be able to go on leave, you better take care of those feet."

Andy nodded. All the way back to his hooch, he was thinking of all the things he wanted to tell them, if he ever figured out who the 'them' was he needed to tell! He would say, "What a crock! I'm not the one that sends me out to wallow in the mud. Now they tell me I have to take care of me, like I have any control over it!" He was frustrated.

There was a great deal of relief, when the three friends saw Suds back at his usual stand that morning. The other two hurried over to talk to him, and Andy followed behind because of his feet. They greeted their friend with big smiles.

"We were worried about you, Man! You okay?" Chicago asked. "How are you?"

"Suds okay now. Bad sick from arm. Suds get shaky thing from fever. It all good now."

"You mean seizures?" Horse asked.

Suds looked at him with surprise, "Horse know shaky thing?"

"Yes, we heard. A head injury, right?" Andy asked. "That's what we heard."

"Head healed but Suds have shakes now when sick. No good," the man nodded. "Suds cover hole in head with hat, but no cover shaky thing."

"I imagine. I'm sorry that you have to deal with that," Andy said.

"Spud walk like old man again. You have rotten foot?"

Andy chuckled, "You got that right! The doc gave me some medicine for it so I should be good as new soon."

"Spud," Suds looked around to make certain no one else could hear but the four of them, "Suds say medic not know. Vietnamese pound special plant, make good medicine. I bring tonight. Spud put on, wrap foot. In morning, mostly no rotten."

"Hmm. Really?" Spud thought, "Have you used it? Does it really work?"

"Suds no bring if no good." He was quite taken back.

Andy could tell he had almost insulted his friend. "No, I'd love to use it. I have to have good feet to get married."

Suds laughed as did his other friends, "Suds think feet not so important for marriage!"

Horse was almost rolling on the ground in hysterics. Andy got indignant. "You're as bad as these two, Suds! I don't think I like any of you!"

Chicago cracked up, "And we're the only friends you can get!"

That evening, they stopped by to pick up the ointment from Suds. He had it in a small packet and on the package was his name and address. He also had his name and address of his uncle in Saigon.

"Spud give address to Horse and Chicago. Suds like good friends. If Suds goes away, Spud can write to Suds' uncle to find."

"Good idea. I'll give you my address at home," Spud volunteered.

Horse said, "We all will. We'll give them to you tomorrow morning. It is important for friends to keep in touch."

Suds smiled, "Suds like that. Suds must go, dirty clothes!"

Later, when the grunts were getting ready to hit the rack, Andy took out the ointment and looked at it.

"You really going to use that stuff?" Chicago asked. "It might be like poison ivy or some medicine man thing."

"You have a problem with a Medicine Man?" Horse asked.

"Not at all . . . , much. I just think that the ointment might be more sanitary."

Andy looked at him and laughed. "We've been wallowing in dirt and mud for months! Now is a really weird time to worry about sanitation! Most modern medicine is made from old medicine man things anyway. They're just in pill form. Besides, that junk the doc has given me sure didn't cure it. What can it hurt?"

"When you have your leg amputated; remember I warned you." Chicago stated.

"Why do you think Suds gave us his address and his uncle's? Do you think something is up? I have a feeling that he isn't going to be around here much longer," Horse observed.

"That's what I thought too. I don't blame him. He could do better in Saigon, I think. I don't know why I think that, but I do. You know, we aren't going to be here forever either. Hey, as soon as I get my feet smeared up, lets get the addresses all copied," Andy suggested.

123

He cleaned his feet and dried them. When he smeared the poultice on his feet, it burned like crazy at first. Had he not promised Suds and talked so big to Chicago, he would have rinsed it off, immediately. Instead, he left it on. After about five minutes, they were just warm. Then he wrapped them and put his socks on over the bandages. Now they felt better than they had in days and didn't itch!

Even though the next day he would be heading for Da Nang, that night his thoughts were mostly about Suds, his feet and the near disaster in the tunnel.

# 252 days left

## 2 days to Honolulu

The next morning, Andy's feet were a lot better. However, he would have been on that bird out of Cu Chi if he had been paralyzed and had to drag himself to get there. His feet had amazing improvement. He saw Suds for a minute before he took off and he thanked him profusely. Then he gave him a big hug and Suds was taken back.

"Suds think Spud very happy," Suds smiled. "If we not see again, keep happy spirit."

"You too, my dear friend," Andy said. "Stay safe."

Andy was surprised how conflicted he felt about leaving. Not that he would have stayed but that he really didn't want to go. What if something happened to Horse and Chicago? They had been together through so much and now he'd be gone. When he came back, they'd be leaving. He was very uneasy about that. He felt things were changing and the important things they had counted on in their precarious place could easily be disrupted.

Mostly he and Chicago teased each other about their grand prowess of their expected performances on their upcoming honeymoons. Horse just shook his head. "You guys will both just sleep! Clean, dry beds, full bellies of real food, no one telling you to get up! I know you two. You'll sleep for a week! Your poor wives will wonder why they took the trip," Horse chided.

"Don't bet on it!" Andy laughed. "There are things more important than sleep!"

"If you say so," Horse chuckled. "Anyway, best wishes, Man. It has been something else. I hope we meet again. If not, I can't imagine having done this without you. You jackasses are the real deal."

Andy hugged Horse. "We'll be back here again soon. Don't talk so gloom and doom. Okay, I'm the first to go, but you two will be leaving on R&R when I get back. Let's not say goodbye. Let's just say 'until tomorrow'."

Horse clapped his back, "Tomorrow."

Chicago almost gave in to tears, "Yah, tomorrow."

Andy was just antsy at Da Nang, and couldn't wait to get on the 'freedom bird' to Hawaii. Once in his seat, he began to relax. He leaned back in comfort, heading for 'the world'. When the stewardess came by, he was almost giddy. Real people did exist! They didn't carry guns or hide in bushes! It was a wonderful revelation.

During the flight, Andy thought about a hundred different things that he wanted to tell his Dad and Mom, and Annie, and Darrell. His head was a jumble.

Annie had written that she and Jeannie, with the help of the folks back home, had set up their double wedding. Jeannie and Darrell were going to get married at the same ceremony, like he and Darrell had talked about since they were kids. Pastor Byron had set it up with a minister in Honolulu. Jeannie's parents and Darrell's parents were going to be there, and Andy's Mom and Dad. Annie's father and his steady girl were trying to get their flights lined up in the last letter than Andy had received.

Andy would be at Schofield Barracks to hear another two-hour briefing and then be released. His parents had packed his civilian clothes, so Andy would not have to rent anything at Schofield. He'd be released from Schofield about one in the afternoon and the wedding was at five. He wouldn't see Annie before the ceremony.

He tried to sleep, but couldn't. His mind was swirling, trying to unwind from one life and focus on the other one. The one that had been put in storage for some time.

It had only been six months since he saw them all, but a lot of water went under the bridge, for them and for him. Some good stuff, and some really bad stuff.

Andy really did appreciate that Darrell and Jeannie were so flexible with their wedding plans to accommodate his wishes. Not many people would do that, but then Darrell was not just anyone. Darrell had written, "At least this way, Jeannie and I have an excuse for a Hawaiian honeymoon. Too bad we'll only see each other at the ceremony, because afterwards, we'll both be otherwise occupied! I doubt the ladies will want us to be hanging out with each other!"

The pilot clicked on the overhead and announced they would be landing in about twenty-five minutes. Andy thought he might have told the weather on the ground, but the cheering on the plane drowned him out. There was not a passenger on that plane that wasn't anxious to land in Hawaii.

Three and a half hours later, Andy signed out. He was behind schedule, but thought he could still make it. He gave his contact information and room location. Then he was a somewhat free man until August 2. He was almost giddy as he walked toward the door of the building.

When he got close to the door, he saw his Dad and Darrell talking to each other at the end of the patio. They were among the several folks there waiting for their loved ones. He flung the door open and ran, as best as his painful feet could carry him, to where his dad was having a cigarette.

He threw his arms around his Dad and then included Darrell in his embrace. After all the greetings, Dad asked him if he was ready to go get married.

Andy sputtered amid chuckled, "I couldn't be more ready. Where is the car? Did you get my message? I can drive in Hawaii. Did you get the rental car with my name on it too? I'd love to drive. I'm so anxious to drive a car."

"Calm down, Andy," Dad grinned. "Yes, I got the message and it is all taken care of. Darrell is the best map-reader in America and he'll give you directions. We are staying at the Hawaiian Regent on Kalakaua Ave on Waikiki Beach. Oh, you know that, huh? Annie said you had to sign out to there or something."

"Yah, all done. Guess they want to know where I'm in case they need me! Ha!" Andy said sarcastically, "They need something, but I'm not it! I can promise you that. How was your flight over here?"

Darrell grinned, "Good. Jeannie flew with Annie and her Dad and his girlfriend, Charlotte, the day before yesterday. My Mom and Dad came in this morning. Your folks and I got in yesterday and since then, he and I are getting this trip to the airport down pat, right Elton?"

"You bet, Darrell. We flew in yesterday with Darrell. Frandsens have been on the Big Island until this morning, two hours after Jessups got here. We can dang near make it to the airport blindfolded!" Andy's Dad chuckled.

"Yah, that's how we drive it! Like we're blind-folded!" Darrell laughed. "Yea gads! We've come into the parking area at the airport every way except right so far!"

"We'll have it down pat when we start taking everyone back out the airport," the older man proclaimed, running his hand through his salt and pepper hair.

"Elton, it is a different street for that!" Darrell pointed out.

"Well, the way I see it, we get them in the general vicinity and the rest is up to them. Let's go, kid. I have a big responsibility. If I don't get the grooms to the church on time, those women will have my hide!"

Andy stopped short, "Are we going directly to the church? I mean, is there a place to change there?"

"Yes to both," his Dad assured him. "You'll be able to wash the Army stink off you before you go down the aisle. What's wrong? Why are you limping?"

Andy gave him a self-conscious look. "Ah, I was hoping no one would notice. It is a lot better than it was. I got that Jungle rot stuff. Mostly my right foot, though. My left foot is almost healed with the stuff that Suds gave me."

His Dad listened and then frowned, "Suds?"

"My Vietnamese friend. He gave me a salve that is homemade. It really did the trick and healed it up better than the junk the medic gave me."

Darrell shook his head, "Why did it not heal up your right foot?"

"Because it was a lot worse. It's been oozing for a while, but it's a lot better. Hell, I could hardly walk before Suds gave me that salve a couple days ago." Then he was beginning to feel uncomfortable with the conversation. "Dad, I brought you some of the Vietnamese Cohn Coffee. or Weasel Poop Coffee. It's the best coffee in the world. I can't wait until you taste it."

His Dad raised his eyebrows and grinned, "The advertisement sounds awful. I'm looking forward to it, but only because you say so. I'll crawl in the backseat and leave the driving to you two. Now be careful. I'll have my eyes closed. I don't know if I can stand to watch it!"

Darrell laughed, "Don't worry. If we're going to get into a big accident, I'll call you so you don't miss it!"

"Thanks," Elton groaned. "Nice to know I can count on you."

On the trip to the church, Andy drove. "You have no idea how nice it feels to get behind the wheel. I have developed a dislike for being driven every place. Usually, they take me somewhere I don't want to go!"

"I imagine," Darrell nodded. "Has it been really tough?"

"Some of it has been a real bitch," Andy nodded. "But I don't want to think about that now. I want to think of good stuff. How is Ginger?"

The rest of the ride, the guys brought Andy up to date on all the gossip from home. They told him about Ginger's almost complete recovery, Zach and Suzy's wedding and about the FBI agent Carl Kincaid, who was now Darrell's business partner."

"Gee, I'm going to have to have everyone wear name tags when I get home!" Andy grinned. "I don't know these people from Adam. And the house has been remodeled! Wow! It will be like a new world."

His Dad patted his shoulder, "No it isn't Andy. It's still your home. Your crazy old home. Little Charlie is still my Chicken Man. Grandpa Lloyd still thinks you are on Iwo Jima and Grandma Katherine still bakes the best caramel rolls in America."

Andy smiled, "I heard about the cooking contest. I guess congratulations are in order, huh Darrell?"

"Well, yah. He and Kevin did do a good job," Elton agreed.

"The only reason that your Dad didn't win is because no one would vote for either him or Kincaid because they both acted like idiots about it!"

Andy's Dad cleared his throat, "Excuse me! I beg your pardon. I did not. It was all Kincaid."

"Yah, Dad," Andy chuckled. "I know. I heard about it from everyone in the clan who knows how to write! And a few who communicate by tape!"

"Well, if that don't beat all," his Dad blustered.

# 250 days left

## 7 days of leave

When they got out of the car at the parking lot of the Lutheran church, Andy took a deep breath. It was the first time that he really noticed their surroundings. The weather was a balmy 76 degrees and the sky was clear. There was a slight breeze that carried the fragrances of tropical flowers. It was a beautiful church built from dark lava rock with a picturesque yard surrounded by every blooming flower Andy had ever imagined.

The men went in the side entrance of the church and down a short hall to the changing room. Thankfully, there was a shower there. Andy couldn't wait to get in it. It even had hot water! As they had promised, his parents had packed his things from home and the first thing he spied was his favorite old cowboy boots. Andy hugged them, "I'm so glad that no one threw them away."

"Your Mom wouldn't let that happen!" Andy's Dad grinned. "She has your back."

Andy looked at his dad, "I know. You guys all do. You have no idea how many times that thought-," then he stopped to regain his composure.

His Dad gave him a quick hug, "I know. Get in the shower. Your Mom will be by to tell you hi and check out your rent-a-tux in a bit. I have to go get her now."

Andy came out of the shower, wrapped in a towel, when his Mom gobbled him up into a huge embrace and kiss. "I'm so glad to see you!"

He hugged her back. He knew she had no idea how much he had waited for her to be there, ever since the night of the snake thing. Damn! Now why did he have to go think of that damned boa. Not today! He returned her embrace and they both had tears.

She smiled through her tears, "Better get dressed. I have to check out how your tux fits."

A few minutes later, Andy had his tuxedo pants on and his Mom was trying to figure out how to tighten the waist. "You've lost weight, Andy. Don't they feed you?"

Andy grinned, "Yah, but I sweat if off. Just so my pants stay up! They should, huh?"

"Oh yah, they will. I can pull these tabs in. I am sure they were put in for just this occasion. If not, we'll use duct tape," his Mom winked.

Andy looked at his Mom and then he gave her a hug, "Mom, I love you. I missed you more than you'll ever know."

She hugged her son back and said, "I love you too, Andy. I am so proud of my boy. You have grownup to be a fine man." Then she wiped her tears, "Okay, let's get this show on the road. It is four-forty. Just think, my baby will be married in twenty minutes."

Andy looked at her and joked, "Wouldn't Pepper be your baby?"

Mom giggled, "I guess so, but you're both my babies."

Elton gave his wife a hug, "Nora, you have to get out of here now. I have to get these two guys out to the front of the church in a couple minutes. I know you two could talk for an hour."

Nora giggled, "No. We'll jabber later. I think we have other fish to fry right now. I have to go help scrape the girls off the ceiling."

Darrell chuckled, while Elton was adjusting his bow tie, "Are they all ready?"

"They are, but you know, they want everything to be perfect," Nora smiled.

Elton walked with the boys to the side entry of the sanctuary. Then he told them to wait for the music and then go stand up on the right hand side of the altar. He was going to go sit with Nora. She would be getting ready to cry, so he had a box of tissues handy. Everyone knew that Andy's stepdad was about as sentimental as they come. The boys knew that he would be in need of the tissues more than Nora.

While the boys stood there, Pastor Wilson came by and introduced himself to Andy. "I've met all the other wedding party, so I guess you must be Andy."

Andy shook his hand, "Yes, sir."

The minister smiled, "Darrell's brother-in-law, Pastor Byron spoke very highly of both of you. When you come out, I'd like Darrell to be in front. That way, I won't marry you guys off to the wrong brides."

The boys chuckled, "That would be a revolting development!"

"It certainly would be!" Pastor Wilson agreed.

The church was dark mahogany and there were stained glass windows. The evening light was dancing across the mahogany pews in rainbows of colors. There were two bouquets of tropical flowers on the altar, and their fragrance filled the sanctuary. The organist looked at her watch and then began to play Clair De Lune.

Andy and Darrell shook each other's hands and then walked out to the front of the church. The minister met them at the altar. The congregation consisted of Elton and Nora Schroeder and George and Alma Jessup on the right side of the aisle. On the left side of the church sat Myrtle Frandsen and behind her, Charlotte Long. Andy had never seen her before, but he assumed that the middle-aged lady with the pleasant smile was Annie's father's girlfriend. They were all bedecked in Hawaiian attire and wearing leis.

The music changed to the Hawaiian Wedding Song and the minister nodded to the small congregation to stand. Jeannie came up the aisle on the arm of her father, Albert Frandsen. She wore a white Victorian dress in satin with a high lace collar. It had long sleeves that were lace from the elbow down. The Princess style skirt was not very full but had a long ruffle on the bottom. In her hair, she wore a garland of braided white flowers and carried one long stemmed rose. She was radiant. Andy had always thought Jeannie was a good-looking gal, but today she was even more fantastic than he had remembered. She caught his eye and gave him a smile. He winked back.

When she got to the bottom of the altar, Darrell came forward and took her arm from her father, Albert Frandsen. They shook hands and Albert gave his new son-in-law a big grin. The couple moved forward and turned. Then Andy looked to the back of the church.

Suddenly, he was worried. He wondered if he would be able to talk. He hadn't been able to talk when he first met Annie! In fact, his whole family gave him grief about it. He hadn't seen her in months! What if she really didn't want to marry him, but was doing it out of patriotism or something? What if he didn't really want to marry her, but just thought that he did? What if when she saw him, she would decide to not marry him? What if she didn't love him anymore? What if this was all a stupid idea? What if-?

Then she appeared on the arm of her father. She wore a dress very similar to Jeannie's except that the bodice had a ruffle and the collar wasn't as high. Her black hair hung straight and shiny under the braided flower crown. She took one look at him with those magnificent eyes and he knew. He knew it was not a stupid idea. Not only was she the most beautiful woman in the world, she was the person that he wanted to share his life with. His eyes filled with tears. As he reached up to wipe a tear, he noticed his stepdad. Elton was already into the tissues. Andy looked at him and they exchanged a silly grin.

Andy stepped down to the front of the altar and met his bride. He shook his father-in-law's hand and nodded. Then he took his Annie's arm. At first, he thought she was trembling, but then he realized it was him.

This was a day that he doubted would ever happen. He thought about that episode in the tunnel just days before, when he and Franklin almost shot each other. He was so grateful he didn't die that day.

The ceremony could have been in Swahili for all Andy knew. He just remembered saying 'I do' and Darrell handing him the ring when the minister asked. The rest was a blur. All he could see was his Annie's large, soft brown eyes and her beautiful smile. Today, she would be his bride. 'Thanks be to God'.

Then the minister said, "You may kiss your brides."

Both young men kissed their wives. Andy didn't give Annie the kiss he wanted to because he was afraid he wouldn't be able to stop. He gave her a sweet kiss and then he and Darrell kissed each other's wives. Then they moved down from the altar and were deluged with hugs and kisses from the assembly of parents, while the musician returned to playing Clair De Lune.

After signing the papers, making it all official and paying everyone who made the ceremony so nice, including the photographer who filmed it on Super 8, they left for the restaurant. On the way back to the dressing rooms, Andy pulled Annie into a doorway. It was a sitting room of some sort. There, he gave her a very passionate kiss and said, "I love you more than you can believe."

They got their things together and drove in a convoy of rental cars to a restaurant where they had made a reservation for the dinner. There they had a wonderful luau-type meal and shared a coconut wedding cake. The small party ate, danced and had a wonderful time. It was quiet but couldn't have been more perfect.

Andy spoke with his father-in-law, Elliott Packineau for the first time. Elliott was of a slight build and about as tall as Andy's dad and had Annie's eyes and smile. He was a friendly man and obviously very protective of his little girl. He was anxious for Andy to meet his steady girl. She was Charlotte Long and they had been dating for about two years. Char was the same height as Elliott and had a slender build. She had long dark blond hair and blue-green eyes. She was very personable and seemed to be down to earth. Elliott said they would be getting married when everyone got back from Vietnam. Annie's brother was over there, Andy was there and Char's youngest son was there. His name was Barron, and he still had about eight months.

Andy's foot began to give him a lot of trouble after a couple hours. By eight o'clock, he was limping and his sock was getting sticky. He knew it was starting to ooze and bleed again. He was very grateful when the group decided to go back to the hotel. Not only could he get his foot out of the shoe but he could be alone with his Annie.

At the Regent, everyone was about as subtle as a sledgehammer. Frandsens said good night right away and reminded Elton they needed to be at the airport at seven for the flight home. Jessups were leaving at eleven in the morning for Maui. The Packineau couple was going to check out the disco and Nora and Elton had plans to go walk on the beach. No one asked what the young couple's plans were. Everyone knew.

The four young people shared the same elevator to their floor and then said good night at Darrell's room. Andy shook Darrell's hand and then they gave each other a hug. "Thanks man."

"You too," Darrell grinned.

Jeannie gave Andy a hug, "It is so good to see you again. We really missed you."

Then his best friends walked to their room hand in hand. Andy knew he was the luckiest guy in the world. Then Annie took his hand, "You have great friends, Andy."

He smiled at her, "They are, but I think I like you better."

Andy carried his bride across the threshold and then caressed her neck with his lips. Soon they were overtaken by the most intense desire and fell passionately onto their bed. Through the windows, the gentle wind moved the sheer curtains. They could hear the surf pounding on the shore and the faint strains of a ukulele in the distance. It was the most wonderful lovemaking either could imagine.

Later that night, Andy got up to have a cigarette. He asked Annie if she wanted something to drink and then poured her a Coke. They put on their robes and sat out on the balcony to watch the waves. It wasn't until they sat down at the small table there that Annie giggled, "You still have your socks on!"

"Ah, I know," Andy was embarrassed. "I guess I can take one off."

Annie looked at him curiously, "Only one?"

"I didn't want to tell you, but Annie, I have jungle rot or something like that on my foot. That is why I've been limping. It is pretty gross. I don't want you to see it."

"What? What do you mean, you don't want me to see it! I'm your wife and plan on being your wife for a long time. Foot rot or no foot rot. Get used to it."

"Wow! I forgot what a bossy old bag you could be," Andy teased.

"Let's see, married a couple hours and the honeymoon's over! That must be record!" Then Annie leaned ahead and gently kissed his cheek, ending on his lips. "Let's fix the foot and get back to more serious matters."

Andy nodded, returning her kiss, "Good idea."

They looked at his foot. It was oozing and bleeding quite a bit. Annie helped him clean it and then put the medication on it. The Army wouldn't let him take the salve from Suds, so he was stuck with their medicine. Then they rewrapped it and put a clean sock on it.

"Tomorrow, we'll go sit in the sun and let it dry out," Annie suggested. "Okay?"

Andy took his wife's hand and pulled her close to him, "Okay. Come here."

# 249 days left

## 6 days of leave

After making love again, the young couple fell asleep in each other's arms. Andy slept soundly for some time than then began to dream. He dreamt that he was trudging along in the jungle like a normal quiet day. In his dream, the mosquitoes began really bothering him. They were on his face and his arms. He tried his best to push them away, but they wouldn't budge. They were in his eyes and so thick that he couldn't even see. They got into his mouth and nose and he could hardly breathe. Finally, he dropped his weapon and began swatting his arm and face as hard as he could to get them to go away.

The next thing he aware of was Annie's voice saying urgently, "Andy, it is me! Annie. Please don't slap me!"

Andy sat straight up in bed. He looked around. It took him a minute to realize where he was and that he had been hitting his beloved Annie and not mosquitoes! He was sick and almost cried. He put his arms around her and apologized.

"God Annie, I am so very sorry. I would never hurt you," he tried to comfort her and himself. "I love you more than life itself. I didn't know what I was doing! I can't believe I did that! Please forgive me."

Annie studied his face intently, "Honey, I know that. I heard you. You were cussing the mosquitoes. It was just a dream. You didn't hurt me. It's okay. I think my hair was on your face."

"I feel just terrible. I don't ever want to hurt you, even a little," Andy was very emotional and trying to find a way to apologize fully. He hated himself for hitting her. He wanted so much to be able to erase it. How could he do that? What the hell was wrong with him?

Annie pulled him into her arms, "Not to worry. It was just a dream. I know you would never hurt me. Calm down, honey. It isn't a big deal." Then she kissed his cheek and smiled, "I'm just glad I'm not a mosquito!"

Andy was still very taken back by the events and wanted badly to believe that it would be okay, but he wasn't certain. All the guys in the hooch were plagued by nightmares, but it seemed to make sense over there. They all just assumed it would go away when they returned to world. He was terrified to go back to sleep for fear that he might hit her again. He could have cried. What a hell of a thing to do on your wedding night!

He stretched out on his back with his arms behind his head. "Annie? What if I never get over this? What if-?"

"Stop it, Andrew. Don't make a big deal out of it. Okay, honey? You have spent a lot of time sleeping with your mosquito friends. I imagine you are just getting used to sleeping with one person instead of a swarm of thousands."

Andy looked at her as she put her arm around his waist and her head on his chest. "We can work it out."

Andy took her in his arms and soon they had forgotten all about the dream.

The sun was up and streaming through the patio window when he woke. He was alone in bed. It took him a minute to figure out where he was and all that had happened the day before. Then he panicked. What if Annie had left him because he hit her? Where was she? He wouldn't blame her if she did. What a horrible thing for him to do! What kind of a person beats on his new bride on their wedding night?

Then he sat up in bed and heard the shower running. He climbed out of bed and put on his robe. He went out on the balcony and with his hands shaking, lit his cigarette. He watched the surf pounding on the beach across the street.

It was beautiful in Honolulu. It was hard to imagine that only a day or so away, people were blowing each other to bits. Here there were smiles, music, bright colors and all types of good food. Over there were cans of rations, camouflage and suspicious looks. He was lost in thought and didn't hear Annie until she pushed the sliding door open a little further before she stepped out.

He looked at her and was amazed at her beauty. She smiled at him and said, "Good morning. Are you up for all day?"

Andy swallowed hard, "Annie. I feel just awful about last night. I could just kill myself. I can't believe that I hurt you."

She took him in her arms, "You didn't hurt me and don't think about it any more. Okay? Things happen. Let's not let it ruin our day, okay?"

Andy kissed her, "I love you. I'm so lucky that you love me."

She patted his chest, and raised her eyebrows, "Remember that on my bad days!" She giggled and then stepped back. "Why don't you get your shower and we can get something to eat! This time change is driving me crazy. It is like ten in the morning back home and I haven't eaten! I am starving."

Andy grinned, "That's my girl. I'll jump in the shower real quick. Can you last a couple minutes?"

"Don't know. But if the curtains are gone when you get out of the shower, you'll have your answer!" Annie smiled as she looked over the balcony. "I wonder if your Dad got Frandsens to the airport. He is so funny. He has been stewing and working so hard to make sure that everyone gets where they need to be. He is trying his best to make everything perfect for everyone. I just love him."

Andy watched the traffic a minute, "I do too. I hope I can be as good of a husband to you as he is to my Mom. He would never hit her."

Annie stood to her full height and spoke forcefully, "Okay. Listen. A bad dream is a bad dream. Anyone can have them. Hush up about it."

Andy didn't know how much to say to her. He stood motionless for a minute, "Annie, some really bad things happened over there. I don't know if I'm going to be able to handle it so good. I'm not as good a person as you might think I am."

She took his hand, "You are my Andy. We'll do whatever we need to do, okay? I'm here for you, good or bad. I know who you are and you are a kind, loving person. That is my real Andy. Now, get your shower."

Andy kissed her cheek, but he still wasn't as confident as he would have liked to have been.

When Andy emerged from the shower, he was relieved that the draperies were still intact. Annie rewrapped his foot and they were off for breakfast. It was just barely five in the morning, Hawaiian time, when they got to the lobby.

Andy's Dad had just pulled the rental car up to the valet and was loading Albert and Myrtle's bags in the trunk. Darrell, Jeannie and Andy's Mom were there too. They walked to the car to tell them goodbye.

"I'm riding along with your Dad, so he doesn't get lost. You coming too?" Darrell asked.

Andy looked at Annie, and she nodded, "You go. I'll be so busy chowing down I won't even miss you."

Nora, Andy's Mom, giggled, "I'll keep an eye on her. Your Dad is hungry too, so he will be back as quickly as he can."

Andy kissed Annie's cheek and then grinned, "Okay. Mom, but I am warning you. Keep her away from draperies!"

They all climbed into the car and took off for the airport. They only had to circle the entrance twice to find the right way in and dropped Frandsens off safe and sound at the gate in plenty of time. Then they headed back to the hotel.

Andy watched the traffic from the back seat. This morning, he didn't feel like driving. He was so upset with himself that he could hardly function. He listened to his Dad and Darrell joke around about the traffic and girls in their bikinis without paying much attention. He tried to be jovial but it was a real effort. He could hardly keep from weeping.

Finally, his Dad caught his glance in the rear view mirror. He quietly asked, "Andy, is everything okay?"

Andy nodded, "Yah. I'm just having jet lag, or culture shock I guess. It is hard to be in the jungle one day and on the beach the next."

"I can imagine it would be. It takes a while to wind down. If you want some quiet time, just say so," his Dad offered.

"Or you can talk to us. There isn't much that we haven't talked about ever," Darrell added. "We'll try to understand, even if we can't."

Andy thanked them both, "I think I'll be okay. I just need to readjust. It is a far cry from a leaky old mess hall to that restaurant last night. I want to thank you guys for all the work you did setting this all up. I know I messed up everyone's plans out of my own selfishness." His voice started to crack. He wasn't going to be able to be as casual as he wanted.

Darrell and his Dad never said a word, but Elton Schroeder pulled over into a nearby parking slot by the beach. He turned off the car and said, "Come, let's go have a cigarette."

Andy felt dread. He knew his Dad and Darrell well enough to know that he wasn't going to worm his way out of this. Damn. He didn't want to talk to them. Maybe it was just a bad dream. He'd be fine. He'd try to convince them he was just tired from the long trip because he really was. That he could do and not even have to lie about it.

They walked toward a concrete picnic table under a huge banyan tree on a slit of grass between the beach and parking area on the ocean side of the street. It was beautiful.

It was then that someone's car backfired in the parking lot. Without a moment's hesitation, Andy hit the dirt with his hands covering his head. As he lay there on the grass, it dawned on him what he had done. He was so embarrassed he wanted to bawl, like a big baby. Darrell and his Dad were stunned, but knew instantly what he had thought.

His Dad knelt down next to him and rubbed his back, "Take it easy, Andy. You are right, it takes a while to unwind. You are tired, but you'll be okay. Now, as soon as you pull yourself together, we'll be here at this picnic table. Okay? Just take it easy. Do you need help getting up?"

Andy shook his head no, but he had quit crying. He was giving himself hell, big time. He sat up cross-legged and just stayed there, holding his head, silently berating himself. He hated people who brought attention to themselves and here he was acting like a major idiot in public. He knew that his Dad and Darrell would understand, but what about everyone else! He looked around. Thankfully, it was early and not many people around. Those that were paid no one attention. He got himself up and brushed himself off. Then he went to the picnic table.

"I'm so sorry you guys, I just need to go back to the barracks. I'll just stay there 'til I go back to my unit. I can't do this. There is something wrong with me. You must think I am a big baby."

"Not at all," Darrell patted his best friend's shoulder. "It was a reflex. I imagine you have done it a time or two. Forget it."

"I can't," Andy started to weep and put his head in his hands at the table. "Jesus, you know what I did last night?"

Elton touched his stepson's arm, "What Andy? What's eating you?"

"I dreamt I was tramping through the boonies like always and the mosquitoes got so thick I couldn't see or breathe. I started swatting them away as hard as I could."

Then he quit talking. He just stopped. There was no way that he wanted to admit to himself or anyone else what he had done. His mind was swirling. He wished he was back in the jungle with Horse and Chicago. They would understand. Or would they?

"Get it out, Andy," his Dad said. "Or it will eat you alive."

Andy wiped his tears and straightened up. "You sound like my buddy over there. Horse. He is always telling us to get it out."

"Well, then do it," without a flinch his Dad said as he offered him a cigarette. Andy looked at him and then took the cigarette. He turned it in his hand a couple times before he lit it. He took a long drag and then cleared his throat, "I don't know what you guys will think of me."

"Andy, I have been in a war. I know that it isn't pretty and I also know that you can't just walk away like it never happened. I still think of things that happened over there and I dream about it sometimes. That is normal. But it is better to talk about it. So, out with it," his Dad stated.

"I woke up when I heard Annie say, 'It's me, it's Annie.' I was hitting her! Can you believe that? I would never hurt her! I love her. Here I was on our wedding night, hitting her!" Andy about lost it.

Darrell put his arm over his friend's shoulder, "Look, I have never been in a war but one time I almost knocked Sammy out of bed when we were kids. We had been haying and got into a beehive. A couple nights later, I dreamt I was being attacked by bees. He had the misfortune of sleeping next to me. I was about to clobber him with my alarm clock when Joey woke me up."

Andy looked at Darrell, "Really?"

"Really. I had no idea what I was doing," Darrell reiterated.

"One time, Jerald and I had been loading cattle all weekend. I went to bed that night and dreamt I was trying to push this heifer into the cattle truck. It was so full that I could hardly shove her in," Andy's Dad shared, with a laugh, "When I woke up, I had shoved your Mom out of bed! She wasn't very happy about it."

"You pushed Mom out of bed?" Andy was shocked. "Did she get hurt?"

"Only a bit, but that wasn't what I got in trouble about," the older man laughed. "It was when I called her 'an old heifer'!"

The three all laughed. Andy did feel better. He especially felt better that his dad had pushed his mom out of bed. Everyone knew they loved each other.

Andy thought a minute, "Maybe men shouldn't sleep."

"Ah, your Mom whacked me a good one once! She said she thought she was beating the carpet on the clothesline, but I still think that she was mad at me. I even had a swollen cheek! That lady packs a wallop!" Then he got serious, "Andy, things like that happen. Your mind is trying to recalculate and reevaluate its circumstances. Don't feel bad about hitting the dirt. Hell, you'll be going back to that mess in a couple days. I don't think it would be wise to break that habit just yet."

Andy pursed his lips, "I'm so relieved that you guys don't think I am nuts."

"Didn't say that," Darrell grinned. "You always have been, but you are normal nuts. Not abnormal nuts."

"Yea Gads," Andy grinned. "You guys are about as much help in the nutty department as pair of jackasses."

Elton grinned to Darrell, "At least we are a pair, huh? I think he should thank his lucky stars for us."

Andy looked at them very seriously, "I do, more often than you'll ever know."

Elton and Darrell sat in silence in a minute and then Elton said, "I don't know about you guys, but I need some breakfast. The ladies have probably cleaned out the whole buffet by now. Let's get moving."

# 249 days left

## 5 days of leave

The rest of the day before had been wonderful. He was glad that he had talked to his Dad and Darrell. It was nice to know that they understood and that alone made him feel more relaxed. Once he was more relaxed, things didn't bother him so much.

After they had a fun breakfast buffet with the entire family, his Dad and Darrell took Jessups to the airport. He and Annie went shopping with Elliott and Char on Waikiki Beach, spending the most time at the International Shopping Plaza. By the time they were finished having lunch there, Andy's foot was really bothering him. He and Annie went back to the hotel. He cleaned and bandaged his foot and then they took a nap.

The young couple woke about three-thirty and went out to sit on the patio to let Andy's foot dry in the sun. About half an hour later, his Mom called and asked if they wanted to get together for dinner or if they had made other plans.

Annie invited his parents to their room to visit about dinner. Andy wasn't very eager for anyone to see his foot, but Annie assured him that it was nothing to be ashamed of.

"I am not ashamed of it, but Mom will freak," Andy explained.

He was correct. His Mom was not very happy about the condition of his foot when she saw it. "My goodness, don't they care if their soldiers can walk? This is ridiculous. What exactly is this stuff anyway?"

"I don't know Mom. Some kind of Jungle rot, but it will heal up. I had it on both feet, but the other foot is okay now. I had some in my arm pit a while back and it finally healed up. It just needs to dry out."

"Why can't it dry out?" Mom was like a badger. She was determined to remedy this situation or at least find a cure. Knowing her, she would call the President and the Secretary of the Army to tell them how to take care of it, and then reverse the charges on the phone call! Nobody wanted to mess with his Mom.

"Because when we are out in the boonies, it is rain and mud. All the time. A person is soaked to the skin. So, this kind of stuff happens. Lots of guys have it. Don't worry, Mom."

"The fact that a lot of guys have it doesn't make me feel any better about it. They should let you stay in camp or whatever when your feet are this bad."

"Mom, I'm sure all the other guys would like to sit in camp, too. It doesn't work that way. Like Horse says, 'This isn't nursery school'."

"I know honey, but I hate it so much," Nora kissed her son's forehead. "You have no idea."

He took her hand, "Yah, Mom. I think I do. I know how you have always been about your 'baby chicks'. Say, tell me about Charlie. How did the Chicken Man do as the ring bearer at Zach's wedding? That must have been something!"

The remaining members of the wedding group went out to dinner together and then to the Don Ho show. They had a great time. That night was uneventful with the exception of some fantastic lovemaking. Andy slept well and didn't dream or fight off any mosquitoes. It was wonderful.

The next morning they attended Sunday services at the Lutheran church where they got married. Pastor Wilson remembered them when he shook hands with them at the door after services. He commented, "It is unusual to ever see the non-local folks I marry again. I hope you enjoyed the service. Darrell, tell your brother-in-law that you are very fine people."

Darrell grinned, "I have been trying to tell him that for years, but so far he doesn't seem to believe me! I don't suppose it would be too much to ask you to put it in writing? And maybe notarize it?"

Pastor Wilson laughed, "I think he knows."

At lunch, the others decided to go to the Pearl Harbor Memorial and Punchbowl Cemetery. Andy really had no desire to see that, so begged off. He told Annie that she could go with them if she wanted, but he was going to just hang around the hotel and sunbathe his foot. She chose to stay with him.

They had a very relaxing day and talked more than they had in months. It was very good for them both. When the others returned from their sight seeing, Darrell called their room to ask them if they wanted to join them all for dinner. Elliott had volunteered to take them out for a Japanese dinner if they wanted. They eagerly accepted.

Before they went out, Andy invited them to stop by their room for a small cup of Cohn coffee. While at the International Market, Andy bought a coffee press and was anxious to make the coffee for everyone. Besides, he wanted some himself.

It was a great success. Almost everyone liked it. Char didn't like coffee and certainly didn't think she would like anything called weasel poop coffee. But the rest of them did and all agreed they needed to get some more. Elton was grateful when Andy presented him with the coffee press and another package of the coffee to take home.

"Dad, I have to ask you. Did you think about coffee when you were in Russia? I think about it all the time. When I'm out in the boonies, that's what I concentrate on," Andy admitted.

"Really?" Annie asked, somewhat surprised.

"Yah, it beats all the other things I need to think about. Mosquitoes, leeches and snakes. I decide how I am going to take my first cup of coffee back in the mess hall. I really look forward to it!" Andy chuckled.

Some of the others just looked at him blankly, but his Dad grinned. "Yah, I did. It was so damned cold over there that is about all I could think of. Holding a cup of steaming coffee and letting the hot vapors defrost my face! I would imagine it with cream or sugar! Why I would be sitting out on guard duty at thirty below and I envision it. If I thought about it hard enough, I could even smell it!"

Andy looked at him in surprise, "You too? I even decide whether or not I'm going to have one teaspoon of sugar or two! Is that bad or what?"

Elliott leaned back, "Well, in the Pacific theatre, I used to try to figure out if I was going to get my shot of whiskey neat, on the rocks or with water. It could keep me going for a while. Guess we all need something pretty blah going on in our heads to keep from thinking."

"It works, too. I remember one tunnel I went down in," just like that he stopped. He had not told his family that he was a tunnel rat. He knew they would worry. Now, he had just blurted it out.

His Dad shot him a glance, knowing that Andy had not intended to bring it up. "Keith and I figured that. So, what about the coffee?"

Andy tried to avoid looking at his Mom or his wife, "Nothing, except that the VC had been enjoying a cup of coffee before we got there. I wondered if it was Cohn or not. Anyway, what is on the agenda for tomorrow?"

Darrell knew that Andy wanted out of that conversation and jumped in with a suggestion. "Jeannie and I were interested in the Polynesian Cultural Center and then we can get tickets and eat there in the evening. They have a Paniolo barbeque-luau thing and a show. I guess that is what they called their cowboys on the big island. What do you guys think?"

"Sounds good to me. What do you think Annie? Dare we go with Dad to a barbeque?" Andy nodded.

"I think we can, if we get him to promise to behave," Annie giggled.

Everyone agreed that would be their plan for the next day. Elton promised to not tell the Hawaiians how to cook, but he insisted he was going to watch them. Maybe he could pick up a pointer or two for the next grilling contest. Everyone rolled their eyes.

Elliott's eyes sparkled, "I charcoal a mean marinated steak. If I could enter your contest, but I'm afraid I'd take the prize, Schroeder. Hands down."

Just like that, they were off and running. The bragging and bluster was so thick that everyone forgot about the tunnels. It seemed the gloves were off for the next year's grilling contest.

That evening they went to a Polynesian Dance show that included dinner and starred Al Harrington who played Ben Kokua, a regular on *Hawaii 5 0* television series. During the show, there was some audience participation. Both Jeannie and Annie were called on stage. They got some quick lessons and then danced a little of the hula. Both their husbands were proud as punch and the girls enjoyed the kisses from the good-looking Al Harrington himself. Andy was beginning to feel more like his old self. He had almost forgotten about the war.

Back in their room, after passionately enjoying each other's bodies, the young couple fell asleep. After a few hours of sleep, Andy woke up. He kissed his wife's shoulder and quietly got out of bed. He put on his robe and took his cigarettes. He went out onto the balcony.

He was worried about Horse and Chicago. He wondered if Chicago would have so many problems on his honeymoon. For all his talk, Chicago was really a big softie, softer than Andy. Horse would be okay, Andy did not doubt that. He was the one they always counted on. He'd be fine. He wondered if Suds had left yet for Saigon. Would his life really be any better there? How long before he could have a real life again?

Andy looked back into the bedroom where his gorgeous wife was sleeping. How would he be able to handle it, if something happened to his Annie? Suds had lost his wife to the VC and he had sustained a terrible injury. His life was ruined by that damned war. How did he cope? He was an amazing person. Suds still managed to keep a happy spirit most of the time and find the good in things. Andy was glad he got to know him and hoped they could get to know each other better.

Then he wondered about Horse. What happened with his girl? All the things those two had shared, secret feelings good and bad, but he had never whispered a breath about what had happened, or even her name. It must have been extremely important to Horse. It was something that really moved him so deeply that he would never speak of it.

He wondered if the squad was out on another patrol. Who went down the tunnels with Franklin? Were they in a hot area? It was killing him not to know. He felt guilty for being in this luxurious hotel with his beautiful new wife while they were still out there. Not that he didn't want to be here because he did. He felt like he had walked out on them.

He was leaning against the railing when Annie came up beside him and put her arms around him. "What's my husband thinking so seriously about?"

"My squad. The guys," Andy was almost ashamed to admit it. "I was wondering what they were doing and if they were okay. I hate to say this, but I almost feel guilty being here."

She hugged him, "I understand that. They've been the most important part of your life for some time now. You guys depend on each other. That's a very close relationship."

Andy turned to watch her, "Do you think I'm weird?"

She smiled, "Not at all. Andy, I talked to my brother Travis when he was home last time and I also talked to my other brother Conrad after he was over there. I have an idea how it is. It is something like Marty and I. We're a team. I love you and want to spend my life with you, but if I am on the job, I want Marty there. He's my partner. We can work together without thinking and I know what to expect. No matter if we're sent to a car wreck, a fire or a shooting, I know that I can depend on Marty. So, I kind of understand, even though we've never been shot at. We did get caught in a grain avalanche once when we were trying to extract a farmer that had been overcome by fumes in his granary. We almost died that time. I know I wouldn't have made it without Marty. That makes a special bond with people that time can't take away."

"I remember hearing about that," Andy shook his head, "I don't deserve anyone as wonderful as you."

"I'm not that wonderful. I have big feet of clay," Annie laughed.

"They are small and dainty," Andy kissed her cheek in front of her ear. "And no Jungle rot."

Annie kissed him back and then giggled, "I can't say I love your right foot!"

Andy feigned indignation, "What about all that 'through sickness and health' stuff?"

"I didn't hear the preacher say anything about foot rot!" Annie giggled.

"Man, you really do have feet of clay," he whispered in her ear. Then he began kissing her neck. "I guess I can get used to it."

Soon, they were back in bed.

# 248 days left

## 4 days of leave

During the night, it got cool and windy. Before long, it was raining. That reminded him of Vietnam. Andy partially woke up and wrapped the blankets tightly around his shoulders. He then pulled his wife next to him, spoon style and fell back to sleep.

Within a short time, he dreamt he was crawling through a tight tunnel. The further he went into the tunnel, the tighter it became. Soon, he could barely move but he had to get through it. He was beginning to panic. He was sweating profusely and couldn't see clearly. It was as if he had crawled into a cobweb and had to fight to get his face free. He couldn't move his hands and was having trouble breathing. He could hear the muffled sounds of the men above him on the ground's surface and the distant pounding of artillery fire.

Then he felt something crawl down the back of his neck! He knew it was either a huge spider or scorpion. He was fighting for every breath and felt the pressure of lack of air on his lungs. Finally he was able to scream.

He jolted himself out of bed and landed on the floor, thrashing to get the blanket from his shoulders. He heard Annie.

"Andy, it is okay. You are with me. We're in Honolulu. You're safe, Andy. Try to calm down. Let me get the light."

She turned on the light and came around the bed to find him on the floor, still partially entangled in his blanket. He was shaking, but beginning to get more oriented to his surroundings. He sat on the floor with his elbows on his knees and put his face in his hands.

Annie put her arms gently around him and tried to calm him. "It's okay, Andy. You are okay. Just breathe as calmly as you can."

He turned to look at her and just fell into her embrace. "Annie. I can't do this. I'm no good to you. Can you take me back to Schofield? I'll stay there until I go back. I don't want to be like this!"

Annie held him and patted his back while he cried. Then she answered, "Andy. I'm not taking you back to Schofield. Honey, don't demand too much from yourself. Please, try to relax. You are doing very well. Bad dreams happen, especially when your mind is trying to work out all the strange events it has dealt with. You need to relax about it. You will be okay. Can you tell me what you dreamt about?"

Andy shrugged, "Ah, just a stupid dream."

"Andy," Annie looked straight at him, "What was it?"

"I don't want to talk about it."

"Secrecy is the playground for the devil. You must tell me everything. How will I ever understand if you don't? Andy, when I married you, I knew that it wasn't going to be a perfect, always happy life. I know that sometimes we'll argue and sometimes want to skin each other. For this to work, we always have to know what is going on with the other person. If we don't, we will be doomed. I can handle almost anything if I at least know what I am dealing with."

Andy watched her while she talked. The only light in the room was the dim bedside lamp, the lightning outside and the dim glow of the light above their balcony. He could hear the rain pelting the window and felt the cool wind blowing gently into the room.

"I don't know what to say. Annie, I don't want you to worry."

She giggled softly, "Too late for that already. Now, tell me what I'm not supposed to be worried about. Honey, would you like some hot tea? I'll put some water in that hot pot if you'd like. I think I would like some."

Andy smiled and kissed her cheek. "That sounds good."

She moved away to put on her robe to make the tea, while he got himself out of the tangle of blankets and put them back on the bed. Then he pulled on his jeans and went over to where she had put the tea bags in their cups. He unwrapped the plastic spoons and as he put them down, she took his hand and gave it a squeeze. Andy smiled at her and she gave him a sweet kiss. "I love you."

When the tea was ready, they sat at the small table by the patio window. It was very pleasant, even though it was raining quite hard. After a sip of the hot tea, he took her hand.

"Annie. I never told you about the tunnels. I didn't want to freak out you and Mom. I have been going down in them for a couple months now."

"I learned that today. Don't ever lie to me again. Promise? Even if you think I won't like it. I know your Mom feels the same. Promise, Andy. If not, I'll go crazy worrying about what you haven't told me!"

"I give you my word. I'm sorry Annie. I just didn't know what to say. It isn't really that bad. I mean, not that dangerous, just terrifying."

"Not that dangerous? How dense do you think I am?" Annie leaned back in doubt. "If you say so."

"Well, I mean, out in the boonies it seems like it is all dangerous. It is just that in the tunnels, a person is alone. Hopefully."

Then he spent the next hour explaining his experiences in the tunnels. He told her everything that he could. They had a sincere and helpful talk. Now, she knew everything. She told her about the dead baby and the near shoot out with Franklin. He told her about when he shot the cobra out of fear, even though it was probably already dead and about when the dirt fell down the back of his neck. She listened to it all and only asked a few questions. Once in a while, she would take his hand or touch his cheek. Only once did she panic, when he told of seeing Franklin's light in the tunnel.

When he was all done, he looked at her. "See, it isn't that dangerous. But I do know that it makes me jumpy as hell. Poor Franklin. If someone drops a cup in the mess hall, he catapults about twenty feet in the air. I guess it's because it is pitch dark down in those things, or something. I don't know."

Annie nodded, "It is frightening. Andy, you probably dreamt about it tonight because you were twisted up in that blanket. Your poor head probably thought if felt like it was in a tunnel. That makes sense. Do you feel better now?"

"Yes, I really do. I just don't want you to worry. I am scared enough for both of us. We don't need both of us going off the deep end. Annie, I'm nothing but a big chicken shit."

"No, you aren't. Being afraid is a sensible thing. You're a coward when you don't do something that needs to be done because you are afraid. You are brave. You do what you need to do, even while you are afraid."

"Do you really believe that? Or is that just talk to keep us chicken livers going back out there?" Andy asked bitterly.

"No. If you weren't afraid in those situations, you'd be a lunatic. That's the truth. I've seen people do a lot of things when they had to, even painful frightening things. One man cut off one of his hands because it was caught under a truck and he couldn't get free any other way. I have also seen people fall apart over nothing. Good grief, some people have a fit because someone puts the wrong dressing on their lettuce! I'd like to just slap them! What you and your squad have faced is real and it is frightening. Reacting to that is normal."

"I don't feel like it sometimes. Sometimes I just want to be a little boy curled up on my Mommy's lap in the rocking chair." Andy watched Annie for her reaction. Her reaction meant so much to him.

Annie giggled softly, "Yah, you would probably squash her! But, that is the way that I'd feel. You want to be some place safe and comforting."

"Some guys don't make it, you know. Some guys just lose it." Then Andy told her about Bradley. It had been bothering him and he really had wanted to talk to her about it He didn't know what she would think of him, especially the part about the snake.

She shook her head, "Good grief! As if you guys don't have enough to contend with, then you have to deal with each other! He sounds like he'd lost his grip."

"Bandaid said that he thought he was wacky when he first got there, because he was wound up so tight. One thing and he would flip out. He lost all sense of reason. I was so horrible. Annie, I didn't even feel bad when I heard that he had been killed in that mortar attack. What the hell kind of a person is that?"

Annie raised her eyebrows, "I don't know. Personally, I would have killed him myself, so don't ask me how I would have felt if I learned that he died. You could've been killed by that snake. I know how much you love snakes in the first place!"

"Yah, I really hate them. When Horse and I talked about it, he said that he felt that same thing when Bandaid told him that Bradley had died. So, I guess, even if I am a cold-hearted SOB, so is he. Huh?"

"Bandaid sounds like a nice guy. Will he be with your platoon until you leave?"

"He was killed, Annie." Andy poured himself more tea and then explained what happened with the pregnant woman and the small children. "I have to tell you, yesterday when we got in the elevator in the lobby and that very pregnant Oriental lady was in there already with her two small kids, I almost panicked. I really had to talk to myself to go in that elevator."

"I noticed that you hesitated. I wondered why. I understand now. Gee, that poor woman must have been desperate, huh? I wonder what all happened to make her do that? It must have been something. War is horrid. It really forces people into decisions that we should never have to make."

"Yah, but there is some good stuff too. Like Suds, giving me that salve for my 'rotten foot' as he calls it. And carrying that weasel poop coffee to me through the jungle in a pack of laundry. He is one hell of a guy. And Chicago, singing that crazy tape for Charlie! Hey, what did Charlie think of that?"

Annie laughed, "Oh good Lord! He loved it. We all went crazy! We all heard that tape a million times! I'm sure that your friend is a nice person, but he really can't sing very well."

"I know. Believe me. Horse and I heard him make the tape and he sang that *Little Green Apples* so many times, we were glad to get back out on patrol!"

"Well, your Mom has the tape that Charlie made for him. Oh, and we have lots of pictures to show you. We need to do that. Don't let me forget," Annie asked. "Charlie sings for a whole tape. We finally had to tell him to go have Elmer help him sing it. It was so funny. Charlie sat on the roof of the doghouse with his tape recorder and sang. Elmer would sit beside him on the ground and howl!"

Andy laughed, "Sounds like Elmer didn't enjoy it very much either. Poor dog."

He could picture it in his mind, and just like that, his mind was filled with the picture of the little boy holding his dog on the leash that day. The dog that seconds later blew up a couple soldiers. His face must have betrayed him, because Annie took his hand, "What is it?"

Then he told her about the little boy. "Annie, anymore I hate to see little kids. I'm half scared of them and don't trust them. I don't want to feel that way, but I don't trust anyone anymore."

"I can see why."

"I'm afraid I'll feel that way about Ginger and Charlie when I get home."

"You won't. You know them. Although little Charlie can be scary in his own way!"

"I know, I have seen him in action! He is quite the guy!" Andy chuckled and shook his head, "What the hell's wrong with people? There are so many nice things that be enjoyed. Why do we spend so much time trying to hurt each other?"

Annie got up and moved to his lap, "I don't know. I think you'll have to ask God about that. That's His department. Right now, I can think of something that could be enjoyed."

"Hmm. I'm going to have to go back to the jungle to get some rest!" Andy began caressing her back. As he kissed her neck, he added, "Maybe I can rest later."

The young couple slept in and didn't get up until almost nine o'clock local time. They dressed and went down to the coffee shop because the buffet had been over for an hour. "Wow! We just like way overslept!"

Annie laughed, "That is because we were up talking half the night. No matter. We needed that, I think."

Andy took her hand, "Annie. Thanks for listening last night. I feel so much better. I promise you, I won't keep things to myself anymore. Okay?"

"Okay," Annie squeezed his hand. "I believe in you. I know how you guys are. If one of your family gives their word, it's something you can count on."

"You are Dad's family too," Andy chuckled. "You know that. Now you are one of his daughters."

Annie gave him a big smile, "Oh Andy. I have been his girl since the Grandpas adopted me!"

"That's right, huh?" Andy chuckled. "They really did glom on to you, didn't they?"

"Before Grandpa Bert passed away, he talked to me. The last thing he told me it was okay for me to be with you now, because he was leaving. Wasn't that sweet? He gave his blessing," Annie had tears in her eyes.

"He waited until the last minute though, didn't her?" Andy snickered, "Did he know that I bought some of those milk cows? Pepper was going to tell him."

"She did, but by then he was so busy ragging on Zach about buying cows, he didn't say too much about it. Grandpa Lloyd did though. He bragged that all of his boys bought cows. Even though Kevin got his late, he still got them."

"Those old guys are something else."

The sun had come out and it turned out to be a nice day. The air was a bit cooler and great for sightseeing. After brunch, the kids met up with the rest of the group and then went to spend the day at the Polynesian Cultural Center. They had a fun time and took a lot of photos. The evening barbeque was delicious and Andy's Dad was sure that he had the secret to their recipe. Everyone figured that is why he was up there chatting up the cooks.

The young couple went back to their room as soon as they got back to the hotel. It had been a great day and Annie and Andy were more confident with each other than they had ever been before.

# 247 days left

## 3 days of leave

They all got up early that morning. It was cool and raining again, but the men were all excited. They had signed up for deep sea fishing that morning. They went to the pier and met up with their captain and guide on the fishing boat that morning at eight. They would be gone until two o'clock.

The ladies had planned on sun bathing, but the since the weather was bad, decided to go shopping instead. Elton groaned, "I can feel my wallet getting lighter already."

Nora raised her eyebrows, "I wouldn't talk Mister. When you and Coot go to town, the banks send out special security guards to pick up all the cash. You guys go nutty."

Elton grinned, "I have to say every word is true. And ask me if I feel bad about it?"

Nora laughed, "I know you don't. Andy, you should see those two. They can fill a pickup in an afternoon, no problem."

Darrell cracked up, "Yah, and Kincaid is still in his wheelchair. I don't know what will happen when he's ambulatory!"

"Dad, am I going to have to go to town with you two to ride shotgun?" Andy joked.

"Only, my son, if you bring a fat wallet and a tight lip!" his Dad chuckled. "We could really raise havoc then!"

The guys had no luck fishing. The sea was choppy and it poured rain a good share of the time, but they had a ball anyway. Elliott seemed like a nice guy and of course, there were not many people Andy would rather be with than his Dad and Darrell.

They talked a little bit about the war. Elliott shared some of the things that his sons had told him and so Andy felt more comfortable talking about a few things. He told them about the little boy and his dog with the grenade. He also told them about the pregnant woman.

Elliott said he had heard of that sort of thing happening in WWII. The Japanese civilians were convinced to not be taken as prisoners. "My god, I saw them jump of cliffs to a certain death to avoid being taken prisoner. Women and small children. Amazing. They must have thought we were the devil personified."

Darrell shrugged, "Well, I guess that is what we thought they were, huh? Isn't that part of the whole war machine thing? To dehumanize the enemy?"

"Yah Darrell," Andy's dad agreed. "There a people who make a living doing that. Can you imagine? Of course, I can't imagine a lot of things. But I bet the ladies have bought up half of Waikiki Beach by now! You poor newly-weds! You'll soon learn that ladies-shopping-in-packs is a dangerous thing."

Elliott and he shared a good laugh over that, and the boys just shook their heads. They were certain that neither of their wives were like that.

The afternoon was spent looking over pictures and hanging out in his parent's room. They ate snacks and sat on the balcony. That evening, Darrell and Jeannie took everyone to a restaurant they had found, the Rueben E Lee. It was a double-decked boat moored on the pier. They had a wonderful dinner there dining by the Pacific surf. On the way back to the hotel, the couples walked hand in hand down Kalakaua Avenue. At the hotel, they split up.

Elliott and Char went back to the disco they had found. Elton and Nora went for a walk on the sea wall and Darrell and Jeannie decided to take off their shoes and walk the sandy beach. That did not work for Andy's foot, even though it was getting better.

Andy and Annie walked hand in hand on the walkway down beach side of Ala Moana Boulevard until they got to a little bar that jutted out over the ocean. There they sat on the patio and watched the surf. They hardly talked but just enjoyed the peaceful evening.

After sitting in silence holding hands for some time, Andy asked, "Are you sorry you married me?"

Annie looked at him in surprise, "Heaven's no! Why do you ask that?"

"I mean, if something would happen, would it have been worth it?"

Annie frowned, "Nothing is going to happen. And no matter, it's definitely worth it. I'm not looking forward to you leaving again in a couple days, but I am looking forward to you returning home in just a few months."

"I still have 246 days left over there!" Andy pointed out.

"How many minutes?" Annie giggled. "I can't wait. Then we can really start our life together. But right now, I'm just thankful we have had this time together."

"Me, too. I just wouldn't want something to happen and you to look back and say that it wasn't worth it."

"Don't be so gloomy. Andy, I love our time together. It will always be what it is. Wonderful," Annie took his hand. "No matter what comes down the road. Okay?"

"Hey Annie," Andy leaned ahead, and spoke very seriously, "I kind of made a guy a promise and you should know about it."

"What promise was that?"

"After a guy in our unit got his family jewels blown off, Horse and I were talking. He sort of asked me that if something like that should happen to him, or if he got killed, that I'd name a kid after him. You know, so the world would know he had been here." Andy cleared his throat. "I hope you don't hate me and I should've asked you, but I said I would."

Annie watched her husband and made a face, "Please don't tell me that his real name is Horse."

Andy laughed, relieved that she wasn't angry, "No. It is Jackson. That isn't too bad, is it?"

Annie looked out over the ocean, "If our first child is a boy, I could live with Jackson. But I'd call him Jack, not Horse. And if it is a girl, we can name her Jacqueline. How does that sound? Jackson Andrew."

Andy burst into laughter, "Oh hell, why don't we name him Andrew Jackson?"

Annie whopped him, 'You moron. I think Jackson Andrew is as close as I want to get."

"How about Jackson Darrell?" Andy asked.

"What about you?"

"What about me? I will be the dad. Can you imagine that? Me actually being a dad?" The thought startled Andy, but he was rather thrilled about it.

"Yes, I can. I've seen how you are with Ginger and Charlie. You will be a good dad. We still have a ways to go before we get that far. You have to get back home."

Andy squeezed her hand, "That is probably very sensible, especially since we have no place to live or anything. But just in case, do we agree on the Jackson thing?"

"Of course. We will be fine, Jackson Andrew's daddy," Annie giggled. "Want to start back to the hotel?"

He took his wife's hand and they were just leaving the bar when he saw his parents. They were walking hand in hand down the street ahead of them. They were far enough ahead of them so that he couldn't hear what they were visiting about, but they were chatting amicably. They shared a laugh about something and then his stepdad put his arm around his wife's waist.

They followed for a bit and then his parents turned to a small grassy area at the top of the beach. They sat on a park bench and shared a very passionate kiss.

Andy looked at Annie, "Wow! I don't know if I should be embarrassed or proud of them."

"I think it is wonderful. But, do you think we should cross the street or pass them?"

"Hmm. I don't know." Andy stopped walking.

Just then his dad looked up and saw him. "Look Mom, we got company."

Nora turned and saw the kids, "They must be hungry! That's when they usually show up!"

Elton got up and took his wife's hand, "Hey, you guys want to go to that ice cream shop down the beach a ways? I saw they serve some really neat looking sundaes. I haven't had a hot fudge sundae since we hit Hawaii."

Nora grinned, "I am getting one with Macadamia Nuts on it."

Andy and Annie looked at each other and giggled. "Okay. It sounds good."

After their sundaes, they went back to the hotel and went to their rooms. In their room, Andy took Annie in his arms, "Do you think that we will still be all mushy like they are, when we are their age?"

"Good grief, Andy. They aren't that old. People don't quit being mushy. Grandma Katherine and Grandpa Lloyd still hug each other and give each other kisses. It isn't age that tears people apart, it is life. A couple has to be careful to not let that happen," Annie explained.

"I don't want it to happen between us. God Annie, I have seen how it tears some guys to shreds when they get a Dear John from their wives or girlfriends. I can't imagine how that must feel."

Annie frowned, "Does that happen a lot?"

"Yah, a lot more than I ever imagined."

"Really? Is it infidelity?"

"Alot of it is, but it is all kinds of stuff. I just can't believe that a person can't remain faithful to someone for more than four months! Good grief. They act like alley cats."

"Andy, I want to be with you forever. So, don't be looking for a Dear John letter. I don't want to get a Dear Ann letter from you, either! Got it, Mister?"

"I got it," then he grinned, "I wouldn't want anyone else to see me with my socks off!"

She whopped him. "I guess I could say I'm honored for the privilege, but that wouldn't be the truth."

# 246 days left

## 2 days of leave

Sometime before dawn, Andy woke up and wanted a cigarette. Since being in Vietnam, he had rarely slept a full night straight through. He seemed destined to wake up at least two or three times. Of course, not having a regular schedule alone was probably the reason. He felt good though; better than he had for a while.

He pulled on his jeans and stepped out to the patio. As he lit his cigarette, he noticed a man crossing the street from the hotel to the benches by the beach. It looked amazingly like Darrell.

Andy watched him for a bit and became convinced it was Darrell. What was he doing wandering around in the middle of the night? Darrell sat on a bench and took a sip from the paper cup he was carrying. Andy was concerned.

He went inside, threw his tee shirt over his head and slipped on his scuffs. Andy knelt down by his wife's side of the bed. Annie was sound asleep. He gently moved the hair back from her face and said, "Annie? Honey? I'm going to go out for a bit. Okay?"

"Huh?" she opened her eyes and tried to focus. "What? You okay?"

"I'm fine, honey," Andy patted her cheek, "I just got up to have a cigarette. I noticed Darrell is sitting over by the beach by himself. I think I should go talk to him."

"Do you think something's wrong?" Annie was more awake now.

"I don't know, but I think I should go talk to him. He has always been there for me," Andy said. "If you don't object."

"No, not at all. You need to see if he's okay. Gosh, you don't suppose they are fighting, do you? I couldn't believe that. He and Jeannie are so good together."

"I don't know. Maybe he just can't sleep. I'll be back as soon as I can," he kissed her. "I love you."

161

"Yah, me too. I hope everything is okay."

Andy hurried out the lobby, stopping only long enough at the coffee vending machine to get a cup. Then he crossed the street. Thankfully, Darrell hadn't moved from his spot. He was staring out toward the ocean, deep in thought. Andy went to the other side of the bench and asked, "May I join you?"

Darrell jumped about two feet and then noticed it was Andy. He smiled slightly, "Help yourself."

Andy sat down but didn't say anything. Darrell continued to sit quietly for a bit and then asked, "You okay? Why are you wandering around in the middle of the night?"

"I'm fine. What is your excuse?" Andy asked, still looking at the methodic undulation of the ocean.

"Don't have one. I don't suppose you'd believe me if I said that I was just enjoying the ocean?" Darrell asked.

"No way in hell."

"Didn't think so. I think if I lived here, I'd sleep on the beach. I love the sound of the surf," Darrell said.

"Yah, it's very relaxing," Andy looked at his friend, "But you don't look very relaxed, my friend. What's bothering you?"

"Ah," Darrell shook his head in despair, "The same old stuff. Andy, I'm such a disappointment to myself and everyone else. I'm just a waste."

"What the hell are you talking about?" Andy was flabbergasted, "You're not a disappointment to anyone. Who said that? Did Jeannie say that? I can't believe it!"

"No. My Jeannie would never say that. You know her, Andy. She is the kindest, most unselfish person in the world. She would never say that, but I imagine she thinks it."

Andy turned, "Why do you say that? Did something happen?"

"Nah, I just woke up thinking. Hell, I'm nothing but a goat farmer. I never finished college, never went to the service, never did a damned thing that amounts to anything. I just milk goats."

"You're the biggest jackass in the world!" Andy almost shouted. "What the hell is wrong with you? You are the best friend anyone could ever have. Everyone in the clan loves you. You're always there to help anyone; any neighbor or anyone who need help! When Sandvahls had all those problems, who was it that went over and did their haying? Who was it that brought in Johnson's harvest when they were in that car accident? Everyone can count on you. Don't do that to yourself, you'll piss me off."

"I knew you'd say that. Look Andy, when we were out on the fishing boat, you guys had all fought for your country, put you lives on the line and did brave things. What the hell did I do? I've never risked my life for anyone. Heroes don't milk goats!" Darrell's voice was shaking and Andy knew he it was really bothering him.

"Darrell, you couldn't go into the service because of your bad heart. We all know that. Hell bells, Man! You have stayed up whole days without sleep to help someone or sit with them when they needed help. You've taken care of the farm for your entire family. Your Dad couldn't have made it this last year without you while he was fighting that cancer. You did his work and yours too. You took him to the hospital and sat with him while he had chemo. You worked while the other boys were in the service or at school."

"Andy, you are in the service." Darrell wasn't giving up.

'Yah, and why is that? Why am I in the service? I'm not some damned war hero. I was an idiot and didn't get the papers mailed off the university in time! I was my own stupidity and I certainly didn't do it to protect my country or anything noble. A lot of the guys over there, joined up because they had a choice of either going to the service or serving a jail sentence for DUI or something. Some of them flunked out of school. Some wanted to get the GI Bill so they could go to college. Some were afraid of what would happen to them if they resisted the draft. Sure, some that enlisted to protect their country, but most are there for other reasons, too. I mean we all care about our country and would do our best to defend it. Some of us are not really sure we are even protecting our country by being there. But that's a whole different thing. I can assure you that I have done nothing that you wouldn't have done, and done alot better. So, don't even talk to me about that."

"But I've done nothing."

"Darrell, you've done more than you can imagine. Hell, some of the guys over there are so worried about their families, their girlfriends and stuff. I never did. I knew. You told me you would watch out of them and I knew you would. You have no idea what a relief that is! You have helped Dad, my brothers and even my goofy sister. You stood in for me at Grandma and Grandpa's funeral. Look at all you've done for Ginger and this Kincaid guy. Mom wrote how you helped him. Don't discount that. You're one hell of person and I'm proud to say you are my friend."

Darrell never moved, "I didn't do any big deal. Just helped out here and there. It was nothing."

Andy was disgusted, "Darrell Jessup. You would be surprised how many people never do a damned thing for anyone but themselves! And the folks that do help each other, don't get to do one big major thing in life one time and win a lifetime award. Most folks just have to piddle away doing little things over and over until you could spit. You don't get to make one big payment of a million dollars. You might pay a million dollars, but it is a penny at a time over a lifetime. Every day; a little here, a little there. You don't get any thanks for it and it may never seem like a big deal! But that is how the real work gets done. One piddly thing at a time. Look at Pastor Byron. He doesn't have a huge television church and have thousands answering an altar call. But he is there, every single day, helping his congregation with all the crappy, annoying stuff that wears us down. Which do you think takes more work? Do you think it would be easier to give one big sermon or listen to 1800 people grump and moan for years?"

Darrell looked at him and chuckled. "I missed you. But Andy, the only reason that I was even able to save the farm was because Kincaid offered to be my silent partner a couple weeks ago. I wouldn't have even been able to afford to come to Hawaii without borrowing from your folks if he hadn't! Now I have a wife and Jeannie deserves more than a goat farmer."

"You dumb shit. If she thought that, she wouldn't have married you. Personally, I don't know what she sees in you, but it must be something. Annie thinks you are the best things since Velcro. If it wasn't for Jeannie, she'd marry you in a heartbeat and leave me in a lurch."

"No, she wouldn't. She loves you," Darrell stated flatly. "You are a real grownup man. I've never moved from being a goofy teenager."

"Now I know you're nutty! Darrell, I worry all the time that I'm not a responsible grownup. I never seem to be as put together or as reliable as you. Everyone knows they can rely on you. I know Annie and I do. What the hell have I got? I still live with my parents, haven't got an education and I crawl up and down holes in some damned jungle. What's that to brag about? When I get out of the service, what will I have? I have a wife that works and no home. But one thing I know that I can count on is my good friend. Darrell, why do you think that Kincaid wanted to be your partner? Because he can see you're a quality guy. You went out of your way to be good to him when you hardly even knew him. You did for Zach, too. You always do. That's you. You would no more let someone do without or suffer if you could help it than a man in the moon. I would guess that God would be pleased to have a lot more like you."

"Whatever, Andy, but I'm a financial failure," Darrell mumbled.

"Oh, I don't think so. You told me that you could have borrowed from either FHA or PCA? Did that fall through?"

"No, that's what I was going to do before Kincaid offered. The papers were all ready to go. But I wouldn't have been able to get here without borrowing from your parents."

"You owned the biggest goat herd in North Dakota before you graduated from high school!"

"Big deal. It was probably the only one, too," Darrell leaned his head in his hands. "No other moron wanted that many goats."

"The fact that I wanted to get married ahead of when we planned, never entered your mind, huh? I was the one who wanted to change everything. You would've borrowed money rather than tell me no. See, that's what kind of a friend you are!"

"Yah, well, I'd have worked for Eddie at the Cheese Factory. I couldn't have made it otherwise."

"I was the selfish one who wanted to change our plans. You could have told me to go to hell and stay with the original plan."

Darrell grinned for the first time, "Oh, Jeannie and I were both glad you did. It was getting to be a real trial to behave. We probably wouldn't have made it much longer. Man that damned EJ really messed everything up for a lot of us guys!"

Andy nodded with a devilish grin, "He sure did. If he kept his pants zipped, Hilda wouldn't have died from that abortion. Man, that cut back on the hanky-panky in our neighborhood faster than anything, huh? No getting a little nooky for us!"

Darrell chuckled, "Yah, and he is in Germany! He doesn't even know it! Well, speaking of wives, I think we both have perfectly good wives waiting for us. We should probably go back to them, huh? Thanks for talking to me Andy. I still don't agree with you, but I do feel better. I'll try to get my head out of my hind end."

"Good idea," Andy laughed, "It really messes up the hairdo."

Later, the day started again when everyone staggered into the buffet at the Regent. They all were in good moods and Andy noticed that Darrell was much more jovial than he had been before.

What a crazy world. Half the people were feeling sorry for themselves because they were in a war and the other half felt bad that they weren't! People felt bad that had no children or felt bad they had too many. Now Andy really believed what his Dad always said. He was glad that was all God's business because it would just gave him a headache.

The group went out to the Dole Pineapple plantation and then had lunch at a pier where the fishing boats unloaded. Afterwards, everyone went back to the hotel to nap or sunbathe.

That evening they all ate at the famous Third Floor of the Regent and had a very fancy meal, Elton's treat. It was a fantastic meal and very top notch. Nora pointed out that she had never eaten anywhere before where the waiter took the napkin ring off her napkin and placed it on her lap for her. She wasn't dissuaded when someone pointed out that probably the waiter took the silver napkin ring off so it wouldn't be stolen!

Andy felt a little out of place with his white tube sock on his bad foot, but was assured by the rest of the group that if he quit rubbing it, no one else would notice. His foot was getting a lot better. He figured if he had another week, it would be all healed, but he didn't. Time was going by way too fast.

His time was running out. He dreaded it and knew that Annie was beginning to think about it. Her dad and Char were leaving the next day for home. Then there was just one more day and his leave would be over.

Andy was torn. He was curious about what was going on back with his squad, if Suds was still there or if Chicago got off as planned. Somehow, he knew that his rack would not be a comforting as the king sized bed he shared with his new wife. The view of ocean beat the view from his barracks door of the pile of debris left from the last mortar attack. And the food, well! What could you say? He felt like he was letting the men in his unit down while he was lolling in Honolulu.

But that night, he slept soundly and all night! When he woke, he wondered if he could actually someday get back to normal.

# 245 days left

## 1 day of leave

That morning when Andy woke up, Annie wasn't in bed. He looked around and saw her standing on the balcony. She was wrapped in her robe and watching the surf.

He pulled on his jeans and went out to join her. He put his arms around her from the back and it wasn't until he kissed her cheek that he realized she was silently crying.

He turned her around. "What is it, baby?" He asked softly. "Why's my girl crying?"

"Oh Andy," she embraced him and buried her face in this chest, "I didn't want to cry. I wanted to be brave but I really don't want you to go back."

He hugged her and kissed her forehead, "I don't want this to be over either but we both know it has to be. Look at it this way; the sooner I go, the sooner it will be over and I can be home. We can be together for the rest of our lives."

"I know, but I don't want you to go. I love being with you," Annie wept softly. Then she stopped abruptly. "Okay Annie," she reprimanded herself, "Grow up."

Andy kissed her eyelids, "Don't cry. Please honey. Come back to bed with me."

A little later, they were standing in line at the buffet. Darrell and Jeannie were there already and Andy's parents came down the hall shortly after them. It was a few minutes before Elliott and Char arrived.

"We're all packed. All we have to do is eat and go. We reserved the hotel shuttle to the airport, so you guys don't have to drive us. You can enjoy your time together," Elliott smiled.

"That would've been no problem. We had planned to take you out there," Darrell said.

Elton chuckled, "We really wanted to make sure that you got on the plane so we could talk about you!"

"Don't worry Schroeder," Elliott joked. "We can't wait to get out of earshot so we can talk about you!"

Both men laughed. Andy was glad that they got along, but then his Mom and Dad were rather easy going. They got along with most folks. He really liked Elliott, and probably Char, although he had hardly talked to her. All in all, meeting the in-laws turned out okay.

Annie was a little shaky yet at breakfast and almost everyone knew what was bothering her. Finally, she just said, "Okay, you guys. I might as well tell you. I'm trying not to be a big blubber baby. I'm trying, honest. Please bear with me if I start crying for no reason."

Nora patted her hand, "I know just how you feel. No need to apologize."

Elton kissed her cheek, "It's better than if you were happy he was going!"

Annie giggled, "Dad, you're so bad. I know that you'll be bawling as much as me when we drop him off."

"Will not," Elton grumped.

"My money is with Annie," Darrell grinned. "We all know you. I bet you that Nora never even got a tissue at the church during the weddings. You were hogging them all."

"Well," Elton said indignantly, "I was allergic to the flowers in that lei thing."

"Yah right!" they all said.

A while later, they all said their goodbyes at the airport shuttle as Char and Elliott put their things in the back of the shuttle. Char gave Andy a hug, "It was nice to meet you. I hope we get to meet again soon. Be safe and take care."

Andy smiled, "It was great to meet you too. I hope to see you at your own wedding soon."

Char smiled, "It won't be this fantastic. The wedding party will get a trip to the Dickinson Elks Club rather than to a beautiful beach hotel."

"We can pretend," Andy grinned.

Then Elliott gave him a big hug. "Take care of yourself, young man. You have your wife to take care of. Andy, I know why Annie's loves you. I think she made a great choice. Welcome to our family."

Andy got tears in his eyes, "Thanks. I really appreciate that."

Elliott looked at him and laughed, "Oh my god! You're a sentimental slob like your Dad!"

"Got a problem with that, Packineau?" Elton chided. "We are just kind-hearted."

Elliott gave Nora a hug, "Any time you want to leave him, let me know! I'm sure I can find you fifty better guys."

Nora giggled, "Oh, I'm used to him. I just don't take him to sad movies!"

They all waved goodbye as the shuttle pulled away. Then they stood there, transfixed. The reality of the end of the holiday settled on all of them. It was depressing.

Elton cleared his throat, "So, what are the big plans for today? Is there anything that we need to get done so we don't forget?"

"We need to pick up the wedding photos this morning," Nora said. "Dad and I can go get them so you kids can enjoy yourselves. You don't want to spend the last day so of your honeymoon hanging around with us old fogeys."

Elton shook his head, "Speak for yourself, Woman."

Nora rolled her eyes, "Come on, Spring Chicken. Let's go pick up the pictures. Besides I want to do some souvenir shopping. Can we meet later to look over the photos?"

"How about for lunch?" Jeannie suggested excitedly. "I'd really like to eat at the Rueben's again. Anyone else?"

Andy put his arm around her, "I don't care about anyone else, I'll eat with you. You know, I don't know if I have ever tasted artichoke hearts in my life before, but those breaded ones are my new favorite food!"

Jeannie grinned, "Okay. You and me, Rueben's for lunch. The rest can show up if they want. We might let them sit with us. Right now, Darrell and I have to go collect some Hawaiian dirt for Ginger's dirt collection."

Elton laughed, "Nora and I found some lava from the volcano on the big Island at a gift store that we got for her. She is quite the dirt kid."

Andy chuckled, "Did you know that the guys in my unit all say bad words for her? She said in a tape that she didn't think that it was fair that

169

she had to go to school when she was sick. Since Uncle Eddie wouldn't say bad words for her about that, she wanted me to do it. The guys heard it and they all volunteered! That is probably the most bad words ever uttered on behalf of someone in the world!"

"I didn't think that going to school was that bad," Jeannie said, rather hurt. "I tried to make the tutoring as interesting as I could."

"That was before she started, Jeannie. She was still in the hospital then. Once you started with her classes, she didn't complain. And pretty soon, she was mailing me pictures that she drew of dirt," Andy chuckled. "I have to say, I could hardly tell one kind from another. A drawing of brown dirt looks a lot like brown dirt!"

The family would meet at Rueben's for lunch about one-thirty. Everyone had a leisurely morning to get everything done before heading back home. Andy and Annie walked along the beach and then stopped at some shops before going back to their room. They took a nap before they joined the rest of the family.

Andy could walk without a limp again. Annie was very pleased about that, feeling that would help him on patrols. However, Andy knew that a couple days back out in the mud, his jungle rot would be right back where he started. He knew he had promised to tell her everything but he kept that to himself.

They got to Rueben's before everyone else and found a table. They enjoyed a Blue Hawaiian and listened to the surf.

"Do you see the ocean in Vietnam?" Annie asked.

"Where we land, yah: it's right by the ocean. My base camp is not by the ocean. It's inland. There are rubber plantations and stuff around. Where we patrol mostly, it is jungle or mountains."

"Are the jungles dense?" Annie asked.

"Yah, I guess. There has been a lot of Agent Orange dumped out there. You know, that defoliant. It kills off the vegetation. I hate to see it. Guess I lived on a farm too long."

Annie frowned, "I've heard some bad stuff about that. What is it like?"

"Smells kind of like an insecticide. Makes your skin sting and you get a rash if you get it on you. They say it has no long-term effects or anything, but it sure smells like poison! If we get in a drench of it, we pull out the gas masks. The poor civilians," then Andy smiled at Annie. "Can we change the subject?"

Annie patted his hand, "Sure honey. I'm sorry."

"No need to be sorry." Andy took her hand and smiled, "Anyway, how much dirt does Ginger have now?"

Annie giggled, "She has expanded her shelves in her room, or I should say that her Dad did. She must have over a hundred jars of dirt! Jeannie had her label them all and everything. It is really neat, actually. Ginger can recognize a good share of it!"

Andy grinned, "That's my Ginger. I wonder what she is going to be like when she grows up? She is not a regular little girl."

"You should see how good she is with Miriam. I mean, Ginger is such a tomboy. I was worried she wouldn't keep an eye out for her. But she does! She watches over her like a hawk. She and Charlie both can't wait 'til she gets over being 'frad jelly' so they can give her the business about everything she has ever done wrong. I honestly think they remember it all too!"

"Frad Jelly?" Andy asked.

"Yah, Aunt Marly said they had to watch out for Miriam because she was fragile. So they think it is frad jelly. Those two keep a pretty good eye on her though. They are relieved because she is now a digger."

His Dad pulled out the chair for his Mom and sat down. "They have really raised cane with my yard. Good grief, there are trenches and dams all over the place, even in the driveway. I'll have to replace the suspension on my car pretty soon!"

Darrell chuckled as they joined the group, "I thought the pipe was to help that."

"Pipe?" Andy was surprised, "My gosh, what kind of digging do they do?"

"Well, Carl makes the plans and Annie is their safety officer," Dad started.

"Yah, I put up yellow flags so folks know not to step into the trenches. Granted they are not deep, but they are good for turning ankles," Annie confirmed.

Dad nodded and continued, "Darrell provides the pipe and they are diverting water from the downspouts of the house across the driveway to the garden. It is a fright!" Andy's Dad laughed. Even though he pretended to be upset about it, every one knew that he was actually kind of proud of the kids. Darrell was no better.

"Those kids were so well behaved when I unloaded that load of bent pipe. They all stood there with the hard hats and their hands on their shovels, like a real construction crew. I had to laugh!" Darrell reported.

"I have the photos, Andy. We can look at them later," His Mom said.

Andy shook his head, "I really miss being home. I really do."

Nora Schroeder gave her son a big hug, "And we miss you too."

"Doesn't really sound like it!" Andy chuckled.

His Dad gave him a serious look, "Well we do. And believe me Sport, there is plenty of yard still to face water diversion. This is just their practice run!"

"I didn't mean it that way," Andy said, "I'm glad you guys are being you guys. Nobody else has a family like mine! I'm really lucky."

"We know. And if you forget, I have it all written down," Darrell joked. "But we do miss you. I can't wait for you to get home. It won't be that long anymore. You'll even be home in time to plan for next summer's excavations! Charlie is planning on building a lake in your Dad's pasture."

Annie giggled, "You bet. No matter how we try to talk him out of it, he is determined that we need it. Yea Gads, can you imagine?"

Dad sighed, "Sadly, I can."

Dad had brought the car, so everyone rode back to the hotel. There they looked over the rest of the photos that Mom had brought and checked out the photos from the wedding. Then they posed for some more and finally decided to get some dinner.

They went to a nearby restaurant and had a nice dinner. At the restaurant, they danced afterwards and had a few drinks, before heading back to the hotel. Andy was getting more and more melancholy.

When they told everyone goodnight, Andy had a hard time. He hated that his time was over and that he would be going back. He wanted to go home with his wife and share in their life. He wanted to get to know the new members of his family and be a part of all their adventures. They were a crazy lot, but he loved them. Things at home were far from perfect. Life was not all fun and games, but it was a good life.

The Army was not his real life. It was a part of it to be sure, but everyone knew that they would all rather be someplace else. He wondered if he would ever be able to see Horse, Swede or Chicago when they got home. They had talked about it, but of course, that was all talk and they knew it.

That night, he and Annie didn't talk much at all. Mostly, they made love and just enjoyed being with each other. There wasn't anything that could be said. They both knew they didn't want to leave and they knew they had to. So, what was the point of talking about it?

During the night, Andy got up and went to the patio to have a cigarette. He watched the ocean's waves as the methodically washed up on the beach. It was idyllic and peaceful. There was Hawaiian music in the air and the perfume of tropical fragrances. This was really a fantastic wedding and honeymoon. He was truly thankful that he had been given this time.

Even though he had told God that if He would just let him have this, he would never ask for anything else; he already was asking for more. He was already begging to be able to return and spend the rest of his life with Annie. He grinned to himself. 'God must just crack up when He hears us with out paltry little prayers. Oh yah, just this one week! Ha! All the while, He knows we won't quit asking for more. That is our nature.'

Annie came up beside him and asked, "What are you smiling about?"

Andy explained it to her and she grinned, "I guess there is never enough, huh?"

Andy became thoughtful, "I don't suppose that is too bad, if we remember to appreciate and be grateful for what we already have. That would be what Aunt Gilda would say."

Annie nodded, "Yah, she would. Well, I'm grateful that we have had this time and I'm still looking forward to the rest of our lives. Andy, I know you must feel a little out of place right now but don't worry. Your home is still your home and no one thinks it would be better without you. You need to remember that. Okay?"

Andy put his arms around her, "How did you know that I was worried about that?"

Annie smiled, "Oh, I think we all knew that. You aren't that cagey, mister."

"Hmm, have to work on that," Andy grinned as they embraced.

"Don't waste your time. We have more important things to do," Annie said.

"What could that be?"

# 244 days left

## *Leave over*

The morning was sunny and slightly breezy. It was starting out to be a perfect day. Andy put off packing his duffel until after breakfast. He didn't want to do that until the last minute. He somehow felt that once that was done, everything would be final.

They had breakfast at the dining room instead of the buffet and had a wonderful meal. "Does the mess hall have pretty good meals?" Jeannie asked.

Andy laughed, "That depends if you have just come back from patrol or if you're leaving! Coming back, it's great. Otherwise, not so much, but it beats those rations. But see, those aren't too bad either if you are hungry enough. It is all relative."

Elton just burst out laughing and his wife looked at him like he was nutty. "What are you laughing about?" Andy's Mom asked, "You're a lunatic."

"No, I know exactly what he means. Just think how good a sugar cookie tastes, unless you have been baking dozens of them."

Nora shook her head and looked at Annie, "They are goofy, pure and simple."

"Is it a big mess hall with a huge kitchen?" Darrell asked.

"It is pretty big and it serves a lot of food, but it is makeshift. The poor thing has been mortared so many times and repaired with whatever is handy, it isn't much better than a shanty. It is leaks like a sieve. During these monsoons, there are buckets sitting all over the place. Sort of gives it character," Andy grinned. He tried to lighten it up because he could see that his Mom was getting upset. "I imagine some of the MP's would be pretty good cooks if they had the time and the ingredients, you know? But it does keep the wolf from the door."

"Just barely," Mom made a disgusted face, "From all the weight you lost, I would think they could do better. Oh well, I guess I'd be jealous if they served vanilla waffles and ham, huh?"

Andy laughed and gave his Mom a hug, "Even if they did, they wouldn't be as good as yours."

"Flattery will get you everywhere," his Mom smiled. "I just wish that it was nicer."

Andy chuckled, "I'll tell the CO that."

Mom whopped him. "Think you're smart, huh? Well, I tell you. The things we hear on the news and see in the papers aren't very good. I'm not happy with a lot of it. That My Lai massacre was horrific. And that Napalm stuff."

Andy became somber, "Mom, there's all kinds of really horrible stuff that goes on over there. Awful stuff. Nobody is a good guy. Not them. Not us. That is the way it is. I wish it wasn't but I have learned the less time I spend thinking about the good or bad, the better off I am. I don't want to paralyze myself or my buddies. I just want to get done with it and get back home.

"I thought I hated the clearings, until I was in the underbrush. I thought I wanted to dig a hole to hide in, until I was in a tunnel. I hate seeing the enemy, but I hate it worse when I don't see them.

"But you know what? I have my buddies and my home. I know I'll eventually get to leave. What about those poor devils that live there? They don't get a leave or know they only need to serve so much time and it's over. That is their home. It will be messed up for years. There has been killing for years and it looks like it isn't going to stop soon. It makes you wonder why they bother getting up in the morning.

"Then you meet someone like Suds, my Vietnamese friend, Nguyen Van Tri. We all him Suds. He has had more bad things happen to him than I can imagine, but he still smiles. He's my friend. Suds does nice things for people, some who treat him worse than dirt; but he does it anyway. He always tells me to keep my 'happy spirit." I've never met a person with a more positive attitude. He is a great person. God must be very happy with a fellow like him."

"What faith is he?" Mom asked.

"I don't really know. I know he isn't Christian and it might be Buddhist, but I don't know. Don't know what it is. But he believes in God. Horse and I think that it is the same God. You know, Horse's Great Spirit and

175

Suds' God are the same God as ours. We might call him a different name, but it is Him. I find that comforting, whether or not it's true. Anyway, I have said way too much. I need to talk about something else now. I'm sorry, I didn't mean to go off on a tangent."

"Nothing to apologize for," his Dad said as he patted his shoulder, "You made more sense than Grandpa Lloyd, although he has his moments."

After lunch, Annie and Andy went back to their room. Before Andy packed, they made love again. It was bittersweet. He really loved her and he knew he was really a lucky bastard after all.

Then he packed, dividing the things that he needed to send back with Annie and the things that he'd take back to Vietnam. Just putting the clothes away, made it all too real to him. He realized though, that comparing it to the first time that he went to Vietnam, he wasn't as frightened. Now, he knew what to expect. The first time, he didn't have a clue what was coming.

In a weird way, he was anxious to get back. He wanted to see Chicago and Horse and hoped that Suds would still be there. Mostly, he wanted it to all get done with; so, the next time he didn't have to go back.

He happened to look up and notice Annie, while he was packing. She was looking out over the ocean, trying to contain her tears. It just about killed him to know how sad she was. He zipped the last zipper and put the bag on the floor. Then he went over to her. He put his arms around her and soon they were making love again.

The phone rang in the room and it was his Dad. "Do you need me to help you bring your bags or anything? We're heading down to the car."

"No, thanks," Andy smiled, "We'll meet you."

He jumped out of bed, washed up a bit and threw his clothes back on, while Annie did the same. Within minutes, they were leaving the room. Before they went out the door, Andy gave her a little kiss. "There will never be enough time to spend with you."

Annie smiled and kissed him back. "My heart goes with you, and yours is with me."

They got to the car and everyone was there. Mom was already crying and Andy gave her a big hug. "Don't worry Mom. I'll be home soon, pestering Kevin and tormenting Pepper. You will wish I'd be leaving again! Just take care of my cowboy boots."

"I will, Andy," Mom embraced him. "I will."

"Okay, let's get this show on the road. The Army doesn't take kindly to having us guys show up late!" Andy stated and then he grinned, "They might skin us!"

"Okay Hotshot!" Dad laughed, "Get in the car. Darrell is the co-pilot, so let him sit in front."

Sooner than anyone wanted, Andy parked in the lot at Schofield. Andy looked around at the many families telling their loved ones goodbye, hugging, crying and trying to encourage each other. 'What a bunch of shit,' he thought. 'Why can't they just call the whole damned thing off?'

They all got out of the car and Dad retrieved his bag from the trunk. After all the tearful hugs, Andy gave his beloved Annie a goodbye kiss. Mostly they just looked into each other's eyes, saying all the things that can't be said.

Then Dad took his arm, "Come on Andy. I'd be honored to walk my son to the door."

Andy hugged Annie, again, who was now weeping with his Mom. He kissed Jeannie, "Take care of my friend."

"You take care of his friend, you hear?" she smiled back. Then Jeannie tried to console both of the other women.

Darrell gave him a big hug and with tears flowing down his cheeks said, "Take it easy, Man. I'll do my best to keep this crew under control. Make sure to get back home. I need help! You hear?"

His face awash with tears, Andy punched him, "I hear. Darrell, I'm counting on you. Don't ever think that isn't important. Got it?"

"Got it."

Dad walked with his son the last twenty feet and then handed him his duffel. "I love you Son. I have been proud to be your father every minute."

"I love you Dad. I really do. Take care of them for me, will you?"

"Count on it."

Andy went through the doors and didn't look back. He couldn't look back, it would have killed him.

He might have considered being embarrassed being so emotional had not everyone else been in the same shape. They only said what needed to be said and got involved in the checking in process. A few minutes later, a bunch of GI's showed up that were still partying. There was about ten of them and they were feeling no pain. It was a helpful diversion from the situation.

By the time Andy boarded the plane well over an hour later, he finally looked back at the patio where he had last seen his family. He guessed he had half hoped they would still be there, even though he knew better. The patio was empty.

As he went up the steps of the plane, he looked over the beautiful island paradise. It had been a miraculous time, no doubt the happiest time of his life. A memory he would never forget.

Then he found his seat and fastened his seatbelt. A minute later, one of the partiers sat down next to him. The poor man was beginning to feel get sick. Andy hoped he wouldn't throw up all the way to Da Nang.

# 243 days left

Alas, Andy did get to share the misery and recuperation of one very sick GI on the way back to Da Nang. The poor fellow had succumbed to the fate of those who excessively partake in the tropical rum drinks. Andy figured what he'd done was far beyond partaking. It may have been more like mainlining! He was so sick. He used every barf bag on the plane and was still throwing up.

He couldn't put together a coherent sentence and apparently the movement of his dehydrated, bloodshot eyeballs inside his head was extremely, tearfully painful. He was unable to focus but his mind probably wouldn't have been able to decipher what he was looking at anyway. For all he knew, he could have been on a plane to Antarctica.

It was certain that being airborne did not help his condition nor did it aid in his recovery. Andy really felt sorry for him and even more sorry for himself having to sit next to him. 'Ah but for the grace of God, there go I,' Andy thought. Andy had to stifle his grin a few times.

When the soldier finally fell asleep, he snored horribly; a big, slobbery snore. His poor head seemed to find comfort leaning on Andy's shoulder. No matter however which way he moved, the sleeping man seemed to follow him like a magnet. Somewhere over the Pacific, Andy amused himself by figuring out how he could jam the GI out the little airplane window. Finally, he fell asleep, too.

He woke up sometime later when the man was retching. Andy knew how he felt and may have been there a time or two himself; but he really wished he didn't have to share it. By the time the plane landed, the pathetic creature next to him was so hung over and pale, Andy wondered if they would have to remove him by stretcher. He was so very grateful he didn't feel like him. However, the situation did take his mind off missing his Annie and his family. No doubt about that.

It was in the very wee hours of the following morning when the truck entered the camp. It was almost like coming home. Andy was actually anxious to find out everything that had gone on while he was gone.

There had been changes. Once the NRVN had started to take over the base, a small shanty village began to spring up on the perimeter of the camp. It had grown in size while he was gone and now was rather large.

These makeshift bunkers housed many of the families of the South Vietnamese service men. Some of them had no home or any safe place to live. Not that outside the base camp was either home or safe. At least they were close to their husband or brother.

There were many little children living in these bunkers and they often wandered around the base and begged for food. While the American soldiers generally sympathized with their plight and actually liked the little kids, the thievery was not looked upon very well. Some of the soldiers were becoming very upset they were there.

Andy used to love little kids, but that had been tested to the point that he was almost as afraid of them. He had begun to feel that far away is the best way to be. He trusted very few civilians at all, whether or not they were family to a NVRN soldier.

He tried to put it into perspective and remember that they were still little kids. He tried to think of Ginger and Charlie. However, it didn't really work. Any more than thinking some little old lady was like his Grandma Katherine. Although, he had to admit, she could probably raise royal hell on some invading force.

He shook his head, 'Forget it. Just do a good job and get home. I have other fish to fry.'

When he got to his hooch, he heard the snoring of the other soldiers and the smells that only an Army tent can have. It was almost welcoming because it was so familiar. It was almost nice to be home.

He was disappointed. His squad was out on patrol, so he couldn't see Chicago and Horse. He put his things away and replaced the photo by his rack with the new one of Annie from their wedding day. He looked at his old rack and had a sarcastic chuckle. 'I think it was all a dream. I will probably wake up and find out that Hawaii never happened.'

When he crawled in bed and pulled the blanket over his shoulder, he noticed his wedding ring. 'It was real. It really was.'

Morning started well before Andy wanted it to. 'No more making love all night and sleeping in. That party is so over.' He shook his head and mumbled to himself, "Okay Schroeder. No more blubber baby. Get on with it."

On his way back from mess, he saw Suds and another Vietnamese man collecting laundry. He waved and Suds motioned for him to come over. Suds stepped away from his line to talk to him.

"Suds leave tonight to be by uncle. I have thing for my good friends."

Suds pulled three boxes out of the bag he was carrying around his neck. 'Maybe you remember Suds. They called To He. They are dragons made of sticky rice and molded by hand around a stick. Then painted bright colors. Suds hope you want.'

Andy opened the top box and took out the To He. It was about the size of a pen and very colorful. He looked at his friend, "They are wonderful. Thank you so much! That was very thoughtful of you. I'm sure that Horse and Chicago will love theirs too. I'll keep it forever. How do I take care of it?"

"Keep in box. It is for remembering Suds," the young man said. He looked to the ground, "Maybe we meet again."

Andy hugged him, even though Suds was uncomfortable with that. "We'll sure try. We will write, okay? Horse said he was going to give you addresses. Did he?"

"Horse did. Suds keep in safe place."

"I hope that things go well for you and that we can spend some good time together. You may not know this, Suds, but many times your happy spirit was the only reason that I kept going. I thought if you can do it, so can I. So don't ever give up. If there is anything that I can ever do for you, please let me know. Promise?"

"Maybe someday Suds see prairies, watch a tornado!" the young man offered with a slight grin.

Andy's tears were rolling down his face while he chuckled, "For sure! If you can come to the farm, you will be my welcome friend. Know that you'll always have a place with me!"

As he started to turn away and then he reached in his pocket. He retrieved the metal key chain that his older brothers had given him for his high school graduation. It was something that Andy had always carried since he received it, even though he had no keys on it. It had his initials AEGS engraved on one side. He handed it to Suds.

"You keep this. I got it from my family. If you ever get to the US and I'm not there, you can show this to my family and they'll know you're my friend. They will offer you a home. Okay?"

Then Suds got tears. "Spud keep."

"No, you keep. Hear me? I want you to have it to remember Spud." Andy knew he had to get out of there before he emotionally collapsed. "Take care my friend. We will meet again, I know. Keep your happy spirit."

Not looking back, he ran off to his hooch carrying the boxes. He got into the barracks, flung himself across his bunk and cried. He didn't give a damn who saw him or what they thought. He just cried.

It was only for a minute or so but he did feel better. Then he got up, wiped his face and put the boxes in his trunk. There were a few other guys around, but no one said a thing. Maybe they knew better or maybe they understood. Andy didn't really care.

He went outside and got to his work detail. Later when he could, he looked over and realized that Suds was gone. He only hoped the poor guy didn't think he was insane or rude. Regardless, there was nothing he could do about it.

Andy thought a minute and then turned his brain off. He wasn't going to think. He went to work.

Later that evening, he heard that the other guys should be coming back sometime during the night. He was glad. He hated it without them. He wrote to his family and he told his brothers that if any Vietnamese ever showed up with his keychain, who it would be. He wrote to his Uncle Byron, their minister, and asked him how long it took a person to get back to normal after being in Vietnam, or if they ever did.

# *240 day left*

It was a few minutes past two when Andy's friends came back. They woke him up and he was so glad to see them. They looked like hell but were a sight for sore eyes.

"How was patrol?"

"Productive," Horse said sarcastically. "Basically, not worth a damn. At least we didn't lose anybody but that wasn't our fault. I don't care about that. How was the wedding?"

"Great. I have a few pictures. It was really great. Seems like years ago now. Counting the minutes, Chicago?"

Chicago grinned, "Yah, but I knocked my damned tooth out when I hit the ground. Rotten deal! My wedding pictures will look like hell. Me, without my front tooth."

Horse hit him, "Your wedding pictures would look like hell anyway if you are in them."

Chicago shook his head, "I ain't no way gonna be missing you!"

Some poor soldier who was trying to sleep yelled, "Will you guys knock it off?"

"Sorry," Andy replied. Then he whispered, "Talk to you guys in the morning."

When the official morning finally arrived, the guys all started talking at once. It was as if they each had so much to say or ask and too little time to do it. Over breakfast, Andy told about his wedding, how he hit the dirt on the beach when the car backfired but left out about hitting Annie. He told them about his nightmares though.

"We have them here all the time," Horse pointed out. "I guess I just sort of figured they would quit when we left. Maybe it takes a while, huh?"

"Hope so," Chicago said. "I sure wouldn't like to put up with those panic attacks back home. What would Sonny think?"

Andy looked away but not before Horse saw the expression on his face. "Annie saw them, huh?"

Andy dropped his head, "Yah. She was very sweet about it, but must have thought she married a madman. I dreamt I was in a tunnel. When I woke up on the floor, I was wrapped up in a blanket and yelling my stupid head off and swinging away. If you are smart; you will warn Sonny before you scare her to death, Chicago."

All three men sat there in dead silence for some time. Then Andy grinned, "Hey, I got the tape from Charlie for you, Chicago. Yea gads, he sings as bad as you do! The family sent him outside to make the tape. Even the poor dog, Elmer was howling when he heard it! But he means well."

"Poor kid. I guess you don't appreciate his talent either, huh?" Chicago smiled, although it was obvious he was still worrying about Sonny and the nightmares.

"Look Chicago," Andy said, "Sonny loves you. If she knows some about it, I'm certain that she'll understand. Just be as honest as you can."

"Were you? Did you tell Annie everything?" Horse raised his eyebrows.

"Most of it, but no. Not everything. How can you explain it? I mean, just how? How can you tell someone how it feels to see some of this stuff? Like seeing another guy's guts hanging from a bush or flicking flesh off your eyelid so you can continue to fire on the enemy? I guess you just don't. But I do think that you had better give your wife a heads up about some of it. Annie said she would rather know than to know I am lying and then imagine even worse stuff."

"Guess that makes sense. You know, just between us," Chicago got very serious, "I feel that I won't make it back from here. I just sort of know I'll never be back in the world. Maybe I shouldn't be getting married. Just stay alone rather than put problems on her."

"You idiot. She already loves you. So she would just feel bad that you broke up with her. And then if you lived, she'd never forgive you." Horse grinned.

Chicago smiled back, but was obviously still very worried. Horse put his fork down, "Maybe you're just worried about not getting back and letting it get to you. You have to keep living like you are going to live forever or else you might as well be dead right now. You have to take chances at life, or you'll be paralyzed and do nothing. If I had known how

Vienna would die-," Horse stopped. He looked at the guys and closed his mouth. In all this time, he had not let anything slip until today.

Chicago and Andy caught each others shocked expression and stared at each other, speechless. Neither knew if they should say anything or respect their friend's privacy. The three sat like stone.

The situation was spared when some soldiers came to sit at the table. Andy and his friends got up to move on since they were finished eating. They never went back to the subject. However, Horse was very quiet after that. Maybe he was afraid they'd bring it up or maybe it had uprooted some memories that he had stored way back in his soul.

They went to work duty and after lunch, Chicago and Horse got ready to go on leave. It was mid-afternoon when Andy saw the truck pull out of camp. He was glad he was busy because he really didn't want them go. He wanted them to have leave but he selfishly wanted them there. He was amazed how dependent they had all become on each other.

That night, they got their orders to go out on a patrol and were told that it could be a long one. Andy wrote letters to his wife and family and hit the rack early. He needed his rest. He was almost glad that he'd be busy again. He thought about who would be going out on patrol. The ones that he was closest to were all gone. Bandaid, Swede, Horse, Chicago and even Franklin was on leave right now. There was still Bole and some others that he knew, but it wasn't the same. Then he thought about Suds. Damn, he hated this.

The birds dropped Andy's platoon into the hill country near to the Cambodian border. Before the helicopters even landed, the air filled with sulfur and smoke. The humid air was thick with battle. The helicopters could not drown out the sound of heavy artillery. The bird dropped them right on the edge of a massive firefight. The platoon they were joining up with was badly pinned down. The gunships were trying to abate the onslaught, but more men were still needed on the ground.

The first bullets Andy saw, hit the dirt just seconds before his feet. This wasn't going to be boring. That was a certainty. The helicopter Andy was riding in took some shelling as it lifted off but made it into the sky safely. Andy's attention was immediately drawn to the situation at hand.

The men moved from the landing zone to more cover as fast as they could. Two men never made it ten feet from the helicopter. One was killed and the other was nearly dead.

The onslaught was on the other side of the landing zone. As Andy moved into the area of the other platoon, he saw the carnage. This was the worst mess Andy had seen so far. Andy's brain scorched with the pleas for help or to be put out of their misery; moaning, praying and crying. The wounded were all seriously close to dying. Andy was thankful to have his job and very thankful he was not a medic. He setup Thumper and soon was back in his mode; slow motion, not thinking just pulverizing the landscape as best he could.

The next helicopter after Andy was shot down as it tried to land. It crashed in some brushy jungle about a couple hundred yards from the landing zone. The last helicopter pulled back up and moved back to wait for a lull.

A lull. That would have been nice, but there wasn't one. The Army and the NVRN were outnumbered at least ten to one. No matter how many enemy were killed, they were replaced almost instantly with two more. And it didn't stop. The North Vietnamese Army just kept coming at them.

Late afternoon, things became quieter and during that time, more helicopters landed with more men and took some of the wounded out.

Andy helped load a man who had his leg blown off. When he slid the stretcher into the helicopter, he noticed the floor of the helicopter that was thick with blood. It must have been at least an inch deep. Andy almost threw up, but there was too much to do.

That bird was no more than off the ground, when it took fire. It was smoking, but Andy thought it might have made it. He didn't think he had heard it crash but there was so many explosions and noise that he wasn't certain. He went back to his position and reloading Thumper as fast as he could.

It may have been three or four hours later, when the fixed wing planes came in. They streamed torrents of Napalm onto the landscape to the north of them. The evening sky instantly filled with smoke and heat. The napalm sucked the oxygen out of the air.

Napalm was a gel like substance made of fuel. It burned at a very high temperature and stuck where it landed. Whoever was unfortunate enough to get it on their skin could not get it off. It was horrid stuff.

Then Puff the Magic Dragon gunships came in. After that, things settled down. The men were able to get the wounded out, remove the dead and fortify their meager little stand as best they could. There were about twenty some Army dead and more ARVN dead. No one knew how many enemy were killed.

By nightfall, he was glad to roll up in his hole. Then Andy realized what was missing. It wasn't raining and it wasn't even muddy! He had not seen one mosquito while on this patrol! He mumbled to himself, 'What the hell kind of a war is this anyway?'

The second day, the soldiers saw a couple gorgeous parrots. They were the most beautiful birds Andy had ever seen. He wondered what they thought of all this commotion. They flew off a few minutes later when the enemy lit up the perimeter with their artillery.

The next eleven days were not much of an improvement over the first. They were under fire most of the time. Fresh troops were brought in daily. The dead and wounded taken out. There were fewer losses than the first day, but they continued. Over the time Andy was there, probably twenty-eight Americans had died and over seventy wounded.

On the twelfth day, the enemy backed out. By that afternoon, it was quiet.

The men knew there would be a 'kill count' made. They all also knew that the numbers were subjective at very least. The enemy removed their dead as quickly and with as much care as the Army did. Our Army kill counts had a tendency to be padded numbers, as did theirs.

However, there were many enemy dead. The next day, Andy helped as the soldiers piled the remains of enemy dead in a large mass grave. Thinking about it even a little, it could make a person real sick. But it was a matter of fact. Men died in large numbers, either them or us. No in between.

The next morning, they received the order to pack up and go home; to leave the land to the enemy. The men all looked at each other. One guy from New Jersey said what they were all thinking, "What the hell? All this and we just leave? Was it worth all those guys that died or blown to bits? For what?"

The soldiers looked at each other and shrugged. Some things cannot be expressed. Andy wondered who made the decision to pick up and leave after all that suffering and death. Surely, there had been some extremely important reason for everyone to fight like this for days? What happened that made this plot of land suddenly not important?

Andy shook his head. His Dad has said not to think about it and he decided that was still the best plan. He was glad to load back into the helicopter.

He looked out over the area as they left. The beautiful jungle land was now cratered, burnt and destroyed. Once that was done, everyone took their toys and went home; apparently satisfied they had really taught those parrots a lesson. 'What a crock.'

# 219 days left

Even though it was very late when they arrived, Andy was anxious to get to camp because the guys would be back. He was looking forward to seeing them again and hearing all about their leave.

He was extremely disappointed to find out they had been sent out on a patrol. He looked at their racks and saw Chicago and Sonny's wedding picture. Chicago's head was turned so it was a side view and no one could see his missing tooth. They looked so happy. Sonny was a stunningly beautiful bride.

Displayed on Horse's rack, a cardboard framed photo from a bar that displayed him and some Army guys partying in Sydney. It looked like he was having a good time, but then those kinds of photos always do. Tucked under Andy's blanket was a tee shirt from the same bar in Australia. Andy smiled and set it aside. He was glad they were back.

It seemed that the war had become more chaotic and in some ways more hateful. There was definitely a feeling of distrust that pervaded everyone. Turning bases over to the South Vietnamese seemed to be a good thing on the face of it, but it also left some uncertainty. It felt as if no one really had a handle on what was going on and there was no definite plan. Maybe because there wasn't.

A couple days later Horse and Chicago arrived back. The three friends got a chance to catch up. They shared stories of their trips and the fun they had. They all had suffered from bad dreams and war related things as Andy had done while in Hawaii. In a weird way, it made Andy feel better. He wasn't under the illusion that he was sane, but at least his friends were as crazy as he was.

The next week, Andy kept himself as busy as possible so he wouldn't miss Annie so much. He wouldn't have traded the honeymoon in Hawaii for anything, but it made it harder to be back in this hell hole.

He and Chicago had some chance to talk and Spud knew Chicago was in the same place. Chicago was more worried about his Sonny. She was going to live with Chicago's mom and younger brother. He was glad about that. Things in Chicago were difficult with all the civil rights marches, riots over bussing, civil rights and the war. The city was ripe with tension. It was turbulent times in the United States and the city of Chicago was absorbed in the whole mess. Chicago wanted his wife to be safe and he worried a lot. He couldn't wait to get them moved to Wisconsin.

Andy was grateful that he didn't have those things to worry about. Where he lived and with his family and Darrell, Annie would be safe. That he could count on.

As for Horse, after the slip about Vienna that one time, no more was ever said. The others were afraid to bring it up and he wasn't about to mention it. From what they could tell, Horse had a good time on leave, but it was a bit hollow since he had no family or close friends to share it with. When Spud mentioned it, Horse simply grinned and pointed out that he wasn't moping around like they were. However, he was never the same after that mention of Vienna and Andy was very concerned.

Chicago enjoyed his tape from little Charlie! Much to everyone's dismay, he felt it necessary to make him another tape. He spent a couple evenings practicing it and managed to empty their hooch in short order. Most of the guys appreciated anything for a kid. In this case had it not been for little Charlie, Chicago would be had his mouth duct taped and stapled shut.

One evening while Chicago was working on his tape to Charlie, Horse and Spud went for a walk to get as far away from him as possible. After walking in silence for a while, Spud asked, "Did you really like Australia?"

Horse nodded, "Yah. I really did. Someday I want to go back when I can see the whole country. It is a fantastic place and I love the people. Did you know it was a penal colony? Isn't that something?"

"Yah, I guess I did know that. I know one of the first colonies in this country were too, huh? Like Georgia or someplace."

"I heard that. So, I suppose you're anxious to get back to your home, huh? What are you going to do when you get back there? Work with your Dad?" Horse lit a cigarette.

"I don't know, Horse. I might go back to college and study law. That seems so far away, I can't even think about it now. What about you?"

Horse sat down on a pile of boxes in their favorite junk pile, "Oh hell, I don't know. I supposed I would go back to Pine Ridge, but here is no work there. You know my family is there but there is nothing else there for me. Maybe I will re-up."

Andy almost fell off the box! "Why in hell would you do that?"

"I don't know. Maybe it's because here I really matter, at least to the guys in my unit. At home, I'm nothing but another drunken Indian," Horse said quietly.

Andy had never seen his friend this down before. He put his hand on his shoulder, "What's eating you Jackson? This isn't like you. You are always the guy who is there to buck the rest of us up."

Horse stared at the dirt. "Don't really know. Everything was fine. I mean it was all bullshit but it was okay until just before we went on leave. I started to think and you know how bad is."

"Yah. I do. Want to talk about it?"

Horse moved a small pile of dirt back and forth with the side of his boot, "No. Probably not."

Andy debated about jumping on him about keeping things bottled up but sensed it was deeper than that. Instead, he patted his shoulder. "Whenever you are ready, but we need to do talk it out before long."

Horse looked at him, "Thanks. I appreciate that."

They sat in silence a short while until some guys came by and challenged them in shooting hoops. Nothing more was said that night.

The next morning, they got word they were heading out toward the west. This time they would be closer to the Cambodian border. They should plan to be gone a while. The guys looked at each other. Things were getting worse out that way. Since they had returned from their R&R, the encounters had become of longer duration and heavier artillery than before. Some felt it was that the enemy was very determined to stop the Vietnamization of the war; while some thought the enemy had been energized by the Tet Offensive. Regardless of the reasons, that had become their new reality.

The birds dropped their unit into an area deep in the jungle near the Cambodian border. It was extremely quiet. They moved away from the LZ rapidly and tramped their way to the north.

Once deep in the dark jungle, Andy's mosquito friends surrounded him. He had to smile. Certainly God was in His heaven and all was right with the world. This was like the 'old days' of a few months ago. This he understood and he was almost confident.

Just before dawn, they encountered many small paddies and signs of agriculture. Suddenly the sky filled with the sounds of aircraft and they scrambled for their gas masks. They were drenched a couple times with good doses of Agent Orange. Once they were clear, they cleaned up as best they could, but of course, most of their clothing was still drenched.

Andy did notice however, that the mosquitoes had left the area. As he walked along, he wondered if a mosquito could get a rash. He doubted it.

It was about noon when they turned toward the west and met up with another unit of men. By two o'clock, they were on the edge of a vast field. They fortified their area on the edge of the jungle and settled in. Obviously, they were waiting for something, although none of the guys knew what.

By evening, they were joined by more men, both US Army and South Vietnamese. Horse, Chicago and Andy sat under the same tree while they ate their rations. "This set up reminds me of the last mission I went on before you guys got back. It was the worst mess I ever did see. It was some serious doings."

"Yah, like the last one we went on before leave," Chicago pointed out. "I never saw so many dead people. None of this sniper—cat and mouse stuff. No matter how we lit them up, they just didn't quit coming," Chicago shook his head.

"I wonder if it isn't because we are fighting more the North Vietnamese Army than the rebel Viet Cong. Although the VC are no pikers! That is for damn certain. At any rate, tomorrow we will know, huh?" Horse pointed out.

"Yah tomorrow," Chicago agreed.

"Tomorrow," Spud concurred.

About two in the morning while Andy was on guard duty, the jungle became suddenly quiet. Andy immediately perked up and his eyes scanned his field of vision acutely. He glanced at the other guard to his right and noticed that he was on edge too. Andy watched the jungle and the abutting field. There was no movement. Nothing.

About a half an hour after this, they all began to settle down a bit. Andy had decided that he was just too nervous tonight for some reason and tried to talk himself out of the feeling of impending doom. Just as he was beginning to think of his coffee again, he heard the lob of a grenade. That is when the most ferocious of hell's battles rose from its peaceful sleep.

They were engulfed by hordes of NVA from the other side of the camp. Not from the trees that afforded cover but seemingly from the fields. It would seem impossible that that many men could sneak across a field without any sign, but they did.

Heavier artillery bombarded them from the jungles to the west and certainly was in place before they even got there. They had probably built their little encampment only meters from the enemy artillery!

Within an hour, they were nearly overrun from the west. It was the most furious fighting Andy had ever seen. By the time back up came by way of the choppers, the western perimeter breached.

Andy shot a few men as they came within a few yards of his location. When that onslaught seemed thwarted, he returned to his Thumper.

A man almost Andy's size jumped on him from the back while he was prone firing Thumper. That was the first hand to hand combat that Andy was ever in, where the ultimate goal was death. He had a flashing thought that he was thankful for all the wrestling matches that he had with his older brothers. The man immediately went for Andy's throat but Andy managed to put his head down toward his chest far enough so the guy couldn't get to him. He only managed to get a gash across the bottom of his ear and his lower neck by his back hairline as he pushed himself over to be on top of the man. Then he grabbed for the man's wrist and bent it backwards while punching at his face with his other hand. The man dropped the knife and Andy grabbed it. He embedded it in the man's chest.

It was almost an instant reflex action and without a single thought of what he was doing. He pushed the man away and onto the ground next to them. The man groaned once and expelled a last gurgle of air. His own knife was still in his heart.

Andy made sure he was dead and went back to Thumper. He kept firing as much as he could. It was a few minutes later when the birds unloaded some nearby NVRN soldiers who quickly helped even the odds. Had it not been for them, they certainly would have been done for. The fight continued until just before daylight when the American fixed wing aircraft came in to turn things around.

They did, and quickly; but only after they had accidentally killed about thirteen of their own men and wounded several others. It was sickening to see their own guys get mowed down by the friendly fire from the sky.

To be fair, they were so overrun; that it would have been difficult to be much help without being so close as to be too close. However, that didn't help the dead and wounded much. However, Chicago pointed out that they would have all been dead had not the aircraft came. They all agreed.

It was almost noon before things were quiet enough for anyone to begin to regroup. Andy almost tripped over the man he had killed when he went to help another GI who had taken a shot in the stomach. Andy helped another GI take the soldier to the medic. It wasn't until the medic asked him if he needed help that Andy remembered that he had been cut.

"Nah, maybe later. You got more important things to worry about now."

"Tie your neckerchief around it to keep any more dirt out and to help it stop bleeding. Don't wait too long to get it taken care of," the medic said without looking up from the man he was giving a morphine shot.

"Thanks, I will," Andy mumbled and went back to help with the others who were wounded.

Around three o'clock as Andy brought another patient to the medics, one guy looked at him and taped up his ear. "You should have had stitches on your neck, but I will just tape them. Try to keep it clean and when we get back to camp get it checked."

Then Andy went to have a cigarette and see about his friends. He wasn't able to find Horse and Chicago until almost five and he was worried. He was beginning to look through the dead and wounded to find them. When he noticed them over on the other side helping carry a gurney, he made a beeline for them.

"I was so worried when I didn't see you," he said as he embraced Chicago. "I thought—, well forget that. I am glad to see you both."

"Us too," looking very tired, pale and worn, Horse grinned. "Hey, Spud, you got a smoke?"

"Sure," Andy handed him a pack.

"I owe you one," Horse smiled weakly.

"For the record, you owe me a carton!" Andy retorted.

"Ah now Spud, don't get all French fried," Horse said and then he collapsed.

Andy and Chicago both grabbed him to try to figure out what had happened. They couldn't see anything until Chicago went to pick him up. He put his hand around his side to boost him up and retrieved it, covered in blood. Andy immediately pulled his shirt out of his pants and found that he had a bleeding wound in his side.

# 202 days left

Chicago and Spud stared at each other for a minute. Nothing could happen to Horse. He was their glue. Either of them could be replaced, but not Horse.

They each grabbed a side of their friend and carried him off to the medics. While they were waiting to hear, Chicago said, "He was helping me carry some of the wounded. He never said a thing. Do you think he didn't know he was wounded?"

The medic overheard, "Sometimes it is adrenaline, sometimes shock. The wound isn't as serious as it looks, just bloody. Your friend lost a lot of blood but once we get him out of here, he will probably be okay. Compared to some of these guys, he is downright healthy. Keep an eye on him and we'll be back to take him back to the base when we can."

"Is his service over?" Andy asked.

"Nah. He'll just have to hole up for a while. He is good for another round or two, if we can control the infection," the medic said apparently unaware how grim that sounded.

The friends took turns sitting by their buddy and helping with the cleanup. The devastation was immense and there were a lot of wounded and several dead. Alot of enemy dead were hauled into another mass grave by the grunts.

Helping throw human bodies unceremoniously in a heap was something that Andy could hardly tolerate. To him it was worse than blowing them up with a grenade, or shooting them. It seemed almost inhumane. It took everything he could do to handle it.

When he came back to sit with Horse, he told Chicago. Chicago leaned back on the tree that Horse was under and listened quietly. "Do you think it would be better to leave them where they lay?"

Andy thought, "Well no, of course not. That would be not only unsanitary but disrespectful."

"So, what do you think? We should dig individual graves for each one? Spud, there's no good solution. The mass grave doesn't bother me as much as the attitude of some of the guys. I hate that some of them make fun of them and stuff. This one guy was being really gross and saying horrible things. I was about ready to deck him. A bit later, I saw him throwing up all over the place. He was just talking like that to cover up how much it bothered him. What is it that Horse always says, 'this isn't nursery school.'

"No, it sure as hell isn't," Andy agreed.

Horse was pretty out of it the whole time that he lay there. He opened his eyes once or twice. Once tried to say Chicago. When he saw Andy, he smiled. That was it. The medics were concerned that he should be transported sooner, but there were so many that needed immediate help more.

It was early the next morning when Horse was taken back to the base. Chicago and Andy helped load him in the copter without a word and Andy grabbed his hand. "See yah Friend."

Chicago looked at him with his goofy permanent smile and said, "Tomorrow."

Horse nodded back, "Tomorrow."

Andy had tears rolling down his cheek, "Yah, tomorrow."

As he watched the bird take off, Andy felt that his whole world was turning inside out. He hated this whole damned thing more than he could imagine hating anything in his whole life. Whatever God thought He was teaching Andy, Andy didn't even want to learn any more. He would just as soon be dead himself as to have to keep throwing human bodies into mass graves and loading his friends into helicopters on gurneys. He almost lost it. Then and there.

Chicago was standing next to him and seemed to read how he was feeling. He grabbed his arm and turned him to look him in the eye. "Dammit. Don't even start, Schroeder! I'm not going to let you do this to me! No way in hell! Hear?"

Andy stammered, "Do what?"

Chicago almost yelled, "Crap out. You can't! We have to stick together. I know I'm not Horse, but shit man, you're all I got over here! Dammit, now, you need to be here for me!" Then the tears started rolling down his cheeks.

Andy was shocked. He had always considered Chicago one of his best friends, but he had to admit that he and Horse were a lot closer, mostly because they were both from the farm. "You're right, Leon. We have to stick together."

Chicago nodded without a smile, "Good."

"And you are wrong, too."

Chicago hit his own forehead, "I should have known. There is no way you would let that go."

"You're as important to me as Horse," then Andy said seriously, and then chuckled, "I just don't like you as well."

Chicago hit him in the arm, "You're such a jackass, I can hardly stand you! We had better get to work before they cut back on our rations."

As they headed back to help, Andy said, "I almost lost it there."

"Me, too. But we can't let Horse think that we can't make it without him. He'd be impossible to be around."

The following day, the word came they were going to move off to the north. There was a field that was logistically valuable to the NVA. They needed it to move their munitions down into some critical valley. This mission was to go in and secure it, denying them access to the area. No one pretended it would be an easy task.

Over the course of the day, most of the US Army and ARVN troops were shuttled by bird to this field that was known only as a number, Field 841. While there were about 400 men on the ground, they were vastly outnumbered.

Andy and Chicago didn't get shuttled into there until the wee hours of the morning. They flew for some distance over jungle, some in heavy foliage and some decimated and barren because of Agent Orange or cratered from warfare. Even the dark shadows beneath the helicopter were unable to cover the ravages on the land.

Off in the distance to the north, they could see the sky lit up with explosions and tracers. There was something massive going on there. Chicago and Spud looked at each other. "I think Horse knew what he was doing when he cut out on us."

Spud raised his eyebrows, "Looks like it."

They were dropped on the edge of the biggest fiasco they had been in to date. The men on the ground were outnumbered at least ten to one. While new troops were being dropped in as fast as possible, the troops on the ground didn't have any where enough resources to get a firm stand.

The helicopters were targeted and had to dodge as much fire as they could to get near the area.

Nevertheless, the onslaught continued. More and more troops were brought in and more and more enemy seemed to simply appear on the horizon. It was straightforward matter of trying to kill them before they killed you.

Morning light was not encouraging. It was obvious that the number of fallen from enemy fire was only a bit more than that from friendly fire. The battlefield was chaos and no one could predict who was where or why. There was little cover and men were just more or less fending for themselves or in small clusters. Only a few areas had any order and even that was haphazard.

The deafening roar of a crowded sky filled with helicopters traffic that would easily rival that at Da Nang airport when Andy landed, mixed with explosions, artillery and the human cries of profanity and pleas for mercy about drove Andy mad. He just wanted the noise to end. He would have sold his soul for quiet.

And the smell. The air was filled with dust, spent explosive, blood, sweat, fuel and fear. Yes, now Andy knew the smell of fear. There was no doubt. They were all going to die. It was probably mid-morning when the realization hit Andy. There was no way that they could hold on much longer, even with men being dropped in.

They were going to die. He didn't feel bad about it at that point. Andy just more or less he accepted the futility of the situation. Not to mention that there was no time to think, eat, sleep or anything like that. A human can only go so long before total collapse occurs. It didn't stop. This field must be very important.

Some front units crawled up a embankment to try to take a bunker. A bullet to the forehead was all the ten received for their effort. Two units were totally decimated before they even got to their positions. One from enemy fire and one from a crippled US gunship that had taken fire itself. It crashed just minutes later in the jungle just beyond the soldiers that had been killed. Andy had watched the whole thing transpire in a matter of a couple seconds. When the plane went down, he threw up. And then he wept.

Someone behind him yelled, "Come on, you Son of Bitch! Get your sorry ass to work! We have a war to fight!"

Andy turned to give the man a dirty look. The soldier was walking toward him and his face suddenly filled with a strangely peaceful smile. Then he fell forward, dead. His chest had been blown apart. His head landed only a couple feet from Andy's boots.

"Holy Jesus," Andy muttered. "Okay, I'll fight this damned war. Don't need to send anymore of your walking dead to convince me!"

The next morning, things changed. As many birds came in as they could to retrieve men. The ground was filled with soldiers clamoring to get on one of the helicopters. That was their only way to be saved from certain death. It was obvious and simple. Stay and die or get on one of those helicopters. Being surrounded, the troops only had one way out.

As the helicopters came near the ground, the flood of desperate soldiers demanding to get on was unfathomable. Andy and Horse's unit was loading when they saw the bird next to them brought down by the weight of the soldiers holding on to the skids hoping to be taken out that. The panic on the ground was unimaginable.

The helicopter pilots were in an untenable position. They were filling over capacity and taking fire all the while. Many of the birds had been shot down on this mission, but the pilots kept going back out. They didn't want to leave a single man there. However, if the weight of the men on the helicopter was too much, they would not get off the ground. Then they'd all die. There was no way to take everyone. It was a choice that King Solomon would have dreaded, and the kind of thing that drove men mad.

Another helicopter pilot had to shoot a few ARVN soldiers who were holding on to the skids so they could get airborne. The men in the copters were stomping on the hands of the soldiers desperately trying to pull themselves into the only route to salvation.

There was nothing noble or patriotic about what was going on. It was a chaotic push for basic survival. Andy had never heard such cries and pleadings in his life. He thought it must be like the gnashing of teeth he had always heard about in the Bible when men were pleading to be saved from hell.

As their helicopter took off, Andy could see the enemy mow down men like so much tall hay while they waited to be rescued. It was horrendous. Andy felt for all of them. He knew how he had felt while waiting to get on his ride out, knowing if he didn't get out soon, he would be dead.

These guys all knew they were going to be slaughtered. Desperate doesn't truly explain how it felt. Or maybe Andy never knew what the word truly meant before.

He thanked God that he was not near the door of this helicopter and had to be the one to make the decision whose grip was going to be stomped. He was very certain however; he would never get over how he felt that day. Ever. Who the hell was he to be granted salvation, while other better men than him were left to be slaughtered?

There was not a word on the bird all the way back to camp. There was not one person wasn't deeply involved in the horror. When they arrived back at camp, they had heard the Army had lost well over 200 men, not to mention the NVRN, and the field was overrun by the enemy about an hour after they'd been pulled out.

Chicago and Spud sat on some boxes as they had a cigarette that night.

"Some bad shit, huh?" Andy said.

"Yah. I know you said I needed to tell Sonny everything; but I'm not telling her about this until I get home. I'll just say it was bad. She would go nuts if she thought they might not let us on a helicopter."

"I thought that too. I guess it is realistic. You know, like too many in a boat. Either you all sink or only some. I'm just glad I didn't have to fight to get on or have to push someone else away. I don't know what I would have done if it had been me. I really don't."

"Me either. Those poor devils that were left were nothing but cannon fodder once the last bird left. I was so glad I didn't have to make the decision who to push off, but still-." Chicago shook his head.

"Yah. Can we change the subject? I'm getting half sick again."

"Good idea," Chicago looked around. "You know, I actually missed this damned place when I was in Hawaii. What's with that?"

Andy chuckled, "It means we're certifiable insane. I did too. Annie said it is because we have such a close bond with each other. But then she never met you, so she must think you're a nice guy or something."

"In Horse's television series, you are going to play the jackass. He is right about that," Chicago growled. "I wonder how he is doing?"

"I thought I'd see what I could find out tomorrow. Today there's probably so much mess that they have no idea what is going on with anyone."

"Probably not," Chicago agreed. "I think I'm going to go get some shut eye. I don't know if I will be able to sleep, but staying awake isn't doing me any good."

"That's for damn sure."

On the way back to their racks, Andy glanced over to where Suds used to have his laundry pick up. "I wonder how Suds is doing? He was a good person. Think we will ever hear from him?"

"If he can get in touch with us, I know we will. Who knows how this mess will to end? He might be dead already. I hope not, but we have to face that."

"You are right. We need to sleep," Andy groaned.

# *196 days left*

The next few days were very quiet. The mood was subdued. Few thought things were faring well and it was a given that the US was pulling out, win or lose. It was disheartening. Those that were still in country were being reshuffled, not replaced. It seemed that they were always short handed.

Since the Paris Peace treaties and General Abram's takeover from Westmoreland, some of the vigor was gone. The Army was less willing to engage and certainly did not want to take many casualties, which sadly brought about an opposite effect. The ARVN were the ones to take the offensive. God bless them, they had the heart, but not the where with all. The US military didn't take the offensive, so the enemy did.

It was easy enough for the big honchos to say the US didn't want to take large numbers of casualties. Hell, neither did the soldiers on the ground! That was a given! Even a moron would know that! But to explain that to the enemy so he wouldn't clobber you while you were sitting on your haunches, didn't seem to work that well. Many soldiers were very discouraged. They may have understood the reasoning and might have even agreed to some extent, but it came down to—were you there to fight this damned war or not? Most guys really didn't care at this point. They just wanted a decision. And they didn't get it.

Chicago and Andy went out on a patrol to the northwest, toward the Cambodian border. Things there were becoming a lot hotter. The US was not supposed to be in either Laos or Cambodia, but that is where the enemy was amassing for a major takeover of South Vietnam. The ARVN was sent across the border however, sometimes by the thousands. Many times, they were victorious, but they were never able to cut the Ho Chi Minh trail. That was the lifeline for the enemy. The cost in life to the ARVN was overwhelming.

This patrol was to go back into an area that Chicago and Andy had been in before. The farmer in Andy had thought it was quite beautiful, with neat little fields. Now it resembled a moonscape, barren and crater-pocked.

Thankfully, this six day trip was very quiet. They searched a couple villages the first day out and Andy went down a blind tunnel. There was nothing there. The first night it started to rain hard. Before nightfall, Andy was curled up in his mud hole, swatting mosquitoes and wondering whatever possessed him not to get the postage to mail that letter to the university.

Days later, they returned to their base without having had to fire their weapons or dodge a bullet. It was almost boring. Wonderfully boring. Andy's right foot was starting to turn red again and he made it a point to take care of it. Since Suds was gone, there was no way he could get more of that miracle salve. Andy's neck was healing up and even though part of his ear was permanently nicked, he was no worse for the wear. All in all, he felt he was pretty lucky.

The guys were able to find out that Horse was doing well in a medical facility near the South China Sea. He was expected to rejoin them in another week or so. That couldn't have been better news.

They were abruptly awakened and loaded into trucks in the late hours one night a few days later. They were given little information except that they were needed to help out a company that was in trouble. It didn't seem like they would long gone, not even a full day.

When the trucks approached the small town from the east, they started to take sniper fire. It was clear this was not going to be the slam-dunk they first thought. Outside of the narrow paved road to the little city, they were met by the numbers of wounded Americans and ARVN. There was also many dead.

The city was nestled on either side of a narrow, deep river. The connection between the two sides was a single bridge. Bravo Company had been split in half by the NVA and Viet Cong. The wounded and dead were on the eastern edge of the city and the enemy had taken over the river edge of the town. While their situation was bad, they at least could get out to the east.

Andy's unit was met up with the remnants of Bravo Company on the western side of the town. Those guys were caught between the bridge and the large numbers of enemy that was closing in from the west. Their only escape would be over the bridge and out through the eastern side. Their movement was thwarted as the bridge was under the control of the NVA. It was only a matter of time before the oncoming mass of NVA would overtake them.

More trucks and men arrived from the east. Several attempts were made to take to the bridge. NVA artillery along the main street kept that from happening. The bridge most certainly had been readied for demolition in the chance the Americans would ever make it there. The remains of Bravo Company were surrounded a few miles west and south of the bridge.

Andy grimaced to Chicago. He returned a look of panic. "Horse is never allowed to leave us again. I decided."

"I agree."

There were two days of futile attempts and the loss of over forty men to take the bridge. As all the other grunts, Andy and Chicago fought house to house. This was close on fighting and the enemy was visible. Unseen, were the snipers. There were alot of them and no one ever saw them. Usually they were only a flash in a window and the sound of someone falling.

It was on-the-job training for the men who had previously fought in jungles and rice paddies. There were mistakes, but the learning curve was rapid. Losing a comrade or being shot at had a tendency to cement information in a soldier's mind effectively.

A nest of enemy armed with grenade launchers and RPG's blockaded one of the city blocks necessary to gain access of the bridge. At least six attempts were made to knock it out to no avail.

Andy, Chicago and a few others were sent to the top of a tall building to try to take out the nest. It took them several hours, but they finally achieved the advantageous position above the nest. Once in place, they were able to knock out them out.

After the firing subsided, Andy looked toward the river. He noticed that a barge was jammed next to the eastern edge of the river and unable to maneuver. It was still above water. A helicopter had been shot down and was stuck precariously on the back end of the barge. On the opposite side of the river, was a tall building that had been shelled repeatedly. It was barely standing. That is when Andy got an idea.

He found Bole and told him his suggestion. "Since the bridge is rigged, there is not much point to trying to get across there. If we could somehow get the building across the river to topple toward the east, maybe the stranded troops could get across the river by way of the downed copter onto the barge. We'd still have to get them out of there, but at least they would be on our side of the river."

Bole thought about it and looked the situation over, "Damn good idea Schroeder. I'll talk to Hamilton and see if it is possible. Until then, keep shelling the road."

A few hours later, they were given the order to keep only a few men to continue to shell the street. The rest were to surreptitiously move out of toward the south. Andy wondered it they were implementing his idea.

As about half the men moved to clear a path to the river south of the main road, fixed wing aircraft came overhead. They bombarded the eastern side of the river and managed to get the building to topple into it. It filled in a lot of that side of the river, but not enough for anyone to cross.

By evening, the soldiers had cleared a small dangerous path toward the river and had taken the barge. They were working furiously to bridge the gap over the river with anything they could find. They managed to get several small round boats out on the barge and helicopter. The decision was made to shuttle across the remaining thirty feet to get to the rubble of the tall building.

As they began to send men across the river, the enemy had figured out what they were doing. They also moved south to thwart the men of Bravo Company from making their way toward the river and put them under heavy fire.

Andy was among the first to cross the river and help clear the way for them. There were people dropping all around. Dead and wounded lay chilly everywhere. Had the fighting not been so unrelenting and the goal so clear, it could've been disheartening. None of the soldiers wanted to leave their brothers surrounded and not at least give one hundred percent to try to get them out. They knew their brothers would do it for them and they were not about to let them down.

By the time they got to the remains of Bravo Company, they had lost several men themselves. The bedraggled men moved toward the river. The enemy descended on them with increased intensity. Thankfully, air support was successful in drawing their attention so the most of the men could get to the river.

Once at the river, they began the tedious task of moving men across the rubble, onto the round boats, crawling across the skeletal remains of the helicopter and onto the barge. The enemy loved the target they made. That is when the Army blew the bridge.

Now the tide had turned. The NVA that were on the eastern side were being squeezed by the river. The bridge was gone and the Army controlled the only makeshift crossing of the river. More ARVN and US troops were arriving from the east.

Seven men and the remains of a fallen soldier were lost to the river during the crossing. They had to cross at night and it was terrifying. Eventually, most of the soldiers made it across.

Now all they had to do was get out of that part of town to safety. The going was a lot easier and the wounded made it to the waiting trucks in about nine hours. They were taken away and the other men were left to finish their business there. Andy's unit was ready to leave the following day.

Andy had never been so tired, or hungry in his life. But for once, he felt they had accomplished something. He knew Horse would be disappointed that he missed 'taking the fort'.

He didn't want to think about the civilians left in the shambles of their city, or all the men who died in the river; but it was a war after all.

Chicago had taken some shrapnel in his thigh and Andy had taken a shot in the upper arm that was only a flesh wound. All in all, they felt they were very fortunate. When they got back to the barracks they felt even better. Horse was sleeping in his rack! Life was good. Damned good.

# 179 days left

It was great to be able to stand down for a couple days. Horse could use the recuperation. Chicago and Spud needed to let their bodies recharge. It had been a harrowing time since their R&R's and they all decided that they were ready for another vacation. It was depressing to realize that they were just now at their halfway point in country.

After breakfast on the second morning, Chicago went back to his bunk for a nap. He was not feeling that well and on antibiotic because of a slight infection from the shrapnel in his thigh.

Andy and Horse walked over to their favorite junk pile and sat down. Andy looked around, "What are we going to do if this ever gets cleaned up?"

Horse shrugged, "Sit on the ground I guess. I'm not too worried. I doubt it will ever get cleaned up. It seems we always get about to this point before something comes up and we quit clearing it."

Horse was serious as he lit a cigarette, "Andy, I think I'm ready to talk to you now. I have kept this stuff bottled up in me for way too long. It's about killing me. When you guys were leaving to get married, I was about to go crazy."

"I'm so sorry. Had we known, we wouldn't have gone on and on about it," Andy said. "What is it, Jackson? What's been eating at you?"

"Well, I know you guys caught it when I dropped Vienna's name that day. I'm glad that neither of you interrogated me about it because I don't think I could have talked about it then. Andy, Vienna and I more than broke up. She is dead, and it is my fault."

Andy was flabbergasted. His mind tried to grasp the information without having a reaction. He knew how important it was to Horse. He lit his cigarette and then asked, "What happened, Horse? Start from the beginning so I can understand. Okay?"

"I think I always knew Vienna, since we were babies. We were the same age and went to school together every year. We started dating when we were thirteen or fourteen. I mean, we had always been together. Everyone knew it. We were going to get married as soon as we were old enough.

"She was beautiful Andy. Not just I thought so. Everyone did. She really was. She lived with her Dad and four brothers. Her Mom had died of tuberculosis a year or so after her little brother was born.

"A couple years ago, her father's friend, this Cabot creep, came to stay with them. He was from Nebraska and I never saw the man sober. He was a glorified ass. If ever anyone had no redeeming virtues, it was him. I hated his guts from the beginning.

"Vienna was afraid of him and usually managed to be gone if no one else was around. A few months before everything went to hell, four more of his friends came to visit. Cabot was always short on money and wasn't above doing whatever he could to get some; that is, except work.

"Vienna's dad was working on a road crew and her brothers were at school. Cabot and his friends had been drinking for a couple days. His friends decided they wanted a woman. Well, no woman would want to be around any of those drunks."

By now, Horse was in tears. He could no longer even talk. Andy put his arm around his friend and let him cry on his shoulder. "Take your time," Andy tried to console him. His mind was racing. "As soon as you're ready, you can tell me. I'm not going any place."

It took him a few minutes before he could pull himself together enough to talk. "Before Vienna got home from school, Cabot made a deal with those guys. He would set it up for Vienna to be alone so they could have her for $60. Sixty damned dollars! Can you believe that? They took him up on it!

"When she got home from school, Cabot left and took her two younger brothers over to the grocery store. Those guys gang raped her, repeatedly. It was a couple hours later when her older brothers got home and they rescued her. Her brothers damn near killed one of those guys. They got scared then and took off. When Cabot got back, the brothers confronted him and he admitted that he had set her up. He was afraid her Dad would kill him so he left too."

Andy shook his head, "Jesus, Horse. That is awful. Did they catch them? Are they in jail?"

"No. Her dad was afraid the State would take his other kids away for letting it happen, so he did nothing. Her aunt took care of her and helped get her fixed up again. She missed a week of school," Horse explained.

"One of her brothers told me about it, and for a while we were going to go hunt those guys down. When my uncle heard about it, he put a screeching halt to that. We were nothing but stupid kids and wouldn't have stood a chance with those five men. We didn't even know where they were, or anything. So we didn't do it."

"Vienna had a hard time getting back into the groove and of course, everyone on the Res knew about what had happened. There was all sorts of talk and whispers. It was hell for her. I was okay then. I didn't care. She was my girl and that was that. It looked like it would work out okay, you know? I really thought it would be okay." Horse almost pleaded with his friend for understanding.

Andy just squeezed his friend's shoulder, "Then what happened?"

"We had tried to behave and had decided not to have sex until we were married and all that. We were going to do it right, you know. I knew that they had raped her but I also knew it wasn't her fault. So that didn't bother me. I mean it did, but it didn't. I was mad that we had waited. Well, you know. But I figured what the hell. I couldn't stand it without her. She was starting to get back to her old self again and things seemed better."

"About six weeks later, she got really withdrawn. It had been bad for her, so I wasn't too surprised. Finally about two months after it happened, she told me. She was afraid she was pregnant. She was totally shattered.

"So, what did I do? I hit the ceiling! I like lost my ever lovin' mind. I had figured that even if they had raped her, she would still be my wife and we'd have our children. I never even imagined this would happen! She was scared and wanted to know what to do. I absolutely didn't want that kid. No way, no how. She didn't either, but neither her dad or I could afford an abortion. She didn't believe in them anyway. She pleaded with me to help her figure out what to do." Horse fell silent as if he was remembering it all.

"Andy, I was the worst thing that could have happened to her. Instead of trying to understand and take care of her, I threw an unadulterated fit. I let my pride and ego get in the way. I screamed at her and told her that there was no way in hell that I wanted their kid growing inside her! No way. I was just awful. I was horrible, Andy. The time that she needed me the most and I just went insane. When I think of some of the stuff I said, I get physically sick. Andy, I didn't even mean or think some of what I was yelling! But that didn't stop me. I left her there crying, standing out by the creek, all alone. Just left her there and stomped off!"

Andy shook the tears from his own eyes, "Man, that is a tough one, but you still loved her. She knew that, right?"

"No, by the time I got through, I really don't think so. After I got home and had time to think over what I had done, I decided that I to go back to her. I would do whatever I could to support her. I really intended to do that. I did Andy. That honestly was my intention.

"About eleven that night, I went over to her house and she had not come home yet. Her brothers and I walked back out down by the creek. We found her slumped against a tree. She had slit her wrists," Horse's tears renewed. "God, Andy. My Vienna was almost dead. Her brothers ran back to get help and I stayed with her. I tried to tell her I loved her and I was sorry, but I don't know if she heard me. Right before she died, she opened her eyes and calmly smiled at me. She said "I love you." Then she just closed her eyes and was gone."

By now, Andy and Horse were both crying. Andy held his buddy a bit and then said, "I'm pretty certain she heard you. She loved you, Horse. She knew it was just a lot for you to handle. It was for her too."

"But Andy, how could I do that? She was the most important person to me in the whole damned world and I let her down when she needed me the most. I just made everything worse," Horse sat quietly for a bit and then lit another cigarette. "I barely made it through her funeral and then I just drank myself into oblivion for a couple weeks. Finally, my uncle caught up with me and literally, pounded some sense into me. He said he could get past me letting her down, but now I was letting everyone else down too. He said he thought maybe he was wrong about me. Maybe that was my real colors! Screwing up once is forgivable but if I was going to make it a habit, I had better get away from him."

"I hated him so bad after we had that fight. You have no idea. But I did get my act together. I went back and graduated high school. I was actually relieved when I got my draft notice. I thought maybe I could pay back for what I had done to Vienna. I know now that it doesn't really work that way. No matter what, she is still gone and she will never be back. God Andy, she'll never be back. And it is my fault."

Andy watched his friend and then straightened his shoulders. "You aren't going to like what I have to say. I hope you know that."

Horse looked at him in surprise.

"I think you're being stupid. You didn't rape her. You didn't make her pregnant. And you sure as hell didn't want her to die! Good grief man. You

211

lost your temper and you were sorry. I know, it must have been hell for her but I believe that she always knew you loved her. I don't doubt that for an instant. I also believe that she forgave you for losing your temper even before she died. Now, you have to quit beating yourself up about it and make your life amount to something!"

Horse studied his friend's face, "Just how in the hell am I supposed to do that?"

Andy picked up a stick and made little gouges in the soil by their feet. "I think first you have to accept that fact that you aren't a super being. You won't always do the right thing at the right time. No one else can either. So you might as well get that out of your thick head. Sure, you can try and we all should, but when we don't make perfection; we need to remember that all the bullshit aside, we are only human.

"Once you get over that hurdle, my Dad would say that you need to think about what happened and think it to death for a while. Try to remember why you did what you did and see if there is something in the whole mess that you should learn. Then hopefully, the next time you can do better."

Horse's face filled with a sarcastic grin. "Hell, Andy. There is no way in hell I'm ever going to get mixed up with a woman again as long as I live. Ever. I won't do that to someone."

Andy shrugged, "Good speech. You are what? Not even nineteen? Yah, well that's one that you won't live up to, so don't tell too many folks. They'll just laugh. Horse, I am not trying to make light of any of this and I know it must be a horrible thing to live with. I can't even imagine. But you need to give yourself some credit for being a good guy. You are and you have always been there with the glue bottle for Chicago, Swede, Suds and me. That isn't as important to you as Vienna was, I know that; but in the great scheme of things, it might be. Dad always says that God doesn't always tell you where He is headed, but it is a good idea to not get off the wagon until the ride is over. Then we'll miss the whole point of it."

"That's all well and good, but it sure didn't help Vienna."

"You weren't the only one that let her down. Her Dad and her aunt did, that Cabot did, everyone had a part in it. You stood by her longer than anyone. I'm sure that she knew that you were just having a fit of weakness. Hell, she let herself down too. She could have not slit her wrists. You didn't tell her to do that. You didn't want her to and you didn't even know she was thinking of it. She must have been seriously considering suicide before you even got mad."

Horse frowned at him, "Why do you say that?"

"Think about it. Did she normally carry a knife with her when she went for a walk?'

Jackson's face was stone and then a glimmer of realization came over him. "No. She never did. You're saying that must have been in the back of her mind before we went out walking. But Andy, I should've understood how upset she was. I should have paid more attention."

"Probably should have. Maybe she didn't have a definite idea, maybe she did. She knew the odds of how it would turn out. She could have had the child and gave it up. My thought is that she was in a turmoil all of her own."

"What do you mean?"

"I have no idea how it would be to be a woman and be pregnant. I can only imagine. That would be enough turmoil for anyone. She had no real good choices. I imagine she was torn between loving her own flesh and blood; and hating it because of the ugly circumstances. I can't begin to imagine how that would feel. She knew you guys loved each other, but she wasn't stupid. I bet she knew that as many doubts as she had about the baby, yours would even be greater. She didn't want to hurt you either. I think that Vienna had been a lot closer to her decision than you ever realized, before you even went for that walk."

Horse sat in silence for a long time. "I need to think on this. You might be a little bit right. But why would she want to leave me?"

"She thought it would hurt you more if she stayed. She might have thought she was giving you freedom. She might not have really understood that you were kindred spirits." Andy clapped his friend on the back, "Shit man, life is a confusing business. Half the time, I don't think that a single one of us have a clue what we're doing."

Horse stood up, "Thanks, Socrates. Just the answer I was looking for. I think we had better get back. Chicago will have more sleep than us and will be impossible to be around."

"Jackson, is this to be just between us or do you want him to know?"

"I'll tell him but I have to figure out how to do it. I'm afraid that he would beat the hell out of me if he knew that I was so rotten to her."

"I doubt that. He's really a good guy."

213

"Yah, Andy. I know. But I need to figure out how to tell him. He's my hero and I would hate to have him know what a worthless bastard I am."

Andy grinned, "Well, thanks a lot there Tonto."

"Don't get all French fried. I knew you would try to understand. I could count on that. You're my best friend, you know. Which by the way, I think is a pretty pathetic state of affairs!"

# *173 days left*

The next day, Chicago had a great mail call. He received a letter from Sonny. She was accepted for a job in Kenosha Wisconsin. She would be an assistant to the professor of Herzing University there. It was an excellent job and she would be able to move his Mom and youngest brother out of inner Chicago to live with her. It was a great relief to Chicago. His older brother would be on leave and could help them get a place and move up there. Her job would start with the new semester, so they needed to be living there by Christmas.

The next thing in his mail call was another tape from Charlie, Andy's little friend. It was a Christmas tape. He sang *Jingle Bells, Santa Claus is Coming to Town* and did that pretty well. However, his rendition of *Silent Night* got Chicago banished from the barracks. He had to go outside to listen to it, far away from anyone else.

Andy knew that Charlie had sung his heart out; loudly, off key and with some of the wrong words, but with deep emotion. Bless Chicago's heart, he got tears when he heard it. Everyone else did too, but for different reasons. When the men heard that Chicago was going to return his tape and sing *O Holy Night*, along with *Rocking Around the Christmas Tree* and *Blue Christmas*, the volunteer rate for the next patrol doubled.

It was hard to believe that it was almost Halloween. The time had gone by more quickly when they were busy, but everyone was pretty depressed that they would be there over the holidays. Somehow or another, Andy had the idea in his head that he would be home for Christmas. Some sort of a delusion, no doubt. When he realized that he wouldn't be, he was really bummed. He wouldn't get out of Vietnam until March.

He wrote to his oldest brother, Keith and asked him to get something for his beloved Annie from him. He knew Keith would do it. Keith and Darlene would be expecting their baby around Halloween. It would be his first real nephew or niece. He was pretty excited about that.

Horse and Chicago had a long talk the next afternoon, and Andy knew that Horse had told him about Vienna. He could tell that Horse was relieved that Chicago didn't blame him, like he'd been afraid that he would. Now, it could be discussed openly between the three of them and maybe help Horse put the tragedy into some sort of perspective.

One night shortly after that, Horse and Andy found themselves sitting on their pile of junk again. In the distance, they could hear the strains of Chicago's voice rehearsing *O Holy Night* with his guitar.

They grinned at each other as Horse lit his cigarette. "The one black man in the world that can't carry a tune or keep a beat, and we have him as our friend! There is something wrong with this system."

Andy laughed, "Yah, Nat King Cole need not live in fear."

"Chicago was really decent when I talked to him about Vienna. He listened and told me that I really screwed up, but that he probably wouldn't have lasted as long as I did. When I told him what you said about she might have made up her mind to do it before she talked to me, he nodded. He said that is the first thing he thought, too. Then he said, 'You know man, don't worry so much. You will probably make a lot better husband than either Andy or I.' Do you think he might be right?" Horse searched his face, "Or was he just yakking?"

Andy listened and thought, "Nah, I think he meant it. You know, he is probably right. You feeling better about things now?"

"No. Not really. I try to think of what you said, but I can't quite accept it," Horse said. "I was thinking about talking to the chaplain, but I don't really like him. He has a peculiar nature."

Andy chuckled, "Peculiar nature?"

"Yah," Horse laughed, "He thinks I'm a pagan or something."

"Does he really think that, or do you think he thinks that?"

"Hell, man. If I have to think about all that much, it's easier to just not talk to him. Don't you get it?"

Andy shook his head, "You are nuts. Hey, why don't you write to my Uncle Byron? He doesn't think Indians are pagans. I know that. And he listens to me all the time, so you know he won't expect you to make sense."

Horse raised his eyebrows, "Yah, but Spud, then I might end up like you!"

"Never mind then," Andy grumped. "Just wallow in it; you ungrateful bum."

"No, I'll write to him. Do you think he would know who I am?"

"Yah, probably. I have mentioned that I am stuck with this nitwit over here. But you'd have to say that you are Horse. I doubt he would know your real name."

"I'll think about it. Okay?" then he looked over to where Chicago was singing, "Now, what are we going to do about that?"

That night, everyone wrote letters home and got organized for a long trip to the bush. They didn't know what it would be, but they were forewarned they would be gone a while. Spud and Horse were relieved that meant that Chicago would send off his tape to Charlie with no more practice! There seemed to be something good in even the worst news.

About three that morning, the men were dropped into the northern end of Iron Triangle. It was an area in Binh Duong Province, a stronghold of the Viet Minh activity during the war. The US and South Vietnamese forces had wanted to destabilize the region as a base for their enemy, but did so with little success.

Cu Chi was inside the Iron Triangle which was located between the Tinh River on the east and the Saigon River on the west, just twenty five miles north of Saigon. Phu Cong was the provincial capital. It was critical for the North Vietnamese army to maintain control over the area. For that reason alone, it was a prime target for the US and South Vietnamese armies.

The tunnel system of Vietnam was expanded after the French war as a base of underground operations for the enemy. At its peak, the system was thought to be over 30,000 miles of tunnels, many concentrated around Cu Chi. The US had made several attempts to eradicate the system because of its threat to Saigon. Between 1966 and 1967, they had launched extensive attacks, Operation Cedar Falls being the largest. That operation involved 16,000 Americans and 14,000 South Vietnamese. It took nineteen days and over seventy Americans were killed. The tunnel rats worked diligently to destroy the tunnel system with explosives, flooding and the aid of B-52 bombers and bulldozers. However after all that, the Americans had still failed to completely demolish the entire system.

The region was still an active center for the Viet Cong and as well as support for the local citizenry who had been so badly impacted by the bombing and the effects of the Agent Orange and Agent Blue. The citizens had not become friends of the US or the South Vietnamese regime.

It was here that the guys would go, once again. Not a man thought that it would be the final campaign there, but they also knew it was important to do. Andy,

Franklin and all the 'little guys' knew what they would be doing. Some days, it wasn't fun to be a tunnel rat.

The mission started out as so many others. Trudging through the bush and the rain was back. Even Andy's legion of mosquitoes had found their way back to their favorite target. Things were back to normal.

Horse teased, "All we need are some leeches and things will be perfect."

The guys were out on the mission for over two weeks. They found many tunnels, all empty. Andy was up and down so many of them it was almost becoming second nature. He noticed he wasn't even afraid of them anymore. Not that he liked them, but it was commonplace. He found no dead people, or even anything of interest. The tunnels were all blown, but it reminded Andy of trying to drown out a gopher hole in a pasture. It gave you something to while away your time, but didn't accomplish a damned thing.

One day, Andy went into an ordinary tunnel When he was nearing the first turn below ground, his elbow bumped something that was protruding and Andy immediately heard the sound of gas expelling. Before he could do more than yank on the rope around his waist, he felt dizzy and then things went dark.

When he woke up, he was above ground and a medic was working on him. He had the worst headache of his life. It took him a couple hours before he was cognizant of what was going on. Chicago and Horse were among the first that he recognized, and they were all glad to see each other. It took Andy almost twenty-four hours after the gas to get back to normal. No one seemed to know just what the gas was, but it came darned close to killing him. After that, Andy's nightmares became more violent and more frequent. Now they occurred almost every night, sometimes more than once a night.

The men encountered many more Pungy pits than they had in the past. They were hateful things and struck fear in the hearts of all the troops. To a man, they had all made pronunciations of what they would want to have their cohorts do if they ever were unfortunate to fall on one. Everyone always agreed, 'Yah a bullet in the head. That would be the thing.' However, it was doubtful that it was more than bravado talk and even more doubtful that their friends would do it. But it was what one always heard.

The men were glad when they received orders to head back to their base. It was nice to sleep indoors in a a real bed. The men were looking forward to eating hot food and standing down for a couple days. It was a well-deserved rest.

Andy's foot was infected again, but not as bad as before. It seemed to be a never-ending thing. He was resigned to the fact it would just remain infected until he got back to the real world. He had become more jumpy and easily irritated after this last patrol. He decided he was just anxious to go home.

The mail was also interesting. Chicago was excited that his wife and brother had found a nice, small home for rent in Kenosha and it would be available the week before Christmas. They had put down the deposit and were making plans to move Sonny and Chicago's mother and youngest brother there.

Horse had been writing to Byron, and he finally received some answers. He said they were very helpful and he felt that for the first time, someone really appreciated how he felt about Vienna. He really was pleased when Pastor Byron confided in him about the death of his girlfriend, Ellen. He shared how he had beaten himself up over it for a long time. Ellen was murdered and Byron had not forgiven himself for not being there to protect her, but instead was deer hunting. Horse could identify and he told Andy that he was looking forward to meeting Byron someday when they got back to the world.

Horse had also received a letter from Swede. He was doing well and back at his home in Minnesota. He related that he's had a difficult time dealing with the nightmares, but assured the guys that they were finally going away. That was a great relief to all of them. He said there was not a day that he didn't think about them and was hoping they could have reunion when they all returned to the world.

Andy got a letter from Suds. He couldn't say much and it was very cryptic, but said he was with his uncle and doing okay. He had a job with Andy's people and hoped someday to visit the prairie and see a tornado. Andy was relieved, but the men couldn't quite decide what Suds was unable to say. Was he working for the Army or the US? Regardless, they were glad for him. He ended it with 'keep your happy spirit.' They all missed him.

Andy heard from his family and friends. Darrell's partner in the farm had just gotten married. Darrell sent some pictures as did his Mom. The whole group was looking forward to the birth of Keith's baby.

He had also received the largest letter in the world from his crazy sister, Pepper. She told him every detail of the business of the garages and gas station. No one could ever accuse her of taking her position as manager lightly. That took nine pages! Then she told about her engagement. That took eleven more! Reading her letter was like listening to her talk! It went on and on and on, but he loved it. She was so happy and thought Chris was so wonderful. It was nice to hear her joy.

His Dad wrote again. He was anxious for Andy to get home. "You have to get here soon, Andy. These crazy people keep dragging more livestock into my barn! It is Grandpa Lloyd's fault. He is making them all buy cows before they get married. I now have a herd cows to milk! A whole herd! Don't tell anyone, but I think I am going to put wheels under Percifull and send her packing. She is getting old and her temperament hasn't improved. That old cow has caused more trouble than a little bit. She needs to go to her rest.

"We now have more horses in the barn, too. Oh Andy, our priest friend, Matt has a horse. His name is Spirit and he is a beauty. Jet black with a small white mark on his forehead. Jerald said Spirit has a brother and he is wondering if you would be interested in him. His name is Wind. Mom and I thought we'd buy him and then when you get home, you can decide if you want him or not. Since Annie has Moonbeam, it would be nice for you to have a horse also. So, you will have to check out Wind when you get home.

"Take care my son and be safe. We are looking forward to your return. There is a lot of snow this winter and I could use another good hand in snow removal! Those Gophers aren't too much help with that kind of shoveling! They prefer to trench. Love Dad."

Andy had to admit, he wanted to be home so much. The horse sounded wonderful. He missed his crazy family and was anxious to see the barn brim full of cows. Then he turned his attention to the letters from Annie. He missed her so.

# 155 days left

The next morning after mail call, the men got the word they were heading back out on another mission like the last. They loaded up again, not looking forward to eating rations for several more days but at least, they were relieved they would be busy. It wasn't quite as depressing that way.

The first ten days were a repeat of the last mission, right down to Andy's 'rotten foot'. There was little action and mostly empty tunnels. There were noticeably more booby traps, in and around the tunnels, which led them all to believe they were getting into a more active area.

The morning of November 16, they were humping their way into a dense area of jungle when the area lit up with incoming. They were almost surrounded and were obviously vastly outnumbered. A terrible firefight erupted and the platoon was in a serious situation.

Only a few hours had elapsed before their numbers were bolstered by more US and ARVN forces. By nightfall, there were at least four hundred men holding off a still larger number of unseen forces. The enemy was concealed rather effectively and was able to pop up and disappear at will. It was very disconcerting.

The men fortified their position as much as possible and welcomed another hundred fifty or so soldiers to their ranks before daybreak. Now they were able to hold their own, but were not able to make any advancement. The fighting now had diminished to a few rounds being shot now and again, but for the most part nothing major.

While they were holding their position, more men were brought in over the next few days. They would soon be expected to make an advance into the area that seemed to be of great value to the enemy.

They remained in the holding position for some days. The enemy activity was less but they were putting forth a definite effort to keep the present lines in place. Neither side was going anywhere. The fighting was static. All the while the US side was continuing to be bolstered, so obviously was the other side. Things were tense and the soldiers were stressed. They kept themselves as occupied as possible to relieve the wait. But they were mostly at the point they wanted the other shoe to simply drop and get it over with.

It rained and rained, and then would tediously rain again. Everything was mud and sloppy. Finally, on the eighth day, the sun came out. The men were able to dry their clothes and clean up. Even thought they were still eating rations, the bit of sunshine cheered everyone considerably and the entire mood of the camp was improved.

The morning of the 26th, the birds came over the horizon. The men all wondered if they were bringing in more men. They were elated to find that the birds were loaded with metal containers of hot food; turkey, dressing, mashed potatoes and pumpkin pie. It was fantastic. The mere thought of a hot meal blew most of their minds, but the fact that it was a Thanksgiving dinner in the middle of the bush was unbelievable!

The men were happier than they had been in months and delighted with the bit of home they were able to share. Even though it conjured up memories and made them all a little homesick; it was truly a time of Thanksgiving. After their dinner, they were amazed when another helicopter came in carrying a container the size of a dairy truck. It contained a satellite phone system. With that, the men were able to make phone calls to their homes! Each man would get a three minute call to their family!

They all lined up and waited their turn. Andy spent most of his time trying to figure out what all he could say in three minutes. He was rather certain that the family would be at his parent's home. Annie would be there too, unless she was working. In that case, he would likely not get to talk to her anyway. He hoped she would be off on Thanksgiving.

Chicago asked Horse to time his speech repeatedly. He would rattle on for three minutes without taking a breath! Finally Horse pointed out that he was not considering that Sonny would say anything. He hadn't thought of that. It threw Chicago into a funk and he had to rethink his entire monologue.

Horse was going to call his Uncle's home because that is where his family would all be meeting if they were getting together. He would speak to whoever was there. He tried to figure out what time it would be at their homes; but since he had no idea how long it would take to get to the front of the line, it was impossible to determine.

The three men waited in line nearly eight and a half hours. Not a one of them even considered it was not worth the wait. Chicago was the first to make his call. When he made his connection he said, "Hello Mom? This is Leon! Really! I love you, can I talk to Sonny?" There was a pause before he said, "Sonny, I love you." Then he cried. He was so overcome with emotion he never said another word until he said goodbye. His well-rehearsed speech went right out the window. He walked away from the phone and broke down in tears. "Dear God, I miss them so much!"

Then Horse got to make his call. He spoke to his uncle. He told them to tell everyone else hello and that he loved them. He sent a Thanksgiving message to Vienna's brothers also and then had to hang up. He went to console poor Chicago who was moaning about all the things he had forgotten to say when he had his chance.

The phone rang at the Schroeder household in the wee hours of the night. Andy's dad answered. "Hello?"

"Dad, this is Andy! I get to make a three minute call. I love you!"

"Andy?" then his Dad yelled, "Annie, Mom come quick. It's Andy." His Dad turned back to the phone, "They're coming! How are you?"

"Dad, I just had a huge turkey dinner with pumpkin pie! Can you believe that?"

"That's great. I miss you and love you son. Bless you. Here's your Mom."

"Andy? It's Mom. I still have your old boots safe and sound. Did you get the news? Keith and Darlene had a baby boy, born November sixth. He is fine."

"That's great, what did they name him?"

"Nathan Frederick. He is healthy and looks just like you did when you were born." Mom giggled.

"Poor kid. That's great Mom. Tell them congratulations for me! I miss you. I love you."

"Me too, Andy. I love you so much. Here is Annie."

Annie was already crying when she took the phone, "Andy! What a wonderful surprise. Dad said you got turkey and pie!"

"Yah and the turkey was hot too! Did you have the usual big dinner?"

"We did. I miss you so much. I can't wait until you get home. I am so glad that Marty and I decided not to take the holiday shift."

"When do you work next?"

"Tomorrow at ten. It is three in the morning here. How are you?"

"Good, Annie. I think about you all the time. I can't wait to see you again. Hey, tell Charlie that Chicago loved his tape and sent him another one. Okay?"

"I will. How are your friends?"

"Good Annie. I will tell them you asked. Hey, I have to go now. I love you. Will you give everyone a hug for me, especially Grandma and Grandpa. I want to be with you so much, Annie."

"I do too. It was wonderful to hear your voice. I love you always."

Then the line went dead.

Andy walked numbly over to his friends. He had tears rolling down his cheeks. He plunked down on the ground. "Shit. I don't know if that made me feel better or worse! I miss them so damned much."

"I know," Horse agreed and Chicago just continued to cry.

"I wish we could get this damned war over with and go home. Annie is fine, how were your families?"

"Fine, but then what can you say in three minutes? Hey Chicago, how did all the rehearsing work out?" Horse chided.

"Oh knock it off. Don't think you made a whole pile of sense when you talked to your family either," Chicago blustered.

"No, don't think any of us did but we got to hear their voices," Horse laughed. "That is the best thing."

Andy looked around, "You know, as miserable as this is, it really has to be the best Thanksgiving ever. I'll never forget it."

A few days later they had been in the bush for twenty-four days. Things were still at a stalemate and it had started to rain again; not hard, but enough to make things miserable. Andy was very certain that it rained constantly in hell. Andy had just finished guard duty and crawled back into his hole for some shuteye when all hell broke lose.

Within minutes, the entire perimeter was on fire. It was clear that the enemy had reinforced in great numbers. Andy was certain they were coming out of every trap door to their underground network. And they had a lot of them.

It was less than an hour before the northern perimeter was breached. Not that the troops didn't put up a good fight, the US and South Vietnamese forces were simply vastly outnumbered. Air cover had been called for, no one had appeared yet to relieve the situation.

Andy could see Horse and Chicago working in unison to keep the enemy at bay. Horse was changing the hot barrel of the Pig as fast as he could. Spud had his hands full with his Thumper and was able to inflict some damage, just not enough. He had slipped back into his adrenalin-induced slow motion. He methodically fired as much as he could. There were targets all over, so it didn't seem to matter where he aimed.

He was vaguely aware that some birds had come in to their rear to either bring in troops or evacuate them, but he was unable to take the time to determine which. Some fixed wing aircraft flew over and lit up the jungle in front of him. His nostrils were filled with sulfur, mud and blood.

A man next to him fell and Andy reached over to pull him to more cover. After he had moved him, he realized that most of his head was gone. He could see that enemy forces were now entering their perimeter from the west also. They received orders to pull back as quickly as possible.

Andy was running through the jungle as fast as he could with all his equipment. Out of the corner of his eye, he could make out Horse and Chicago running about fifteen feet to the right side him. They arrived at the place they were to take their new positions and were within ten feet of each other. Andy couldn't help but think how rare that was.

There was a massive barrage of artillery fire and then another order to pull back. Andy had no idea how long this had gone on or if there was more help on the way. He didn't know if this was going to be his end or not. He was just running as fast as he could. He wasn't even afraid, he was just running.

Then he saw the onslaught from the east. The enemy was coming from every direction. The men were retreating as fast as they could. Andy knew there were birds landing and taking off to the south and now he was rather certain they were evacuating. He was reminded of the last situation he had been in and certainly hoped this time there were enough birds so no one would have to be left behind.

The sky was filled with smoke belching machinery, bullets, artillery and screams of men shouting orders, spewing profanity or begging for mercy. The sound was deafening. There was no time to think and the adrenalin only seemed to make their legs go faster, but not fast enough. The air was nearly impossible to inhale because of debris, smoke and rain. They were no longer looking where their feet were landing, they were just moving as fast as they could.

They came into a denser area of jungle. Chicago was carrying the heavy Pig and Horse was keeping up to him loaded down with all the artillery he could carry. Andy ran along behind them with his Thumper and as many grenades as he could carry.

Two men ahead of them screamed as they landed in a large deep Pungy pit. As Andy came up beside them, he realized they were both dead. One had a spike through his neck and other right through his chest. His sergeant yelled at him to keep moving.

About fifty feet from that point, Chicago was in the lead. Suddenly, he disappeared from view. Andy saw Horse stop and fall to his knees. As Andy approached he saw the sight he had hoped and prayed he'd never see. Chicago was curled on his side at the bottom of a Pungy pit with the weight of the Pig on top of him.

# 131 days left

Andy threw Thumper down in the dirt and was on his knees on the other side of the pit from Horse. The noise and confusion around them had become background noise. Both he and Horse were oblivious to the battle raging around them, focused only on their friend.

The drab afternoon sky seemed appropriate for the day. The light wasn't bright but it wasn't dark. The pouring rain seemed fitting. The ground was soggy and sunk under their weight. The Pungy pit was filling with water in the bottom from the torrents of pelting rain. The sides were smooth and slimy with mud, only demarcated by streams of water ravaging downward.

Horse had taken off the artillery around his neck and was reaching frantically for Chicago. The weight of the Pig was pressing down on Chicago's side and holding him there. They could see that there was one spike through the lower part of his right leg and another through the muscle of his thigh.

Thankfully, Chicago was only about four feet down, unlike the last two men who had fallen at least six feet. His right arm was impaled just below the elbow. There was another spike protruding from the muscle high on his shoulder. They could not tell if it had penetrated through his body cavity although they were both certain that some of the hideous rods had.

The men thought they should be able pull Chicago out since he wasn't that deep. Andy helped Horse pull the heavy Pig off their friend. Chicago lay on his side perfectly still, his eyes closed. His face still had that stupid permanent smile, but he was totally gray.

Horse looked at Andy in panic, "Is he dead?"

"Don't know. Can't tell. He is on his side so maybe not. You think? We should be able to get him out," Andy thought aloud.

The men were discussing this as if they were discussing some impersonal project. They were not thinking of Chicago as their friend as much as a weight that had to be removed. It seemed strange since it was something more personal either of them had ever felt before.

Then Horse looked at Andy in despair. "Think we should pull him up? Will it make him worse?"

"Don't know." Andy yelled. "But we have to try."

Each guy was spread eagle on the soil on either side of the pit trying to get enough traction to pull with all their might. They reached down and grabbed onto Chicago's torn green jacket and attempted to pull him up and free.

The ground was so soaked that it made pulling him extremely difficult. He was stuck rather well and by their effort of pulling, the men were pulling themselves down into the hole. At one point, Horse almost slipped on top of Chicago and Andy had to brace his fall. They were both holding on to Chicago with one hand until Horse could get moved back far enough. This wasn't going to be easy.

He groaned and the pulling was painful enough for Chicago to emit a blood curdling scream. At least they knew he wasn't dead. They looked at each other.

Andy asked. "I think he is coming lose."

"Pull again, your direction this time. I think he fell in from that side," Horse determined.

The men reached down again and pulled with all their might. This time Chicago screamed and opened his eyes. He looked at the men in anguish and yelled, "Dear God, just leave me. Get out. Tell Sonny I love her."

Horse glared at him, "Tell her yourself. Pull!"

Andy and Horse pulled with all their adrenalin enhanced strength but were still unable to extract the man from the hole. Each time they released their pull and his body moved back down into the pit. The poor man screamed anew with the horrendous pain.

By now Chicago was gushing blood and his face was filled with tears. He begged. "Please leave me. End it for me. God, have mercy. Please shoot me!"

"No way in hell," Horse said forcefully, "Get your sorry ass out of this damned hole. You aren't crapping out on us."

"God, I can't take it. Please, give me a bullet!" Chicago pleaded.

Andy and Horse looked at each other for what seemed like an eternity, but it was only an instant. There were men all around yelling at them to move on. There was a closing window when they could make their escape from certain death. The pulling on him was only opening his wounds to bleed more. He had already lost a lot of blood. He was begging to die. They knew it had been his wish that if he ever landed in one of those pits. Artillery fire was pulverizing the ground near them. The enemy was getting closer by the second. The helicopters were filling and leaving.

Andy had never felt such anger and desperation in his life. He was furious, with the enemy, the hole, the Army, the government and God. It was one thing if he was going to die, but not before his got his friend out of that stupid hole! No one left someone they cared about die in some stupid four foot hole!

He yelled to his Lord, "Dammit God, You get down in that damned hole and push him out of there! We are doing our part. You hear me?"

Horse looked at him and snapped, "Shut up and pull!"

They reached down and gave another mighty pull. The pit released his body to them. Andy held him in place while Horse moved around to Andy's side of the pit and together they rolled him up toward them. They were finally able to drag him out.

His right side was punctured in several places and he was bleeding profusely. The two men wrapped him as tightly as they could with anything they could find to stop the bleeding and each grabbed one side of him. He was in agony and begged they leave him.

Horse yelled at him, "We can talk about all this tomorrow!"

Andy nodded, "Tomorrow."

Even Chicago mumbled, "Tomorrow."

They moved as fast as they could toward the direction the rest of the men who were in the middle of a massive evacuation. It seemed miles.

The sky was full of helicopters which were hovering for their turn to land to take on the helpless men. The pilots were dodging each other and incoming fire to save these men. Many took fire, but none of them left without carrying out as many men as possible. The pilots were dedicated to saving as many as they could, even at risk to themselves.

The large fixed wing Puffs artillery fire obliterated the area where the enemy had emerged. It seemed like a good idea, but most of the men knew that any enemy that far back were probably down in the safety of their tunnels by now.

Somewhere along the way, Chicago closed his eyes and went totally limp. Blood spurted out of his nose and his huge dimpled crease filled with blood. Andy saw it and thought of how out of place Chicago's permanent smile was now. They both thought he might be gone, but Horse and Spud kept dragging him along. They had come too far now to let go of their badly mangled friend.

The helicopter the nearest to them had filled and took off. In the midst of all the confusion, men were yelling and crying; some pleading and even a few shaking their fists. Some were trying to return fire to the advancing enemy, only to wound some of their own men who were running toward them. It was a mass of human chaos, not unlike what Andy had seen before.

This time, he was not scared. He just didn't care because he was furiously mad. Crazy angry! He didn't give a damn about anything except getting Chicago onto one of those helicopters. He didn't even care if he was already dead. At least Sonny could get him home again for burial. His single obsession was to get that man out of there.

He and Horse moved toward another helicopter which took off before they got to it. They looked around for a medic but there was no one in sight. Everyone was in major evacuation mode. Then they saw another helicopter.

They were about two hundred feet from that helicopter when they heard the sound of artillery pounding the ground beside them. They felt the ground vibrate and felt the concussion across the bottom of their legs. Horse managed about ten feet beyond where Andy fell. They all three were down.

# *126 days left*

Andy's eyes opened to a blinding light. It was deathly quiet and mostly white light. He wondered if he was dead. He couldn't remember how he got to wherever he was. He knew he wasn't in Vietnam, nor was he home. He was unable to move and really felt nothing. No pain or sensations of any kind. He decided that must be dead. Then he closed his eyes.

The next time he opened his eyes, he heard a voice saying, "Schroeder" but whoever was saying it, pronounced his name wrong. They said Schrohder not Schrayder. That couldn't be Heaven because they would certainly know how to pronounce your name in Heaven. Then he wondered if he went to Hell. But it wasn't raining, so it couldn't be Hell. He closed his eyes again.

Andy heard a noise and it sounded real. It sounded like something metal bumping something wooden. Then he heard the voice again, "Andrew Schroeder?"

He answered without opening his eyes because he wasn't sure he remembered how to open them. "Schrayder," he corrected, weakly.

Then the voice said, "Sorry. Can I call you Andrew?"

Andy's eyes opened by themselves now and he saw a young man dressed in a white uniform. "Andy," Andy answered and then frowned. He tried to determine where he was.

"You're on a hospital ship in the Philippines," the thoughtful man explained. "You are going to be okay. You were evacuated from Vietnam. Do you remember any of it?"

The young nurse moved some tubes connected to his arm. Andy became extremely uninterested in the conversation and closed his eyes again. He fell back to sleep.

It was later that he opened his eyes again. This time he was alone but he could see much better. He was in a room with institutional green walls.

He wondered to himself who sold that color paint, because he must be a millionaire by now. Everything was painted that color.

This time, he didn't go back to sleep. He looked around and began to take in his surroundings. His legs seemed to be moving by themselves. He couldn't figure that out because he couldn't feel them but he could see them go back and forth. Then he tried to sit up.

That was the first time that he felt pain. Severe pain. He was unable to move and the effort to try to sit up produced excruciating painful results. He tried to figure out where he was. He panicked a little but then remembered the man who said he had been evacuated. Where did he say his was? Some island?

He lay there quite confused for a while and trying to find out what else he could move. He could move his head and his right hand, but not his left. His right hand didn't hurt but his right elbow did. He wondered how that could be. Then he fell back to sleep.

The next time he was aware of anything was when the young man woke him to ask him some questions. "Andy, are you feeling any pain?"

"No. I thought my elbow hurt."

"You had a little shrapnel removed from it. It will be okay before long."

"Thank you," Andy answered for some reason. Then he asked, "My feet are going. Why are my feet going?"

"You have had extensive surgery on both of your legs. You are now in a continuous motion machine. Your legs have to stay moving until you can walk again. We don't want you knees to freeze up."

"Did they get cold?"

"No. Not that kind of freezing. Do you remember anything before you came here?"

"No. Did I freeze my feet?"

"No. Andy, both of your legs were badly injured."

"Rotten foot?

"Huh?" the attendant asked, "I don't understand."

"I had rotten foot. My foot was all rotten from the jungle. I didn't have the salve from Suds anymore."

The man looked at his chart, "Oh, you mean that severe skin infection on your right foot? That is getting better now. It is healing up."

"Good," Andy smiled. "Then my feet can rest, huh?"

"Not yet, Andy. Why don't you get some sleep and we can talk about this all later? I can explain it to you better after you have more rest."

"Okay," Andy said as he closed his eyes. He didn't want to say anything to the man, but salve from Suds would work a lot better than that moving thing they had.

Andy had no sense of time, but when he woke up the next time, he was in a lot of pain. He must have made a noise because the young man said, "I'm here, Andy. I will give you another shot in a little bit, okay?"

"Now?"

"In a bit. How are you feeling?"

"Why are my feet moving? It hurts like hell."

"You had extensive surgery on both legs and until they heal more, we have to keep them moving so they don't seize up on you. Do you know where you are?"

"Some boat I guess," Andy replied.

Then the nurse told him what had happened. He had been evacuated from a battlefield in Vietnam. He first was in the hospital at Cu Chi and then transferred to Cam Ranh Bay. From there, he was transported to this hospital ship in the Philippines.

"Where is Horse?" Andy was beginning to remember some things. "Horse, my friend?"

"I'm sorry. I don't know about a person named Horse. If you can give me more information, I'll try to find out for you."

"I can't remember his other name. My legs hurt so bad now. Can you do something so it isn't so bad? I don't want to be a blubber baby. Ginger wouldn't like that."

The man smiled, "I'll go get your shot now and we can talk later. Okay?"

The man returned in a few minutes with his shot and then said, "Andy, I'll try to find out more about what happened for you so when you wake up the next time, I can tell you more. You try to rest now."

When Andy woke the next time, he knew it was dark outside. The lights in the room were dim but it was somewhat easier to see than in the bright light. He wondered where the man was who had helped him. Then he had to throw up.

Soon he was aware that a woman was helping him while he threw up. It was impossible to do because he couldn't sit up because his feet were moving. This was so ridiculous. He could barely turn on his side, because both legs were tethered to a machine. He had to twist around and throw up into a little basin. It made him hurt all over. Another lady came in and gave him a shot.

The next time he woke, he felt better. He was relieved to see the young man again. "Hello," Andy said.

"Hi Andy," the man said. "Sorry to wake you. I hear you had a rough night last night. Apparently you had a reaction to some of your medication, huh?"

"I don't know," Andy replied. "I was sick though. What is your name?"

"My name is Jon. I will be your nurse again today. How is the old stomach this morning?"

"Okay. My legs are numb. Why are they going back and forth?"

"Andy, you were shot right across the back of both your knees. You lost both of your knees and some of your right leg. You have had a couple surgeries and now have been fitted with some dandy artificial knees. These guys are metal and much more sturdy than the real ones."

Andy frowned at him, "Knees?"

"Yah. I found out as much information as I could to tell you what happened. You and another man were carrying a wounded man to a helicopter when you all took fire. All three of you received leg injuries. Yours was the worst of that however. You also lost quite a bit of your right calf bone. It was a good thing we were giving you a new knee anyway, because we extended the metal rod to fill in for the bone loss."

Andy frowned again, "That's ducky. Will I be able to walk?"

"Of course. You will have to learn how again but you'll do fine. You took a lot of shrapnel. That in your right elbow will probably cause you the most trouble. But you will be okay. Don't worry. Almost as good as new."

Andy studied the man. "How almost is almost?"

"We can go into more detail later. Just be assured your artificial knees will be on the inside of your skin and not on the outside like an artificial leg,"

"Nice. I guess." Andy thought a bit, "How long do these legs have to keep moving? It is driving me crazy. I can't move with my legs in these machines."

"About six weeks, but not constantly after a while."

"Six weeks?" Andy was devastated.

"Yah, but not constantly. Okay? Tomorrow we will try to get you up and walking a little. Then you can have the machines off while we do that."

"Okay. Can we do that now?"

"No, sorry. It isn't like a regular knee replacement, because the artillery fire wasn't as neat as a surgeon's knife."

"Oh." Andy fell silent. "How is Horse? Is Chicago okay?"

The man pulled up as stool. "Here is what I found out. There was a Jackson Fielding who was helping you carry another man. Fielding—,"

Andy corrected him, "Horse. His name is Horse."

"Okay, Horse was shot the same time as you. He sustained some injuries to his legs like you did, but the damage was below his knee. He didn't have to have knee replacements. The doctors are working to try to save his left ankle now. Hopefully he will do okay."

"Is he here, too?"

"No, he was sent to a hospital ship on the coast of Japan. Once he has the last surgery there, he will be shipped back to the US. First stop, San Francisco."

"What about me? Will I go to San Francisco?"

"I'm not certain yet where they are going to send you."

"Did Chicago make it?"

"Would that be Leon Washington?"

"Yes. He fell into a Pungy pit. I hope his isn't dead."

"Andy, I only found out that he survived to make it to Cam Ranh Bay. He was stabilized there but very critical. He was flown out of there. I am trying to find out where and how he is. Okay? I will let you now the very minute I can find out anything."

"Thank you, Jon."

"You're welcome Andy.

"Does my wife know where I am? And Mom and Dad?"

"Yes, Andy. Your family was informed."

"I hope you told them I was okay. They'll be worried sick."

"I didn't talk to them but I know they have been kept informed. When you get a little better, we might be able to set up a phone call. Okay?"

"That would be good. They all worry so much, you know." Then Andy closed his eyes quite exhausted, "Jon, where is my stuff?"

"The Army has it and will take it to wherever you go. Don't worry."

"I had a picture of Annie. You should see my wife. She is beautiful."

"I bet she is, Andy. Why don't you rest now?"

Andy went back to sleep.

# 122 days left

Jon came in the next morning with a big grin. Andy was still rather doped up, but asked, "What are you grinning about?"

"Got some news for you. Ready?" the man raised his bed a little.

"I take it is good news huh?" Andy asked drowsily. "Are you taking this damned machines off my legs?"

"Kind of. You and I are getting you out of bed, if you think you want to try," Jon smiled.

"Really? Let's do it. I can't wait to get these metal monsters off my legs!" Andy almost yelled.

"Not so fast there, fella!" Jon laughed. "We'll be doing it soon. I have some other news for you that you might be interested in, also."

"What would that be?"

"Your friend Horse did well with his surgery and will be transferred to Fort Meade Hospital in South Dakota by Christmastime."

Andy just beamed. "That is fantastic. Will he be okay? Will he be able to go back to the service? Will I?"

"No. Both of your military careers are over. We sort of want guys with both their legs, knees and ankles. He will be in the hospital for about a month, but then should be able to go home."

Andy thought it over and then asked, "What day is it?"

"It is December 8," the fair-haired man answered. "And if you are better soon, we can have you call home on Sunday. Would you like that?"

"That's great. Did you hear anything about Chicago?"

"Yes, but his news is not as good. He was about out of blood before they got him to a refill station! Man, he was lucky. He has some very serious injuries. He is still at the Army Hospital in Camp Zama, Japan. Most of his injuries are doing very well, but he is having problems with a bad one to his lung. It was not only punctured, but torn. He may still lose that lung. I was able to get messages to both those guys from you and let them know you were doing okay."

Andy got tears in his eyes, "Thanks. I think I love you."

"My wife might get a little jealous about that. Oh, and by the way," Jon reached into his pocket, "I found this in some old helmet that was setting around. Wanna see it?"

Andy frowned, "Yah, I guess."

Jon handed him the photo of Annie, the poem from Bole and the Bible verse that Pastor Byron had given Andy when he left for Vietnam. He held the worn pieces of paper in his hand and wept. "God bless you man. You have no idea how much this means to me. Thank you for finding them for me."

Andy caressed the photo of Annie with his other hand. "I love her so much."

"She is a beautiful girl, Andy. Oh, and I found this in your stuff. A braid or something. Here. I imagine you know what it is."

There was Ginger's braid of mahogany red hair that she had given to him so they wouldn't be lonely for each other. Andy was certain that it was lost forever. He hugged the nurse. "You have no idea how much this means to me!"

"Yah," Jon grinned, "I think I might. So, anytime you're ready, we can get you out of your favorite machine. Once you get master walking around, we will be shipping you out to Fargo VA hospital. I hear that is not too far from your home."

"Only about two hundred miles! How soon?" Andy's face lit up.

"As soon as you quit yapping and get on your feet, mister."

"Can I be home by Christmas?"

"Doubt in your home, but maybe back to Fargo."

"Close enough."

Standing upright required a lot more energy than Andy could have ever possibly imagined. First, it took a while to get everything unhooked and all his tubes rearranged. To keep his legs in the machine, they had to be unstrapped from the foot and thigh slides. These two slides contracted and forced the knee to bend. It could be set for the degree of bend, but it was always set to be a little less than comfortable. At first, the angle of bend was not that great, but since the wounds were all fresh, it was extremely painful. If it didn't hurt a little, it probably wasn't doing its job.

When his right leg was removed from the continuous motion machine, he sat up and rubbed it. Oh, that felt so good. But it also hurt, more than he would have believed. There were stitches all over his leg and knee.

There was one long incision over a foot and a half long that extended right over the top of his knee extending at least eight inches up and down from his kneecap. His right leg was also bandaged in the calf. It looked like it had been in a food chopper.

He noticed the reddened skin of the 'rotten foot' that extended up to the sides of his foot. He had to smile. It was getting better, but it was still there. He could never mix up his feet with someone else's.

When he tried to move his leg so Jon could remove the large machine from under it, Andy had a surprise. It weighed at least a ton and he had little strength with it. The muscles in his upper leg were not willing to contract properly and from below his knee it was dead weight. The movement that he had was only from the machine. Tears came to his eyes and he groaned.

"Take it easy, there," Jon encouraged. "Slowly. Your legs have been through a lot. You can't force them to behave like you are used to."

Andy looked at Jon and nodded. 'That's for sure,' he thought. By the time he got his leg moved, he had broken out in a sweat and was nearly exhausted. 'How will I ever be able to stand up?' he wondered.

Jon must have read his mind. "Don't worry, Andy. You can do this. We got all day. Just take your time."

"I'm such a wimp."

"Look Andy, fighting to regain your health is just as difficult as facing an enemy. This is just a different enemy."

Andy looked at him and nodded. He still felt like a wimp.

Once his right leg was resting on the mattress, they started to remove the machine from his left leg. It didn't hurt as bad and wasn't as bandaged up. That however, did not mean that it moved any easier. When the leg was finally freed, Andy lay back on his pillows and closed his eyes. He was totally worn out and discouraged.

"Wanna take a minute and rest before we get you up?" Jon asked.

Jon left Andy alone and went to tend to another patient in the ward. Andy had only begun to notice the other men around him as he woke up more. He didn't talk to anyone and very few of them did more than sleep. There might have been twenty guys in there. All seemed to have their legs either in traction, casts or those stupid machines like Andy's.

Too soon, Jon came back. "Okay, Champ. Now spin slowly around to the left side. I think that leg has more strength. We will get you up on that side. Okay?"

Andy nodded, but suggested maybe they should put the whole thing off another day or so. Jon said no. Then Andy tried to sit up. At least he could move his butt, which he was unable to do before since the machines pulled on his legs. He was able to get upright.

He had to have help from Jon and was so weak he could hardly stay sitting up. His right elbow deemed his right arm worthless so he had to depend on his left arm for leverage. Spinning was not a term he would have used to describe his trying to turn around on the bed. Crawling was more like it.

Finally he got his legs down and was sitting on the edge of the bed. The change in gravity on his legs yielded new pain. It was more like a burning ache than a bone hurt like before. Jon just smiled when Andy tried to explain the difference.

"Your blood vessels are getting used to the new orientation of your body. When you think we can do it, we will slowly scoot you off the bed and onto your feet. Hold on to me and don't be macho. Have I got your word? I don't want you going ass over teakettle."

Andy smiled. It had been a while since he heard that phrase. "You got my word. I will hold on for dear life. What do I hold on to while I walk?"

"I think today, we will just stand. How does that sound? Maybe we can try again this afternoon and walk. But we need to go at this slowly."

"I want to do it, Jon. I want to do it."

"I know you do; but Andy, if you fall we could have to go back to point zero. You don't want to start all over again, do you?"

"I guess not."

Then the two men stood Andy on his feet. There was no question that Andy would hold on to Jon. He was so weak and dizzy that he couldn't even have slipped off his bed without Jon's aid. Andy was so glad he was tall and strong. He was the only reason Andy didn't topple over.

They stood there until Andy got his bearings and then was able to finally let go of his grip on Jon. He must have stood for about five minutes and was beginning to get very tired and weak.

"Okay Champ," Jon grinned, "Are you ready to take a bit of a rest now?"

Andy nodded. He didn't want to feel like a weakling, but he was really all in. He had everything he could do to keep from falling back onto his bed. It must have taken at least another half an hour to get him back into bed, his tubes all untangled and restrung, his legs strapped back into those hateful machines and then to put his head back on his pillow. It felt so damned good to get his head back down.

Jon looked at him as he lay back. "Good work."

"Ah shit. At this rate, I will be here forever," Andy groaned. "I feel like a baby."

"Not really. Getting over the injuries will test what your made of more than anything. You did very well. You have been lying around for a few days now and it takes it toll. If you get lazy, I will be here with a whip."

Andy grinned weakly, "I can see you have a streak of that."

"Shh. Don't let the other guys know. Now get some sleep. I'll bring you another shot in a little bit." Jon patted him on the shoulder. "Now I am going to turn your little machines on so your legs can practice doing the can-can."

"Thanks," Andy scowled. Then he fell asleep.

That afternoon, the orderlies cleaned up all the men as well as they could be. They were told they would have an important visitor. An hour later, a field commander came through the ward with a box of purple hearts and made bedside presentations to all the men there. Andy was proud, but wished his Dad had been there. Jon took photos of every man as he receive his award and told them he would get the photos to them as soon as they were developed. It was real nice of him. Andy was glad that he had Jon taking care of him. He was a good guy.

# 121 days left

The next morning was an exciting day. This would be the first day that Andy could walk. He was worried. Jon had told him that he would have to learn how to walk again and he wasn't certain that he could do that. How does one learn that?

Jon told Andy to unstrap himself from the machines. It took him a long time, but he did it. However, by the time he was free of the machines, he was huffing and puffing at the point of near exhaustion.

Jon smiled, "I thought you might enjoy it more, as much as you hate them."

"Yah, I did," Andy moaned. "I just don't have any strength."

"As soon as you can unstrap your machines, get yourself out of bed and walk to the head; you can get rid of some of those tubes."

"That would be a blessing. Do you think I can do that by tomorrow?"

"Maybe the next day, Champ. First you have to become acquainted with your Erector Set."

"What?"

"Some folks call it a walker. It is this handy dandy metal thing that you use to walk with."

"I thought I'd use crutches."

"Nope. They don't work so well with knee replacements, especially when you mess up both of them at once. You had to show off and take the two for one special. Now you have to use the Erector Set. It looks geriatric, but trust me you will be glad to have it. It has three sides and is much more stable than a crutch. Besides, your right arm isn't a lot of help."

"It looks like it came from an old folk's home," Andy grumbled.

"Well, it is either this or roller skates," Jon chuckled. "Your choice."

Andy frowned at him, "You enjoy your work, don't you?"

Jon laughed, "I guess it beats cleaning shrimp."

Andy had to laugh, "I could learn to dislike you."

After they got Andy out of bed and on his feet, Jon slid the walker toward him. Andy grabbed onto it with a death grip. His left arm was the strongest, but he could hold on to it with his right only it was very painful.

"Don't delude yourself, Andy. If you have a lot of pain, you won't have the strength that you think. Your body doesn't work that way."

Andy stood there shaking while holding on to his 'erector set.' "Now what the hell am I suppose to do? Stand here and quiver? I can't move!" Andy almost was in tears.

"Just calm down. As soon as you get your standing under control, I'll help you move the walker forward so you can take a step. Are you having a lot of pain?"

"No, not pain. More like panic," Andy replied.

"Good. Panic we can deal with," Jon grinned.

"Easy for you to say."

After a minute or so, Andy began to get control and was able to quit shaking. Then Jon said, "Okay, now. You move whichever foot you want ahead and I will slowly move the walker ahead. And don't take a big step. A shuffle is good at first. Then you won't have to pick either foot up off the ground. Okay?"

And so he did. Slowly he walked, or more accurately scuffed, about ten feet. Then they turned the erector set around and he scuffed back. By the time he got back in his bed, hooked up to the machine and got to relax, the major part of the morning was gone.

Just as he was looking forward to his shot and a long nap, Jon had another little surprise for him. "We are going to increase the degree on the machines. Okay? We need to get a little more bend."

Jon watched Andy's face while he turned the dial up. When he saw that Andy was beginning to grimace a little from pain, he set the dial. "You'll be glad, Andy. Really. If you don't get a good bend in your leg, you will be crippled. You don't want that."

Andy glared at him. Maybe he didn't give a damn. Maybe he just wanted to sleep. He hated this almost as much if not more than those damned mosquitoes. Then he wondered about his little friends, and if they had a new pincushion. Then he fell asleep.

By Sunday, Andy had improved enough to get himself in and out of bed and walk to the john. The catheters were removed and he felt more human. He was still on strong pain medication. When he talked to Jon about it, Jon explained. "Look this is what they did. The doctors opened up your leg in the front. That is why the big incision. Then they folded the skin back and removed what was left of your knees. They did that by sawing off your big leg bone, the femur, about eight inches above the knee and then sawing off your lower leg, the calf bone. On your right leg, you had shattered that bone a lot, so they had to take off to about eight inches above your ankle. Then they put the artificial knee in. It has two like caps on it. One end fits on the bottom of the stub of your femur and the other that fits on top of your calf bone. Then they secure it with Duct tape and Elmer's glue. And whallah!"

Andy socked him, "You jackass."

"I know. I can't resist it sometimes. Seriously, then they secure the artificial leg and knee joint and sew it shut. But all your blood vessels and nerves and muscle have been shoved around quite a bit, so they put up a fuss. Pain, swelling and itching. Besides that, now your leg has to deal with this crazy metal thing in there. It will take some getting used to, Andy. It will be more sensitive to cold and heat then your bone, and you will not be able to kneel on it again."

"Why not?"

"It will be excruciatingly painful. Don't know why, but I know it is a fact. You will have to learn how to get out of a bathtub or up off the ground a different way than you did before. You will be able to bend it back and forth, but you won't have the sideways movement you used to enjoy. Walking on irregular surfaces or loose rocks will be difficult. However, most folks learn to accommodate for that. Twisting on one leg will be a no-no, but no one has to tell you that. And carrying heavy weights will make the top part of your calf bones hurt like hell, because they are taking the brunt of it all now. The pain alone will stop that before it happens. At first, you will need to practice bending those knees back and forth through the pain until you can go up steps and bend your leg like normal. The more you do it, the easier it will become. Okay?"

Andy listened carefully, "Will I be able to ride horse?"

Jon bit the inside of his lip, "In time. Not right off. Probably will take awhile before you can build up the muscle tone in your legs, but you should be able to. No rodeo stuff, but yah."

"Crawling under cars? My Dad has a mechanic shop. I work there."

"No crawling on your knees. That is a never again thing. But you can get under a car with one of those scooter boards."

Andy grinned, "You have never worked on a car, I take it? They are not called scooter boards."

"Should be called that," Jon grinned. "No. I was too busy dissecting little critters in biology class."

"Will these knees require a lot of care?"

"These guys will probably wear out in about ten years or so, unless you get too rambunctious. Then they have to be replaced. Try to get them changed out one at a time though. It is easier than both at once. You get them both done at once like now, and then you don't have a leg to stand on!" Jon chuckled at his own joke.

"How long has it been since you've had a day off? Man you really need to get out of here." Andy shook his head.

"Been awhile my friend, but as long as you guys insist on getting shot up, I have to work. It is a tough life!" Jon grinned. "Now, I'm going to give you a shot and you can go night-night. When you wake up, we will call your family."

Andy fell asleep almost as soon as he had his shot. He had wanted to think about what he was going to say, but didn't have time. The next thing he knew, Jon was there patting his shoulder, "Hey Sleeping Beauty. I got a phone time for you. I just need to throw you in your wheel mobile and zip you down there. Let's go, unless you would rather nap."

"Cute, Jon." Andy said as he started to sit up.

"Might be a good idea to raise the back of your bed," Jon shook his head. "I hate to break it to you, Andy, but you are my slowest learner."

Andy frowned at him, "I bet you have no friends, do you?"

"Nope, but as long as I control the pain meds, I get by. Everybody is nice to me." Jon winked.

The phone rang twice before his Dad answered. "Hello?"

"Hi Dad, this is Andy!" Then the tears overflowed and he could hardly contain himself. "How are you?"

"I'm fine, Andy. How are you doing? We have been so worried about you. Let me call Annie and your Mom okay?" Dad yelled for them to come to the phone and then came back on the line. "How is it going?"

"Pretty good Dad. I wish you were here. Bright sun, beaches and big surf. It is good."

"What kind of pills are you getting?" his Dad laughed. "I think I want some."

"Really Dad, I am on a hospital ship and am doing pretty good. I can get out of bed and to the bathroom on my own now. I have to use a walker. I got two artificial knees, you know. But I will be fine. I should get sent to Fargo before long. Then maybe you can come and see me."

"Of course, we will be there, as soon as we can. You can walk then? You don't need a wheelchair?"

"Nope. I can walk. I won't be able to ride horse until later though, but Jon, my nurse, says I'll be able to do that again. I miss you guys so much."

His Dad was talking through his tears, too, "I miss you my boy. I am so glad you are doing okay. Mom and I already decided to buy Wind, so you will be able to ride him when you feel well enough. Thank God you are okay."

"Dad, can you ask Uncle Byron to keep Chicago and Horse in the prayer circle at church. Chicago is in pretty bad shape, but he is alive. Horse should be back in South Dakota by Christmas."

"We already have their names in, Andy. If there is anything you want us to do for them or their families, just let us know. Well, I have to go now. Your Mom is chomping at the bit. I love you and I am so proud of you."

"Dad, I got a Purple Heart. Jon took a picture when I got it. I will send it to you, okay?"

"Okay son. Take care and get well soon."

His Mom came on the phone, "Andy? I'm so glad to be able to talk to you. I was about out of my mind."

"I figured that. I know how you are. Mom, I'm okay. Can you tell Ginger, that I still have her braid and I am trying not to be a blubber baby? Okay?"

"Sure, I will. The kids are all so worried about you. But little Charlie is beside himself about Chicago."

"He isn't doing that well, Mom. He is in a hospital in Japan, but my nurse checked and it looks like he will pull through. Tell Charlie to make him another tape. He will like that. I will find out where he should mail it, okay?"

"I miss you so much. Keep strong and get better fast so you can come home to us soon. Okay? Did I hear Dad say you will be in Fargo?"

"That's the plan now. I will let you know."

"That isn't far away. Take care and here is someone you might want to talk to."

Annie took the phone, "Andy, I love you."

"I love you too, Annie. You are my best girl. I miss you so much."

"You had me worried sick. No more of that, you hear?"

"I will try not to. My nurse found your picture so I have it with me again. How are you doing?"

"Better once I heard you were doing okay. You have no idea what I went through when I heard you were wounded."

"I can about imagine."

"I want to be with you. Are you being taken care of okay?"

"Yes, I have good care. My nurse is mean though."

"Good," Annie giggled, "And I hope she is ugly."

"No, but she is a he. A muscle bound man with an ugly nature!" Andy teased. Jon looked over from where he was reading a magazine and grinned.

"That's even better. Andy, do you have any idea when you will be home?"

"Not yet, but Jon thinks before too long. They don't want to keep us hanging around here."

"It cannot be soon enough. I can't wait to have you home with me."

"Me either."

Jon pointed to his watch.

"Is Pepper getting all spastic about her wedding?"

"Getting? She has been for a month already! Hopefully, you will be home for it. They aren't getting married until January second."

"I hope I can be. I have to go now. Annie, I miss you so much you have no idea."

"I think I have a pretty good one. I love you."

"I love you too."

Andy hung up and wiped the tears from his eyes. "My family says you had better be nice to me or you will have to explain it to them," he teased.

"Didn't sound like it from where I sat," Jon joked. "So when is this big wedding?"

"My sister is getting married January second. Think I will be home by then?" Andy asked.

"We will see," Jon smiled with an evil grin. "I will turn your machines up on high."

"Oh good grief."

# 117 days left

Monday afternoon, Jon told him that he had found out that Chicago had to have one lobe of his lung removed, and that now he was doing much better. The doctors hoped that in a couple weeks they could move him to the Jesse Brown VA Medical Center in Chicago.

"Will he be okay?" Andy asked.

"Well Jesse Brown has a great reputation, so I would think that he would be. I got his address for you to give to that Charlie you talked to yesterday. He will be in Japan a few more weeks, but the aim is to have him in Chicago by the holidays," Jon smiled. "And you, my little friend. Your rent check bounced so we are throwing you overboard! Later tonight, we will be moving you."

"How and to where?"

"I got you a cheap ticket on a garbage scow, so if you keep quiet in the hold, I should be able to smuggle you into the States," Jon laughed.

Andy shook his head and looked at this guy in wonder. He thought he must have a hell of a job. He knew he sure wouldn't want it.

"No, they will be birding you to Clarks Field and then you will go by plane. You should be in Fargo in about twenty-four hours, more or less. You know, the transferring takes time and they might all want to gawk at you."

"Seriously man, you need a long leave." Andy grumped.

"I know. Will you tell my CO?" Jon grinned. "They are going to pretty much knock you out, so you won't get to enjoy the scenery. But guess what? We are going to keep your little machines here. You can't take them along."

"You mean I am done with them?" Andy was hopeful.

"Nope. Fargo is polishing up a couple new ones for you to use when you get there."

"Delightful," Andy scowled. "Hey Jon, could you give me your address? I might want to write to you sometime. Just to explain to you how nice people are supposed to act."

"Sure," Jon seemed pleased. "I would be delighted to hear from you. It might surprise you to know that most guys never speak to me again after I take their Erector Sets away."

Andy smiled, "Doesn't surprise me one bit."

Later, the staff removed the machines for the last time and got Andy ready to be transported. He was pleased that Jon stopped back up even though he was off duty to tell him goodbye. "Take care of yourself, Andy. I have enjoyed getting to know you."

Andy smiled, "Me too. How long you got left?'

"Seven months."

"Maybe we can catch up again sometime. Thanks Jon."

"Bye Andy."

Andy was asleep before he left the ship. The entire next couple days were a fog. He remembered smells and sensations, but only seeing a few things. He had been very hot and then very cold. Both made his legs hurt like hell. He was either shivering or sweating, but little in between.

He had never in his life had so much pain, even though it was dulled with a drugged stupor. He didn't know which was worse, begin drugged or hurting?

His elbow was giving him a hard time and sometimes it felt like it does when one hits their crazy bone. It even made his fingers tingle. He hated that.

Unable to move on his own, he was pushed, slid, jammed, covered or uncovered, lifted and hauled all over and every which way. He always heard engines and people talking, and things being moved around. Once in a while, he heard human moans. He didn't like that. Every bounce and jolt seemed to produce a new pain. It was miserable.

The sleep, if one called it that, was garbled with disjointed dreams and nothingness. He dreamt vividly and in living color. Sometimes the dreams were all black. Nothing but blackness. Some of the dreams seemed so real and yet so bizarre.

In one, he and Horse sitting on their favorite pile of junk at camp. He could hear Chicago trying to sing. Then he dreamt about Bradley and the damned snake curling around his leg. In his dream, Bradley was laughing at him while he held the dead woman and her baby from the first tunnel he had gone down.

He dreamt a lot of being in the jungle with guns poking out at him from every direction through the dense vegetation. And it was always pouring down rain.

He thought he was being smothered by the mosquitoes once. He dreamt he was in the pig pen at the farm in some mud and it was filled with leeches. When he tried to pull himself out, Annie kept pushing him back down. He hit her. He woke up and felt sick, and threw up.

In one dream, he and Franklin had gone down a tunnel and decided to have Thanksgiving dinner there. Then the little boy that had been shot because of his dog was there but they didn't have enough food for him.

He dreamt that Darrell and Horse were at his wedding in Hawaii. Horse was marrying Vienna, who was alive and well. He was so happy. Chicago was singing *Blest Be the Tie That Binds*. Suds was playing the organ.

Then he dreamt that his Mom had thrown his favorite boots away because she thought he didn't have any legs. He was frantically looking for his boots. How could she do that? He woke up screaming that his legs were still there and that she should go find the boots!

Then he became aware that he was in a room and someone was there with him. He was in a stationary building. There was a nurse there attending to him.

"Hello," she said, "Have a bad dream?"

Andy nodded, his throat was so dry he couldn't talk. He noticed that his feet were moving again. He looked down to see they were put back into the continuous motion machines.

"Andy," the lady continued, "You had quite the reaction to the medication they gave you. You can't be taking that stuff. We will make a note of it so they never give it to you again. You really had some frightful dreams."

Andy nodded. That he truly believed.

"Where am I?" he asked hoarsely.

"You are in Fargo, now. We will get you back to normal and then your family is coming down to see you? They should be here tomorrow. Will you like that?"

Andy nodded. Yah, he would really like that. He couldn't truly grasp that he was home in North Dakota again. He tried to sit up, but was too weak.

"Hold on there, Andy," the girl said, "You need to pull yourself together before you start ramrodding around here. You need to get your bearings. Today is December fifteenth. Your wife and your parents will be here tomorrow. With any luck at all, we will have you out of here before Santa comes. Okay?"

"Where will I go?"

"We are going to send you home. As soon as you work those bad drugs out of your system and get back on your feet, we are going to ship you home. Does that sound good? You can come back and visit us for a follow up."

Andy nodded. It sounded very good, but he was so tired. He fell back asleep.

He woke later and there was someone else there beside him. "Hello. Are you ready to sit up for me? Maybe you would like some real dinner?"

Andy looked at the woman, "Dinner?" he asked hoarsely.

"Yes," she said as she removed the cover from the plate on his bedside table. "It looks like hamburger steak and mashed potatoes. Can I crank up your bed so you can try to eat?"

Andy nodded. The dinner was rather tasteless, but the water was good. His lips felt better and he went back to sleep. When he woke later, he had to go to the bathroom.

He put on his light and was half out of bed before the attendant got there.

The man chuckled, "Really have to go, huh?"

Andy nodded. When he returned to bed he asked the man, "What time is it?"

"It is about three in the morning. You seem rather perky. How you feeling?"

"Good. I slept and I didn't even dream."

"You were having some fantastic nightmares when you first arrived. I'm glad you got some real sleep. You had better try to get some more. We will be cranking everyone out of their slumber in a couple hours. You know how we operate."

Andy nodded. That he did know. Then his asked the man, "Did someone tell me that my wife would be here today, or did I dream it?"

"Not a dream. She will be here, and your parents. They thought they would be here about ten-thirty."

"Do I look like hell?

The man chuckled, "Yah, but there is nothing we can do about that. I'll help you clean up and put on something decent before she shows up though. Will that be okay?"

"Yah. I would like that."

"No point in scaring them half to death, huh?" the man smiled. "Anything else I can do for you now?"

Andy thought, "No. I'm sure there is something I am forgetting, but I will be okay." Then he looked at the man, "I will be, right?"

"Yes, you will be. You should get out of here in a few days. We just need to check you out and make sure that all systems are go. You're doing fine. Just don't take that medicine again. You were pretty far out there."

Andy laughed, "God, you should have seen my dreams from my side."

"I heard about them, thank you very much. That was enough. Now go to sleep."

# 111 days left

When the lab tech came in to take Andy's blood, he was already awake. Andy felt better than he had in days. And he was so excited.

He had his breakfast, and as the man had promised, he helped Andy get cleaned up. It felt so good to shave and have his hair trimmed. The men picked out the newest of the hospital gowns they could find and then got him back into bed.

Andy begged that they take off the hateful machines until after he saw his family. The physician approved it when he made his rounds.

"Young man," the older doctor said, "We are going to cut you lose in a couple days. I understand you can continue your therapy in Bismarck and if I can extract a promise that you'll be vigilant with the machines and your exercises, you can go home day after tomorrow. Your family said they have a room on the main floor and can accommodate your needs. Do I have your word?"

"Of course, Sir! I promise. I will do my exercises religiously. How long do I have to have the machines on?"

"I'll give you a paper than explains it. As you start moving around more, you don't need to use it as much, but a minimum of four or five hours a day."

"That much? For how long do I have to do that?"

"At least until we see you again in mid January. Then we can reassess the situation. But Andy, I want you to know that if you slough off now, you will continue to pay for it. You have to work those knees or they will freeze up on you and you will be pretty much a cripple. So take it seriously."

"I will, sir. I will."

"Okay, then. See you tomorrow morning. If all your tests come back okay, you will be ready to go. Then I will sign your release so you can leave the next day."

"Thank you sir," Andy smiled. The doctor left the room and Andy removed his legs from the machines. "Okay guys, we have to have an understanding. I want you to work, so don't be giving me any grief."

The attendant came in and moved the machines to the floor and got his bed straightened around. He was all ready for his family to arrive. He waited until he fell asleep.

When he woke up a little later, Annie was already engulfed in his arms. She was embracing him with tears flowing down her cheeks. They shared the most passionate kiss that they could in a relatively public place. He was so glad to have her with him and he wanted her so badly. He hoped they would never have to be apart again.

They kissed and then Andy heard someone clear their throat. It was his Dad. "Want us to leave?"

Andy looked at him and laughed, "No way in hell. Come here."

They all embraced and then Andy hugged his Mom. "I love you guys so much. Did you hear that I can go home day after tomorrow? Home! I really get to be home. Can you believe that?"

"I am glad you are going to be home for Christmas, but I think I would rather that you would be well," his Mom kissed his cheek.

"I am good. Really. And I am a lot better now. Just think, I am home for good. No more good byes. I am not leaving again. I hope you guys know that."

His Dad grinned, "I give you a month and you will be looking for an excuse to get away from us. Apparently you forgot what we are like."

"No, I didn't. I love all you crazy people."

"Ginger is about batty for you to get home! And Charlie." Mom grinned. "And Grandma is baking peach kuchen today, so it will be ready when you get there."

"Is Grandpa in the house? He will get to it first, you know?" Andy raised his eyebrows.

"Grandma is making enough so he can have some too. Grandpa is so happy that you left Iwo Jima," Dad added. "And wait until you see your little nephew, Nathan. He is a good one. I think you will like him."

"I can't wait. What is his middle name again?" Andy asked.

"Frederick, after Darlene's dad," Mom explained. "We call him Nate. He is going to be President some day."

Andy hugged Annie again, "His idea or yours?"

256

The next day, Andy's doctor was pleased with the test results and he was given the word he could go home. He was beside himself.

He wondered if Horse was going to get home for Christmas. He sincerely missed him. He really wanted to talk to him about so many things. It seemed like they had all been somehow cheated by their abrupt departures.

Andy decided he would call him as soon as he got home. He had written to Chicago and a nurse was going to mail it for him. He really hoped that he would be stateside soon. He was dying to find out how he was doing. And he was worried about Sonny.

Even though he had left Vietnam, he knew it had not left him. He had made some wonderful friends and some pretty rotten enemies there. He had been more relieved, more grateful, more frightened and more disgusted there than any place in the world. And yet, part of him still wanted to be there. He knew good people who were still there and it tore him apart that he wasn't there to help them. He was lucky. He was home. They were not. It made him feel guilty. Logically, he knew better, but this had little to do with logic.

He wondered how it would all end. Would the people of that small nation ever be able to go out and plant their fields in peace? Would his friend Suds ever have a good life? He certainly deserved it. He should have an opportunity to live it. And all those little kids that had lost their parents and seen nothing but destruction all their lives; what would become of them? It wasn't fair for any reason that he could understand.

He couldn't wait to talk to Pastor Byron about his anger toward God. He knew he needed to work that out. He still didn't understand why he had to be sent there, why anyone had to be sent there, or why anyone had to live in it. He couldn't come to grips with why it was acceptable to kill some people when you were expected to protect some others that were worse. He just didn't get it. What was it he was supposed to learn?

He remembered how little he prayed and how empty he felt. He knew that his faith was very small and yet it was still there. He wondered if he'd ever be able to go to church and listen to a whole sermon. He really wondered.

He as also very aware of the tests he had failed. He knew that he was capable of hate and violence, killing someone, letting down people that he cared about, not trusting those who probably deserved trust and being totally selfish in some situations. He had also learned that he was capable of hurting his Annie, someone he never in the world wanted to hurt.

However, Andy also knew he had grown there. He had found that he had a reserve of strength that he could tap. He knew he was capable of handling bad situations in a reasonable manner. He thought he was now a grownup; but interestingly, it didn't seem to matter that much anymore. Now he knew that grownups could be just as irresponsible and as impossible as any kid. They were just older.

And he had learned that friends and allies come in all sizes, colors and shapes and from some pretty strange places. He was fully aware that no one went through this world totally on their own steam. Everyone needed a lot folks, and he was very aware that he did. He was also extremely grateful that he had so many good people to count on.

He had lost some good friends over there. Bandaid was gone. He was such a decent guy and had died doing a good deed. That didn't seem right. He remembered the man who was blown apart bringing him some more grenades. Sadly, he also remembered those God-awful Pungy pits. He didn't think very highly of humanity, but he also loved it. That was twisted. Mostly he had discovered that he was all too human.

Yah, he no longer had to keep his countdown. He knew when he would be home. He also knew there were many folks he had left behind who still didn't have that luxury. Some had no home to return to. Swede, Chicago and Horse were all through with their countdown. Yet none of them knew how their battles would all end. He hated it, but he was grateful for the bond they shared. A part of him belonged to them and they belonged to him. And that would never change.